Enid Blyton's

MYSTERIES

The Enid Blyton Newsletter

Would you like to receive The Enid Blyton Newsletter? It has lots of news about Enid Blyton books, videos, plays, etc. There are also puzzles and a page for your letters. It is published three times a year and is free for children who live in the United Kingdom and Ireland.

If you would like to receive it for a year, please write to: The Enid Blyton Newsletter, PO Box 357, London, WC2N 6QB, sending your name and address. (UK and Ireland only.)

THE ENID BLYTON TRUST
FOR CHILDREN

We hope you will enjoy this book. Please think for a moment about those children who are too ill to do the exciting things you and your friends do.

Help them by sending a donation, large or small, to THE ENID BLYTON TRUST FOR CHILDREN. The Trust will use all your gifts to help children who are sick or handicapped and need to be made happy and comfortable.

Please send your postal order or cheque to:
The Enid Blyton Trust for Children,
3rd Floor, New South Wales House,
15 Adam Street, Strand,
London WC2N 6AH

Thank you very much for your help.

Enid Blyton's

MYSTERIES

containing
The Mystery of the Burnt Cottage
The Mystery of the Disappearing Cat
The Mystery of the Secret Room

complete and unabridged

DEAN
in association with
Methuen Children's Books

The Mystery of the Burnt Cottage first published 1943
The Mystery of the Disappearing Cat first published 1944
The Mystery of the Secret Room first published 1945
This edition published 1992 by Dean,
in asscociation with Methuen Children's Books,
an imprint of Reed Consumer Books Limited,
Michelin House, 81 Fulham Road, London SW3 6RB
and Auckland, Melbourne, Singapore and Toronto
Reprinted 1993
Copyright © Darrell Waters Limited
1943, 1944, 1945

ISBN 0 603 55062 2

Enid Blyton is a registered trademark of
Darrell Waters Limited

A CIP catalogue record for this book
is available at the British Library

Printed in Great Britain by The Bath Press

THE MYSTERY OF
THE BURNT COTTAGE

CONTENTS

1   THE BURNING COTTAGE

IT was at half-past nine on a dark April night that
all the excitement began.

The village of Peterswood was perfectly quiet
and peaceful, except for a dog barking somewhere.
Then suddenly, to the west of the village, a great
light flared up.

Larry Daykin was just getting into bed .when
he saw it. He had pulled back his curtains so that
the daylight would wake him, and he suddenly saw
the flare to the west.

' Golly ! What's that ! ' he said. He called to
his sister. ' Daisy ! I say, come here and look.
There's a funny flare-up down in the village somewhere.'

His sister came into the bedroom in her night-
dress. She looked out of the window.

' It's a fire ! ' she said. ' It looks pretty big,
doesn't it ? I wonder what it is. Do you think it's
some one's house on fire ? '

' We'd better go and see,' said Larry, excited.
' Let's get dressed again. Mummy and Daddy are
out, so they won't know anything about the fire.
Come on, hurry.'

Larry and Daisy dressed quickly, and then ran
down the stairs and out into the dark garden. As
they went down the lane they passed another house,
and heard the sound of hurrying footsteps coming
down the drive there.

'It's Pip, I bet!' said Larry, and shone his torch up the drive. The light picked out a boy about his own age, and with him a small girl of about eight.

'Hallo, Bets! You coming too?' called Daisy, surprised. 'I should have thought you'd have been asleep.'

'Larry!' called Pip. 'It's a fire, isn't it? Whose house is burning, do you think? Will they send for the fire-engine?'

'The house will be burnt down before the firemen come all the way from the next village!' said Larry. 'Come on—it looks as if it's down Haycock Lane.'

They all ran on together. Some of the villagers had seen the glare too, and were running down the lane as well. It was exciting.

'It's Mr. Hick's house,' said a man. 'Sure as anything it's his house.'

They all poured down to the end of the lane. The glare became higher and brighter.

'It's not the house!' cried Larry, 'It's the cottage he works in, in the garden—his workroom. Golly, there won't be much left of it!'

There certainly wouldn't. The place was old, half-timbered and thatched, and the dry straw of the roof was blazing strongly.

Mr. Goon, the village policeman, was there, directing men to throw water on the flames. He saw the children and shouted at them.

'Clear orf, you! Clear orf!'

'That's what he always says to children,' said Bets. 'I've never heard him say anything else.'

8

It was not the least use throwing pails of water on the flames. The policeman yelled for the chauffeur.

'Where's Mr. Thomas? Tell him to get out the hose-pipe he uses to clean the car.'

'Mr. Thomas has gone to fetch the master,' shouted a woman's voice. 'He's gone to the station to meet the London train!'

It was Mrs. Minns, the cook, speaking. She was a fat, comfortable-looking person, who was in a very scared state now. She filled pails of water from a tap, her hands trembling.

'It's no use,' said one of the villagers. 'Can't stop this fire now. It's got too big a hold.'

'Some one's phoned for the fire-engine,' said another man. 'But by the time it gets here the whole place will be gone.'

'Well, there's no fear of the house catching,' said the policeman. 'Wind's in the opposite direction luckily. My word, what a shock for Mr. Hick when he comes home.'

The four children watched everything with excitement. 'It's a shame to see such a nice little cottage go up in flames,' said Larry. 'I wish they'd let us do something—throw water, for instance.'

A boy about the same size as Larry ran up with a pail of water and threw it towards the flames, but his aim was bad, and some of it went over Larry. He shouted at the boy.

'Hey, you! Some of that went over me! Look what you're doing, for goodness' sake!'

'Sorry, old boy,' said the boy, in a funny drawling sort of voice. The flames shot up and lighted the whole garden well. Larry saw that the boy was plump, well-dressed and rather pleased with himself.

' He's the boy who has come to live with his father and mother in the inn opposite,' said Pip in a low voice to Larry. ' He's awful. Thinks he knows everything, and has so much pocket-money he doesn't know what to do with it ! '

The policeman saw the boy carrying the pail. ' Here you ! ' he yelled. ' Clear orf ! We don't want children getting in the way.'

' I am not a child,' said the boy indignantly. ' Can't you see I'm helping ? '

' You clear orf ! ' said Mr. Goon.

A dog suddenly appeared and barked round the policeman's ankles in a most annoying way. Mr. Goon was angry. He kicked out at the dog.

' This your dog ? ' he called to the boy. ' Call him orf ! '

The boy took no notice but went to get another pail of water. The dog had a wonderful time round Mr. Goon's trousered ankles.

' Clear orf ! ' said the policeman, kicking out again. Larry and the others chuckled. The dog was a nice little thing, a black Scottie, very nimble on his short legs.

' He belongs to that boy,' said Pip. ' He's a topping dog, absolutely full of fun. I wish he was mine.'

A shower of sparks flew up into the air as part of the straw roof fell in. There was a horrible smell of burning and smoke. The children moved back a little.

There came the sound of a car down the lane. A shout went up. ' Here's Mr. Hick ! '

The car drew up in the drive by the house. A man got out and ran down the garden to where the burning cottage stood.

' Mr. Hick, sir, sorry to say your workroom is almost destroyed,' said the policeman. ' Did our best to save it, sir, but the fire got too big a hold. Any idea what caused the fire, sir ? '

' How am I to know ? ' said Mr. Hick impatiently. ' I've only just got back from the London train. Why wasn't the fire-engine sent for ? '

' Well, sir, you know it's in the next town,' said Mr. Goon,' and by the time we knew of the fire, the flames were already shooting through the roof. Do you happen to know if you had a fire in the grate this morning, sir ? '

' Yes, I did,' said Mr. Hick. ' I was working here early this morning, and I had kept the fire in all night. I was burning wood, and I dare say that after I left a spark flew out and set light to something. It may have smouldered all afternoon without any one knowing. Where's Mrs. Minns, my cook ? '

' Here, sir,' said poor, fat, trembling Mrs. Minns. ' Oh, sir, this is a terrible thing, sir ! You never like me to go into your work-cottage, sir, so I didn't go in, or I might have seen that a fire was starting ! '

' The door was locked,' said the policeman. ' I tried it myself, before the flames got round to it. Well—there goes the last of your cottage, sir ! '

There was a crash as the half-timbered walls fell in. The flames rose high, and every one stepped back, for the heat was terrific.

Then Mr. Hick suddenly seemed to go mad. He caught hold of the policeman's arm and shook it hard. ' My papers ! ' he said, in a shaking voice. ' My precious old documents ! They were in there ! Get them out, get them out ! '

' Now, sir, be reasonable,' said Mr. Goon, looking at the furnace not far from him. ' No one can save anything at all—they couldn't from the beginning.'

' My PAPERS ! ' yelled Mr. Hick, and made a dart towards the burning workroom, as if he meant to search in the flames. Two or three people pulled him back.

' Now, sir, now, sir, don't do anything silly,' said the policeman anxiously. ' Were they very valuable papers, sir ? '

' Can't be replaced ! ' moaned Mr. Hick. ' They are worth thousands of pounds to me ! '

' Hope they're insured, sir,' said a man near by. Mr. Hick turned to him wildly.

' Yes—yes, they're insured—but money won't repay me for losing them ! '

Bets did not know what being insured was. Larry told her quickly. ' If you have anything valuable that you are afraid might be stolen or burnt, you pay a small sum of money to an insurance company each year—and then if it does happen to be destroyed, the company will pay you the whole cost of your valuable belongings.'

' I see,' said Bets. She stared at Mr. Hick. He still seemed very upset indeed. She thought he was a funny looking man.

He was tall and stooping, and had a tuft of hair

that stuck out in front. He had a long nose, and eyes hidden behind big spectacles. Bets didn't much like him.

'Clear all these people away,' said Mr. Hick, looking at the villagers and the children. 'I don't want my garden trampled down all night long. There's nothing any one can do now.'

'Right, sir,' said Mr. Goon, pleased at being able to 'clear orf' so many people at once. He began to walk towards the watching people.

'Clear orf,' he said. 'Nothing to be done now. Clear orf, you children. Clear orf, every one.'

The flames of the cottage were burning low now. The fire would burn itself out, and that would be the end. The children suddenly felt sleepy after their excitement, and their eyes smarted with the smoke.

'Pooh! My clothes do smell of smoke,' said Larry, disgusted. 'Come on—let's get back home. I wonder if Mummy and Daddy are back yet.'

Larry and Daisy walked up the lane with Pip and Bets. Behind them, whistling, walked the boy with the dog. He caught them up.

'That was a real thrill, wasn't it?' he said. 'Good thing no one was hurt. I say, what about meeting to-morrow, having a game or something? I'm all alone at that hotel opposite Mr. Hick's garden—my mother and father are out golfing all day.'

'Well——' said Larry, who didn't particularly like the look of the boy, 'Well—if we are anywhere about, we'll pick you up.'

'Right,' said the boy. 'Come on, Buster. Home, boy!'

The little Scottie, who had been circling round the children's legs, ran to the boy. They disappeared into the darkness.

'Conceited fat creature!' said Daisy, speaking of the boy. 'Why should he think we want to know him? I say, let's all meet in your drive to-morrow, Pip, and go down to see what's left of the cottage, shall we?'

'Right,' said Pip, turning in at his drive with Bets. 'Come on, Bets. I believe you are nearly asleep!'

Larry and Daisy went on up the lane to their own home. They yawned. 'Poor Mr. Hick!' said Daisy. 'Wasn't he upset about his precious old papers!'

2   THE FIVE FIND-OUTERS—AND DOG

THE next day Larry and Daisy went to see if Pip and Bets were anywhere about. They could hear them playing in the garden and they shouted to them.

'Pip! Bets! We're here!'

Pip appeared, followed by the much smaller Bets, panting behind him.

'Seen the burnt-up cottage this morning?' asked Larry.

'Yes. And I say, what do you think—they say

somebody burnt it down on purpose—that it wasn't an accident after all ! ' said Pip, excited.

' On *purpose* ! ' said Larry and Daisy. ' But whoever would do a thing like that ! '

' Don't know,' said Pip. ' I overheard somebody talking about it. They said that the insurance people had been down already, and some fire expert they brought with them said that petrol had been used to start up the fire. They've got some way of finding out these things, you know.'

' Golly ! ' said Larry. ' But who would do it ? Somebody that didn't like Mr. Hick, I suppose ? '

' Yes,' said Pip. ' I bet old Clear-Orf is excited to have a real crime to find out about. But he's so stupid he'll never find out a thing ! '

' Look—there's that dog again,' said Bets, pointing to the little black Scottie appearing in the garden. He stood sturdily on his squat legs, his ears cocked, looking up at them as if to say ' Mind me being here ? '

' Hallo, Buster ! ' said Larry, bending down and patting his knee to make the dog come to him. ' You're a nice dog, you are. I wish you were mine. Daisy and I have never had a dog.'

' Nor have I,' said Pip. ' Here, Buster ! Bone, Buster ? Biscuit, Buster ? '

' Woof,' said Buster, in a surprisingly deep voice for such a small dog.

' You must get him a bone *and* a biscuit,' said Bets. ' He's trusting you and believing you, Pip. Go and get them for him.'

Pip went off, with the squat little Scottie trotting beside him trustingly.

Soon they were back, Buster carrying a bone and a big biscuit in his mouth. He set them down on the ground and looked inquiringly at Pip.

'Yes, they're for you, old chap,' said Pip. 'He's not a bit of a greedy dog, is he? He waits to be told before he begins!'

Buster crunched up the bone and then swallowed the biscuit. They seemed to fill him with joy and he began to caper round and about the children, inviting them to chase him. They all thought him a wonderful little dog.

'It's a pity he has such a silly fat sausage for a master,' said Larry. Every one giggled. The dog's young master did look rather sausagey and fat. Just as they were chuckling, they heard the sound of footsteps and saw Buster's master coming to join them.

'Hallo,' he said. 'I thought I heard you playing with Buster. Buster, what do you mean by running off like that! Come here, sir!'

Buster bounced over to him in delight. It was quite plain that he adored the plump boy who owned him.

'Heard the news?' asked the boy, patting Buster. 'About some one having fired that work-room on purpose?'

'Yes,' said Larry. 'Pip told us. Do you believe it?'

'Rather!' said the boy. 'As a matter of fact, I suspected it before any one else did.'

'Fibber!' said Larry at once, knowing by the conceited tone of the boy's voice that he hadn't suspected anything of the sort.

' Well, look here,' said the boy. ' I've been staying in the hotel opposite Mr. Hick's garden—and last evening I saw a tramp wandering about there ! I bet he did it ! '

The others stared at him. ' Why should he do it ? ' asked Pip at last. ' Tramps don't go in and pour petrol over things and set them on fire just for fun.'

' Well,' said the boy, thinking hard, ' this tramp may have had a spite against Mr. Hick. You can't tell. Mr. Hick hasn't got a very good name about here for being good-tempered. He may have kicked the old tramp out of the place, or something, that very morning ! '

The others thought about this. ' Let's go into the summer-house and talk,' said Pip, feeling excited. ' This is a sort of mystery, and it would be fun if we could help to solve it.'

The boy with Buster walked into the summer-house too, without being asked. Buster scrambled on to Larry's knee. Larry looked pleased.

' What time did you see the tramp ? ' asked Pip.

' About six o'clock,' said the boy. ' A dirty old fellow he was too, in a torn mackintosh, and a frightful old hat. He was skulking along the hedge. Buster saw him and tore out, barking.'

' Did you notice if he had a tin of petrol in his hand ? ' asked Larry.

' No, he hadn't,' said the boy. ' He'd got a stick of some sort. That's all.'

' I say,' said Daisy suddenly. ' I say ! I've got an idea ! '

They all looked at her. Daisy was a great one for ideas, and usually she had good ones.

'What's the idea this time?' asked Larry.

'We'll be detectives!' said Daisy. 'We'll set ourselves to find out " WHO BURNT THE COTTAGE." '

'What's a detective?' asked eight-year-old Bets.

'It's somebody who solves a mystery,' said Larry. 'Somebody who finds out who does a crime.'

'Oh, a find-outer,' said Bets. 'I'd love to be that. I'm sure I would make a very good find-outer.'

'No, you're too little,' said Pip. Bets looked ready to cry.

'We three older ones will be proper detectives,' said Larry, his eyes shining. 'Pip, Daisy and me—the Three Great Detectives!'

'Can't I belong?' said the fat boy at once. 'I've got plenty of brains.'

The others looked at him doubtfully. His brains didn't show in his face, anyway.

'Well, we don't know you,' said Larry.

'My name is Frederick Algernon Trotteville,' said the boy. 'What are your names?'

'Mine is Laurence Daykin,' said Larry, 'and I'm thirteen.'

'Mine's Margaret Daykin, and I'm twelve,' said Daisy.

'I'm Philip Hilton, aged twelve, and this is Elizabeth, my baby-sister,' said Pip.

The boy stared at them. 'You're none of you called by your names, are you?' he said. 'Larry for Laurence, Pip for Philip, Daisy for Margaret and Bets for Elizabeth. I'm always called Frederick.'

For some reason this seemed funny to the others.

The boy spoke in a drawling, affected kind of voice, and somehow the name of Frederick Algernon Trotteville just seemed to suit him.

' F for Frederick, A for Algernon, T for Trotteville,' said Pip suddenly, with a grin. ' F—A—T ; it describes you rather well ! '

Frederick Algernon Trotteville looked rather cross at first, then he gave a grin. ' I *am* rather fat, aren't I ? ' he said. ' I've an awful appetite, and I expect I eat too much.'

' Your parents ought to have known better than to give you three names whose initials spelt FAT,' said Daisy. ' Poor old Fatty ! '

Frederick Algernon sighed. He knew quite well that from now on he would be Fatty. He had already been Tubby and Sausage at school—now he would be Fatty in the holidays. He gazed at the little company of four friends.

' Can I belong to the detective-club ? ' he asked. ' After all, I did tell you about a tramp.'

' It isn't a club,' said Larry. ' It's just us three older ones banding together to solve a mystery.'

' And me too ! ' cried Bets. ' Oh, do say I can too ! You're not to leave me out ! '

' Don't leave her out,' said Fatty unexpectedly. ' She's only little, but she might be some use. And I think Buster ought to belong too. He might be awfully good at smelling out hidden things.'

' What hidden things ? ' said Larry.

' Oh, I don't know,' said Fatty vaguely. ' You simply never know what you are going to find when you begin to solve a mystery.'

' Oh, let's all belong, Fatty and Buster too.

Please ! ' cried Bets. Buster felt the excitement and began to whine a little, pawing at Larry with a small black foot.

The three bigger ones felt much more inclined to let Fatty join them once they realized that Buster could come too. For Buster's sake they were willing to have Fatty, plump, conceited and stupid. Buster could be a sort of bloodhound. They felt certain that real detectives, who solved all sorts of mysteries, would have a bloodhound.

' Well,' said Larry. ' We'll all belong and try to solve the Mystery of the Burnt Cottage.'

' We're the Five Find-Outers and Dog,' said Bets. Every one laughed. ' What a silly name ! ' said Larry. But all the same, it stuck, and for the rest of those holidays, and for a very long time after, the Five Find-Outers and Dog used that name continually for themselves.

' I know all about police and detectives,' said Fatty. ' I'd better be the head of us.'

' No, you won't,' said Larry. ' I bet you don't know any more than the rest of us. And don't think that we're so stupid as not to see what a very good opinion you've got of yourself ! You might as well make up your mind straightaway that we shan't believe half the tall stories you tell us ! As for being head—I shall be. I always am.'

' That's right,' said Pip. ' Larry's clever. He shall be the head of the bold Find-Outers.'

' All right,' said Fatty ungraciously. ' I suppose it's four against one. Blow—is that half-past twelve, —yes, it is. I must go.'

' Meet here this afternoon sharp at two,' said

Larry.   'We will discuss the finding of clues then.'

'Glues?' said Bets, not hearing the word properly.   'Oh, that sounds exciting.   Are glues sticky?'

'Idiot,' said Pip.   'What use you are going to be in the Find-Outers, I simply can't imagine!'

3   THE FIRST MEETING

AT two o'clock sharp the Five Find-Outers and Dog met together in Pip's big garden.   Pip was waiting for them, and he led them to the old summer-house. 'This had better be our headquarters,' he said. 'We shall keep wanting to meet and discuss things, I expect.   It's a good place for that because it's at the bottom of the garden, and nobody can overhear us.'

They all sat down on the wooden bench that ran round the old summer-house.   Buster jumped up on to Larry's knee.   Larry liked that.   Fatty didn't seem to mind.

'Now,' said Larry, 'as I'm the head of us I'd better start things going.   I'll just go over what we all know, and then we'll discuss what we should do.'

'I do think this is exciting,' said Bets, who was very much enjoying being one of the Big Ones.

'Don't interrupt, Bets,' said Pip.   Bets made her face solemn and sat still and straight.

'Well, we all know that Mr. Hick's cottage work-room, which stands at the end of his garden, was burnt down last night,' said Larry. 'Mr. Hick was not there till the end, because his chauffeur had gone to meet him off the London train. The insurance people say that petrol was used to start the fire, so some one must have done it on purpose. The Find-Outers have made up their minds that they will find out who has done this crime. Is that right?'

'Quite right, and very well put,' said Pip, at once. Buster wagged his tail hard. Fatty opened his mouth and began to speak in his high, affected voice.

'Well, I suggest that the first thing we do is to . . .' But Larry interrupted him at once.

'I'm doing the talking, Fatty, not you,' he said. 'Shut up!'

Fatty shut up, but he didn't look at all pleased about it. He put on a bored expression and rattled the money in his pocket.

'Now what we must do to find out who did the crime, is to discover who, if anyone, was near the workroom or in the garden that evening,' said Larry. 'Fatty tells us he saw a tramp. Well, we must find that tramp and somehow try to discover if he had anything to do with the fire. There's Mrs. Minns, the cook, too. We must find out about her.'

'Oughtn't we to find out if anyone had a spite against Mr. Hick?' put in Daisy. 'People don't go burning down cottages just for fun. It must have been done to pay Mr. Hick out for something, don't you think?'

'That's a very good point, Daisy,' said Larry. 'That's one of the things we will have to discover —who had a spite against Mr. Hick.'

' I should think about a hundred people had,' said Pip. ' Our gardener said that he's got a very bad temper and nobody likes him.'

' Well, if we could find out if anyone with a spite was in the garden yesterday evening, we've as good as got the man ! ' said Larry.

' Also we must find clues,' put in Fatty, who could not be quiet any longer.

' Glues,' said Bets joyfully. She loved the sound of that word. ' What *are* glues ? '

' Bets, you really are a baby,' said Pip. ' It's not glues, it's clues.'

' Well, what are clues ? ' asked Bets.

' Clues are things that help us to find out what we want to know,' said Larry. ' For instance, in a detective story I was reading the other day, a thief dropped a cigarette end in the shop he was burgling, and when the police picked it up, they found it was an unusual kind of cigarette. They went round trying to find out who smoked that kind, and when at last they found out, they had got the thief ! So the cigarette end was a clue.'

' I see,' said Bets. ' I shall find heaps of glues —I mean clues. I shall love that.'

' We must all keep our eyes and ears open for clues of any sort,' said Larry. ' Now, for instance, we might find footprint clues. You know—footprints leading to the cottage, made by the criminal.'

Fatty laughed scornfully. The others looked at him. ' What's the joke ? ' asked Larry coldly.

' Oh, nothing,' said Fatty. ' It just made me laugh a bit when I thought of you hunting for footprints in Mr. Hick's garden. There can't be less than about a million, I should think—with all the people who were there watching the fire last night.'

Larry went red. He glared at Fatty's round face, and Fatty grinned back.

'The man who started the fire might have been hiding in the hedge or somewhere, waiting for his chance,' said Larry. 'Nobody went into the hedge last night. We might find footprints there, mightn't we ? In the ditch, where it's muddy ? '

'Yes, we might,' said Fatty. 'But it's no good looking for footprints leading to the cottage ! Mine are there, and yours, and old Clear-Orf's, and a hundred others.'

'I vote we don't let Clear-Orf know we are solving the mystery,' said Pip.

'It's *his* mystery ! ' said Daisy. 'He's as pleased as a dog with two tails because he's got a real crime to solve.'

'Well, we'll keep out of Clear-Orf's way,' said Larry. 'Won't he look silly when we tell him who really did do it ! Because I'm sure we shall find out, you know, if we all work together and try hard.'

'What shall we do for a beginning ? ' asked Pip, who was longing to do something.

'We must look for clues. We must find out more about the tramp in the torn mackintosh and old hat that Fatty saw,' said Larry. 'We must find out if any one has a spite against Mr. Hick. We must find out if any one had the chance of getting into the workroom that day, to fire it.'

'It wouldn't be a bad idea to talk to Mrs. Minns, the cook,' said Daisy. 'She would know if any one had been about that day. And hasn't Mr. Hick got another man-servant besides his chauffeur ? '

' Yes, he's got a valet, but I don't know his name,' said Larry. ' We'll find out about him too. Golly, we've got a lot to do.'

' Let's all go and look for glues first,' said Bets, who quite thought she would find all kinds of things round and about the burnt cottage, which would tell at once who the wrong-doer might be.

' Right,' said Larry, who rather wanted to hunt for clues himself. ' Now, listen—we may be turned off if any one sees us poking about at the bottom of Mr. Hick's garden. So I shall drop a shilling somewhere, and if we are questioned I shall say I've dropped a shilling, and then they'll think we are looking for it. It'll be quite true—I *shall* drop a shilling ! '

' All right,' said Pip, getting up. ' Come on. Let's go now—and after that I should think the next thing to do is for one of us to go and have a talk with Mrs. Minns. I bet she'll be glad enough to jabber about everything. We might learn a lot of useful things from her.'

Buster leapt down from Larry's knee, his tail wagging. ' I believe he understood every word ! ' said Bets. ' He's just as keen to look for glues as we are ! "

' You and your glues ! ' said Larry, laughing. ' Come on, Find-Outers ! This is going to be exciting ! '

THE five children and Buster made their way down
the drive and into the lane. They passed Mr.
Hick's house, and went on down the winding lane
until they came to where the cottage had been burnt
down. There was a tiny wooden gate that opened
on to an overgrown path leading to the cottage.
The children planned to go down that, because
then, they hoped, nobody would see them.

There was a horrid smell of smoke and burning
still on the air. It was a still April day, very sunny
and warm. Celandines lay in golden sheets everywhere.

The children opened the wooden gate and went
up the overgrown path. There stood what was left
of the workroom, a ruined, blackened heap. It
had been a very small cottage, once two-roomed,
but the dividing wall had been taken down by Mr.
Hick, and then there had been one big room suitable
for him to work in.

' Now,' said Larry, half-whispering. ' We've
got to look about and see if we can find anything
to help us.'

It was plainly no use to look about where all the
watchers had been the night before. The garden
was completely trampled down just there, and the
criss-cross of footprints was everywhere. The
children separated, and very solemnly began to hunt
about alongside the overgrown path to the cottage,

and in the tall hedges that overhung the ditches at the bottom of the garden.

Buster looked too, but as he had a firm idea that every one was hunting for rabbits, he put his nose down each rabbit hole, and scraped violently and hopefully. It always seemed to him a great pity that rabbits didn't make their holes big enough for dogs. How easy, then, to chase a scampering bunny !

' Look at Buster hunting for clues,' said Pip, with a giggle.

The children looked for footprints. There were none on the path, which was made of cinders, and showed no footmarks at all, of course. They looked about in the celandines that grew in their hundreds beside the path. But there was nothing to be seen there either.

Pip wandered off to a ditch over which hung a drooping hedge of bramble and wild rose. And there he found something ! He gave a low and excited call to the others.

' Here ! I say, come here ! I've found something ! '

At once every one crowded over to him, Buster too, his nose quivering. ' What is it ? ' said Larry.

Pip pointed into the muddy ditch beside him. Nettles grew there, and they were trampled down. It was plain that some one had stood there in the ditch —and the only reason for standing in nettles in a muddy ditch was to hide !

' But that's not all ! ' said Pip, excited. ' Look —here's where the person came in and went out ! '

He pointed to the hedge behind, and the children

saw a gap there, with broken and bent sprays and twigs, showing where some one had forced his way in and out.

' Oooh,' said Daisy, her eyes very wide. ' Is this a clue, Larry ? '

' A very big one,' said Larry, pleased. ' Pip, have you seen any footprints ? '

Pip shook his head. ' The man who hid here seemed to tread on the nettles all the time,' he said. ' Look, you can see where he went—keeping in the ditch. See where the nettles are broken down.'

The children cautiously followed the broken-down patches of nettles. The ditch curved round to the back of the cottage—but there, unfortunately, so many people had trampled the night before, that it was impossible to pick out any footsteps and say, ' Those are the man's ! '

' Well, look here, although we can't find any footsteps in the garden that belong to the hiding man, we might be able to find some on the other side of the hedge,' said Fatty. ' What about us all squeezing through that gap where the man got in and out, and seeing if we can spy anything the other side.'

They all scrambled through the hole in the hedge. Fatty was the last. His eye caught sight of something as he squeezed through. It was a bit of grey flannel, caught on a thorn.

He gave a low whistle and clutched at Larry, who was just in front of him. He pointed to the scrap of flannel.

' The man tore his coat as he got through this gap,' he said. ' See that ? My word, we *are* getting

28

"Here, I say, I've found something."

on ! We know that the man wore a grey flannel suit now ! '

Larry carefully took off the scrap of grey rag from the thorn. He put it into a match-box, wishing that he, and not Fatty, had noticed it.

' Good for you ! ' he said. ' Yes—that may be a very valuable clue.'

' Has Fatty found a glue ? ' asked Bets, in excitement. Every one crowded round to hear what Fatty had discovered. Larry opened the match-box and showed the bit of grey flannel.

' Now we've only got to find some one who wears a suit of grey flannel, a bit torn somewhere, and we've got the man ! ' said Daisy, pleased.

' I think we're much cleverer than Clear-Orf,' said Pip.

' I've got awfully sharp eyes, you know,' said Fatty, feeling tremendously pleased with himself. ' Fancy, no one but me saw that ! I really have got brains.'

' Shut up ! ' said Larry. ' It was just chance, that's all, that you saw it.' He put the scrap back into his match-box.

Every one felt a bit excited. ' I like being a Find-Outer,' said Bets happily.

' Well, I don't know why,' said Pip. ' You haven't found out anything yet. I found the place where the man hid, and Fatty found a bit of his coat ! *You* haven't found a thing ! '

It was Larry who found the footprint. He found it quite by accident. The gap in the hedge led to a grassy field, where it was impossible to see any prints at all. But the farmer had been along and taken a few squares of turf from a certain part, and at one side, near the edge, was a distinct footprint !

' It's the farmer's, I expect,' said Pip, when Larry showed it to him.

' No—there's the farmer's print,' said Larry, pointing to a big hob-nailed print, which appeared up and down the bare patch. ' This is a smaller print altogether. I shouldn't think it's more than size eight, and the farmer's footprint looks like size twelve ! It's enormous. I think this *must* be the print of the man we are looking for. Let's see if we can find another.'

The children hunted about. Nothing could be seen on the grass, of course, so they went to the edges of the field. And there Daisy found three or four more footprints, some on each side of the stile that led out of the field into a lane beyond.

' Are these the same prints ? ' she called. The others came running. They looked hard. Larry nodded his head. ' I believe they are,' he said. ' Look—these shoes have rubber soles with criss-cross markings on them. Pip, run back to that other print, and see if the marking is the same, will you ? ''

Pip tore over to the patch from which the farmer had removed the turf. Yes—the criss-cross marking showed up quite clearly in the print. It was the same shoe, no doubt about that !

' Yes ! ' he yelled. ' It's the same ! ' The others were thrilled. They really were getting on !

' Well,' said Larry, looking down the lane. ' I'm afraid it's not much good going any farther, because

the surface of the lane is hard, and won't show anything. But we've found out what we wanted to
know. We've found out that a man hid in the hedge
for some reason, and we know that he wore shoes
of a certain shape and size, with rubber soles that
had criss-cross markings! Not bad for a day's
work!'

'I'll make a drawing of the prints,' said Fatty.
'I'll measure the exact size, and make an exact copy
of the marks. Then we've only got to find the shoes,
and we've got the man!'

'We know what sort of shoes he wore and what
kind of suit,' said Larry, thinking of the scrap of
grey cloth in his match-box. 'I bet old Clear-Orf
won't have noticed anything at all.'

'I'd better go back to the hotel and get some
paper to copy the footprints,' said Fatty importantly.
'It's a good thing I can draw so well. I won first
prize last term for Art.'

'What art?' said Larry. 'The art of boasting?
Or the art of eating too much?'

'Aren't you clever?' said Fatty crossly, who
did not at all like this sort of teasing.

'Yes, he *is* clever!' said Daisy, 'but he doesn't
boast about his brains as you do, Frederick Algernon
Trotteville!'

'Let's go back to the burnt cottage and see if
there's any other clue to be found there,' said Pip,
seeing that a quarrel was about to flare up.

'Yes,' said Bets. 'I'm the only one that hasn't
found a glue, and I do want to.'

She looked so sad about this that Fatty hastened
to comfort her.

32

'Well, Buster hasn't found anything either,' he said. 'He's looked hard, but he hasn't discovered a single thing. Don't worry, Bets. I expect you will soon find something marvellous.'

They all went back to the gap in the hedge and squeezed through. Fatty went off to the little hotel opposite the garden to get a piece of paper and a pencil. The others stood and stared at the ruined cottage.

'What are you doing here?' suddenly said a rough voice. 'Clear orf!'

'Golly! It's old Clear-Orf!' whispered Larry. 'Look for my shilling, all of you!'

The four children began to hunt around, pretending to be looking for something.

'Did you hear what I said?' growled the policeman. 'What are you looking for?'

'My shilling,' said Larry.

'Oh! I suppose you dropped it when you came round interfering last night,' said Mr. Goon. 'I don't know what children are coming to nowadays—always turning up and messing about and hindering others and being a general nuisance! You clear orf!'

'Ah! My shilling!' said Larry, suddenly pouncing on his shilling, which, when he had arrived, he had carefully dropped beside a patch of celandines. 'All right, Mr. Goon. We'll go. I've got my shilling now.'

'Well, clear orf, then,' growled the policeman. 'I've got work to do here—serious work, and I don't want children messing about, either.'

'Are you looking for glues?' asked Bets, and

33

immediately got such a nudge from Pip that she almost fell over.

Luckily Clear-Orf took no notice of this remark. He hustled the children out of the gate and up the lane. 'And don't you come messing about here again,' he said.

'Messing about!' said Larry indignantly, as they all went off up the lane. 'That's all he thinks children do—mess about. If he knew what we'd discovered this morning, he'd go green in the face!'

'Would he really?' said Bets, interested. 'I'd like to see him.'

'You nearly made *me* go green in the face when you asked old Clear-Orf if he was looking for clues!' said Pip crossly. 'I thought the very next minute you'd say *we* had been looking for some and had found them, too! That's the worst of having a baby like you in the Find-Outers!'

'I would *not* have said we'd found anything,' said Bets, almost in tears. 'Oh, look—there's Fatty. We'd better warn him that Clear-Orf is down there.'

They stopped Fatty and warned him. He decided to go down and do his measuring and copying later on. He didn't at all like Clear-Orf. Neither did Buster.

'It's tea-time, anyway,' said Larry, looking at his watch. 'Meet to-morrow morning at ten o'clock in Pip's summer-house. We've done awfully well to-day. I'll write up notes about all our clues. This is really getting very exciting!'

5 FATTY AND LARRY LEARN A FEW THINGS

AT ten o'clock the next morning the five children and Buster were once again in the old summer-house. Fatty looked important. He produced an enormous sheet of paper on which he had drawn the right and left footprint, life-size, with all its criss-cross markings on the rubber sole. It was really very good.

The others stared at it. 'Not bad, is it?' said Fatty, swelling up with importance, and, as usual, making a bad impression on the others by boasting. 'Didn't I tell you I was good at drawing?'

Larry nudged Pip and whispered in his ear. 'Pull his leg a bit,' he said. Pip grinned, and wondered what Larry was going to do. Larry took the drawing and looked at it solemnly.

'Quite good, except that I think you've got the tail a bit wrong,' he said. Pip joined in at once.

'Well, I think the ears are the wrong shape too,' he said. 'At least, the one on the right is.'

Fatty gaped, and looked at his drawing to make sure it was the right one. Yes—it was a copy of the footprints all right. Then what were Larry and Pip talking about?

'Of course, they say that hands are the most difficult things to draw,' said Larry, looking at the drawing carefully again, his head on one side. 'Now, I think Fatty ought to learn a bit more about hands.'

Daisy tried to hide a giggle. Bets was most amazed, and looked at the drawing, trying to discover the tail, ears and hands that Larry and Pip were so unaccountably chatting about. Fatty went purple with rage.

' I suppose you think you're being funny again,' he said, snatching the drawing out of Larry's hand. ' You know quite well this is a copy of the footprints.'

' Golly ! So that's what it is ! ' said Pip, in an amazed voice. ' Of course ! Larry, how could we have thought they were anything else ? '

Daisy went off into a squeal of laughter. Fatty folded up the paper and looked thoroughly offended. Buster jumped up on to his knee and licked his master's nose.

Bets put everything right in her simple manner. ' Well ! ' she said, astonished, ' it was all a joke, wasn't it, Larry ? I looked at that drawing and I could quite well see it was a really marvellous copy of those footprints we saw. I couldn't imagine what you and Pip were talking about. Fatty, I wish I could draw as well as you can ! '

Fatty had got up to go, but now he sat down again. The others grinned. It was a shame to tease poor old Fatty, but really he did have such a very good opinion of himself !

' I've just shortly written down a few notes about yesterday,' said Larry, drawing a small notebook out of his pocket. He opened it and read quickly the list of clues they already had. He held out his hand for Fatty's drawing.

' I think it had better go with the notes,' he said.

' I'll keep both the notes and the drawings and the scrap of grey cloth somewhere carefully together, because they may soon become important. Where shall we keep them ? '

' There's a loose board just behind you in the wall of the summer-house,' said Pip eagerly. ' I used to hide things there when I was little like Bets. It would be a fine place to put anything now— no one would ever think of looking there.'

He showed the others the loose board. Buster was most interested in it, stood up on the bench and scraped hard at it.

' He thinks there's a rabbit behind it,' said Bets.

The notebook, the match-box with the grey rag, and Fatty's drawing were carefully put behind the loose board, which was then dragged into place again. All the children felt pleased to have a hidey-hole like that.

' Now what are our plans for to-day ? ' said Pip. ' We must get on with the solving of the mystery, you know. We don't want the police to find out everything before we do ! '

' Well, one or more of us must interview Mrs. Minns, the cook,' said Larry. He saw that Bets did not understand what ' interviewing ' was. ' That means we must go and see what the cook has to say about the matter,' he explained. Bets nodded.

' I could do that,' she said.

' You ! ' said Pip scornfully. ' You'd tell her right out all that we had done and found and everything ! You can't even keep the very smallest secret ! '

' I don't tell secrets now,' said Bets. ' You know

I don't. I haven't told a single secret since I was six years old.'

'Shut up, you two,' said Larry. 'I think Daisy and Pip might go and see Mrs. Minns. Daisy is good at that sort of thing, and Pip can keep a look out to see that Clear-Orf or Mr. Hick don't come along and guess what Daisy is doing.'

'What shall I do, Larry?' asked Fatty, quite humbly, for once in a way.

'You and I could go and talk to the chauffeur,' said Larry. 'He might let out something that would be useful to us. He usually washes down the car in the morning.'

'What about *me*?' said Bets, in dismay. 'Aren't I to do anything? I'm a Find-Outer too.'

'There's nothing you can do,' said Larry.

Bets looked very miserable. Fatty was sorry for her. 'We shan't want Buster with us,' he said. 'Do you think you could take him for a walk over the fields? He just loves a good rabbitty walk.'

'Oh yes, I could do that,' said Bets, brightening up at once. 'I should like that. And, you never know, I might find a glue on the way.'

Every one laughed. Bets simply could *not* remember the way to pronounce that word. 'Yes —you go and find a really important glue,' said Larry.

So Bets set off with Buster at her heels. She went down the lane towards the fields, and the others heard her telling Buster that he could look for rabbits and she would look for glues.

'Now then, to work!' said Larry, getting up. 'Daisy, you and Pip go down to Mrs. Minns.'

' What excuse shall we give for going to see her ? '
asked Daisy.

' Oh, you must think of something yourself,'
said Larry. ' Use your brains. That's what
detectives do. Pip will think of something, if you
can't.'

' Better not all go down the lane together,' said
Pip. ' You and Fatty go first, and see if you can
find the chauffeur at work, and Daisy and I will
come a bit later.'

Larry and Fatty went off. They walked down
the lane and came to Mr. Hick's house, which stood
a good way back, in its own drive. The garage was
at the side of the house. A loud whistling came
from that direction, and the sound of water.

' He's washing the car,' said Larry, in a low
voice. ' Come on. We'll pretend we want to see
some one who doesn't live here, and then ask if
he'd like us to help him.'

The boys went down the drive together. They
soon came in sight of the garage, and Larry went
up to the young man who was hosing the car.

' Morning,' he said. ' Does Mrs. Thompson
live here ? '

' No,' said the young man. ' This is Mr. Hick's
house.'

' Oh,' said Larry, in a vexed tone. Then he
stared at the car.

' That's a fine car, isn't it ? ' he said.

' Yes, it's a Rolls Royce,' said the chauffeur.
' Fine to drive. She's very dirty to-day, though.
I've got all my work cut out to get her clean before
the master wants her this morning ! '

'We'll help you,' said Larry eagerly. 'I'll hose her for you. I often do it for my father.'

In less than a minute the two boys were at work helping the young chauffeur, and the talk· turned on to the fire.

'Funny business that fire,' said the chauffeur, rubbing the bonnet of the car with a polishing cloth. 'The master was properly upset about losing those valuable papers of his. And now they say it was a put-up job—some one did it on purpose! Well—Peeks did say that it was a wonder no one had given Mr. Hick a slap in the face for the way he treats everybody!'

'Who's Peeks?' said Larry, pricking up his ears.

'Peeks was his man-servant—sort of valet and secretary mixed,' said the chauffeur. 'He's gone now—went off the day of the fire.'

'Why did he go?' asked Fatty innocently.

'Got kicked out!' said the chauffeur. 'Mr. Hick gave him his money, and he went! My word, there was a fine old quarrel between them, too!'

'Whatever about?' said Larry.

'Well, it seems that Mr. Hick found out that Peeks sometimes wore his clothes,' said the chauffeur. 'You see, he and the master were much of a size, and Peeks used to fancy himself a bit—I've seen him prance out in Mr. Hick's dark blue suit, and his blue tie with the red spots, and his gold-topped stick too!'

'Oh,' said Fatty. 'And I suppose when Mr. Hick found that out he was angry and told Peeks to go. Was Peeks very upset?'

'You bet he was!' said the chauffeur. 'He came out to me, and the things he said about the master would make anybody's ears burn. Then off he went about eleven o'clock. His old mother lives in the next village, and I guess she was surprised to see Horace Peeks marching in, baggage and all, at that time of the morning!'

The two boys were each thinking the same thing. 'It looks as if Peeks burnt the cottage! We must find Peeks and see what he was doing that evening!'

There came a roar from a window overhead. 'Thomas! Is that car done yet? What are you jabbering about down there? Do I pay you for jabbering? No, I do not.'

'That's the master,' said Thomas, in a low tone. 'You'd better clear out. Thanks for your help.'

The boys looked up at the window. Mr. Hick stood there, a cup of tea or cocoa in his hand, looking down furiously.

'Mr. Hick and cup,' said Larry, with a giggle. 'Dear old good-tempered Hiccup!'

Fatty exploded into a laugh. 'We'll call him Hiccup,' he said. 'I say—we've got some news this morning, haven't we! I bet it was Peeks, Larry. I bet it was!'

'I wonder how Daisy and Pip are getting on,' said Larry, as they went down the drive. 'I believe I can hear them chattering away somewhere. I guess they won't have such exciting news as we have!'

6 MRS. MINNS DOES A LOT OF TALKING

DAISY and Pip were getting on very well indeed. As they had stood outside Mr. Hick's garden, debating what excuse they could make for going to the kitchen door, they had heard a little mew.

Daisy looked to see where the sound came from. ' Did you hear that ? ' she asked Pip. The mew came again. Both children looked up into a tree, and there, unable to get down or up, was a small black and white kitten.

' It's got stuck,' said Daisy. ' Pip, can you climb up and get it ? '

Pip could and did. Soon he was handing down the little creature to Daisy, and she cuddled it against her.

' Where does it belong ? ' she wondered.

' Probably to Mrs. Minns, the cook,' said Pip promptly. ' Anyway, it will make a marvellous excuse for going to the kitchen door, and asking ! '

' Yes, it will,' said Daisy, pleased. So the two of them set off down the drive, and went to the kitchen entrance, which was on the opposite side of the house to the garage.

A girl of about sixteen was sweeping the yard, and from the kitchen nearby there came a never-ending voice.

' And don't you leave any bits of paper flying around my yard, either, Lily ! Last time you swept that yard you left a broken bottle there, and half a newspaper and goodness knows what else ! Why your mother didn't teach you how to sweep and dust and bake, I *don't* know ! Women nowadays just leave their daughters to be taught by such as me, that's got all their work cut out looking after a particular gentleman like Mr. Hick, without having to keep an eye on a lazy girl like you ! '

This was all said without a single pause. The girl did not seem to be paying any attention at all, but went on sweeping slowly round the yard, the dust flying before her.

' Hallo,' said Pip. ' Does this kitten belong here ? '

' Mrs. Minns ! ' shouted the girl. ' Here's some children with the kitten.'

Mrs. Minns appeared at the door. She was a round, fat woman, short and panting, with sleeves rolled up above her podgy elbows.

' Is this your kitten ? ' asked Pip again, and Daisy held it out to show the cook.

' Now where did it get to this time ? ' said Mrs. Minns, taking it, and squeezing it against her. ' Sweetie ! Sweetie ! Here's your kitten again ! Why don't you look after it better ? '

A large black and white cat strolled out of the kitchen, and looked inquiringly at the kitten. The kitten mewed and tried to jump down.

' Take your kitten, Sweetie,' said Mrs. Minns. She put it down and it ran to its mother.

' Isn't it exactly like its mother ? ' said Daisy.

' She's got two more,' said Mrs. Minns. ' You come in and see them. Dear little sweets ! Dogs I can't bear, but give me a cat and kittens and I'm happy.'

43

The two children went into the kitchen. The big black and white cat had got into a basket, and the children saw three black and white kittens there too, all exactly alike.

' Oh, can I stay and play with them a bit ? ' asked Daisy, thinking it would be a marvellous excuse to stop and talk to Mrs. Minns.

' So long as you don't get into my way,' said Mrs. Minns, dumping down a tin of flour on the table. She was going to make pastry. ' Where do you live ? '

' Not far away, just up the lane,' answered Pip. ' We saw the fire the other night.'

That set Mrs. Minns off at once. She put her hands on her hips and nodded her head till her fat cheeks shook.

' What a shock that was ! ' she said. ' My word, when I saw what was happening, any one could have knocked me down with a feather.

Both the children felt certain that nothing short of a bar of iron would ever knock fat Mrs. Minns over. Daisy stroked the kittens whilst the cook went on with her talk, quite forgetting about the pastry.

' I was sitting here in my kitchen, treating myself to a cup of cocoa, and telling my sister this, that and the other,' she said. ' I was tired with turning out the larders that day, and glad enough to sit and rest my bones. And suddenly my sister says to me, " Maria ! " she says, " I smell burning ! " '

The children stared at her. Mrs. Minns was pleased to have such an interested audience.

' I said to Hannah—that's my sister—I said

" Something burning ! That's not the soup catching in the saucepan surely ? " And Hannah says, " Maria, there's something burning terrible ! " And then I looked out of the window and I saw something flaring up at the bottom of the garden ! '

' What a shock for you ! ' said Daisy.

' Well ! ' I says to my sister, ' it looks as if the master's workroom is on fire ! Glory be ! ' I says. ' What a day this has been ! First Mr. Peeks gets the sack and walks out, baggage and all. Then Mr. Smellie comes along and he and the master go for one another, hammer and tongs ! Then that dirty old tramp comes and the master catches him stealing eggs from the hen-house ! And now if we haven't got a fire ! '

The two children listened intently. All this was news to them. Goodness ! There seemed to have been quite a lot of quarrels and upsets on the day of the fire. Pip asked who Mr. Peeks was.

' He was the master's man-servant and secretary,' said Mrs. Minns. ' Stuck-up piece of goods he was. I never had much time for him myself. Good thing he went, *I* say. *And* I shouldn't be surprised if he had something to do with that fire, either ! '

But here Lily had something to say. ' Mr. Peeks was *far* too much of a gentleman to do a thing like that,' she said, clattering her broom into a corner. ' If you ask me, it's old Mr. Smellie.'

The children could hardly believe that any one could be called by such a name. ' Is that his *real* name ? ' asked Pip.

' It surely is,' said Mrs. Minns, ' and a dirty neglected old fellow he is too ! What his house-

keeper can be about, I don't know. She doesn't
mend him up at all—sends him out with holes in
his socks, and rents in his clothes, and his hat
wanting brushing. He's a learned old gentleman,
too, so they say, and knows more about old books
and things than almost any one in the kingdom.'

'Why did he and Mr. Hick quarrel?' asked
Pip.

'Goodness knows!' said Mrs. Minns. 'Always
quarrelling, they are. They both know a lot, but
they don't agree about what they know. Anyway,
old Mr. Smellie, he walks out of the house muttering
and grumbling, and bangs the door behind him so
hard that my saucepans almost jump off the stove!
But as for him firing the cottage, as Lily says, don't
you believe a word of it! It's my belief he wouldn't
know how to set light to a bonfire! It's that stuck-
up Mr. Peeks who'd be spiteful enough to pay
Mr. Hick back, you mark my words!'

'He would not,' said Lily, who seemed determined to stick up for the valet. 'He's a nice young
man, he is. You've no right to say things like that,
Mrs. Minns.'

'Now, look here, my girl!' said the cook,
getting angry, 'if you think you can talk like that
to your elders and betters, you're mistaken! Telling
me I've no right to say this, that and the other!
You just wait till you can scrub a floor properly, and
dust the tops of the pictures, and see a cobweb when
it's staring you in the face, before you begin to talk
big to me!'

'I wasn't talking big,' said poor Lily. 'All I
said was . . .'

'Now don't you start all over again!' said Mrs. Minns, thumping on the table with the rolling-pin as if she was hitting poor Lily on the head with it. 'You go and get me the dripping, if you can find out where you put it yesterday. And no more back-chat from *you*, if you please!'

The children didn't want to hear about Lily's faults, or where she put the dripping. They wanted to hear about the people that Mr. Hick had quarrelled with, and who might therefore have a spite against him. It looked as if both Mr. Peeks and Mr. Smellie would have spites against him. And what about the old tramp too?

'Was Mr. Hick very angry with the tramp when he found him stealing the eggs?' asked Pip.

'Angry! You could hear him all over the house and the garden too!' said Mrs. Minns, thoroughly enjoying talking about everything. 'I said to myself, "Ah, there's the master off again! It's a pity he doesn't use up some of his temper on that lazy girl Lily!"'

Lily appeared out of the larder, looking sulky. The children couldn't help feeling sorry for her. The girl put the dripping down on the table with a bang.

'Any need to try and break the basin?' inquired Mrs. Minns. 'It's a bad girl you are to-day, a right down bad girl. You go and wash the back steps, madam! That will keep you busy for a bit.'

Lily went out, clanking a pail. 'Tell us about the tramp,' said Pip. 'What time did Mr. Hick see him stealing eggs?'

'Oh, sometime in the morning,' said Mrs. Minns,

rolling out pastry with a heavy hand. 'The old fellow came to my back door first, whining for bread and meat, and I sent him off. I suppose he slipped round the garden to the henhouse, and the master saw him there from the cottage window. My word, he went for him all right, and said he'd call the police in, and the old tramp, he went flying by my kitchen door as if a hundred dogs were after him !'

'Perhaps *he* fired the cottage,' said Pip. But Mrs. Minns would not have it that any one had fired the cottage but Mr. Peeks.

'He was a sly one,' she said. 'He'd come down into my kitchen at nights, when every one was in bed, and he'd go to my larder and take out a meat-pie or a few buns or anything he'd a mind to. Well, what I say is, if some one can do that, they'll set fire to a cottage too.'

Pip remembered with a very guilty feeling that once, being terribly hungry, he had slipped down to the school larder and eaten some biscuits. He wondered if he was also capable of setting fire to a cottage, but he felt sure he could never do that. He didn't think that Mrs. Minns was right there.

Suddenly, from somewhere in the house, there came the sound of a furious flow of words. Mrs. Minns cocked her head up, listened and nodded.

'That's the master,' she said. 'Fallen over something, I shouldn't wonder.'

Sweetie, the big black and white cat, suddenly flew into the kitchen, her fur up, and her tail swollen to twice its size. Mrs. Minns gave a cry of woe.

'Oh, Sweetie ! Did you get under his feet again ! Poor lamb, poor darling lamb !'

The poor darling lamb retired under the table, hissing. The three kittens in the basket stiffened in alarm, and hissed too. Mr. Hick appeared in the kitchen, looking extremely angry.

' Mrs. Minns ! I have once more fallen over that horrible cat of yours. How many more times am I to tell you to keep her under control ? I shall have her drowned.'

' Sir, the day you drown my cat I walk out ! ' said Mrs. Minns, laying down the rolling-pin with a thump.

Mr. Hick glared at the cook as if he would like to drown her as well as the cat. ' Why you want to keep such an ugly and vicious animal, I cannot think,' he said. ' And good heavens above—are those kittens in that basket ? '

' They are, sir, said Mrs. Minns, her voice rising high. ' And good homes I've found for every single one of them, when they're old enough.'

Mr. Hick then saw the two children, and appeared to be just as displeased to see them as he had been to see the kittens.

' What are these children doing here ? ' he asked sharply. ' You ought to know better, Mrs. Minns, than to keep your kitchen full of tiresome children and wretched cats and kittens ! Tell them to go ! '

He marched out of the door, first setting down the empty cup and saucer he was carrying. Mrs. Minns glared after him.

' For two pins I'd burn your precious cottage down if it wasn't already gone ! ' she called after Mr. Hick, when he was safely out of hearing. Sweetie rubbed against her skirt, purring loudly. She bent down and stroked her.

' Did the nasty man tramp on you ? ' she asked fondly. ' Did he say nasty things about the dear little kittens ? Never you mind, Sweetie ! '

' We'd better be going,' said Daisy, afraid that Mr. Hick might hear what Mrs. Minns was saying, and come back in a worse temper than ever. ' Thank you for all you've told us, Mrs. Minns. It was most interesting.'

Mrs. Minns was pleased. She presented Pip and Daisy with a ginger bun each. They thanked her and went, bubbling over with excitement.

' We've learnt such a lot that it's going to be difficult to sort it all out ! ' said Pip. ' It seems as if at least three people might have done the crime— and really, if that's the kind of way that Mr. Hick usually behaves I can't help feeling there must be about twenty people who would only be too glad to pay him back for something ! '

7   THE TRAMP—CLEAR-ORF— AND FATTY!

THE four children met in the old summer-house all full of excitement. Bets and Buster were not yet back, but they couldn't wait for them to come. They had to tell their news.

' We saw the chauffeur ! He's called Thomas,' said Larry. ' He told us all about the valet called

Peeks. He was chucked out on the day of the fire, for wearing his master's clothes ! '

' I'm sure he did the crime,' said Fatty eagerly. ' We must find out more about him. He lives in the next village.'

' Yes, but listen ! ' said Daisy. ' It might be old Mr. Smellie ! '

' *Who* ? ' said Larry and Fatty, in astonishment. ' Mr. *Smellie* ! '

' Yes,' said Daisy, with a giggle. ' *We* thought it couldn't be a real name, too, when we heard it, but it is.'

' Mr. Hiccup and Mr. Smellie,' said Fatty unexpectedly. ' What a lovely pair ! '

Larry chuckled. ' Daisy and Pip don't know about Mr. Hick and cup,' he said. He told them. They laughed.

' It isn't *really* very funny, but it *seems* as if it is,' said Daisy. ' At school things seem like that sometimes too—we scream with laughter, and afterwards it doesn't really seem funny at all. But do let us tell you about Mr. Smellie, and the quarrel he had with Mr. Hiccup.'

She told Larry and Fatty all that Mrs. Minns had said. Then Pip told about the old tramp who had been caught stealing eggs. And then Daisy described how Mr. Hick himself had come into the kitchen and rowed Mrs. Minns for letting her cat get under his feet. ' They had a proper quarrel,' said Daisy,' and Mrs. Minns actually called after Mr. Hick and said she felt like burning down his cottage if it hadn't already been done ! '

' Golly ! ' said Larry, surprised. ' It looks as

if old Mrs. Minns might have done it herself then
—if she felt like it to-day, she might quite easily
have felt like it two days ago—and done it ! She
had plenty of chance.'

'You know, we have already found four suspects,' said Fatty solemnly. 'I mean—we can quite
properly suspect four persons of firing that cottage—
the old tramp, Mr. Smellie, Mr. Peeks and Mrs.
Minns ! We *are* getting on.'

'Getting on ?' said Larry. 'Well, I don't know
about that. We seem to find more and more people
to suspect, which makes it all more and more difficult. I can't think how in the world we're going
to discover which it is.'

'We must find out the movements of the four
suspects,' said Fatty wisely. 'For instance, if we
find out that Mr. Smellie, whoever he is, spent the
evening of the day before yesterday fifty miles away
from here, we can rule him out. And if we find that
Horace Peeks was at home with his mother all that
evening, we can rule *him* out. And so on.'

'What we shall probably find is that all four
people were messing about somewhere near the
place,' said Pip. 'And how in the world are we
going to trace that old tramp ? You know what
tramps are—they wander about for miles, and
nobody knows where they go or where they come
from.'

'Yes—the tramp's going to be difficult,' said
Daisy. 'Very difficult. We can't rush all over the
country looking for a tramp. And if we did find
him, it's going to be difficult to ask him if he set fire
to the cottage.'

52

'We needn't do that, silly,' said Larry. 'Have you forgotten our clues?'

'What do you mean?' asked Daisy.

'Well—we've only got to find out what size shoes he wears, and if they've got rubber soles, criss-crossed with markings underneath, and if he wears a grey flannel coat,' said Larry.

'He doesn't wear a grey flannel coat,' said Fatty. 'I told you—he wore an old mackintosh.'

The others were silent for a moment. 'Well, he might have a grey flannel coat underneath,' said Daisy. 'He might have taken his mackintosh off for a moment.'

The others thought this was rather feeble, but they had no better suggestion.

'Time enough to worry about grey flannel coats and mackintoshes when we've found the tramp,' said Pip. 'That *is* going to be a problem, I must say!'

'Hark—isn't that old Buster barking?' said Fatty suddenly. 'I bet that's Bets coming back. Yes—she's calling to Buster. I say—haven't we got a lot of news for her?'

The sound of Bets' running feet was heard up the drive, and then down the garden path to the summer-house. The four big ones went to the door to welcome her. Buster shot up to them, barking madly.

'Bets! We've got such a lot of news!' called Larry.

'We've had a most exciting time!' cried Daisy.

But Bets didn't listen. Her eyes were shining brightly, her cheeks were red with running, and she could hardly get her words out, she was so excited.

'Pip! Larry! I've got a glue! Oh, I've got a glue!'

'What?' asked the other four together.

'I've found the tramp!' panted the little girl. 'Do say he's the biggest glue we've found!'

'Well—he's really a suspect, not a clue,' began Larry, but the others interrupted him.

'Bets! Are you sure you've found the tramp?' asked Pip excitedly. 'Golly—we thought that would be almost impossible.'

'Where is he?' demanded Fatty, ready to go after him immediately.

'How do you know it's the tramp?' cried Daisy.

'Well, he was wearing a dirty old mackintosh and a terrible old hat with a hole in the crown,' said Bets. 'Just like Fatty said.'

'Yes—the hat did have a hole in the crown,' said Fatty. 'Bets, where is this fellow?'

'Well, I went for a walk with Buster, as you know,' said Bets, sinking down on the grass, tired out with running. 'He's a lovely dog to take for a walk, because he's so interested in everything. Well, we went down the lane and into the fields, and along by the river, ever so far. We came to a field where sheep and lambs were, and there was a hay-rick nearby.'

Buster barked a little, as if he wanted to tell about it all too. Bets put her arm round him. 'It was Buster who found the tramp—wasn't it, darling? You see, I was walking along—and suddenly Buster went all stiff—and the hairs rose up along the back of his neck—and he growled.'

'Ur-r-r-r-rrr!' said Buster obligingly.

54

' He honestly understands every word, doesn't he ? ' said Bets. ' Well, Buster went all funny, like that, and then he began to walk stiffly towards the hay-rick—you know, just as if he had bad rheumatism or something.'

' Animals always walk like that when they are suspicious, or frightened or angry,' said Fatty, grinning at Bets. ' Go on. Don't be so long-winded.'

' I went with Buster,' said Bets, ' as quietly as I could, thinking there might be a cat or something the other side of the rick. But it was the tramp ! '

' Golly ! ' said Larry, and Pip whistled.

' You're a very good Find-Outer,' said Fatty warmly.

' I did so badly want to find out something,' said Bets. ' But I suppose really and truly it was Buster who did the finding, wasn't it ? '

' Well, he wouldn't have, if you hadn't taken him for a walk,' said Larry. ' What was the tramp doing ? '

' He was asleep,' said Bets. ' Fast asleep. He didn't even wake when Buster sniffed at his feet.'

' His *feet* ! ' said Pip. ' What sort of shoes did he have on ? Did they have rubber soles ? '

Bets looked dismayed. ' Oh ! I never thought of looking. And I so easily could have seen, couldn't I, because he was fast asleep. But I was so excited at finding him that I just never thought of looking at his shoes.'

' There's no time to be lost,' said Pip, jumping up. ' He may still be fast asleep. We'd better go and have a look at him and his shoes and his clothes.

Fatty can tell us at once if he's the tramp he saw in Mr. Hick's garden or not.'

Excited and rather solemn, the Five Find-Outers and Dog set off down the lane to the fields that ran beside the river. They went fast, in case the tramp had awakened and gone on his way. It was so marvellous that Bets should actually have found him —they couldn't possibly risk losing him !

They came to the rick. A gentle sound of snoring told them that the tramp was still there. Fatty picked up Buster and crept round the rick without making a sound.

On the other side, curled up well, lay a tramp. He was an old fellow, with a stubbly grey beard, shaggy grey eyebrows, a red nose, and long, untidy hair that straggled from under a terrible old hat. Fatty took a look at him. He tiptoed back to the others.

' Yes—it's the tramp all right ! ' he whispered, thrilled. ' But it's going to be difficult to pull aside his mackintosh to see if he's got a grey coat underneath. And he's got his feet sort of curled up underneath him. We shall have to get right down on the ground to see what sort of sole his shoes have got underneath.'

' I'll go and try,' said Larry. ' You others keep Buster quiet here, and watch out in case any one comes.'

Leaving the others on the far side of the rick, Larry crept round to the side where the tramp slept. He sat down near him. He put out his hand to pull aside the old mackintosh to see if the man wore grey underneath. The trousers appearing below the coat were so old and dirty that it was quite impossible to tell what colour they had once been.

The tramp moved a little and Larry took back his hand. He decided to try and see the underneath of the man's shoes. So he knelt down, put his head to the ground and did his best to squint at the tramp's shoes.

The tramp suddenly opened his eyes. He stared in the greatest astonishment at Larry.

'What's bitten *you*?' he suddenly said, and Larry almost jumped out of his skin.

'Think I'm the king of England, I suppose, kneeling in front of me with your head on the ground like that!' said the tramp. 'Get away. I can't abide children. Nasty interfering little creatures!'

He curled himself up again and shut his eyes. Larry waited for a second or two, and was about to try squinting at the man's shoes again when he heard a low whistle from the other side of the rick. That meant some one was coming. Well, they would all have to wait till the passer-by was gone. Larry crept round to join Pip and the rest.

'Some one coming?' he asked.

'Yes—old Clear-Orf!' said Fatty. Larry peeped round the rick. The village policeman was coming up from the other direction, along a path that did not go near the rick. He would soon be gone.

But as he came along he suddenly caught sight of the old tramp sleeping by the rick. The children drew back hurriedly as Mr. Goon walked quietly and quickly over to the rick. There was a ladder leaning against the rick and Larry pushed Bets and the others up as quickly as he could. They would

57

He did his best to squint at the tramp's shoes

be less likely to be seen on top than below. Fortunately the rick had been cut well out, when hay
was taken to the various farm-animals, and it was
easy to balance on the cut-out part.

The policeman crept up quietly. The children,
peering over the rick, saw him take out a notebook.
Fatty gave Larry such a nudge that the boy nearly
fell.

' Look ! Look what he's got down in his notebook ! He's got a drawing of that footprint *we* saw !
He's been cleverer than we thought ! '

Clear-Orf tiptoed up to the tramp and tried his
best to see what sort of shoes he had on. He, too,
did as Larry had done and knelt down, the better
to see. And the tramp opened his eyes !

His astonishment at seeing the policeman kneeling in front of him was enormous. It was one thing
to see a boy behaving like that, but quite another
thing to see a policeman. The tramp leapt to his
feet with a howl.

' First it's a boy bowing down to me and now
it's a bobby ! ' he said, jamming his old hat down on
his long grey hair. ' What's it all about ? '

' I want to see your shoes,' said Clear-Orf.

' Well, see them, then ! Look at them well,
laces and all ! ' said the tramp, rapidly losing his
temper.

' I want to see the soles,' said the policeman
stolidly.

' Are you a cobbler or a policeman ? ' asked the
tramp. ' Well—you show me the buttons on your
shirt, and I'll show you the soles of my shoes ! '

The policeman began to breathe very heavily,

and his face got red. He snapped his notebook shut.

'You better come-alonga-me,' he said. The tramp didn't think so. He skipped out of the way and began to run across the field, very nimbly indeed for an old fellow. Clear-Orf gave a roar, and turned to run after him.

And at that moment Fatty, excited beyond words, fell off the hay-rick, and landed with a thud on the ground below. He gave such an agonized yell that the policeman stopped in amazement.

'What's all this-ere?' he said, and glared at Fatty. Then he caught sight of the other children peering anxiously down from the top of the rick, afraid that Fatty had broken all his bones. He was most astonished.

'You come on down!' he roared. 'Always children messing about! You wait till the farmer catches you! How long have you been there? What do you mean, spying like this?'

Fatty gave a frightful groan, and the policeman, torn between his desire to rush after the disappearing tramp, and to pull Fatty to his feet and shake him, went up to him.

'Don't touch me! I think I've broken my left leg and my right arm, dislocated both my shoulders and broken my appendix!' said Fatty, who sincerely believed that he was practically killed.

Bets gave a squeal of horror and jumped down to see what she could do to help poor Fatty. The others leapt down too, and Buster danced delightedly round Clear-Orf's ankles. The policeman kicked out at him.

' Clear-orf,' he said. ' Dogs and children !
Always messing about and getting in the way.
Now that fellow's gone, and I've missed a chance
of questioning him ! '

He waited to see if Fatty was really hurt. But,
except for a good shaking, and some fine big bruises,
Fatty was not hurt at all. His fat had kept him from
breaking any bones !

As soon as the policeman saw the others helping
Fatty up, brushing him down, and comforting him,
he took a look round to see if he could make out
where the tramp had gone. But he was nowhere
to be seen. He turned to the five children.

' Now, clear-orf,' he said. ' And don't let me
see you hanging round again.'

Then, with great dignity, Mr. Goon made his
way heavily to the path, and walked down it without
turning his head once. The children looked at each
other.

' We were getting on so well till Clear-Orf came,'
sighed Daisy. ' I wonder where that tramp went to.'

' I'm going home,' said Fatty miserably. ' I
feel awful.'

' I'll take you home,' said Daisy. ' You come
too, Bets. Do you boys want to see if you can trace
the tramp ? '

' Yes,' said Larry. ' Might as well whilst we've
got the chance. I don't wonder Fatty fell off the
rick. It was pretty exciting, wasn't it ? '

' Fancy old Clear-Orf having a drawing of that
footprint in his notebook,' said Pip thoughtfully.
' He's smarter than I thought. Still—we've got
something he hasn't got—a bit of grey flannel ! '

Fatty, Daisy, Bets and Buster went off together. The other two set off in the direction the tramp had taken. They meant to find him again if they could !

8   WHAT MUST BE DONE NEXT?

LARRY and Pip ran quickly in the direction the tramp had gone. It seemed silly that, although all the children had seen him, and Clear-Orf too, nobody had managed to find out what kind of soles his shoes had !

There was no sign of the tramp at all. The boys met a farm-labourer and hailed him.

' Hie ! Have you seen an old tramp going this way ? '

' Yes. Into that wood,' said the man, and pointed to a small copse of trees in the distance. The boys ran there, and looked about among the trees and tangled undergrowth.

They smelt the smoke of a fire, and their noses and eyes soon guided them to it. By it, on a fallen tree, sat the dirty old tramp, his hat off now, showing his tangled, straggly hair. He was cooking something in a tin over the fire.

When he saw Larry he scowled. ' What ! You here again ? ' he said. ' You get away. What do you mean, following me about like this ? I haven't done nothing.'

' Well,' said Larry boldly, ' you tried to steal

eggs from Mr. Hick's hen-house the other day. We know that ! But that's nothing to do with us.'

'Mr. Hick ! So that's his name,' said the old tramp, sticking a skewer in whatever it was that he was cooking. 'I didn't steal his eggs ! I didn't steal nothing at all. I'm an honest old fellow, I am, and everybody will tell you the same ! '

'Well—what were you doing hiding in the ditch at the bottom of his garden ? ' said Larry. The tramp looked astonished.

'I never hid in no ditch,' he said. 'I wasn't the one that did the hiding. Ho, dear me no ! I could tell you something, I could—but I'm not going to. You put that policeman after me, didn't you ? '

'No,' said Larry. 'He came along unexpectedly and went over to you. He didn't know we were anywhere about.'

'Well, I don't believe you,' said the old tramp. 'You set that bobby after me. I know you did. I'm not going to be mixed up in anything that don't concern me. But there was funny goings-on that night, ho yes, I should think there were.'

The old fellow suddenly groaned and rubbed his right foot. His big toe stuck out of the shoe, which was too small for him. He took the shoe off, showing a sock that was practically all holes, and rubbed his foot tenderly.

The boys looked at the shoe, which the tramp had thrown carelessly to one side. The sole was plainly to be seen. It was of leather, and so much worn that it could not possibly keep any damp out.

'No rubber sole ! ' whispered Larry to Pip.

' So it couldn't have been the tramp hiding in the ditch. Anyway, I don't believe he knows a thing. And look at the old coat he's got under the mack— it's green with age, not grey ! '

' What you whispering about ? ' said the tramp. ' You get away. Can't I live in peace ? I don't do no harm to nobody, I don't, but children and bobbies, they come after me like flies. You leave me alone. I'd be as merry as a blackbird if I had a pair of shoes that fitted me poor old feet. You got a pair of shoes that would fit me ? '

' What size do you take ? ' asked Pip, thinking that perhaps he could get an old pair of his father's boots for the footsore old tramp. But the tramp didn't know. He had never bought a pair of shoes in his life.

' Well, if I can get an old pair of my father's boots, I'll bring them to you,' said Pip. ' Or better still, you come and get them. I live in the red house in the lane not far from Mr. Hick's house. You come there to-morrow, and I'll perhaps have got some boots for you.'

' You'll set that bobby after me again if I come back,' grumbled the tramp, taking out something peculiar from the tin, and beginning to eat it with his hands. ' Or that Mr. Hick will. Well, he'd better be careful. I know a few things about Mr. Hick and his household, I do. Yes, I heard him shouting at quite a few people that day, besides me. Ho yes. There was funny goings on there, but I'm not mixed up in them, I tell you.'

Larry looked at his watch. It was getting late. ' We'll have to go,' he said. ' But you come along to Pip's house to-morrow, and you can tell us anything you want to. We shan't give you away.'

The boys left the old tramp and tore home to their dinner, very late indeed. Their mothers were not pleased with them.

'Whatever have you been doing?' asked Pip's mother. 'Where have you been?'

Pip couldn't possibly tell her, because the Find-Outers and their doings were very secret. 'I was with the others,' he said at last.

'You weren't, Pip,' said his mother. 'Bets and Daisy have been here a long time—and that fat boy too, whatever his name is. Don't tell stories.'

'Well, I was with Larry,' said Pip. Bets saw that he was in difficulties and she tried to rescue him by suddenly changing the subject.

'Fatty fell off a hay-rick this morning,' she said. It certainly changed the subject. Her mother stared at her in horror.

'Who did? That fat boy? Did he hurt himself? Whatever were you doing on a hay-rick?'

Pip was afraid that Bets was going to say why they were all on the rick, so *he* changed the subject quickly too.

'Mummy, has Daddy got a very old pair of boots he doesn't want?' he asked innocently. His mother looked at him.

'Why?' she asked. Pip was not usually interested in his father's old clothes.

'Well, I happen to know some one who would be very glad of them indeed,' said Pip.

'Why?' asked his mother again.

'Well, you see, his toes are sticking right out

65

of his shoes,' explained Pip, trying to interest his mother in the matter.

' Whose toes ? ' asked his mother, astonished.

Pip stopped. Now he would have to bring in the tramp, and that was part of the secret. Bother ! Whatever they talked about seemed to lead back to something the Find-Outers were doing.

' It's just a poor old tramp,' said Bets. Pip glared at her.

' A tramp ! ' said her mother. ' Surely you are not making friends with people like that, Pip ? '

' No,' said Pip desperately. ' I'm not. I'm only sorry for him, that's all. You always say, Mummy, that we should be sorry for people not so well-off as ourselves, and help them, don't you ? Well, that's why I thought of giving him some old boots, that's all.'

' I see,' said his mother, and Pip gave a sigh of relief. ' Well, I'll find out if there is an old pair of Daddy's boots, and if there is, you shall have them. Now, do get on with your dinner.'

After he had finished his very late meal, Pip escaped into the garden and went to find Bets, who was in the summer-house.

' Bets ! Was Fatty all right ? He wasn't really hurt, was he ? '

' No. He's got some lovely bruises though,' said Bets. ' The best I've ever seen. I guess he'll boast about them till we're sick of hearing about bruises. Didn't he make a thump when he fell ? Did you and Larry find the tramp ? What happened ? '

' Well, he's not the person who hid in the ditch, nor the one whose coat got caught on the brambles,' said Pip. 'We saw both his shoes and his coat. He heard all the quarrels that went on. Larry and I thought we'd ask him a few questions to-morrow when he comes to get the boots. I believe he could tell us quite a few things if he was certain we wouldn't put the police after him. He may even have spotted who was hiding in the ditch!'

'Oooh,' said Bets, thrilled. 'Oh, Pip, wasn't it funny when the tramp woke and saw Larry kneeling in front of him—and after that, old Clear-Orf doing the same thing!'

'Yes, it was funny,' said Pip, grinning. 'Hallo, there's Fatty and Buster.'

Fatty limped into the garden, walking extremely stiffly. He had tried to make up his mind whether to act very heroically, and pooh-pooh his fall, but limp to make the others sorry for him, or whether to make out that he had hurt himself inside very badly and frighten them.

At the moment he was behaving heroically. He smiled at Bets and Pip, and sat down very gingerly.

'Do you hurt much?' asked Bets sympathetically.

'Oh, I'm all right,' said Fatty, in a very, very brave voice. 'A fall off a rick isn't much! Don't you worry about *me*!'

The others stared at him in admiration.

'Do you want to see my bruises?' asked Fatty.

'I've seen them,' said Bets. 'But I don't mind seeing them again. I like bruises best when they begin to go yellow, really. Pip hasn't seen them, have you, Pip?'

Pip was torn between wanting to see the bruises,

67

and not wanting Fatty to boast and show them off. Fatty didn't wait for him to answer, however. He began to strip off various garments, and display bruises of many sizes and shapes. They were certainly good ones.

' I've never seen such beauties,' said Pip, unable to stop himself admiring them. ' I never have bruises like that. I suppose it's being fat that makes them spread so. Won't you look lovely when you go yellow-green ? '

' That's one thing about me,' said Fatty, ' I'm a wonderful bruiser. Once, when I ran into the goal-post at football, I got a bruise just here that was exactly the shape of a church-bell. It was most peculiar.'

' Oh, I wish I'd seen it,' said Bets.

' And another time,' said Fatty, ' some one hit me with a stick—just here—and the next morning the bruise was exactly like a snake, head and all.'

Pip reached out for a stick. ' I'll give you another snake if you like,' he said. ' Just tell me where you'd like it.'

Fatty was offended. ' Don't be mean,' he said.

' Well, shut up about snakes and church-bells then,' said Pip, in disgust. ' Bets has only got to say " Oh, how wonderful," and you make up the tallest stories I've ever heard. Hallo—here are Larry and Daisy.'

Fatty didn't like to say any more about his bruises, though he was simply longing to show them to the others. Larry had been thinking a lot about everything whilst he had gobbled up his late dinner, and he had his plans all ready. He didn't even ask poor Fatty how he felt after his fall, but started off straightaway with his ideas.

' Look here,' he said, ' I've been thinking about Clear-Orf. I don't like him knowing about those footprints. We don't want him to solve this mystery before we do. For all we know he's got his eye on Peeks and Mr. Smellie too, as well as the tramp. We *must* get in first. It would be too awful if horrid old Clear-Orf found out everything before we did ! '

' It would,' agreed every one wholeheartedly. Buster wagged his tail.

' We must see this man-servant, Peeks,' said Larry. ' It's most important. I don't suspect that old tramp any more now that I've seen his shoes and coat. Anyway, I'm certain that if he had fired the cottage, he would have fled away out of the district as soon as ever he could. As it is, he's still about. I don't believe he did it. I'm much more inclined to think that Peeks did it. We must find out.'

' We must,' agreed every one again.

' I shall question the tramp closely to-morrow,' said Larry, rather grandly. ' I feel certain he can tell us plenty. Fatty, do you think you and Daisy could find out about Peeks to-morrow ? I'll stay here with Pip and Bets and question the tramp.'

' Right ! ' said Fatty and Daisy joyfully. If only they could get ahead of Clear-Orf ! They simply must beat him !

9   LILY COMES INTO THE STORY

FATTY really was too stiff to want to do anything more that day, so Larry, Pip and Daisy left him in the garden with Bets and Buster, reading quietly. They thought they would go down to Mr. Hick's house and talk to Mrs. Minns again.

' We ought really to find out if Mrs. Minns could have fired the cottage herself,' said Larry. ' I don't feel as if she did, but you can't go by feelings if you are a detective. Also, we must get Horace Peeks's address.'

' We'll take some fish for Sweetie, the cat,' said Daisy. ' I think there was some left over that cook might let me have. Mrs. Minns will be awfully pleased to see us if we take a present for Sweetie.'

The cook gave her a fish-head, wrapped up in paper. Buster smelt it and wanted to follow Daisy, but Fatty held him firmly by the collar.

' It's no good him coming,' said Daisy. ' He'd be sure to chase Sweetie, and then Mrs. Minns would chase *us* ! '

They went down the lane together. ' Leave me to do the talking,' said Larry.

Daisy laughed. ' Don't you worry—it will be Mrs. Minns who does it ! ' she said.

They arrived at the kitchen door and looked inside. Lily was there, writing a letter. She looked as if she had been crying. ' Where's Mrs. Minns ? ' asked Larry.

' Upstairs,' said Lily. ' She's in a bad temper.
I upset a jug of milk all over her, and she keeps on
saying I did it on purpose.'

' Were you here on the night of the fire ? ' asked
Larry. Lily shook her head.

' Where were you, then ? ' asked Larry. ' Didn't
you see the fire ? '

' I saw it when I came back from my evening
off,' said Lily. ' Never you mind where I was. It's
got nothing to do with you ! '

' I know,' said Larry, surprised at Lily's violent
tone. ' What I can't understand is—why didn't
Mrs. Minns or her sister smell the fire when it
began ! '

' Here's Mrs. Minns's sister now,' said Lily,
looking up as a very fat woman, with twinkling eyes
under a big hat trimmed with flowers, came up to
the kitchen door. She looked in and seemed surprised to see the children.

' Hallo, Mrs. Jones,' said Lily sulkily. ' Mrs.
Minns is upstairs changing her dress. She won't
be a minute.'

Mrs. Jones came in and sank into a rocking-chair,
breathing heavily. ' My, it's hot to-day,' she said.
' Who are all these children ? '

' We live up the lane,' said Pip. ' We've brought
a fish-head for Sweetie.'

' Where are all the kittens ? ' asked Daisy, looking
at the empty basket.

' Oh ! ' said Lily. ' I hope they haven't gone
out of the kitchen and upstairs. Mrs. Minns told
me to keep the door shut ! '

' Perhaps the kittens are outside,' said Larry,

71

shutting the door that led into the hall. He didn't particularly want Mr. Hick to hear the talking in the kitchen and come in. ' Oh—there's Sweetie ! '

The big black and white cat came into the kitchen, her tail straight up in the air. She smelt the fish-head and went to Daisy. Daisy unwrapped it and put it into the cat's dinner-bowl in a corner of the kitchen. Sweetie immediately took it out of the bowl and began to eat it on the floor.

' Was Sweetie frightened of the fire the other night ? ' asked Pip, thinking it was about time to start on the subject.

' She was kind of restless,' said Mrs. Jones.

' Oh, were *you* here ? ' said Daisy, pretending to be surprised. ' Goodness—how was it you didn't know the cottage was burning then ? '

' I did,' said Mrs. Jones indignantly. ' Didn't I keep saying to Maria, " Maria, there's something burning ! " I've a very good nose, but Maria hasn't. I kept sniffing round the kitchen, and I even put my nose into the hall, thinking there might be something burning there.'

' Didn't Mrs. Minns go and see if there was anything burning too ? ' asked Larry.

' Ah, Maria didn't want to move that evening,' said Mrs. Jones. ' She'd got her rheumatism back something cruel. She was stuck, real stuck.'

' What do you mean, stuck ? ' asked Larry, with interest.

' Well, she sat down in this rocking-chair at tea-time, and she says to me, " Hannah," she says, " I'm stuck. Me rheumatism's got me again, and I can't move." So I says to her, " Maria, you just stay put. I'll get the tea and everything. Mr. Hick is out, so there's no dinner to get. I'll just stay with you till your poor legs are better." '

The children listened, and each of them thought the same thing. ' If Mrs. Minns was stuck in a chair all the evening with rheumatism, then she couldn't have fired the cottage ! '

' And didn't poor Mrs. Minns get up at all out of the rocking-chair ? ' asked Daisy. ' Not till you really knew there was a fire, I mean ? '

' No—Maria just stayed put,' said Mrs. Jones. ' It wasn't till me nose told me there really was something burning terrible that Maria got up. I went to the kitchen-door and sniffed—and then I went out into the garden—and I saw the flare down at the bottom there. I shouted out, " There's a fire, Maria ! " and she turned as white as a sheet. " Come on, Maria ! " I says, " We've got to do something." But poor Maria, she can't get out of her chair, she's so stuck ! '

The children drank all this in. It certainly could have been nothing to do with Mrs. Minns. If she had been so ' stuck ' with rheumatism, she wouldn't have been likely to rush round setting fire to cottages. And anyway her sister was with her all the time. It was quite plainly nothing to do with Mrs. Minns. That was another Suspect crossed off !

Mrs. Minns opened the kitchen door and came in, looking angry. She had been upstairs to take off her milk-drenched dress. She glared at Lily, and then looked in surprise at the three children.

' Well, Maria,' said Mrs. Jones, ' how's the rheumatics ? '

'Good afternoon, Mrs. Minns,' said Daisy. 'We came to bring a fish-head for Sweetie.'

Mrs. Minns beamed. She was always touched when any one did anything for her precious cat. 'That's nice of you,' she said. 'My rheumatism's better,' she said to her sister. 'Though what it will be like after being drenched with milk, I *don't* know. Really, things are coming to a pretty pass when that girl Lily throws milk all over me."

'I didn't do it on purpose,' said Lily sulkily. 'Can I go to the post with this letter?'

'No, that you can't,' said Mrs. Minns. 'You just get the tea ready for Mr. Hick. Go on now—stop your letter-writing and get a bit of work done for a change.'

'I want to catch the post,' said Lily, looking ready to cry.

'Well, you won't,' said Mrs. Minns unkindly. Lily started to cry, and the children felt sorry for her. She got up and began to get out cups and saucers.

The children wondered how to mention Horace Peeks. They wanted to get his address so that they might go and see him.

'Has Mr. Hick got a new man-servant yet?' asked Larry, at last.

'He's been seeing some to-day,' said Mrs. Minns, sinking into an arm-chair, which creaked dolefully beneath her weight. 'I only hope he gets one that doesn't put on airs and graces like Mr. Peeks, that's all.'

'Does Mr. Peeks live near here?' asked Pip innocently.

'Yes,' said Mrs. Minns. 'Let me see now—where does he live? Oh, my memory—it gets worse every day!'

There came a most unwelcome interruption just as it seemed that Mrs. Minns was on the point of remembering Horace Peeks's address. The kitchen door shot open, and three kittens flew through the air, landing on the floor with mews and hisses. Every one looked round in amazement.

Mr. Hick stood at the door, his front tuft of hair bristling like a parrot's crest.

'Those kittens were in my study!' he shouted. 'Are my orders never to be obeyed? Unless they are out of the house by this evening, I'll drown the lot!'

He was about to bang the door when he caught sight of the three children. He advanced into the kitchen and pointed a finger at them. 'Didn't I turn you out before? How dare you come here again?'

Larry, Pip and Daisy got up and fled. They were not cowards, but really Mr. Hick was so very fierce that it honestly seemed as if he might throw them out, just as he had flung the kittens into the kitchen!

They ran up the drive—but half-way to the gate Larry stopped. 'Wait till old Hiccup has gone out of the kitchen,' he said. 'We simply *must* get Horace Peeks's address. We can't do anything about him till we know where he is.'

They waited for a minute or two and then went back very cautiously to the kitchen. Mrs. Minns was talking to her sister, and Lily was still clattering about with the tea-things. The children put their heads round the door.

'What do you want now?' asked Mrs. Minns good-naturedly. 'My word, you ran away like frightened mice! Made me laugh to see you!'

'You were just trying to think of Horace Peeks's address when Mr. Hick came in,' said Larry.

'Was I, now?' said Mrs. Minns. 'Well, it came into my mind in a flash, like—and now it's gone again. Let me see—let me see. . . .'

She was thinking hard, and the children were waiting breathlessly, when the sound of heavy footsteps came up to the kitchen door and a loud knock was heard.

Mrs. Minns went to the door. The children saw that it was Mr. Goon, the policeman! They never seemed to be able to get away from old Clear-Orf.

'Morning, Mam,' said Clear-Orf to Mrs. Minns, and he took out his large black notebook. 'About this here fire—I think you've given me all the information I require. But I'd just like to ask you a few questions about that fellow Peeks.'

The children frowned at one another. So Clear-Orf was after Peeks too!

'Do you know his address?' asked Clear-Orf, looking at Mrs. Minns out of his bulging pale-blue eyes.

'Well,' said Mrs. Minns, 'if that isn't a peculiar thing, Mr. Goon—I was just trying to think of his address at the very moment you knocked! These children wanted to know it.'

'What children?' said Clear-Orf in surprise.

He put his head in at the door and saw Larry, Daisy and Pip.

'You again!' he said in disgust. 'Clear orf! You kids are always popping up. You're a regular nuisance. What do you want Peeks's address for? Just nosey, I suppose?'

The children said nothing. Mr. Goon pointed backwards with his thumb. 'Go home!' he said. 'I've private business to do here. Clear orf!'

There was nothing for it but to 'clear orf,' and the children did so, running up the drive to the gate. They were very angry.

'Just as Mrs. Minns was thinking of the address!' said Larry.

'I hope she doesn't think of it and tell Clear-Orf,' said Pip gloomily. 'If she does, Clear-Orf will go over and see Peeks before we do.'

'Blow!' said Daisy. They all felt very disheartened. They were just going out of the gate when they heard a low whistle from the bushes nearby. They turned back to see who it was.

Lily appeared, a letter in her hand. She looked frightened, but determined. 'Will you post this letter for me?' she asked. 'It's to Mr. Peeks, to warn him that people are saying he started the fire. But he didn't, he didn't. I know he didn't! You post the letter, will you?'

There was a shout from the kitchen. 'Lily! Where are you!'

Lily disappeared at once. The children ran out of the gate, excited and surprised. They stopped behind a hedge when they had gone a little way, and examined Lily's envelope. It had no stamp on. The girl had forgotten it in her hurry.

' Golly ! ' said Larry, ' here we've been all the afternoon trying to get Horace Peeks's address and couldn't—and now, suddenly, it's just been presented to us, given into our hands ! '

' What a bit of luck ! ' said Daisy, thrilled. ' I *am* pleased.'

' The thing is—do we want Peeks to be warned ? ' said Larry. ' You see—if he did do the crime, he ought to be caught and punished. There's no doubt about that. If he is warned beforehand that people are suspecting him, he might run away. Then we shouldn't solve the mystery.'

They all stared at one another. Then Pip had an idea. ' I know ! We'll go and find Peeks after tea to-day, instead of waiting for to-morrow. We'll see him and try to make up our minds if he did it or not. If we think he didn't do it, we'll give him Lily's letter ! '

' Good idea ! ' said the others, pleased. ' After all, we can't post a letter without a stamp—but we can deliver it by hand.' They looked at the address.

Mr. H. Peeks,
    Ivy Cottage,
      Wilmer Green.

' We'll go on our bikes,' said Larry. ' Come on —we must tell the others ! '

10 INTERVIEWING MR. HORACE PEEKS

THE three of them went back to Fatty and Bets. Buster greeted them uproariously.

' Hallo,' said Fatty, ' how did you get on ? '

' Awfully badly at first,' said Larry, ' and then, right at the end, we had a slice of good luck.'

He told Bets and Fatty about the afternoon and they listened with the greatest interest. They all examined Peeks's address, and were thrilled.

' So now Pip and Daisy and I are going on our bikes to Wilmer Green,' said Larry. ' It's only about five miles. At least, we'll have tea first and then go.'

' I want to go too,' said Bets at once.

' I'd *like* to go, but I believe I'm too stiff,' said Fatty.

' You stay with Bets,' said Pip. ' We don't want to appear in a crowd. It might put Peeks on his guard.'

' You keep leaving me out,' said Bets sadly.

' No, we don't,' said Larry. ' Do you really want a job ? Well, find out Mr. Smellie's address, see ? Fatty will help you. It may be in the telephone book, or somebody may know it. We shall want his address to-morrow, because we must go and see him too. All the Suspects must be interviewed ! '

' Two of them are crossed off now,' said Pip. ' Mrs. Minns didn't do it—and I'm sure the tramp didn't either. That only leaves Mr. Smellie and

Mr. Peeks. I do wish we could find some one wearing rubber-soled shoes with those markings. It would be such a help ! '

' I'll find out Mr. Smellie's address ! ' said Bets joyfully, pleased at having something real to do. ' I'll bring the telephone book out here to Fatty.'

The tea-bell rang. The children ran indoors to wash, and were soon sitting down eating bread and butter and jam. Larry and Daisy stayed to tea, but Fatty had to go back to the hotel, as his mother was expecting him.

After tea Fatty came back and joined Bets. Larry and Pip and Daisy got out bicycles and cycled off. They knew the way to Wilmer Green quite well.

' What excuse shall we make for asking to see Horace Peeks ? ' said Larry, as they cycled quickly along.

Nobody could think of a good excuse. Then Pip had an idea. ' Let's go to the house and just ask for a drink of water,' he said. ' If Peeks's mother is there I expect she'll talk nineteen to the dozen, and we may find out what we want to know—which is—where was Horace Peeks on the evening of the fire ? If his mother says he was at home with her all the evening we can cross him off.'

' Good idea ! ' said Larry. ' And I'll tell you what I'll do, too ; just before we get to the house I'll let the air out of my front tyre, see—and pumping up the bike will make a further excuse for staying and talking.'

' Right ! ' said Pip. ' I do think we are getting clever.'

After some hard cycling they came to the village

of Wilmer Green. It was a pretty place, with a duck-pond on which many white ducks were swimming. The children got off their bicycles and began to look for Ivy Cottage. They asked a little girl where it was, and she pointed it out to them. It was well set back from the road, and backed on to a wood.

The children rode to it, dismounted and went into the old wooden gate. Larry had already let the air out of his front tyre and it was almost flat.

'I'll ask for the water,' said Daisy. They went up to the door, which was half-open. There was the sound of an iron going thump, thump, thump.

Daisy knocked on the door. 'Who's there?' said a sharp voice.

'Please could we have a drink of water?' asked Daisy.

'Come in and get it,' said the voice. Daisy opened the door wide and went in. She saw a sharp-faced old lady ironing a shirt. She nodded her head towards a tap over a sink.

'Water's there,' she said. 'Cup's on the shelf behind.'

The two boys came in whilst Daisy was running the water. 'Good evening,' they said politely. 'Thank you so much for letting us have some water. We've cycled quite a way, and we're awfully hot,' said Larry. The old lady looked at him approvingly. He was a good-looking boy, and had beautiful manners when he liked.

'Where have you come from?' she asked, thumping with her iron.

'From Peterswood,' said Larry. 'I don't expect you know it, do you?'

'That I do,' said the old lady. 'My son was in service there with a Mr. Hick.'

'Oh, how funny!' said Daisy, sipping the cup of water. 'We were down in Mr. Hick's garden the other night, when there was a fire.'

'A fire!' said the old woman, startled. 'What fire? I hadn't heard anything of that. Not Mr. Hick's house, surely?'

'No—only his cottage workroom,' said Pip. 'No one was hurt. But surely your son would have told you about it, wouldn't he—didn't he see it?'

'When was the fire?' asked the old lady.

Pip told her. Mrs. Peeks stopped ironing and thought. 'Well, now, that was the day Horace came home,' she said. 'That's why he didn't know anything about it. He'd had a quarrel with Mr. Hick, and he gave notice. He got here in the afternoon and gave me a real start.'

'Then he must have missed the fire,' said Pip. 'I expect he was with you all the evening, wasn't he?'

'No, he wasn't,' said Mrs. Peeks. 'He went out after tea on his bike, and I didn't see him again till it was dark. I didn't ask him where he went. I'm not one for poking and prying. I expect he was down at the Pig and Whistle, playing darts. He's a rare one for darts, is our Horace.'

The children exchanged glances. So Horace disappeared after tea—and didn't come back till dark! That seemed very suspicious indeed. *Very* suspicious! Where was he that evening? It would have been so easy to slip back to Peterswood on his bike, hide in the ditch, and set fire to the cottage when no one was about—and then cycle back unseen in the darkness !

Larry wondered what sort of shoes Horace wore. He looked round the kitchen. There was a pair of shoes waiting to be cleaned in a corner. They were about the size of the footprint. But they didn't have rubber soles. Perhaps Peeks was wearing them now. The children wished he would come in.

' I must just go and pump up my front tyre,' said Larry, getting up. ' I won't be a minute.'

But although he left the other two quite five minutes to talk, there didn't seem anything more to be found out. They said good-bye to Mrs. Peeks and went to join Larry.

' Didn't find out anything else,' said Pip in a low voice. ' Hallo—who's this ? Do you think it is Horace ? '

They saw a weedy-looking young man coming in at the gate. He had an untidy lock of hair that hung over his forehead, a weak chin, and rather bulging blue eyes, a little like Mr. Goon's. He wore a grey flannel coat !

All the children noticed this immediately. Daisy's heart began to beat fast. Could they have found the right person at last ?

' What you doing here ? ' asked Horace Peeks.

' We came to ask for a drink of water,' said Larry, wondering if he could possibly edge round Horace to see if there was a tear in his grey coat anywhere !

' And we found out that we come from the same place that you lived in only a little while ago,' said Daisy brightly. ' We live at Peterswood.'

'That's where I worked,' said Horace. 'Do you know that bad-tempered old Mr. Hick? I worked for him, but nothing was ever right. Nasty old man.'

'We don't like him very much ourselves,' said Pip. 'Did you know there was a fire at his place the day you left?'

'How do you know what day I left?' asked Mr. Peeks, astonished.

'Oh, we just mentioned the fire to your mother and she said it must have been the day you left, because you didn't know anything about it,' said Pip.

'Well, all I can say is that Mr. Hick deserved to have his whole place burnt down, the mean, stingy, bad-tempered old fish!' said Horace. 'I'd like to have seen it!'

The children looked at him, wondering if he was pretending or not. 'Weren't you there, then?' asked Daisy, in an innocent voice.

'Never you mind where I was!' said Peeks. He looked round at Larry, who was edging all round him to see if he could spot a tear in the grey flannel coat that Horace was wearing. 'What are you doing?' he asked. 'Sniffing round me like a dog! Stop it!'

'You've got a spot on your coat,' said Larry, making up the first excuse he could think of. 'I'll rub it off.'

He pulled out his handkerchief—and with it came the letter that Lily had given to him to give to Horace Peeks! It fell to the ground, address side upwards! Horace bent to pick it up and stared

84

in the utmost astonishment at his own name on the envelope !

He turned to Larry. ' What's this ? ' he said.

Larry could have kicked himself for his carelessness. ' Oh, it's for you,' he said. ' Lily asked us to post it to you, but as we were coming over here we thought we might as well deliver it by hand.'

Horace Peeks looked as if he was going to ask some awkward questions, and Larry thought it was about time to go. He wheeled his bicycle to the gate.

' Well, good-bye,' he said. ' I'll tell Lily you've got her letter.'

The three of them mounted their bicycles and rode off. Horace shouted after them. ' Hie ! You come back a minute ! '

But they didn't go back. Their minds were in a whirl ! They rode for about a mile and a half, and then Larry jumped off his bicycle and went to sit on a gate. ' Come on ! ' he called to the others. ' We'll just talk a bit and see what we think.'

They sat in a row on the gate, looking very serious. ' I was an idiot to drag that letter out of my pocket like that,' said Larry, looking ashamed of himself. ' But perhaps it was as well. I suppose letters ought to be delivered—oughtn't they ? Do you think Horace started the fire ? '

' It looks rather like it,' said Daisy thoughtfully. ' He had a spite against Mr. Hick that very day, and his mother doesn't know where he was that night. You didn't notice if his shoes had rubber, criss-crossed soles, did you, Larry ? And was his grey flannel coat torn in any way ? '

' I couldn't see his shoe-soles, and as far as I

could see, his coat wasn't torn at all,' said Larry.
'Anyway, that letter will warn him now, and he'll
be on his guard!'

They talked for a little while, wondering what
to do about Peeks. They decided that they would
set him aside for a while and see what Mr. Smellie
was like. It seemed to rest now between Horace
Peeks and Mr. Smellie. It was no good deciding
about Peeks until they had also seen Smellie!

They mounted their bicycles again and set off.
They free-wheeled down a hill and round a corner.
Larry went into some one with a crash! He fell
off and so did the other person!

Larry sat up and stared apologetically at the
man in the road. To his horror it was old Clear-
Orf!

'What! You again!' yelled Mr. Goon, in a
most threatening voice. Larry hurriedly got up.
The other two were farther down the road,
laughing.

'What you doing?' yelled Mr. Goon, as Larry
stood his bicycle upright, ready to mount again.

'I'm clearing orf!' shouted Larry. 'Can't
you see? I'm clearing orf!'

And the three of them rode giggling down the
hill, pausing to wonder every now and again if old
Clear-Orf was on his way to see Horace Peeks!
Well—Horace was now warned by Lily's letter—so
Mr. Goon wouldn't get much out of him, that was
certain!

11   THE TRAMP TURNS UP AGAIN

IT was seven o'clock when the three of them rode up Pip's drive. Bets was getting worried, because her bedtime was coming very near, and she couldn't bear to think that she would have to go before she heard the news that Larry, Daisy and Pip might be bringing.

She jumped for joy when she heard their bicycle bells jangling as they rode at top speed up the drive. It was such a lovely evening that she, Fatty and Buster were still in the garden. Fatty had examined his bruises again, and was pleased to see that they were now a marvellous red-purple. Although they hurt him he couldn't help being very proud of them.

'What news? What news?' yelled Bets, as the three travellers returned.

'Plenty!' cried Larry. 'Half a tick—let's put our bikes away!'

Soon all five and Buster were sitting in the summer-house talking. Fatty's eyes nearly dropped out of his head when he heard how Larry had dragged the letter out of his pocket and dropped it by accident at Horace Peeks's feet.

'But Clear-Orf's on the trail all right,' said Pip. 'We met him as we were going home. Larry knocked him off his bike, going round the corner. Clear-Orf must be brighter than we think. He's a little way behind us, that's all!'

'Well, we'd better get on Mr. Smellie's track

as soon as possible to-morrow,' said Fatty. ' Bets and I have got his address.'

' Good for you,' said Larry. ' Where does he live ? '

' It was in the telephone book,' said Bets. ' It was very easy to find because there was only one Mr. Smellie. He lives at Willow-Dene, Jeffreys Lane.'

' Why, that's just at the back of our garden,' said Larry, in surprise. ' Isn't it, Daisy ? Willow-Dene backs on to half our garden. I never knew who lived there, because we've never once seen any one in the garden, except an old woman.'

' That would be Miss Miggle, the housekeeper,' said Fatty.

' How do you know ? ' asked Daisy, in surprise.

' Oh, Bets and I have been very good Find-Outers to-day,' said Fatty, with a grin. ' We asked your gardener where Willow-Dene was, and he knew it, because his brother works there. And he told us about Miss Miggle, and how difficult she finds it to keep old Mr. Smellie clean, and make him have his meals, and remember to put his mack on when it rains, and so on.'

' What's the matter with him, then ? ' said Larry. ' Is he mad or silly or something ? '

' Oh no. He's a something -ologist,' said Bets. ' He studies old, old papers and documents, and knows more about them than any one else. He doesn't care about anything but old writings. The gardener says he's got some very, very valuable ones himself.'

' Well, as he conveniently lives so near us, per-

haps Larry and I could interview him to-morrow,'
said Daisy, very much looking forward to a bit more
' find-outing,' as Bets kept calling it. ' I think we're
getting rather good at interviewing. I bet we're
better than old Clear-Orf. Any Suspect would
know at once that Mr. Goon was after him and
would be careful what he said. But people talk to
children without thinking anything about it.'

Larry got his notes out from behind the loose
board in the summer-house. ' We must add a bit
to them,' he said, and began to write. Pip got out
the match-box and opened it. He wanted to see if
the bit of grey flannel was at all like the grey coat
that Horace Peeks had worn. It did look rather
like it.

' Still, Larry couldn't see any torn bit,' said
Pip. ' And I had a good look at his trousers too, but
I couldn't see any tear in them.'

The children stared at the grey flannel. Pip
put it back into the box. He unfolded Fatty's
beautiful drawing of the footprints, and grinned as
he remembered the tail, ears and hands that he and
Larry had so solemnly talked about when they first
looked at the footprints in the drawing.

' You know it's not half a bad drawing,' said
Pip. Fatty brightened up very much, but he was
wise enough not to say a word this time. ' I shall
learn these criss-cross markings by heart, so that
if ever I come across them at any time I shall know
them at once.'

' I'll learn them too,' said Bets, and she stared
seriously at the drawing. She felt quite certain
that if ever she spotted a footprint anywhere in the

mud with those special markings, she would know them immediately.

' I've finished my notes,' said Larry. ' I can't say that our clues have helped us at all. We must really find out if Peeks wears rubber-soled shoes— and we mustn't forget to look at Mr. Smellie's either.'

' But they may not be wearing them,' objected Fatty. ' They might have them in the cupboard, or in their bedroom.'

' Perhaps we could peep into Mr. Smellie's boot-cupboard,' said Larry, who hadn't the faintest idea how he would set about doing such a thing. ' Listen —there are four Suspects. One was Mrs. Minns, but as she had rheumatism all the evening of the fire, and was stuck fast in her chair, according to her sister, *she* couldn't have started the fire. So that leaves three Suspects. The tramp was another Suspect, but as he does not wear rubber-soled shoes, or a grey coat, and did not get away quickly as we might have expected him to, we can practically rule him out too. So that leaves two Suspects.'

' I think it was Horace Peeks,' said Pip. ' Why shouldn't he tell us where he was on the evening of the fire ? That's very suspicious.'

' Well, if Mr. Smellie can tell us where *he* was, that will only leave Horace Peeks,' said Larry. ' Then we will really pay all our attention to him, find out what his shoes are like, and if he has a grey coat indoors with a tear, and what he was doing on that evening and everything.'

' *Then* what do we do ? ' asked Bets. ' Go and tell the police ? '

'What! Tell old Clear-Orf and have him taking all the credit and praise to himself?' cried Larry. 'I should think not. We ought to go to the Inspector of Police himself, Inspector Jenks. He's head of all the police in this district. Daddy knows him quite well. He's a very, very clever man, and he lives in the next town.'

'I should be frightened of him,' said Bets. 'I'm even a bit frightened of Clear-Orf.'

'Pooh! Frightened of that old stick-in-the-mud with his froggy eyes?' said Fatty. 'You want to be like Larry, sail down a hill on your bike and knock him off, crash, round the corner!'

Every one laughed. Then a bell rang and the five got up, with Buster running round their legs. Fatty said good-night and went to have dinner with his father and mother at the hotel. Larry and Daisy got their bicycles and rode home. Pip went in to supper and Bets went off to bed. Buster went with Fatty. His young master retired to bed very early that night for he was still stiff and his bruises were painful. Buster had a good look at them when Fatty undressed, but didn't seem to think much of them.

'To-morrow that old tramp will come to get the boots Mummy has looked out for him,' said Pip to Bets. 'We'll ask him a few questions.'

'What questions?' asked Bets.

'We'll ask him straight out if he saw Horace Peeks in the ditch, hiding,' said Pip. 'If he says yes, that will be a great help to us.'

None of the children slept very well that night for they were all excited over the happenings of the day. Bets dreamt of Clear-Orf, and woke with a squeal, dreaming that he was putting her in prison for starting the fire! Fatty slept badly because of his bruises. It didn't matter how he lay, he seemed to lie on two or three.

It had been arranged that the next day Pip and Bets and Fatty should stay in their garden, on the look out for the tramp. Pip should question him carefully. Larry had told him what to ask.

' Have the boots out so that he can see them and want them badly,' said Larry. ' But don't let him have them till he's answered your questions. No answers, no boots. See ? '

So the next day Fatty and Buster joined Pip and Bets, and the four of them waited for the tramp to turn up.

The tramp did turn up. He slipped slyly in at the back gate, looking all round and about as if he thought some one was after him. He still had on the terrible old shoes, with toes sticking out of the upper parts. Pip saw him and gave a low call.

' Hallo ! Come over here ! '

The tramp looked over to where Pip was standing. ' You're not setting that bobby after me ? ' he asked.

' Of course not,' said Pip impatiently. ' We don't like him any more than you do.'

' Got the boots ? ' asked the tramp. Pip nodded. The old fellow shambled over to him and Pip took him to the summer-house. There was a small wooden table there, and the boots were on it. The tramp's eyes gleamed when he saw them.

' Good boots,' he said. ' They'll fit me proper.'

'Wait a minute,' said Pip, as the tramp put out his hand to take them. 'Wait a minute. We want you to answer a few questions first, please.'

The tramp stared at him, and looked sulky. 'I'm not going to be mixed up in no trouble,' he said.

'Of course not,' said Pip. 'We shan't split on you. What you tell us we shall keep to ourselves.'

'What do you want to know ?' asked the tramp.

'Did you see any one hiding in Mr. Hick's garden on the evening of the fire ?' asked Fatty.

'Yes,' said the tramp. 'I saw some one in the bushes.'

Bets, Pip and Fatty felt quite breathless. 'Did you really *see* them ?' asked Pip.

'Course I see them,' said the tramp. 'I see plenty of people in the garden that evening, so I did.'

'Where were you ?' asked Bets curiously.

'That's none of your business,' said the tramp roughly. 'I wasn't doing no harm.'

'Probably watching the hen-house, waiting for a chance of an egg or two, even though old Hiccup had chased him away,' thought Pip, quite correctly.

They all stared at the tramp, and he stared back. 'Was the person who was hiding in the bushes a young man, with a lock of hair falling over his forehead ?' asked Pip, describing Horace Peeks. 'Did he have sort of bulgy eyes ?'

'Don't know about his eyes,' said the tramp. 'But he had a lock of hair all right. He was whispering to some one, but I couldn't see who.'

This was news. Horace Peeks hiding in the

bushes with somebody else ! Were there two people concerned in the crime then ?

It was a puzzle. Could Horace Peeks and Mr. Smellie have planned the fire together ? The children didn't know what to think.

' Look here,' began Pip. But the tramp had had enough.

' You give me them boots,' he said, and he stretched out his hand for them. ' I'm not saying no more. Be getting myself into trouble if I don't look out. I don't want to be mixed up in anything, I don't. I'm a very honest fellow.'

He took the boots and put them on. He would not say a word more. ' He seems to have gone dumb,' said Pip. They watched the tramp walk away in his new boots, which were a little too big for him, but otherwise very comfortable.

' Well, the mystery is getting deeper,' said Fatty. ' Now we seem to have *two* people hiding in the garden, instead of one. There's no doubt one was dear Horace. But who was the other ? Perhaps Larry and Daisy will have some news for us when they come.'

Buster had growled nearly all the time the tramp had been in the summer-house. Fatty had had to hold him tight, or he would have flown at the dirty old fellow. Now he suddenly began to bark joyously.

' It's Larry and Daisy,' said Bets. ' Oh, good. I wonder if they've got any news.'

12   MR. SMELLIE—AND A RUBBER-
SOLED SHOE

LARRY and Daisy had spent an exciting morning.
They had decided to interview old Mr. Smellie as
soon as possible, and get it over. They talked over
the best way of tackling him.

'We can't very well go and ask for a drink of
water or anything like that,' said Daisy. 'I simply
can't imagine what excuse we can make up for going
to see him.'

They both thought hard for some minutes.
Then Larry looked up. 'What about throwing our
ball into Mr. Smellie's garden ?' he said.

'What good would that do ?' asked Daisy.

'Well, silly, we could go after it—climb over
the wall, don't you see—and hope that he will see
us and ask what we're doing,' said Larry.

'I see,' said Daisy. 'Yes—it seems quite a
good idea.   We'll do that.'

So Larry threw his ball high and it went over
the trees, and fell in the middle of the lawn next
door. The children ran down to the wall at the
bottom. In a moment or two they were over it and
in the bushes at the end of Mr. Smellie's garden.

They went boldly out on to the lawn and began
hunting for the ball. They could see it quite well,
for it was in the edge of a rose-bed on the lawn.
They called to one another as they hunted, hoping
that some one in the house would hear them and
come to a window.

Presently a window opened at the right side of the house, and a man looked out. His head was quite bald on top, and he had a straggling beard that reached almost to the middle of his waistcoat. He wore heavy horn-rimmed glasses that made his eyes look very big.

' What are you doing ? ' he called.

Larry went and stood under the window and spoke extremely politely.

' I hope you don't mind, sir, but our ball fell in your garden, and we're looking for it.'

A gust of wind blew into the garden and flung Daisy's hair over her face. It tugged at Mr. Smellie's beard, and it rustled round the papers on the desk by him. One of them rose into the air and flew straight out of the window. Mr. Smellie made a grab at it, but didn't catch it. It fell to the ground below.

' I'll get it for you, sir,' said Larry politely. He picked up the paper and handed it back to the old man.

' What a very queer paper,' he said. It was thick and yellow, and covered with curious writing.

' It is parchment,' said Mr. Smellie, looking at Larry out of short-sighted eyes. ' This is very, very old.'

Larry thought it would be a good idea to take a great interest in old papers. ' Oh, sir ! ' he said. ' Is it really very old ? How old ? How very interesting ! '

Mr. Smellie was pleased to have any one taking such a sudden interest. ' I have much older ones,' he said. ' I spend my time deciphering them—

He picked up the paper

reading them, you know. We learn a great deal of old history that way.'

'How marvellous!' said Larry. 'I suppose you couldn't show me any, sir, could you?'

'Certainly, my boy, certainly,' said Mr. Smellie, positively beaming at Larry. 'Come along in. I think you will find that the garden door is open.'

'Could my sister come too?' asked Larry. 'She would be very, very interested, I know.'

'Dear me, what unusual children,' thought Mr. Smellie, as he watched them going in at the garden door. They were just wiping their feet when a little bird-like woman darted out of a room nearby and gazed at them in surprise.

'Whatever are you doing here?' she said. 'This is Mr. Smellie's house. He doesn't allow any one inside.'

'He's just asked us in,' said Larry politely. 'We have wiped our feet very carefully.'

'Just asked you in!' said Miss Miggle, the housekeeper, filled with astonishment. 'But he never asks *any* one in—except Mr. Hick. And since they quarrelled even he hasn't been here.'

'But perhaps Mr. Smellie has visited Mr. Hick!' said Larry, still wiping his feet, anxious to go on with the conversation.

'No, indeed he hasn't,' said Miss Miggle. 'He told me that he wasn't going to visit any one who shouted at him in the disgusting way that Mr. Hick did. Poor old gentleman, he doesn't deserve to be shouted at. He's very absent-minded and a bit queer sometimes, but there's no harm in him.'

'Didn't he go down and see the fire when Mr.

Hick's workroom got burnt ? ' asked Daisy. Miss Miggle shook her head.

' He went out for his usual walk that evening,' she said. ' About six o'clock. But he came back before the fire was discovered.'

The children looked at one another. So Mr. Smellie had gone out that evening—could he possibly have slipped down to Mr. Hick's, started the fire and come back again ?

' Did you see the fire ? ' asked the housekeeper, with interest. But the children had no time to answer, for Mr. Smellie came out to see what they were doing. They went with him into his study— a most untidy room, strewn with all kinds of papers, its walls lined with books that reached right up to the ceiling.

' Gracious ! ' said Daisy, looking round. ' Doesn't any one ever tidy this room ? You can hardly walk without stepping on papers ! '

' Miss Miggle is forbidden to tidy this room,' said Mr. Smellie, putting his glasses on firmly. They had a habit of slipping down his nose, which was rather small. ' Now let me show you these old, old books—written on rolls of paper—in the year, let me see now, in the year . . . er, er . . . I must look it up again. I knew it quite well, but that fellow Hick always contradicts me, and he muddles my mind so that I can't remember.'

' I expect your quarrel a day or two ago really upset you,' said Daisy, most sympathetically. Mr. Smellie took off his glasses, polished them and put them back on his nose again.

' Yes,' he said, ' yes. I don't like quarrels. Hick

99

is a most intelligent fellow, but he gets very angry if I don't always agree with him. Now *this* document . . .'

The children listened patiently, not understanding a word of all the long speech that Mr. Smellie was making. He quite forgot that he was talking to children, and he spoke as if Larry and Daisy were as learned as himself. They began to feel very bored. When he turned to get another sheaf of old papers, Larry whispered to Daisy. 'Go and see if you can find any of his shoes in the cupboard outside in the hall.'

Daisy slipped out. Mr. Smellie didn't seem to notice that she was gone. Larry thought he would hardly notice if he, Larry, went too !

Daisy found the hall cupboard. She opened the door and went inside. It was full of boots, shoes, goloshes, sticks and coats. Daisy hurriedly looked at the shoes. She turned up each pair. They seemed about the right size, but they hadn't rubber soles.

Then she turned up a pair that *had* rubber soles ! How marvellous ! Perhaps they were the very ones ! She looked at the markings—but for the life of her she couldn't quite remember the markings in the drawing of the footprint. Were they or were they not just like the ones she was looking at ?

' I'll have to compare them,' thought the little girl at last. ' I must take one shoe home with me and go down to see the footprint drawing. We shall soon see if they are the right ones.'

She stuffed a shoe up the front of her jersey. It

made a very funny lump, but she couldn't think where else to hide the shoe. She crept out of the hall cupboard—straight into Miss Miggle !

Miss Miggle was tremendously astonished to see Daisy coming out of the boot cupboard. ' Whatever are you doing ? ' she asked. ' Surely you are not playing hide-and-seek ? '

' Well—not *exactly*,' said Daisy, who didn't quite know what to say. Miss Miggle carried a tray of buns and milk into the study, where Mr. Smellie was still lecturing to poor Larry. She put the tray down on the table. Daisy followed close behind her, hoping that no one would notice the enormous lump up her jersey.

' I thought the children would like to share your eleven o'clock lunch with you, sir,' said Miss Miggle. She turned to look at Daisy. ' Gracious, child— is that your hanky up the front of your jersey. What a place to keep it ! '

Larry glanced at his sister and was amazed to see the curious lump behind her jersey.

' I keep all kinds of things up my jersey-front,' said Daisy, hoping that no one would ask her to show what she had. Nobody did. Larry was just about to, but stopped himself in time on seeing that the lump was decidedly the shape of a shoe !

The children had milk and buns, but Mr. Smellie did not touch his. Miss Miggle kept at his elbow, trying to stop him talking and to make him eat and drink.

' You have your milk now, sir,' she kept saying. ' You didn't have your breakfast, you know.' She turned to the children. ' Ever since the night of the fire poor Mr. Smellie has been terribly upset. Haven't you, sir ? '

' Well, the loss of those unique and quite irreplaceable documents in the fire gave me a shock,' said Mr. Smellie. ' Worth thousands of pounds they were. Oh, I know Hick was insured and will get his money back all right, but that isn't the point. The documents were of the greatest imaginable value.'

' Did you quarrel about those that morning ? ' asked Daisy.

' Oh no ; you see, Hick said these documents here, that I've just been showing you, were written by a man called Ulinus,' said Mr. Smellie earnestly, ' and I know perfectly well that they were written by three different people. I could not make Mr. Hick see reason. He flew into a terrible temper, and practically turned me out of the house. In fact, he really frightened me. He frightened me so much that I left my documents behind.'

' Poor Mr. Smellie,' said Daisy. ' I suppose you didn't know anything about the fire till the morning ? '

' Not a thing ! ' said Mr. Smellie.

' Didn't you go near Mr. Hick's house when you went for your evening walk ? ' asked Larry. ' If you had, you might have seen the fire starting.'

Mr. Smellie looked startled. His glasses fell right off his nose. He picked them up with a trembling hand and put them on again. Miss Miggle put a hand on his arm.

' Now, now,' she said, ' you just drink up your milk, sir. You're not yourself this last day or two.

You told me you didn't know where you went that evening. You just wandered about.'

'Yes,' said Mr. Smellie, sitting down heavily in a chair. 'That's what I did, didn't I, Miggle? I just wandered about. I can't always remember what I do, can I?'

'No, you can't, sir,' said kind Miss Miggle, patting Mr. Smellie's shoulder. 'The quarrel and the fire have properly upset you. Don't you worry, sir!'

She turned to the children and spoke in a low voice. 'You'd better go. He's got himself a bit upset.'

The children nodded and slipped out. They went into the garden, ran down to the bottom and climbed over the wall.

'Funny, isn't it?' said Daisy. 'Why did he act so strangely when we began to ask him what he did the evening of the fire? Do you suppose he did start it—and has forgotten all about it? Or remembers it and is frightened? Or what?'

'It's a puzzle,' said Larry. 'He seems too gentle a man to do anything so awful as burn a cottage down—but he might be fierce in some queer way. What *have* you got under your jersey, Daisy?'

'A rubber-soled shoe with funny markings,' said Daisy, bringing it out. 'Do you think it is like the footprint?'

'It looks as if it might be,' said Larry, getting excited. 'Let's go straight to the others and compare it with the drawing. Come on! I can hardly wait!'

LARRY and Daisy rushed up to the others.   They
stared at the shoe in her hand in excitement.

' Daisy !   Oh, Daisy !   Have you found the
rubber-soled shoes that belong to the man who
burnt the cottage ? ' cried Fatty.

' I think so,' said Daisy importantly.   ' You see,
Larry and I went to see Mr. Smellie, as we had
planned to do—and whilst he was talking to Larry
I slipped away and looked in his hall cupboard
where shoes and things are kept.   And among the
shoes I found one pair that had rubber soles—and
I'm almost certain the markings are the same as
in those footprints we saw.'

The children crowded round to look.   ' It certainly looks very like the right shoe,' said Pip.

' It *is*,' said Fatty.   ' I ought to know, because
I drew the prints ! '

' Well, *I* don't think it is,' said Bets unexpectedly.
' The squares on the criss-cross pattern aren't quite
so big.   I'm sure they're not.'

' As if *you* could tell ! said Pip scornfully.   ' I
think we've got the right shoe—and we'll prove it.
Get the drawing out of the summer-house, Fatty.'

Fatty went to get it.   He took it from behind the
loose board and brought it out to the others.   They
unfolded it, feeling very thrilled.

They all gazed at the drawing, and then at the
underneath of Mr. Smellie's shoe.   They looked

very, very hard indeed, and then they sighed in disappointment.

'Bets is right,' said Fatty. 'The squares in the pattern of the rubber sole are not quite so big as in my drawing. And I know my drawing is quite correct, because I measured everything carefully. I'm awfully good at things like that. I never make . . .'

'Shut up,' said Larry, who always felt cross when Fatty began his boasting. 'Bets, as you say, is quite right. Good for you, young Bets!'

Bets glowed with pleasure. She really *had* learnt that drawing off by heart, as she had said she would. But she was as disappointed as the others that Daisy had not found the right shoe after all.

'It's awfully difficult being a Find-Outer, isn't it?' said Bets. 'We keep finding out things that aren't much help, or that make everything even more difficult. Pip, tell Larry and Daisy what the tramp said.'

'Oh yes—you must hear about that,' said Pip; and he began to tell Larry and Daisy what had happened with the tramp.

'So now, you see, it's a bigger puzzle than ever,' finished Pip. 'The tramp saw Peeks all right, hiding in the bushes—but he heard him whispering to some one else! Was it old Mr. Smellie, do you think? You say that he went out for a walk that evening, and we know that Peeks was out at that time too. Do you suppose they planned the fire together?'

'They might have,' said Larry thoughtfully. 'They must have known one another—and they

might have got together that day and made up their
minds to punish old Hiccup for his unkindness.
However can we find out ? '

' Perhaps we had better see Mr. Smellie again ? '
said Daisy. ' Anyway, we must put back his shoe
somehow. We can't keep it. Any one seen Clear-
Orf to-day ? '

Nobody had, and nobody wanted to. The
children talked over what they were to do next.
At the moment everything seemed rather muddled
and difficult. Although they had ruled out Mrs.
Minns and the tramp from their list of Suspects, it
seemed impossible to know whether Peeks or
Smellie, or both, had really done the crime.

' It wouldn't be a bad idea to go and see Lily, '
said Fatty suddenly. ' She might tell us a few
things about Horace Peeks. After all, she wrote
him a letter to warn him. She might know more
than we think ! '

' But Lily wasn't there that evening, ' said Daisy.
' It was her evening off. She said so. '

' Well, how are we to know she didn't go
back to Hiccup's and hide in the garden ? ' said
Fatty.

' It seems as if half the village was hiding in
that garden on the evening of the fire, ' said Larry.
' The old tramp was there—and we think Smellie
was—and we know Peeks was—and now you say
perhaps Lily was too ! '

' I know. It's really funny to think how full
Hiccup's garden was that evening ! ' grinned Fatty.
' Well—don't you think it would be a good thing
to go and see Lily ? I don't suspect *her* of anything

—but it would be just as well to see if she can tell us anything to help us.'

' Yes—it's quite a good idea,' said Larry. ' Blow —there's your dinner-bell, Pip. We'll have to leave things till this afternoon. We'll all go down and see Lily—we'll take something for the cat and kittens again. And what about Mr. Smellie's shoe ? When shall we take that back ? '

' We'd better take it back this evening,' said Daisy. ' You take it back, Larry, when it's dark. You may find the garden door open, and you can just slip in and put the shoe back.'

' Right,' said Larry, and he got up to go. ' We'll be back after lunch, Find-Outers. By the way— how are your bruises, Fatty ? '

' Fine,' said Fatty proudly. ' I'll show you them.'

' Can't stop now,' said Larry. ' I'll see them this afternoon. So long ! '

' One's going yellow already,' said Fatty. But Larry and Daisy were gone. Pip and Bets were running to the house, afraid of getting into trouble if they waited any longer. Fatty went off with Buster, hoping that the others wouldn't forget about his bruises in the afternoon.

They all met together again at half-past two. Daisy had stopped at the fishmonger's and bought some fish for the cats. It smelt very strong, and Buster kept worrying her to undo the paper. Nobody asked Fatty about his bruises.

He was offended, and sat gloomily whilst the others discussed what to say to Lily. Bets noticed his face and was surprised.

'What's the matter, Fatty?' she asked. 'Are you ill?'

'No,' said Fatty. 'Just a bit stiff, that's all.'

Daisy took a look at him and gave a little squeal of laughter. 'Oh, poor Fatty! We said we'd look at his bruises and we haven't!'

Every one laughed. 'Fatty's an awful baby,' said Larry. 'Cheer up, Fat-One. Show us your bruises and let us admire every one of them, big, medium and small.'

'They're not worth mentioning,' said Fatty stiffly. 'Come on—let's get going. We'd better get off quickly, or it will be tea-time before we've finished talking.'

'We'll see his bruises at tea-time,' whispered Daisy to Larry. 'He's gone all sulky now!'

So they set off down the lane to find Lily. They felt certain they would not be caught by Hiccup this time because Pip had seen him go by in his car not long before.

'One or two of us must talk to Mrs. Minns,' said Larry,' and the others had better try and get Lily out into the garden and talk to her. We'll see how things go.'

But, as it happened, everything was very easy. Mrs. Minns was out, and there was no one in the kitchen but Lily. She was pleased to see the children and Buster.

'I'll just put Sweetie and the kittens out in the hall, and shut the door,' she said. 'Then that little dog can come in. I like dogs. What's his name? Buster! That's a nice name for a dog. Buster! Buster! Would you like a bone?'

Soon the cat and kittens were safely out of the way and Buster was gnawing a bone on the floor. Lily got out some chocolate from a drawer and handed it round. The children liked her. She seemed much more cheerful without Mrs. Minns to shout at her.

'We gave that note to Horace Peeks,' said Larry. 'We found him all right.'

'Yes, I got a letter from him to-day,' said Lily. She looked rather sad suddenly. 'That nasty Mr. Goon went up and saw him and said all kinds of horrible things to him. Horace is that worried he doesn't know what to do.'

'Did Mr. Goon think he had started the fire, then?' asked Daisy.

'Yes,' said Lily. 'A good many people are saying that. But it isn't true.'

'How do you know?' asked Fatty.

'Well, I *do* know,' said Lily.

'But you weren't here,' said Larry. 'If you weren't here, you can't possibly know who did or didn't start the fire. It *might* have been Horace for all you know.'

'Now, don't you say a word if I tell you something, will you?' said Lily suddenly. 'Promise? Say "Honour bright, I'll not tell a soul."'

The five children recited the seven words very solemnly, and Lily looked relieved.

'Well, then,' she said, 'I'll tell you how I know it wasn't Horace that did it. I know because I met him at five o'clock that day, and I was with him till I got in here at ten o'clock, which is my time for being in!'

The five children stared at her. This was indeed news.

'But why didn't you tell every one that?' asked Larry, at last. 'If you said that, no one would say that Horace burnt down the cottage.'

Lily's eyes filled with tears. 'Well, you see,' she said, 'my mother says I'm too young to say I'll marry any one, but Horace Peeks, he loves me, and I love him. My father said he'd thrash me if he caught me walking out with Horace, and Mrs. Minns said she'd tell my father if ever she caught me speaking a word to him. So I didn't dare to go out to the pictures with him, or even to talk to him in the house.'

'Poor Lily,' said Daisy. 'So when you heard every one talking against him, you were very upset and wrote to warn him?'

'Yes,' said Lily. 'And, you see, if I tell that I was out with him that night, my father will punish me, and maybe Mrs. Minns will send me off, so I'll lose my job. And Horace can't say he was with me because he knows it will be hard for me if he does.'

'Where did you go?' asked Fatty.

'I went on my bicycle half-way to Wilmer Green,' said Lily. 'We met at his sister's there and had tea together, and a bite of supper. We told his sister all about how poor Horace had lost his job that day, and she said maybe her husband would give him some work till he could find another job.'

Fatty remembered that the tramp had seen Horace Peeks in the garden that evening, and he looked sharply at Lily. Could she be telling all the truth ?

'Are you sure that Horace didn't come here at all that night ? ' he said. The others knew why he said it—they too remembered that the tramp had said he had seen Horace Peeks.

'No, no ! ' cried Lily, raising her voice in fright. She twisted her handkerchief round and round in her hands, and stared at the children. ' Horace wasn't anywhere near here. I tell you, we met at his sister's. You can ask her. She'll tell you.'

Larry felt certain that Lily was frightened and was not telling the truth. He decided to be bold.

' Lily,' he said, in a very solemn voice, ' *some*body saw Horace in the garden that evening.'

Lily stared at Larry with wide, horrified eyes. ' No ! ' she said. ' They couldn't have seen him. They couldn't ! '

' Well, they did,' said Larry. Lily stared at him for a moment, and then began to sob.

' Who could have seen him ? ' she said. ' Mrs. Minns and her sister were here in the kitchen. Mr. Hick and the chauffeur were out. There wasn't any one about ; I know there wasn't.'

' How do you know, if you weren't here ? ' asked Larry.

' Well,' said Lily, swallowing a sob. ' Well, I'll tell you. I *was* here ! Now don't you forget you've said honour bright you won't tell a soul ! You see, this is what happened. I rode off to meet Horace, and when I met him he told me he'd left some of his things at Mr. Hick's, and he wanted them. But he didn't dare to go and ask Mr. Hick for them.

So I said to him, " Well, Horace," I said, " Mr. Hick's out, and why don't you come along and get them now, before he comes back ? " '

The children listened breathlessly. They were getting the truth at last !

Lily went on, twisting her handkerchief round and round all the time. ' So when we'd had a cup of tea, we rode off here, and we left our bikes behind the hedge up the lane. Nobody saw us. We walked down, behind the hedge, till we got to Mr. Hick's. Then we both slipped into the bushes and waited a bit to see if any one was about.'

The children nodded. The tramp had said that he had heard Peeks whispering to some one—and that some one must have been Lily !

' I soon found out that Mrs. Minns had got her sister talking to her,' went on Lily, ' and I knew they'd sit there for ages. I said to Horace that I'd get his things for him if he liked, but he wanted to get them himself. So I kept watch whilst he slipped into the house by an open window, got his things and came out into the bushes again. Then we went off on our bikes, without seeing a soul.'

' And Horace didn't slip down the garden to the workroom ? ' asked Larry. Lily looked indignant.

' That he didn't ! ' she said. ' For one thing I'd have seen him. For another thing, he wasn't gone more than three minutes. And for another thing, my Horace wouldn't do a thing like that ! '

' Well—that lets Horace out,' said Larry, saying aloud what every one else was thinking. ' He couldn't have done it. I'm glad you told us all this, Lily. Golly—I do wonder who did it then ? '

' It only leaves Mr. Smellie,' said Bets, without thinking.

Bets's words had an astonishing result. Lily let out a squeal, and stared at Bets as if she couldn't believe her ears. She opened and shut her mouth like a fish, and didn't seem able to say a word.

' Whatever's the matter ? ' asked Larry, in surprise.

' What did she say that for ? ' asked Lily, almost in a whisper. ' How does she know that Mr. Smellie was here that night ? '

Now it was the children's turn to look surprised. ' Well,' said Larry, ' we don't know for certain. We only just wondered. But why are you so astonished, Lily ? What do *you* know about it, anyway ? You didn't see Mr. Smellie, did you ? You said that no one saw you and Horace.'

' That's right,' said Lily. ' But *Horace* saw some one ! When he got in through the window, and went upstairs to get his things, he saw some one creeping in through the garden door. And it was Mr. Smellie ! '

' Golly ! ' said Larry and Pip. They all stared at one another. ' So Mr. Smellie *did* go down here that night ! ' said Larry.

' No wonder he was so startled when you asked him if he went anywhere near Mr. Hick's on the evening of the fire,' said Daisy.

' *He* did it ! ' said Bets trumphantly. ' Now we know. *He* did it ! He's a wicked old man.'

'Do you think he did it?' Fatty asked Lily. She looked puzzled and perplexed.

'*I* don't know,' she said. 'He's a nice, quiet old gentleman, *I* think, and always had a kind word for me. It's not like him to do such a violent thing as set something on fire. But what I *do* know is— it wasn't Horace.'

'No—it doesn't look as if it could have been Horace,' agreed Larry. 'I see now why you didn't say anything before, Lily—you were afraid. Well, we shan't tell any one. It seems to me that we must now turn more of our attention to Mr. Smellie!'

'No doubt about that!' said Fatty. 'Well— we've certainly found out a few things this afternoon!'

14   CLEAR-ORF TURNS UP AT AN AWKWARD MOMENT

THE children stayed talking to Lily for a little while, and then, as it was getting near tea-time they had to go. The girl was relieved to have told somebody of her troubles, and she saw them off, after they had once more promised to keep to themselves all that she had told them.

They were all having tea at Pip's, which was nice because they could talk everything over. They were very excited indeed.

'Things are moving!' said Pip, rubbing his hands together. 'They certainly are moving! I don't believe Horace Peeks had anything to do with it at all. Not a thing. I think it was Mr. Smellie. Look how scared he was when you and Daisy spoke to him about his walk that evening. Why should he be scared if he hadn't done anything wrong ? '

' And we know his shoes are the right size, even if the rubber-soles don't match the drawing,' said Daisy.

' Maybe he *has* got a pair that *do* match,' said· Fatty, ' but he's hidden them somewhere in case he did leave footprints behind. He might have thought of that.'

' Yes, that's so,' said Larry. ' If only we could find some one with a torn grey flannel suit—that really would settle matters ! '

' We really ought to search and see if we can find those shoes,' said Daisy. ' I should think they are in his study somewhere. You know he told us that Miss Miggle isn't allowed to tidy up in there. He could easily pop them into a cupboard there, or behind those rows of books or somewhere.'

' Daisy, that's a clever idea of yours,' said Larry, pleased. ' I believe you're right. Shall I creep in to-night and have a hunt ? '

' Are we allowed to get into people's houses and hunt for their shoes ? ' said Pip doubtfully.

' Well, we can't ask anybody that,' said Larry. ' We'll just have to do it. We're not doing anything wrong. We're only trying to find out something.'

' I know. But grown-ups are funny,' said Pip. ' I'm sure most of them wouldn't like children creeping about their houses looking for clues.'

' Well, I don't see what else to do,' said Larry.

'I really don't. Anyway, silly, we've got to put back the shoe that Daisy took, haven't we?'

'Yes,' agreed Pip. 'That certainly must be done. Don't get caught, that's all!'

'I shan't,' said Larry. 'Sh—here comes your mother, Pip. Talk about something else.'

Pip's mother asked Fatty how he was after his fall. Fatty was delighted, because the others had quite forgotten to ask about his bruises again.

'Thank you, I'm all right,' he said, 'but my bruises are rather extraordinary. I've got one the shape of a dog's head—rather like Buster's head, really.'

'Really?' said Pip's mother, astonished. 'Do let me see it!'

Fatty spent a wonderful five minutes showing all his bruises, one after another, especially the one shaped like a dog's head. It was difficult to see how he made out that it was shaped like one, but Pip's mother seemed most interested. The children scowled. How annoying grown-ups were! Here they had been trying to stop Fatty from continually showing off and boasting, and now Pip's mother was making him ten times worse.

In a few minutes Fatty was telling her all about the bruise he had had once that was shaped like a church-bell, and the other that looked like a snake.

'I'm a really marvellous bruiser,' he said. 'I shall be a wonderful sight to-morrow when I'm in the yellow stage.'

'Come on,' whispered Larry to Pip. 'I can't stick this. This is Fatty at his worst.'

Leaving Fatty talking eagerly to Pip's mother,

the four children crept off. Buster stayed with Fatty, wagging his tail. He really seemed as much interested in his young master's bruises as the grown-up!

'Let's go for a bike-ride and leave old Fatty to himself,' said Pip, in disgust. 'I can't bear him when he gets like this.'

So the four of them went for a bike-ride and Fatty was surprised and hurt to find that he was all alone in the garden, when Pip's mother left him. He couldn't think why the others had gone, and he spent a miserable hour by himself, thinking how unkind they were.

When they came back, he greeted them with a volley of complaints.

'You *are* mean! Why did you go off like that? Is that the way to behave, Pip, when people come to tea with you? You're horrid!'

'Well, we thought you'd probably be about an hour boasting to Pip's mother,' said Larry. 'Don't look so fierce, Fatty. You shouldn't be such an idiot!'

'Going off like that finding clues and things without me,' said Fatty angrily. 'Aren't I a Find-Outer too? What have you been doing? Seeing Horace Peeks—or Lily again? You *are* mean!'

'We didn't see any one,' said Bets, feeling sorry for Fatty. She had so often been left out of things because she was younger than the others, and she knew how horrid it was to feel left-out. 'We only went for a bike-ride.'

But Fatty was really offended and hurt. 'I don't think I want to belong to the Find-Outers any more,' he said. 'I'll take my drawing of the footprints and go. I can see you don't want me. Come on, Buster.'

Nobody wanted Buster to leave the Find-Outers —and they didn't really want Fatty to, either. He wasn't so bad once you got used to him.

Daisy went after him. 'Come back, silly,' she said. 'We do want you. We want to discuss what to do to-night about Mr. Smellie's shoes. You come and say what we ought to do, too. I want to go into Mr. Smellie's house and keep guard for Larry, whilst he is hunting for the shoes we think Mr. Smellie has hidden. But he won't let me.'

Fatty went back to the others, still looking rather sulky.

'Larry, I do wish you'd let me creep into Mr. Smellie's house with you,' said Daisy. 'Fatty, don't you think I really ought to keep guard for him?'

'No, I don't,' said Fatty. 'I think a boy ought to go with Larry. I'll go, Larry. You shall do the hunting and I'll watch out that nobody discovers you.'

'No, I'll go,' said Pip, at once.

'You wouldn't be able to slip out without being seen,' said Larry. 'Fatty could. His parents don't seem to bother about him much. All right, Fatty —you come and help me then. I thought I'd wait till about half-past nine, and then scout about and see if old Smellie is still in his study. It's no use trying anything till he's gone to bed. He may be one of these people that stays up till about three o'clock in the morning, of course. We'll have to see.'

'Well, I'll be along about half-past nine,' said Fatty. 'Where's the shoe? In the summer-house? I'll bring it with me, in case your mother wants to know where you got it from. It'll be dark then and no one will see what I'm carrying.'

Fatty cheered up very much when he found that there was something really exciting he could join in. He forgot his sulks, and discussed where to meet Larry.

'I shall climb over the wall at the bottom of the garden,' said Larry. 'But you, Fatty, had better go up the road in front of Mr. Smellie's house, and go into the drive there, and round to the back that way. Meet me somewhere at the back of the house. See?'

'Right,' said Fatty. 'I'll hoot like an owl to tell you when I'm there.'

'Can you hoot?' said Bets, in surprise.

'Yes, listen,' said Fatty. He put his two thumbs side by side, frontways, and cupped his hands together. He blew carefully between his thumbs, and at once a mournful quavering hoot, just like an owl's, came from his closed hands. It was marvellous.

'Oh, you *are* clever, Fatty!' said Bets, in great admiration. Fatty blew again, and an owl's hoot sounded over the garden. He really was very good at it.

'Simply wonderful!' said Bets. Fatty opened his mouth to say that he could make much better bird and animal noises than that, but caught a look in Larry's eye that warned him in time to say nothing. He shut his mouth again hurriedly.

'Well,' said Larry, 'that's settled then. You meet me at half-past nine behind Mr. Smellie's house, and hoot like an owl to tell me you're there. I shall probably be hiding in the bushes somewhere, waiting for you.'

The children all felt excited as they went to bed that night. At least, Fatty didn't go to bed, though Larry did. But then Larry's mother usually came to tuck him up and say good-night, and Fatty's didn't. So Fatty felt quite safe as he sat, fully-dressed, in his bedroom, reading a book to make the time pass.

At ten past nine he switched off his light and put his nose outside his bedroom door. There was no one about. He slipped along the passage and down the stairs. Out of the garden door he went, and into the hotel garden. In half a minute he was in the lane, and running up it with the shoe tucked under his coat.

At just before half-past nine he came to Mr. Smellie's house, and stopped outside the front gate. The house was quite dark. Fatty walked up and down outside for a moment or two to make quite certain that there was no one about.

He didn't see some one standing quite still by one of the big trees that lined the road. He walked down in front of the house once more, making up his mind to go into the drive—and then quite suddenly he felt a strong hand on his shoulder !

Poor Fatty almost jumped out of his skin. 'Oooh !' he said, frightened, and the shoe dropped from beneath his coat !

'Ho !' said a voice that Fatty knew only too

well. ' Ho ! ' A torch was flashed into his face, and the voice said ' Ho ! ' again, this time more loudly.

It was Clear-Orf's voice. He had been standing quietly beside the tree, and had been astonished to see Fatty come up the lane, and walk softly up and down in front of the house. Now he was even more astonished to find that it was ' one of them children ! ' He bent down and picked up the shoe. He stared at it in the greatest astonishment.

' What's this ? ' he said.

' It looks like a shoe,' said Fatty. ' Let me go ! You've no right to clutch me like that.'

' What are you doing with this shoe ? ' asked Clear-Orf, in an astonished voice. ' Where's the other ? '

' I don't exactly know,' said Fatty truthfully. The policeman shook him angrily.

' None of your cheek,' he said. He turned the shoe upside down and saw the rubber-sole. At once the same thought flashed across his mind as had flashed across Daisy's when she had first seen it— the markings were like those on the footprint !

Mr. Goon stared at the shoe in amazement. He flashed his torch at Fatty again. ' Where did you get this ? ' he asked. ' Whose is it ? '

Fatty looked obstinate. ' Some one found it and gave it to me,' he said at last.

' I shall keep it for the time being,' said Mr. Goon. ' Now you just come-alonga-me for a minute.'

But Fatty didn't mean to do that. With a sudden quick twist he was out of Clear-Orf's grasp and tearing up the lane as fast as he could go. He went right to the top, and then round and into the lane in which Larry's house stood. He slipped into Larry's drive when he came to it and made his way to the bottom of the garden, his heart beating loudly. He shinned up to the top of the wall and dropped down. He made his way cautiously to the back of the house.

Then he hooted like an owl. 'Oooo-oo! Oooo-ooo-ooo-OOOOO!'

15   A FRIGHT FOR LARRY AND FATTY

IN another moment poor Fatty almost jumped out of his skin again! Some one clutched his arm hard. He had been expecting an answering whistle or hoot from somewhere about, but he had not guessed that Larry was behind the bush that he himself was standing by.

'Oooh!' said Fatty, startled.

'Sh!' came Larry's voice in a whisper. 'Have you got the shoe?'

'No,' said Fatty, and explained quickly what had happened to it. Larry listened in dismay.

'You *are* an idiot!' he said. 'Giving one of our best clues away to old Clear-Orf like that! He'll know we are after the same ideas as he is now!'

'The shoe wasn't a clue,' argued Fatty. 'It was a mistake. We thought it was a clue, but it wasn't. Anyway, Clear-Orf's got it, and I really couldn't help it. He nearly got me too. I only just managed to twist away.'

'What shall we do?' asked Larry. 'Shall we go in and hunt now? There's no light in the study. Old Mr. Smellie must have gone to bed.'

'Yes, come on,' said Fatty. 'Where's the garden door?'

They soon found it, and to their great delight it was still unlocked. As there was a light from the kitchen, the two boys thought that Miss Miggle was still up. They decided to be very cautious indeed.

They slipped in at the door. Larry led the way to the study where he and Daisy had talked to Mr. Smellie that day. 'You'd better stay on guard in the hall,' he said. 'Then if Miss Miggle or Mr. Smellie do happen to come along you can warn me at once. I shall open one of the windows of the study if I can do it without making a lot of noise —then I can slip out of it if any one thinks of walking into the room.'

Larry went into the study. He had a torch with him, and he shone it round the untidy room. There were papers everywhere! Papers and books on the desk, papers and books on the floor and on the chairs. There were books in the bookcases that lined the wall, and books on the mantelpiece. It was quite plain that Mr. Smellie was a very learned man!

Larry began to hunt for the shoes he hoped to find. He pulled out a few books from each shelf in the bookcase and ran his hand behind. But there was nothing there. He looked under the piles of paper everywhere but he found no shoes.

Fatty was outside in the hall, keeping guard. He saw the hall-cupboard where Daisy had found the shoe, and he thought it would be a good idea to peep into it. Daisy might possibly have overlooked some shoes that might be the right one. He slipped into the cupboard.

He was so very busy turning up the shoes and boots in the cupboard that he didn't hear some one slipping a latch-key into the front door. He didn't hear some one coming into the hall and quietly closing the front door. So he had no time at all to warn poor Larry to escape! He only heard Mr. Smellie when the old man walked into the study and switched on the light!

It was too late to do anything then, of course! Larry was caught with his head inside a cupboard, not knowing that any one was in the room until the light was suddenly switched on!

He took his head out of the cupboard in horror. He and Mr. Smellie stared at one another, Larry in fright, and Mr. Smellie in anger and amazement.

'Robber!' said Mr. Smellie angrily. 'Thief! Wicked boy! I'll lock you up and telephone to the police!'

He pounced on Larry and took hold of him with a surprisingly strong hand. He shook the boy hard, and Larry gasped. 'Please, sir,' he began, 'please, sir.'

But Mr. Smellie was not going to listen to anything. His precious papers were all the world to him, and the sight of somebody rummaging through them filled him with such fury that he was unable to listen to a word. Shaking Larry hard, and muttering all sorts of terrible threats, he pushed the boy before him into the hall. Poor Fatty, overcome with shame at having failed to warn Larry, shivered in the hall cupboard outside, not daring to show himself.

'Bad, wicked boy!' he heard Mr. Smellie say as he pushed poor Larry up the stairs. Larry was protesting all the time, but Mr. Smellie wouldn't listen to a word. 'I'll fetch the police in. I'll hand you over!'

Fatty trembled. It was bad enough to be caught, but it was even worse to think that poor Larry might be handed over to that horrid old Clear-Orf. He heard Mr. Smellie take Larry to a room upstairs and lock him in. Miss Miggle, amazed at the sudden noise, came rushing into the hall to see what the matter was.

'Thieves and robbers!' cried Mr. Smellie. 'That's what the matter is! I came home just now, walked into my study—and there I found thieves and robbers after my papers!'

Miss Miggle imagined that there must have been two or three men there, and she gaped in astonishment.

'Where are the robbers?' she asked.

'Locked in the box-room upstairs,' said Mr. Smellie. Miss Miggle stared at Mr. Smellie in even greater surprise. She couldn't believe that he had taken two or three men upstairs by himself and locked them into the box-room.

She saw that Mr. Smellie was trembling with excitement and shock. 'Now you just go and sit down quietly before you telephone the police,' she said soothingly. 'You're all of a shake! I'll just bring you something to drink. The robbers are safe enough upstairs for a bit.'

Mr. Smellie sank down on a chair in the hall. His heart was thumping, and he was breathing hard. 'Be all right in a minute,' he gasped. 'Ha! I got the best of the robbers!'

Miss Miggle ran to the kitchen. Fatty listened breathlessly. Somehow he felt certain that old Mr. Smellie had gone back into the study. He didn't know that he was sitting on a chair just at the foot of the stairs.

'I'd better take this chance of rescuing poor Larry,' thought Fatty, in desperation. He opened the cupboard door and made a dart for the stairs. Mr. Smellie was most amazed to see another boy appearing, this time out of the hall cupboard. He could hardly believe his eyes. Was his house alive with boys that night?

He made a grab at Fatty. Fatty was startled and let out a yell. He tried to run up the stairs, and dragged Mr. Smellie behind him for a few steps. The old man had got his strength back again by now, and, filled with anger at the sight of what he thought was yet another thief, he clung to Fatty like a limpet. The boy went up a few more steps, with Mr. Smellie almost tearing the coat off his back.

Then Fatty stumbled and sat down heavily on a stair about half-way to the top of the flight. Mr. Smellie fell on top of him, almost squashing the boy flat.

'Ow-wow!' yelled poor Fatty. 'Get off! You're hurting me!'

Miss Miggle dropped the glass she was holding and rushed into the hall. What in the wide world could be going on ? Was the whole house full of robbers ? She was just in time to see Fatty wriggle out from under Mr. Smellie and roll down the stairs to the bottom, with many bumps and loud groans.

She saw at once that he was only a boy, and she spoke to him severely.

' What's the meaning of this ? How dare you come into some one else's house ? What's your name and where do you live ? '

Fatty decided to be very upset and hurt. Miss Miggle was a very kind soul, and perhaps she would let him off if she thought he was nothing but a bad little boy out on an escapade.

So Fatty lifted up his voice and howled. Larry heard him, and wondered whatever could be happening. He banged at the locked door, adding to the noise and commotion. Miss Miggle looked quite bewildered.

' He's locked my friend into a room upstairs,' howled Fatty. ' I was just going up to rescue him when Mr. Smellie caught me and pummelled me and threw me down the stairs. Oh, I'm covered with bruises ! What my mother will say when she sees them I really don't know. She'll have Mr. Smellie up for injuring a child ! She'll call in the police ! '

' Now you can't possibly be bruised yet,' said Miss Miggle. ' I'm sure such a kind old man as Mr. Smellie wouldn't hit you, and he wouldn't throw you down the stairs. Don't be a naughty little story-teller ! '

'I'm not, I'm not!' said Fatty, pretending to weep. 'I'm covered with bruises. Look—here—and here—and there—and there! Oh, fetch a doctor, fetch a doctor!'

To Miss Miggle's extreme astonishment and to Mr. Smellie's horror, the boy in the hall was really and truly covered with the most terrifying purple, green and yellow bruises. They stared at Fatty as he showed them his curious markings. It did not occur to either of them that the boy had had them for one or two days already.

'Mr. Smellie!' said Miss Miggle, in a most reproachful tone. 'Just look at the poor child! How could you knock a little boy about like that? What his parents will say I really do not dare to think.'

Mr. Smellie was simply horrified when he thought that he had been the cause of Fatty's awful bruises. He swallowed hard once or twice, and stared at Fatty. 'Better put something on the bruises,' he suggested at last.

'I'll do that whilst you phone for the police,' said Miss Miggle, remembering the other robbers whom she still supposed were locked up in the box-room above.

But Mr. Smellie didn't seem to want to phone for the police now. He looked a bit sheepish, and said, 'Well, Miss Miggle, perhaps it would be better to ask the boys for an explanation of their curious behaviour in my house before I call in the police.'

'Will you let my friend out, please?' said Fatty. 'We didn't come here to rob you. It was only a joke, really. Let's call it quits, shall we? If you don't say anything to the police, we won't tell our mothers —and I won't show my bruises.'

Mr. Smellie cleared his throat. Miss Miggle looked at him. ' So the robbers and thieves were only two small boys ! ' she said. ' Dear, dear ! Why didn't you call *me* ? I could have settled the matter without all this noise and commotion and throwing down the stairs ! '

' I didn't throw him down the stairs,' said Mr. Smellie, going up to let Larry out of the box-room. Very soon Larry was down in the hall with Fatty, and Mr. Smellie took them both into his study. Miss Miggle came in with some stuff to put on Fatty's bruises. Larry looked most astonished but didn't say a word.

' Dear, dear, I never in my life saw such dreadful bruises on any child ! ' said Miss Miggle, dabbing each bruise with the stuff from her bottle.

' I'm a wonderful bruiser,' began Fatty. ' I once had a bruise shaped exactly like a church-bell.'

' What were you two boys doing in my house to-night ? ' said Mr. Smellie sharply. He didn't want to hear any history of bruises. Larry and Fatty were silent. They really didn't know what to say.

' You'll have to tell him that,' said Miss Miggle. ' You didn't come in here for any good purpose, I'll be bound. Now be good boys and own up.'

Still the boys were silent. Mr. Smellie suddenly lost his temper. ' Unless you tell me what you came here for I *will* hand you over to the police ! ' he said.

' Well, I don't know what they'll say when they see all my bruises,' said Fatty.

' I've an idea those bruises were made before

to-night ! ' said Mr. Smellie, getting sharper and sharper. ' I know what yellow means in a bruise, if Miss Miggle doesn't ! '

The boys said nothing. ' Names and addresses ? ' barked Mr. Smellie, getting out a pen. ' I'll see your parents as well as the police.'

The idea of their fathers and mothers knowing that they had been caught wandering about some one else's house at night was much more alarming than having in the police. Larry suddenly surrendered.

' We came to bring back a shoe we took this morning,' he said in a low voice. Both Miss Miggle and Mr. Smellie stared as if they thought Larry had gone mad.

' A *shoe* ? ' said Mr. Smellie at last. ' Why a shoe ? And why only *one* ? What are you talking about ? '

' We were looking for a shoe that fitted a footprint,' said Larry desperately.

This was even more puzzling to the two listeners. Mr. Smellie tapped his pen impatiently on his desk. ' Explain properly,' he said. ' I give you one minute. At the end of that time I telephone the police and also your parents, if you haven't given me a full and proper explanation of your most extraordinary conduct.'

' It's no use,' said Fatty to Larry. ' We'll have to tell him the real reason, even if it does warn him and put him on his guard.'

' What *are* you talking about ? ' said Miss Miggle, who was getting more and more astonished.

' Put me on my guard ! ' said Mr. Smellie.

'What do you mean ? Really, I begin to think that you two boys are completely mad.'

'We're not,' said Larry sulkily. 'But we happen to know something about you, Mr. Smellie. We know that you were in Mr. Hick's house on the evening of the fire.'

The effect of these words was most astonishing. Mr. Smellie dropped his pen on the floor and sprang to his feet. His glasses fell off his nose, and his beard shook and quivered. Miss Miggle also looked immensely surprised.

'You *were* there, weren't you ? ' said Larry. 'Somebody saw you. They told us.'

'Who told you ? ' spluttered Mr. Smellie.

'Horace Peeks saw you,' said Larry. 'He was in the house himself that evening, getting some of his things before Mr. Hick came back—and he saw you. How will you explain that to the police ? '

'Oh, Mr. Smellie, sir, what were you doing down there that evening ? ' cried poor Miss Miggle, at once thinking that her employer might possibly have fired the cottage.

Mr. Smellie sat down and put his glasses on his nose again. 'Miggle,' he said, 'I see that you suspect me of firing Mr. Hick's workroom. How you can think such a thing after serving me all these years, and knowing that I cannot even kill a fly, I don't know ! '

'Well, why did you go there, then ? ' asked Miss Miggle. 'You'd better tell me, sir. I'll look after you, whatever you've done ! '

'I don't need any looking after,' said Mr. Smellie, with some sharpness. 'All I went down

to Mr. Hick's for was to get the papers I had forgotten to bring away with me after my quarrel with
the fellow that morning. I certainly went into his
house—but I did not go near the workroom. I got
my papers—and here they are on the table. I
showed them to this boy and his sister this very
morning ! '

16   SURPRISES AND SHOCKS

ALL three stared at Mr. Smellie, who was quite
clearly speaking the truth.

' Golly ! ' said Larry. ' So that's why you went
there. Didn't you hide in the ditch, then ? '

' No, of course not,' said Mr. Smellie. ' I
walked down the drive quite openly, found the
garden door open and went in and collected my
papers. Then I walked out. I hid nowhere—
unless you think that standing by the gate for a
little while, to make sure no one was about, was
hiding.'

' Oh,' said Larry. This was terribly puzzling.
If what Mr. Smellie said was true, then there were
no Suspects left at all. But *Some*body must have
done the deed !

' And now will you kindly tell me what you took
my shoe for ? ' asked Mr. Smellie.

Larry told him, and then Fatty told him who
had now got the shoe. Mr. Smellie was annoyed.

' That interfering policeman ! ' he said. ' He

has been up and down past my house goodness
knows how many times to-day. I suppose he has
been suspecting me too. Now he's got my shoe.
I do think you boys deserve a good whipping.'

'Well, sir, we are only trying to find out who
started the fire,' said Fatty. He told Mr. Smellie
all they had done so far. Miss Miggle listened
in admiration and amazement. She was divided
between indignation that the boys should have
suspected Mr. Smellie so strongly, and astonishment that they should have found so many clues
and suspects.

'Well,' said Mr. Smellie at last. 'I think it's
about time you went home, you two. I can assure
you that I had nothing whatever to do with the fire,
and have no idea who had. I shouldn't think it
would be Horace Peeks. More likely the old tramp.
Anyway, my advice to you is to leave it to the police.
You children will never find out things like that.'

The boys stood up. 'Sorry about your shoe,
sir,' said Fatty.

'So am I,' said Mr. Smellie dryly. 'It's got
my name inside. So I've no doubt Mr. Goon will
be along here in the morning. Good-night. And
try not to suspect me of any more fires, thefts,
killings, or anything of that sort, will you? I am
really only a harmless elderly fellow interested in
nothing but my old papers!'

The boys left, distinctly subdued. They couldn't
help thinking that Mr. Smellie hadn't had anything to do with the firing of the cottage. But, then,
who had?

'I'm tired,' said Larry. 'Meet to-morrow at

Pip's place. Your bruises came in useful, Fatty. Without them I don't believe we'd have got free ! '

' They looked fine, didn't they ? ' said Fatty cheerfully. ' Well, good-night. We've had an adventurous evening, haven't we ? '

The other three were amazed and admiring when they heard all that had happened to Larry and Fatty. But they were even more puzzled than amazed.

' It's a most extraordinary thing,' said Pip thoughtfully. ' We keep finding that all kinds of people were hiding in the garden that night—and all of them were there for some definite reason. Even the tramp—he was after eggs. And yet we can't put our fingers on the real wrong-doer. *Could* the tramp have done it ? *Could* Horace have set fire to the cottage, although he was only gone three minutes ? *Could* Mr. Smellie have done it ? Horace says he saw him in the house, getting his papers— but it's possible he might have fired the cottage after that.'

' Yes. But somehow I feel certain he didn't now,' said Larry. ' Let's go down to Hiccup's garden and have a Big Think. We may have missed something.'

They all went down. They saw Lily hanging out the clothes, and whistled to her. With a quick look round to see that Mrs. Minns was not about, she ran to them.

' Lily ! Where exactly did you and Horace hide in the bushes ? ' asked Larry. ' Were you in the ditch by the workroom ? '

' Oh no,' said Lily, and she pointed to some

bushes by the drive. 'We were there. We never went near the ditch.'

'And old Smellie says he only hid for a moment by the gate. But *some*one hid in the ditch ! ' said Fatty thoughtfully. 'Let's go there, every one.'

They went to the ditch. The nettles were rising up again by this time, but it was still easy to see where they had been flattened by some one. The children squeezed through the gap and went to look at the footprint on the space where the turf had been taken away. It was still there, but fainter now.

'You know,' said Daisy suddenly, 'you know, these footprints—the one here and the ones round about the stile—all point one way. They are coming towards the house, but not going away. Whoever hid in the ditch came across the fields to the house —but there are no footprints at all to show that he went back that way.'

'He might have gone out of the front gate, silly,' said Fatty. 'Well, I must say I feel defeated to-day. Our clues don't tell us anything now—and all our Suspects seem to be innocent. I feel a bit tired of finding out things that lead us nowhere. Let's do something else to-day. Let's go for an all-day picnic.'

'Oooh *yes*,' said every one. 'We'll go back for our bikes. We'll go to Burnham Beeches and have a lovely time.'

Bets' mother would not allow her to go, because it was too far for an eight-year-old to ride. The little girl was very disappointed.

'I'd rather Bets didn't go for a picnic to-day

anyway,' said her mother. ' She looks a bit pale. Leave Buster behind and let her go for a walk with him. She'll like that.'

Bets did love taking Buster for walks, but it hardly made up for missing a picnic. Fatty was very sorry for her when she stood at the gate waving to them as they went off on their bikes.

' I'll bring you back heaps of primroses ! ' he called. ' Look after Buster, won't you ? '

Buster wagged his tail. He meant to look after Bets, not have Bets look after *him* ! He too felt sad when he saw the children going off without him. But he knew that he could never run fast enough to keep up with bicycles.

It had been raining in the night and everywhere was muddy. Bets thought she had better put on her rubber boots. She went to get them. Buster pattered after her on muddy paws.

' It's a pity *you* can't wear goloshes or something, Buster,' she said. ' You get awfully muddy.'

The two of them set off for a walk. Bets went down the lane to the river. She chose a little path that ran alongside the river for some way, and then turned back again across a field that led to the stile where the children had seen the exciting footprints a few days before.

Bets danced along, throwing sticks for Buster, and remembering not to throw stones for him to fetch because Fatty said they broke his teeth. She stooped down to pick up a stick—and then stood still in the greatest astonishment.

There, plainly to be seen on the muddy path in front of her, was a line of footprints exactly like the ones the children had found by the stile ! Bets by now knew the prints by heart, for she had gazed at Fatty's drawings so often. She felt absolutely certain that they were the same. There was the rubber sole with its criss-cross markings, and the little squares with the blobs at each corner !

'Ooh, look, Buster,' said Bets at last. She could feel her heart thumping with excitement. Buster came to look. He sniffed at the footprints and then looked up at Bets, wagging his tail.

'They're the same prints, aren't they, Buster, dear ? ' said Bets. 'And listen, Buster—it only rained last night—so some one must have walked along here since then—and that some one is the person we're after—though we don't know who ! Oh, Buster—what's the best thing to do ? I do feel so excited, don't you ? '

Buster capered round the little girl as if he understood every single word she said. She stood for a moment or two looking down at the line of footprints.

'We'll follow them, Buster,' she said. 'That's what we'll do ! We'll follow them. See ? I don't know how long it is since the person walked along here, but it's not very long, anyway. Come on— we may even catch up with the person who made the prints. Oh, this *is* exciting ! '

The little girl followed the footprints with Buster. He put his nose down to them and followed them too, though it was really the smell he was following, not the marks themselves. Along the muddy path they went, and then crossed a road to the other side. Then up another footpath, where they showed quite plainly, and then into a lane. Here they were not so easy to follow, but Buster's nose was most useful, for he could follow the smell, even where there was no footprint to be seen.

'You really are very clever, Buster,' said Bets, in great admiration. 'I wish my nose was like yours. Yes—that's right—that's another of the prints— and here's another—and another. Look—they're going to the stile.'

So they were. It was plain that the owner of the prints had crossed the stile and jumped down on to the field beyond. Bets grew more and more excited.

'The prints are going the same way as the other prints did!' she said to Buster. 'Look! Now, Buster, dear, use your nose well across this field because I can't see anything on the grass, of course.'

Buster went across the field in a straight line, his black nose held close to the ground. He could smell exactly where the person had walked. Soon Bets came to a bare muddy bit and there she saw a footprint clearly outlined. 'You are going the right way, Buster,' she said. 'Keep your nose down! Hurry! Maybe we shall find the person if we're quick! I believe these footprints have only just been made.'

The footprints did not lead to the gap in the hedge. Instead they led over another stile and up the lane that led to Bets' own house. But at Mr. Hick's gate the prints turned and went up Mr. Hick's own drive!

Bets was amazed. So the man who fired the cottage had actually gone back to it to-day! She wondered if he had gone to the front door or the back door. She went up the muddy drive, her face down, watching the prints. They went right to the front door. Just as she got there the door opened and Mr. Hick appeared. He seemed astonished to see Bets.

' Well, what are *you* doing here ? ' he asked.

' Oh, Mr. Hick,' gasped Bets, too excited to think that she might be giving away any of the Find-Outers' secrets. ' I'm following these footprints, and they go right to your door. Oh, Mr. Hick, it's most awfully important to know who made them. Has any one been to see you to-day ? '

Mr. Hick looked surprised, and he frowned at Bets and Buster. ' I don't understand,' he said. ' Why is it so awfully important ? '

' Well, if only I knew who made these footprints I should be able to tell the others who fired your cottage the other evening,' said Bets importantly.

Mr. Hick looked completely bewildered, and he stared very hard indeed at Bets. ' You'd better come in, he said at last. ' This is very extraordinary. What is a child like you doing, following footprints —and how do you know anything about it ? Come in. No—leave the dog outside.'

' Let him come too,' said Bets. ' He'll be very, very good. He'll scratch your door down if you leave him outside.'

So Buster went in too, and soon the three of them were sitting in Mr. Hick's study, which, like Mr. Smellie's, was littered with papers and books.

' Now,' said Mr. Hick, trying to speak in a pleasant voice, which was very difficult for him.

' Now, little girl, you tell me why you followed those footprints and what you know about them. It may be a help to me.'

Bets, proud to have a grown-up listening to her so closely, poured out the whole story of the Find-Outers and what they had done. She told Mr. Hick about the clues and the Suspects, and he listened without saying a single word.

Buster made himself a perfect nuisance all the time. He would keep going over to Mr. Hick, sniffing at him, and trying to nibble his feet. Mr. Hick got most annoyed, but Buster wouldn't leave him alone. In the end Bets had to take him on her knee and keep him there.

When she had finished her story, right up to that very morning, she looked eagerly at Mr. Hick. ' Now will you tell me who came here to-day ? ' she asked.

' Well,' said Mr. Hick slowly, ' as it happens, two of your Suspects came here. Mr. Smellie came to borrow a book—and Horace Peeks came to ask me for a reference.'

' Oh ! So it might be either of them,' said Bets. ' I do wonder which of them wore the rubber-soled shoes with those markings. Well, anyway, now we know for certain it was one of those two. Mr. Hick, you won't tell a single soul what I've told you this morning, will you ? '

' Certainly not,' said Mr. Hick. ' A lot of people seem to have been in my garden that day I went up to town, didn't they ? Wait till I get my fingers on the one who played that dirty trick on me, and burnt all my valuable papers ! '

' I'd better go now,' said Bets. She stood up, and put Buster down. He immediately rushed to Mr. Hick and began to sniff at his trousers in a way that Mr. Hick thoroughly disliked. He kicked Buster away and the dog yelped.

' Oh, *don't*!' said Bets, dismayed. 'You shouldn't kick a dog, Mr. Hick. That's cruel.'

' You go now and take that dog with you,' said Mr. Hick. ' And my advice to you children is— don't meddle in things that concern grown-ups. Leave the police to do the finding-out !'

' Oh, we *must* go on,' said Bets. ' After all, we *are* the Find-Outers !'

She went up the drive with Buster and saw the footprints once again. One row went up the drive and one row went down. How Bets wished she knew whether the prints had been made by Smellie or Peeks ! She longed and longed for the others to come home. She could hardly wait to tell them her news. She wondered if they would mind her telling Mr. Hick all that she had told him. But, after all, it couldn't matter *him* knowing. He would do all he could to help them, Bets was sure—and he had faithfully promised not to tell any one at all.

The others came back after tea, tired and happy after a lovely day at Burnham Beeches. Fatty presented Bets with an enormous bunch of primroses.

Bets could not wait for one moment to tell them her news. She was simply bursting with it—but just as she was in the middle of it, there came a very nasty surprise !

Up the garden appeared Pip's mother, and with

her was Clear-Orf, looking very smug and also very forbidding.

' Old Clear-Orf ! ' said Larry, in a low tone. ' Whatever does he want ? '

It was soon quite clear what he had come for ! Pip's mother spoke to the children in a very stern voice.

' Children ! Mr. Goon has come to me with a very extraordinary story of your doings in the last few days. I can hardly believe what he says ! '

' What's the matter ? ' asked Pip, scowling at Clear-Orf.

' Pip, don't scowl like that,' said his mother sharply. ' Apparently all of you have been interfering in matters that concern the police. Even Bets ! I simply cannot understand it. Mr. Goon even tells me that you and Frederick, Larry, got into Mr. Smellie's house last night. What *will* your mothers say ? And even little Bets has been following foot-prints and imagining herself to be a detective ! '

' Who told Mr. Goon that ? ' burst out Bets. ' Nobody knows but me—and Mr. Hick ! '

' Mr. Hick rang me up, and I have just been to see him,' said Mr. Goon, speaking with great dignity. ' He told me all your goings-on—inter-fering little busybodies ! '

Bets burst into loud sobs. ' Oh, Mr. Hick told me he wouldn't tell *any* one ! ' she wailed. ' Oh, he did promise me faithfully ! He's a wicked, wicked man ! He's broken his faithful promise. I hate him ! '

' Bets ! Behave yourself ! ' said her mother.

' Of course, Bets *would* go and give everything

away!' said Pip sulkily. That's what comes of having her in the Find-Outers. Little idiot! She goes and tells everything to Mr. Hick, he rings up Clear-Orf, and now we're all in the soup!'

'What are you muttering about, Pip?' said his mother. 'Who is Clear-Orf?'

'Mr. Goon,' said Pip defiantly. 'He's always telling us to clear-orf.'

'Ho!' said Mr. Goon, swelling himself out like an angry frog, his blue eyes bulging fiercely. 'Ho! Didn't I always find you hanging about, you kids? Regular pests you are. Now you just listen to me for a few minutes.'

There was absolutely nothing to be done but listen to Mr. Goon. The five children stood there, red and angry, Bets still sobbing. Only Buster didn't seem to care, but sniffed happily round Clear-Orf, who fended him off every now and again.

Clear-Orf had a lot to say about 'nosey children' and 'little nuisances' and 'interfering with the law.' He ended up with a threat.

'And if I come across any of you nosing about again, or if Mr. Hick reports you to me, you'll all get into Very Serious Trouble,' he said. 'Ho yes —VERY SERIOUS TROUBLE. You keep out of matters that don't concern you. And as for you, Master Laurence and Miss Daisy, and you Master Frederick, *your* parents are going to hear about this as well. You mark my words, you'll be sorry you ever interfered with the Law.'

'We didn't,' said Pip desperately. 'We only tried to help.'

'Now, no back-chat!' said Mr. Goon majestically. 'Children can't help in these things. They only get into trouble—Very Serious Trouble.'

And with that Mr. Goon departed with Pip's mother, a burly, righteous-looking figure in dark blue.

17   VERY STRANGE DISCOVERIES

A STORM of anger broke over poor Bets when Mr. Goon had gone.

'Idiot!' said Pip. 'Going and blabbing everything out to old Hiccup!'

'Honestly, you've ruined everything, Bets,' said Daisy.

'This is the end of the Find-Outers,' said Larry gloomily. 'That's what comes of having a baby in it like Bets. Everything's spoilt.'

Bets sobbed loudly. Fatty was sorry for her. He actually put his arm round her and spoke kindly, though he felt as impatient as the others at the break-up of their plans and hopes.

'Don't cry, Bets. We all do silly things. It was clever of you and Buster to track those prints, I must say. And wouldn't I like to know which of those two, Peeks or Smellie, wore those shoes!'

Pip's mother appeared again, looking stern. 'I hope you are feeling ashamed of yourselves,' she said. 'I want you all to go down and apologize to Mr. Hick for interfering in his concerns. He is naturally very annoyed to think that you have been messing about each day in his garden.'

' We didn't do any harm,' said Pip.

' That's not the point,' said his mother. ' You children simply *can*not be allowed to go on to private property, and into private houses without permission. You will all go down immediately to Mr. Hick and apologize. Do as I say at once.'

The children set off together down the drive, with Buster at their heels. They were all sulky and mutinous. They hated having to apologize to some one they detested. Also they all felt that it was terribly mean of Mr. Hick to have given Bets away like that, when he had solemnly promised not to.

' He's a nasty piece of work,' said Larry, and every one agreed.

' I don't care *who* fired his workroom,' said Fatty. ' I'm glad it *was* burnt down, and his precious papers too.'

' You shouldn't say things like that,' said Daisy, though she felt much the same herself at that moment.

They arrived at the house and rang the bell. Bets pointed out the footprints and they all gazed at them with interest. Bets was right. The prints were exactly like the ones in Fatty's drawing. It was too bad that they had to give up the search for the criminal just as they had almost found the man !

Mrs. Minns opened the door and was surprised to see the little company. Sweetie, who was at her heels, fled away with tail up in the air as soon as she saw Buster.

'Please, will you tell Mr. Hiccup—er, I mean Mr. Hick—that we want to see him?' said Larry. Mrs. Minns looked even more surprised, and was about to answer when a voice called from the study.

'Who's that, Mrs. Minns?'

'Five children and a dog, sir,' answered Mrs. Minns. 'They say they want to see you.'

There was a pause. 'Bring them in,' said Mr. Hick's voice, and very solemnly the children and Buster went into the study. Mr. Hick was there, sitting in a big chair, his legs crossed, and his crest of hair looking rather alarming.

'What have you come for?' he asked.

'Mother said we were all to apologize to you, Mr. Hick,' said Pip. And, with one voice, the children chanted in a most mournful tone, 'We apologize, Mr. Hick!'

'Hmmm,' said Mr. Hick, looking more amiable. 'I should think so, indeed!'

'You said you wouldn't tell any one,' burst out Bets. 'You broke your promise.'

Mr. Hick didn't consider that promises made to children need be kept at all, so he didn't feel guilty or say he was sorry. He was about to say something when several aeroplanes passed over the garden, rather low. The noise made him jump and Buster growled. Larry ran to the window. He was extremely good at spotting any kind of aeroplane that flew overhead.

'It's those Tempests again!' he cried. 'I've only seen them twice over here. Look at their curious tail-fins.'

'They were over here two or three days ago,'

said Mr. Hick, with interest. ' I saw them. There were seven. Are there seven to-day ? '

Larry counted them. All the children looked out of the window—except Fatty. He didn't look out of the window. He looked at Mr. Hick with a most bewildered expression on his face. He opened his mouth as if to speak, and then firmly closed it again. But he still went on staring at Mr. Hick, very deep in thought.

The Tempests came over again, roaring low. ' Let's go out and see them,' said Larry. ' We can see them better out-of-doors. Good-bye, Mr. Hick.'

' Good-bye. And don't poke and pry again into matters that don't concern children,' said Mr. Hick stiffly. ' It was probably Horace Peeks that fired my workroom. The police will soon make out a case against him. He wore rubber-soled shoes this morning when he came to see me, and there is no doubt that he made those prints up and down the drive.'

' Oh,' said the children, feeling very sorry for poor Lily. She would be terribly upset they knew. Only Fatty said nothing, but looked hard at Mr. Hick again, a curious expression on his face. They all went out—but the Tempests were now gone again, leaving a faint throbbing behind them.

' Well, that's done,' said Larry, with relief. ' How I hated apologizing to that mean fellow ! I suppose Peeks did do it, after all—fire the cottage, I mean.'

Fatty was very silent as they all walked down the lane towards the river. They meant to go for a short walk before supper-time. Bets looked at Fatty.

'What's the matter?' she asked. 'Are your bruises hurting you?'

'No. I'd forgotten all about them,' said Fatty. 'I was thinking of something very, very, very queer!'

'What was it?' asked the others, interested. Fatty stopped and pointed up into the sky. 'You know those planes we saw?' he said. The others nodded.

'Well,' said Fatty, 'they were Tempests, and they have only been over here twice—once to-day—and once on the evening of the day that the cottage was fired!'

'Well—what about it?' said Larry impatiently. 'Nothing queer about that, surely!'

'Listen,' said Fatty, 'when we spoke about those Tempests, what did Mr. Hick say? He said that he saw them when they were over here two or three days ago—and he counted them and there were seven. Which was quite correct.'

'What are you getting at?' asked Pip, frowning.

'I'm getting at something queer,' said Fatty. 'Where was Mr. Hick on the evening that the fire was started?'

'On the London train!' said Larry.

'Then how could he have seen and counted the Tempests that flew over *here*?' said Fatty.

There was a startled silence. Every one thought hard. Larry spoke first. 'It *is* queer!' he said. 'Those planes *have* only been here twice—every one spoke about them. And if Hiccup saw them that evening—then he must have been *here*!'

148

'And yet his chauffeur met the London train and he walked off it!' said Daisy. 'He couldn't possibly have seen the planes if he was really on the train, because at that time the train had hardly started out from London!'

'And so,' said Fatty, a note of triumph in his voice, 'and so, Find-Outers, we have yet another Suspect. Mr. Hick himself!'

'Oooh,' said Bets, amazed. 'But he wouldn't fire his own cottage!'

'He might—to get the insurance money on his valuable papers,' said Fatty. 'People do do that sometimes. I expect he sold the papers—then set fire to the workroom and pretended the papers were burnt, in order to get more money. Golly! Can it really be possible?'

'We can't tell any one,' said Daisy.

'I should think not!' said Larry. 'Whatever in the world shall we do about it?'

'We must find out how it was that Mr. Hick got on the London train that night,' said Fatty. 'Look—we're near the railway line here. The London trains always come by here, and there's one due. Let's see what happens.'

The children climbed on to the fence by the railway and sat there, waiting. Soon they saw a cloud of smoke in the distance. The train was coming. It came roaring along—but when it reached one portion of the line, it slowed down, and finally it stopped.

'It always stops there,' said Bets. 'I've noticed that. Perhaps it gets water or something.'

It was too far away to see why it had stopped.

Anyway it soon started up again, and puffed by the five children. Buster ran away behind a bush when it came. He was afraid of the noise.

Fatty was again thinking very deeply. So was Larry. 'Listen,' said Fatty. 'Is it possible for any one at night to wait for the train just there, and hop into an empty carriage, do you think? Then, at Peterswood Station, if he had a season ticket, people would never know he hadn't come all the way from London.'

'Fatty, I believe you're right!' said Larry. 'I was just thinking the very same thing myself. I believe Hiccup could have done it. Pretended to go to London—slipped back—hid in the ditch, leaving those few footprints behind him—fired the cottage—slipped back to the railway line just there —waited till the train stopped, as it always does— hopped into an empty carriage in the dark—and then got out as cool as a cucumber, to be met by his car and chauffeur at the station!'

The more the children thought about this, the more certain they felt that Mr. Hick might have done it. 'After all,' said Bets, 'a man that could break his faithful promise could do *any*thing, simply *any*thing.'

'Whatever is Buster doing?' said Fatty, hearing some excited barks coming from the little dog, some way back in the copse of trees behind them. 'Buster! BUSTER! What's the matter? Found a rabbit?"

Buster yelped and then appeared, dragging something black and muddy. 'Whatever *has* he got?' said Bets.

Every one looked to see. 'It's an old shoe!' said Daisy, laughing. 'Buster, what do you want with an old shoe?'

Buster went to Bets and laid the shoe down at her feet. Then he stood looking up at her, as if he was telling her something, wagging his tail hard. Bets picked up the shoe. She turned it over.

'*Look!*' said Bets. 'The real proper shoe at last! The one that made the footprints!'

The others nearly fell off the fence in their excitement. Bets was perfectly right. It was THE SHOE!

'Buster followed the footprints and knew their smell, and when he smelt the shoes hidden over there he knew the smell again, and that's why he brought them to *me*,' cried Bets. 'We had followed the prints together, you see. Oh, and now I know why he kept on and on sniffing round Mr. Hick's shoes when I went to see him. He could smell the same smell!'

'Clever dog,' said Fatty, patting Buster. 'Where's the other shoe, old fellow? Find it, find it!'

Buster rushed off to a bush not far away and began to scrape violently beneath it. Soon he unearthed the other shoe and laid it at Fatty's feet. The children picked it up.

'Well!' said Fatty. 'This is very queer. I suppose old Hiccup got the wind up after Bets had told him she had followed the footprints, and went out and buried the shoes in case the police should find them in his house, or spot him wearing them. And good old Buster smelt them out. Clever, good, marvellous dog ! Big bone for you to-morrow, Buster, a GREAT BIG BONE ! '

' And now—whatever are we going to do about everything ? ' said Larry, going back to the path. ' It's no good telling the police. We're in disgrace and wouldn't be listened to. It's no good telling our parents. We're in enough trouble as it is.'

' Let's go and sit down by the river and talk about it,' said Pip. ' Come on. We'll simply *have* to decide something. Things are getting very serious.'

18   AN UNEXPECTED FRIEND

THE children made their way along the path that led to the river. They found a sheltered place on the 'high bank of the river and sat down. Buster growled a little but sat down with them.

' What are you growling for, Buster ? ' said Bets. ' Don't you want to sit down ? '

Buster growled again and then stopped. The children began to talk.

' It's a queer thing,' said Pip, ' we've found the man who started the fire—and we've got all the facts—we know how he got on to the London train —we know that his shoes fit the footprints—we know that he was afraid and hid those shoes—which we've found—and we know why all the other Suspects were down in the garden that evening. We know everything—and yet we can't do anything about it because Mr. Goon would be sure to pretend that *he* found out everything ! '

' Yes—it's no good telling the police,' said Fatty gloomily. ' And it's no good telling our parents either, because they would just ring up Mr. Goon. Isn't it perfectly sickening to think that we've solved the mystery and found out simply everything, and we can't get the criminal punished. Horrid Mr. Hick ! He ought to be punished. Don't you think it was mean the way he tried to lay the blame on poor old Peeks when he thought we were getting to know too much ? '

' Yes,' agreed every one.

' It was funny the way he gave himself away by mentioning those aeroplanes,' said Larry. ' It was really smart of Fatty to spot that, I think.'

' It certainly was,' said Daisy warmly, and the others nodded.

Fatty swelled up at once. ' Well, as I've told you before,' he said, ' I really *have* got brains. Now, at school . . .'

' Shut up, Fatty,' said every one together, and Fatty subsided and shut up, still feeling pleased, however, that the others admired him for spotting such a curious clue.

They all went on talking about the burnt cottage and the Suspects and clues for a little while longer, and then Buster growled so fiercely and so long that every one was surprised and puzzled.

' What *is* the matter with Buster ? ' said Bets. ' Has he got a tummy-ache or something, do you think ? '

She had hardly finished saying these words when

a large round face appeared above the rim of the high river bank. It was a kindly face, set with big intelligent eyes that had a real twinkle in them.

' Oh ! ' said every one, startled.

' Pardon me,' said the face. ' I'm afraid I've frightened you. But, you see, I was sitting down here, below the bank, in my favourite corner, fishing. Naturally I kept quiet, because I didn't want to disturb the fish. I couldn't help hearing what you were talking about—it was most interesting, *most* interesting, if you'll pardon my saying so ! '

Buster barked so loudly that the children could hardly hear what the hidden person was saying. He climbed up on to the bank beside them, and they saw that he was a very big fellow, burly and strong, dressed in a tweed suit and enormous brown shoes.

The man sat down beside them and took out a bar of chocolate, which he broke into bits and offered the children. They couldn't help liking him.

' Did you hear everything we said ? ' asked Bets. ' It was really all a secret, you know. We're the Find-Outers.'

' The Fine Doubters ? ' said the man, puzzled. ' What do you doubt then ? '

Every one giggled. ' No—the Finddddd-Outers,' said Daisy, sounding the letter D loudly at the end of Find. ' We find out things.'

' Ah ! I see,' said the big man, lighting a pipe. Buster was now quite friendly towards him and licked his hand. The big man patted him.

' What are you ? ' asked Bets. ' I haven't seen you before.'

A large round face appeared above the bank

'Well—if you don't mind my saying so—I'm a bit of a Find-Outer myself,' said the man. 'I have to solve mysteries too. Most interesting it is—I'm sure you agree with me ? '

'Oh *yes*,' said every one.

'I gather that you are in a spot of bother at the moment ? ' said the man, puffing at his pipe. 'You have solved your mystery—but you can't make your discoveries known ? Is that right ? '

'Yes,' said Larry. 'You see—Mr. Goon, the policeman here, doesn't like us, and has complained to our parents about some things we did. Well— I dare say some of them were pretty awful, really —but we did them in a good cause. I mean—we wanted to find out who burnt down Mr. Hick's cottage.'

'And now that you have found out, you have got to keep quiet about it,' said the man, puffing away. 'Most annoying for you. Tell me more about it. As I say—I'm a bit of a Find-Outer too, in my way—so I enjoy talking over a mystery as man to man, if you see what I mean.'

The children looked at the big, burly fellow on the bank. His keen eyes twinkled at them, and his big hand patted Buster. Larry looked round at the others.

'I think we might as well tell him everything, don't you ? ' said Larry. They nodded. They all trusted the big fisherman, and somehow knew that their secrets were safe with him.

So Larry, interrupted sometimes by Daisy, Fatty and Pip, told the whole story of the Find-Outers, and what they had discovered. The big man listened keenly, sometimes putting in a question, nodding his head every now and again.

'Smart boy, you,' he said to Fatty, when Larry came to the bit about how Mr. Hick had given himself away by saying that he had seen the seven Tempests on the evening of the fire. Fatty went red with pleasure, and Bets squeezed his hand.

The story was finished at last. The big man knocked out his pipe and looked round.

'An extremely good piece of work, if I may say so,' he said, beaming round. 'I congratulate the Five Find-Outers—and Dog! And—I think I can help you a bit.'

'How?' asked Larry.

'Well, we must get hold of that tramp again,' said the big man. 'From what you say he said to you, he probably saw Mr. Hick in the garden too—hiding in the ditch—and that would be valuable evidence. And er—certainly the police ought to know about all this.'

'Oh,' said every one in dismay, thinking of Clear-Orf, and how he would say that he himself had found out everything. 'And we could never, never find that tramp again!' said Larry. 'He may be miles and miles away.'

'I'll find him for you all right,' promised the big man.

'And old Clear-Orf—that's Mr. Goon, you know—won't listen to a word we say, I'm sure,' said Fatty gloomily.

'I'll see that he does,' said the astonishing man, getting up. 'Leave it to me. Call at your police station to-morrow at ten o'clock, will you ? I'll be there, and we'll finish up everything nicely.'

He picked up his rod and put it over his shoulder. 'A most interesting talk,' he said. 'Valuable to both of us, as I hope you will agree.'

He strode off in the evening twilight, and the children watched him go. 'Ten o'clock to-morrow at the police station,' said Fatty, feeling rather uncomfortable. 'Whatever's going to happen there ? And how is that man going to find the tramp ? '

Nobody knew. Larry looked at his watch, gave a yell and leapt to his feet. 'I say—it's *awf*ully late. We *shall* get into a row. Come along, quickly.'

They hurried home, with Buster at their heels. 'Good-bye ! ' they called to one another. 'Ten o'clock to-morrow at the police station. Don't be late ! '

19   THE END OF THE MYSTERY

THE next morning the Five Find-Outers and their dog arrived punctually at the police station. With them they brought their clues, as the big man had requested. There was Fatty's drawing of the foot-prints, the bit of grey cloth in the match-box, and the rubber-soled shoes that had been scraped up by Buster.

'You know, the only clue that wasn't any use was the bit of grey flannel,' said Larry, opening the box. 'We never found out whose coat it belonged to, did we ? And yet it must belong to some one who went through that gap ! Perhaps Mr. Hick wore a grey suit that night. If so, he hasn't worn it since, because he's always had on dark blue whenever we've seen him.'

They went into the police station feeling a little awed. Mr. Goon was there, without his helmet, and also another policeman the children didn't know. They stared at Mr. Goon, expecting him to rise up and say ' Clear-Orf ! '

But he didn't. He told them to sit down in such polite tones that the children were overcome with astonishment. They sat down. Buster went to inspect the policeman's legs, and Clear-Orf didn't even kick out at him.

' We were to meet some one here,' said Fatty. Clear-Orf nodded.

' He'll be along in a minute,' he said. As he spoke, a small police-car drove up, and the children looked round, expecting to see their friend, the big man. But he wasn't in the car.

To their surprise there was some one else in it that they knew. It was the old tramp ! He was muttering to himself, and looking rather scared.

' I'm an honest old fellow, I am, and nobody never said I wasn't. I'll tell anything I know, course I will, but I won't do nothing to get meself into trouble, that I won't. I've not done nothing wrong.'

There was a plain-clothes policeman in the car with him, besides the driver. Bets was surprised when Larry told her that the man in the dark grey suit was a policeman.

' I thought they never, never wore anything but their uniforms,' she said.

Then another car drove up, driven by an extremely smart-looking man in blue uniform. He wore a peaked cap, and the other policemen saluted him smartly when he heaved himself out of the car. The car was big, but the man was big too !

The children gazed at him—and Bets gave a squeal. ' It's the fisherman ! It's the man we saw yesterday ! Hallo ! '

' Hallo, there ! ' said the big man, smiling.

' We've found the tramp, Inspector,' said the plain-clothes policeman to the big man. The children looked at one another. So their friend was an Inspector of Police ! Golly !

' An Inspector is a very, very high-up policeman,' whispered Pip to Bets. ' He's terribly clever. Look at old Clear-Orf. He's trembling like a jelly ! '

Clear-Orf was not really trembling, but it was plain that he was quite overcome by the visit of the Inspector to his small police station. His hands shook as he turned over the pages of his notebook.

The Inspector beamed at the children. ' Nice to see you again, if I may say so,' he said. He spoke to Clear-Orf, making Mr. Goon jump. ' You are lucky to have five such smart children in your district, Goon,' he said.

Clear-Orf opened and shut his mouth but said nothing. He didn't want smart children in his district, especially any that were smarter than he was ! But he couldn't very well say so to his Inspector.

Then the tramp was brought before the Inspector

and questioned. He answered willingly enough, once he had been assured that he would only do himself good, not harm, by answering truthfully. The children listened intently.

'Tell us all the people you saw in Mr. Hick's garden that night,' said the Inspector.

'Well,' said the tramp. 'There was meself, hiding under a bush near the workroom, not doing ńo harm to nobody—just taking a rest, like.'

'Quite,' said the Inspector.

'Then I saw that fellow who got the sack that morning,' said the tramp. 'Peeks, his name was. He was hiding in the bushes, along with some one else I couldn't see. But by the voice I reckoned it was a girl. Well, I see him going into the house and out again, through a window.'

'Ah,' said the Inspector.

'Then I see an old fellow,' said the tramp. 'I heard him having a quarrel with Mr. Hick that day —name of Smellie, wasn't it ? Yes. Well, he came walking down the drive, quiet-like, and he slipped into the house by a door, just before Peeks came out again.'

'Go on,' said the Inspector. 'Did you see any one else ? '

'Yes, I did,' said the tramp. 'I see Mr. Hick himself ! '

Every one listened breathlessly. 'I was lying under that there bush,' said the tramp, 'thinking that there was a lot of people in the garden that evening, when I heard some one squeezing through the gap in the hedge, not far from me. I looked through the sprays of the bush and I **saw it was**

Mr. Hick himself. He stood there in that ditch
for a long time, and then he went to a big clump of
blackberries and fished up a tin out of the middle
where it was hidden.'

Fatty gave a little whistle. It was extraordinary
to hear the tramp relating the whole story that they
had so carefully pieced together. That tin must
have contained petrol !

' Then Mr. Hick went to the little cottage nearby,
stayed there a while, came out and locked the door,
and hid in the ditch again,' said the tramp. ' I lay
under my bush as still as a mouse. After a time,
when it was really dark, I heard Mr. Hick getting
out of the ditch and going down the lane towards
the railway. Then I saw a light in the cottage and
I guessed it was on fire, and I went off mighty quick.
I didn't want to be found there and accused of
firing it.'

' Thank you,' said the Inspector. ' Was there
any one else at all that you saw ? '

' Not a soul,' said the tramp.

' A very pretty plot,' said the Inspector. ' Mr.
Hick wants money. He manages to pick a quarrel
with a good many people that day, so that if by
chance the insurance company suspect foul play,
there are many people who have reason to fire his
cottage out of spite. He gets his chauffeur to take
him to the station in the afternoon, to catch the
train to town. He must have got out at the next
station, and walked back over the fields to his garden,
where he hid until he fired the cottage. Then he
walked back to the railway, waited at the place where
the London train always halts for a minute, and

gets into an empty carriage, unseen in the darkness. He arrives at Peterswood Station, is met by his chauffeur and driven home, to be told that his workroom is on fire. Very pretty indeed.'

'And now, I think, we must ask Mr. Hick a few questions,' said the plain-clothes man.

'That is so,' agreed the Inspector. He turned to the children. 'We will let you know what happens,' he said. 'And, if I may say so, I am very proud to have met the Five Find-Outers—and Dog. I trust that we shall work together on other mysteries in the future. I should be extremely grateful for your help—and I am sure Mr. Goon feels the same as I do.'

Mr. Goon didn't at all, but he could do nothing but nod and try to smile. He was angry to think that the five 'pests' had actually solved the mystery before he had, and that the Inspector was praising them.

'Good-day, Goon,' said the Inspector pleasantly, walking out to his car.

'Good-day, Inspector Jenks,' said poor Clear-Orf.

'Can I give you children a lift?' inquired the Inspector. 'Am I going your way?'

He was, for he was going to Mr. Hick with the plain-clothes man. The children piled into the big car, bursting with importance, and hoping that every one in the village would see them riding with their friend, the great Inspector!

'I suppose you couldn't possibly put in a word for us with our parents, could you?' asked Pip.

' You see, Mr. Goon complained so bitterly of us. If you spoke well of us, it would be a great help.'

' It would be a pleasure,' beamed the Inspector, starting up his powerful car. ' I'll call in after I've interviewed Mr. Hick.'

He kept his word. He called on Pip's mother later in the day, and very much impressed her with his admiration for the Find-Outers.

' They are very smart children,' he said. ' I am sure you will agree with me. I am proud to know them.'

The children crowded round him eagerly. ' What about Mr. Hick ? What did he say ? '

' I questioned him closely, and let him know that we knew everything and had got his shoes too,' said the Inspector. ' He denied it at first, but when asked to explain how it was that he heard those aeroplanes coming over here at the time when he had vowed he was in London, he broke down and confessed everything. So I am afraid Mr. Hick will have to leave his comfortable house and spend some considerable time with the police ! He is even now on his way, and poor Mrs. Minns is in a most excited state.'

' I expect Lily will be glad that Horace isn't suspected any more,' said Daisy. ' And we'd better go and tell Mr. Smellie all about it too, so that he will forgive us for getting into his house and taking his shoe. Will Mr. Goon give him back his shoe, Inspector Jenks ? '

' It has already been done,' said the big man. ' Well, I must be going. I hope I shall see you again some day. You did very well indeed with your clues and your list of Suspects.'

' There was only one clue that wasn't any good,' said Larry, pulling out his match-box with the bit of grey flannel in. ' We never found any Suspect with a grey flannel coat, and a tiny bit torn out of it.'

' Well, if you don't mind my saying so, I have an idea that I can explain that clue,' said the big Inspector, looking wise.

' Oh, do tell us,' said Bets.

The Inspector pulled Larry to him, swung him round, and showed the others a tiny tear in his grey flannel jacket, just by the arm-pit at the back.

' That's where your bit of grey cloth came from ! ' he said, with a deep chuckle. ' You all got through that gap in the hedge when you went to find foot-prints, didn't you ? And Larry must have caught himself a bit on a prickle—and the boy behind him spotted the bit of grey rag on the twig and thought it was a clue ! Good thing you didn't see that Larry's coat was torn, or you might have written *him* down as a Suspect too ! '

The children laughed. ' However was it that nobody noticed Larry's coat was a bit torn ? ' said Bets, astonished. ' Well—to think of all the things we found out—and we didn't find that out ! '

' Good-bye,' said the Inspector, getting into his car. ' Thanks for your help. It's a very satisfactory ending, as I'm sure you will agree with me ! '

' Rather ! ' said every one. ' Good-bye ! It *was* a bit of luck meeting you ! '

The car roared off up the lane. The children turned back into the garden.

' What an exciting week we've had,' said Daisy.
' I suppose now the Find-Outers must come to an
end, because we've solved the mystery ! '

' No,' said Fatty. ' We'll still be the Five Find-
Outers and Dog, because you simply *never* know
when another mystery will come along for us to
solve. We'll just wait till it comes.'

They are waiting—and one will come, there's
no doubt about that.

But, of course, that will be quite another story !

THE MYSTERY OF THE DISAPPEARING CAT

CONTENTS

1   THE BIG BOY NEXT DOOR

BETS was feeling very excited. Her big brother
Pip was coming home from school that day for the
long summer holidays. She had been without him
for three months, and had felt very lonely. Now
she would have him again.

'And Larry and Daisy will be home to-morrow!'
she said to her mother. 'Oh, Mummy! it will be
fun to have so many children to play with again.'

Larry and Daisy were Pip's friends. They were
older than Bets, but they let her play with them.
In the Easter holidays the four of them, with another
boy and his dog, had had a great adventure finding
out who had burnt down a cottage.

'We were the Five Find-Outers,' said Bets,
remembering everything. 'We found out the
whole mystery, Mummy, didn't we? Oh, I do wish
we could solve another mystery these holidays too!'

Her mother laughed. 'Oh, it was just a bit of
luck that you solved the mystery of the burnt
cottage,' she said. 'There won't be any more
mysteries, so don't expect any, Bets. Now hurry
up and get ready. It's time to meet Pip.'

Pip was most excited to be home again. When
he got back with Bets he tore round the garden,
looking at everything. It seemed to him as if he
had been away for years.

His little sister tore round with him, chattering
at the top of her voice all the time. She adored
Pip, but he didn't take very much notice of her.

To him she was only just a little girl, still a baby, who liked her dolls, and cried when she fell down.

' Larry and Daisy are coming back to-morrow,' she panted, as she rushed round after Pip. ' Oh, Pip ! do you think we can be the Find-Outers again ? '

' Only if there is something to find out, silly,' said Pip. ' Oh ! I forgot to tell you, Fatty is coming for the holidays too. His parents liked Peterswood so much when they stayed here at Easter, that they have bought a little house, and Fatty will be here for the hols.'

' Oh, *good* ! ' said Bets happily. ' I like Fatty. He's kind to me. We shall really be the Five Find-Outers again then ; and oh, Pip ! I suppose Buster is coming, isn't he ? '

' Of course,' said Pip. Buster was Fatty's little black Scottie dog, loved by all the children. ' It will be nice to see old Buster again.'

' How do you know about Fatty coming ? ' asked Bets, still trotting round after Pip.

' He wrote to me,' said Pip. ' Wait a minute—I've got the letter here. He sent a message to you in it.'

The boy felt in his pockets and took out a crumpled letter. Bets took it from him eagerly. It was very short, written in extremely neat handwriting.

' DEAR PIP,—Just to say my parents have bought White House, not far from you, so I'll be seeing you in the summer hols. Hope we have another mystery to solve. It would be fun to be the Five Find-Outers and Dog again. Give my love to little Bets. I'll pop down and see you as soon as I get back.—Yours,
' FREDERICK ALGERNON TROTTEVILLE.'

'Why doesn't he sign himself Fatty?' asked Bets. 'I think Frederick Algernon Trotteville sounds so silly.'

'Well, Fatty *is* silly sometimes,' said Pip. 'I hope he won't come back full of himself. Do you remember how he kept boasting about his marvellous bruises last hols, when he fell off that hayrick?'

'Well, they *were* most awfully good bruises,' said Bets, remembering. 'They did turn a wonderful colour. I wish my bruises went like that.'

Larry and Daisy came back the next day about three o'clock. After tea they raced off to see Pip and Bets. It was lovely to be all together again. Bets felt a little left-out after a bit, because she was the only one who did not go to boarding-school, and did not understand some of the things the others said.

'I wish I wasn't only eight years old,' she thought for about the thousandth time. 'Larry's thirteen, and the others are twelve—ages older than me. I shall never catch them up.'

Just as they were all exchanging their news, and laughing and chattering gaily, there came the scampering of feet up the drive, and a small black Scottie dog hurled himself into the middle of them, yapping excitedly.

'It's Buster! Oh, Buster, you're back again!' cried Daisy in delight. 'Good old Buster!'

'Dear old Buster! You're fatter!'

'Hallo, Buster-dog! Glad to see you, old fellow!'

'Darling Buster! I've missed you so!'

They were all so engaged in making a fuss of the excited little dog that they didn't see Fatty,

Buster's master, walking up to them. Bets saw him first. She jumped to her feet with a squeal, and rushed to Fatty. She flung her arms round him and hugged him. Fatty was pleased. He liked little Bets. He gave her a hug back.

The others grinned at him. ' Hallo, Fatty ! ' said Larry. ' Had a good term ? '

' I was top of my form,' said Fatty, not looking very modest about it.

' He's the same old Fatty,' said Pip with a grin. ' Top of this, that, and the other—full of brains as usual—best boy in the school ! '

' Shut up,' said Fatty, giving Pip a friendly punch. ' I suppose *you* were bottom of *your* form ! '

It was lovely to lie on the grass, play with Buster, and think of the eight or nine long sunny weeks ahead. No lessons. No rules. No being kept in or writing out lines. The summer holidays were really the nicest of all.

' Any news, Bets ? ' asked Fatty. ' Any mysteries turned up ? Any problems to solve ? We're still the Five Find-Outers and Dog, don't forget ! '

' I know,' said Bets happily. ' But there isn't any mystery at present, Fatty. I haven't even seen old Clear-Orf for weeks.'

Clear-Orf was the burly village policeman, Mr. Goon. The children always called him Clear-Orf, because that was what he said whenever he saw them. He didn't like children, and they didn't like him.

' Bets just hasn't any news at all,' said Pip. ' Nothing at all seems to have happened in Peterswood since we left to go to school.'

Bets suddenly remembered something. ' Oh,

I've just remembered,' she said. 'Somebody has come to live next door.'

The house next door had been empty for a year or two. The other children looked at Bets. 'Any children there?' asked Pip.

'No,' said Bets. 'At least, I don't think so. I've seen a big boy there, but I think he works in the garden. I hear him whistling sometimes. He whistles awfully nicely. Oh, and there are lots of cats there—very funny cats.'

'*Cats?* What sort of cats?' said Pip in surprise, and Buster pricked up his ears and growled at the mention of cats.

'They've got dark-brown faces and tails and legs,' said Bets, 'and cream-coloured fur. I saw the girl who looks after them carrying one once. It looked very queer.'

'She means Siamese cats,' said Larry. 'Have they got bright blue eyes, Bets?'

'I don't know,' said Bets. 'I wasn't near enough to see. Anyway, cats have green eyes, not blue, Larry.'

'Siamese cats have bright blue ones,' said Fatty. 'I know, because my aunt once had one—a beauty, called Patabang. They are valuable cats.'

'I'd like to go in next door and see them some day,' said Daisy, thinking that a cat with bright blue eyes, dark-brown face, legs, and tail, and cream-coloured fur sounded very lovely. 'Who's the owner, Bets?'

'Somebody called Lady Candling,' said Bets. 'I've never seen her. She is away a lot, I think.'

The children lay on their backs talking. Buster went from one to another, licking their faces and making them squeal and push him away.

173

Then there came the sound of a cheerful whistling just over the wall. It was a fine whistle, clear and melodious.

' That's the big boy next door I told you about,' said Bets. ' Doesn't he whistle nicely ? '

Larry got up and went to the wall. He hopped up on a big flower-pot and looked over the wall. He saw a boy there, about fifteen, a big lad with a round red face, startlingly blue eyes that looked rather surprised, and a big mouth full of very white teeth. The lad was hoeing the bed below the wall.

He looked up when he saw someone peeping over. He grinned, showing all his white teeth.

' Hallo,' said Larry. ' Are you the gardener next door ? '

' Lawks ! no,' said the boy, grinning even more widely. ' I'm just the boy—the gardener's boy, I'm called. Mr. Tupping is the gardener—him with the hooky nose and bad temper.'

Larry didn't think that Mr. Tupping sounded very nice. He glanced up the garden, but Mr. Tupping and his hooky nose were not in sight.

' Could we come over and see the cats one day ? ' asked Larry. ' It's Siamese cats, isn't it, that Lady Candling has ? '

' Yes. Lovely creatures they are,' said the boy. ' Well, you'd better come when Mr. Tupping is out. He reckons that the whole place is his, cats and all, the way he behaves. Come in to-morrow afternoon. He'll be out then. You can get over this wall. The kennel-girl will be here—Miss Harmer her name is. She won't mind you seeing the cats.'

' Righto ! ' said Larry, pleased. ' We'll be over here to-morrow afternoon. I say—what's your name ? '

But before the boy could answer him, an angry voice sounded from not far off.

' Luke ! Luke ! Where have you got to ? Didn't I tell you to clear away that rubbish ? Drat the boy, he's no use at all.'

Luke raised startled blue eyes to Larry, and put his hoe over his shoulder. He looked scared.

' That's him,' he said in a whisper. ' That's Mr. Tupping. I'll be going now. You come on over to-morrow.'

He went up the path. Larry slipped back to the others. ' He's the garden boy,' he said. ' His name's Luke. He looks nice, but a bit simple. I shouldn't think he could say boo to a goose.'

Bets felt certain she couldn't either, because geese were big and hissy. ' Are we to see the cats to-morrow ? ' she asked. ' I heard you saying something about them.'

' Yes. To-morrow afternoon, when Mr. Tupping the gardener is out,' said Larry. ' We'll hop over the wall. Better not take old Buster though —you know what he is with cats ! '

Buster growled when he heard the word. Cats ! What did the children want to go and see cats for ? Silly useless animals, with paws full of nasty pins and needles ! Cats were only good for one thing, and that was—to chase !

2   HORRID MR. TUPPING!

THE next afternoon the children remembered that they were to go and see the Siamese cats. Larry went to the wall and whistled for Luke.

The boy came along after a while, smiling and showing his white teeth. ' It's safe to come,' he said. ' Mr. Tupping is out.'

Soon all the children were over the wall. Fatty helped Bets. Buster was left behind and was most annoyed about it. He barked angrily, and stood up on his hind legs, pawing the wall desperately.

' Poor Buster,' said Bets, sorry for him. ' Never mind, Buster—we'll soon be back.'

' No dogs allowed in here,' said Luke. ' Because of the cats, you know. They're prize cats. Won no end of money, so the kennel-girl says.'

' Do you live here ? ' asked Larry, as they all walked up the path towards some big greenhouses.

' No. I live with my stepfather,' said Luke. ' My mother's dead. I got no brothers or sisters. This is my first job. My name's Luke Brown, and I'm fifteen.'

' Oh,' said Larry. ' I'm Laurence Daykin, and I'm thirteen. This is Margaret, my sister. She's twelve. We call her Daisy. This is Frederick Algernon Trotteville. He's twelve too, and he's called Fatty."

' I'd rather be called Frederick, thanks,' said Fatty, in a cross voice. ' There's no reason for me to be called Fatty by every Tom, Dick, and Harry ! '

'You aren't Tom, Dick, or Harry, you're called Luke, aren't you ? ' said Bets to Luke. He grinned.

'I'll call you Frederick if you like,' he said to Fatty. 'By rights I should call you Master Frederick, but I guess you don't want me to.'

'I'm Elizabeth Hilton, and I'm eight, and I'm called Bets,' said Bets, afraid that Larry was going to leave her out. 'And this is Philip, my brother. He's twelve and he's called Pip.'

They told Luke where they lived, and he told them where he lived—in a tumbledown cottage by the river. By this time they had left the green-houses behind and were going through a beautiful rose - garden. Beyond it rose a green - painted building.

'That's the cat-house,' said Luke. 'And there's Miss Harmer.'

A plump young woman, dressed in corduroy coat and breeches, was near the cat-house. She looked surprised to see the five children.

'Hallo,' she said, 'where have *you* come from ? '

'We came over the wall,' said Larry. 'We wanted to see the cats. They're not ordinary ones, are they ? '

'Oh no,' said Miss Harmer. She was a big, strapping girl of about twenty. 'There they are—do you like them ? '

The children gazed into the big cage-like build-ing. There were quite a number of cats there, all with the same striking colouring—dark-brown and cream, with brilliant blue eyes. They stared at the children, and miaowed in most peculiar voices.

'They're lovely,' said Daisy, at once.

'I think they look queer,' said Pip.

'Are they really cats? They look a bit like monkeys,' said Bets. The others laughed.

'You wouldn't think they were monkeys once you felt their sharp claws!' said Miss Harmer, with a laugh. 'All these cats are prize ones—they have been to shows and won a lot of money.'

'Which one has won the most money?' said Bets.

'This one over here,' said Miss Harmer, and she led the way to a smaller cage, like a very large kennel on legs. 'Well, Dark Queen? Aren't you a beauty? Here are some visitors to tell you how lovely you are!'

The big Siamese cat in the large, airy cage rubbed her head against the wire-netting, mewing loudly. The kennel-girl scratched her gently on the head.

'Dark Queen is our very, very special cat,' she said. 'She has just won a prize of a hundred pounds. She is worth much more than that.'

Dark Queen stood up, and her dark-brown tail rose in the air, swaying gently to and fro. Bets noticed something.

'She's got a few creamy hairs in the middle of her dark tail,' she said to Miss Harmer.

'Yes,' said the kennel-girl. 'She was bitten by one of the others there, and the hairs grew cream instead of brown. But they will turn brown later. What do you think of her?'

'Well—she seems just exactly like all the others,' said Daisy. 'I mean—they are exactly alike, aren't they?'

'Yes, they are,' said Miss Harmer. 'They have exactly the same colouring, you see. But I can always tell the difference, even when they are all mixed up together.'

'Fancy being worth more than a hundred pounds!' said Fatty, staring at Dark Queen, who stared back with unwinking blue eyes. 'Luke, you've got eyes as blue as Dark Queen's. You've got Siamese cat's eyes!'

Everyone laughed, and Luke looked rather foolish.

'Could you get Dark Queen out?' asked Daisy, who was longing to hold the beautiful cat. "Is she tame?'

'Oh *yes*,' said Miss Harmer. 'They are all tame. We only keep them in cages because they are so valuable. We couldn't let them roam free in case someone stole them.'

She took a key from a nail, and unlocked the cage-door. She lifted Dark Queen out, and held her. The beautiful cat rubbed against her, purring in a deep voice. Daisy stroked her, and to her delight the cat jumped into her arms.

'Oh, isn't she friendly?' said Daisy joyfully.

Then there came a great disturbance! Buster suddenly rushed along the path and flung himself on Fatty, barking joyfully. Dark Queen leapt straight out of Daisy's arms, and disappeared into the bushes. Buster, surprised, stared for a moment, and then, with a loud and joyful yelp, plunged after her. There was a terrific scrimmage.

Miss Harmer squealed. Luke's mouth fell open and he looked frightened. All the cats set up a miaowing. Fatty called fiercely:

'Buster! Come here, sir! BUSTER! Do you hear me? COME HERE, SIR!'

But no amount of calling could get Buster away

if there was a cat to chase. Miss Harmer ran in despair to the bushes. Only Buster was there, his nose bleeding from a scratch, his tongue hanging out, his eyes very bright and excited.

'Where's Dark Queen?' wailed Miss Harmer. 'Oh, this is awful! Puss, puss, puss!'

Bets began to cry. She couldn't bear to think that Dark Queen had gone. She thought she heard a noise in some bushes right at the end of the path and she ran off to see, tears running down her fat cheeks.

Then there came another commotion. Someone walked up to the cages, came round them—and it was Mr. Tupping, the gardener! Luke stared at him in fright.

'What's all this?' shouted Mr. Tupping. 'Who are you? What are you doing in my garden?'

'It isn't your garden,' said Fatty boldly. 'It's Lady Candling's, and she's a friend of my mother's.'

It wasn't a bit of good telling Mr. Tupping that it wasn't his garden. He felt that it belonged to him; he felt that every flower was his, every pea, and every smallest currant. And here were children and a dog in *his* garden! He detested children, dogs, cats, and birds.

'You get out of here,' he shouted in an angry voice. 'Go on! Get out at once! Do you hear me? And if I catch you here again I'll box your ears and tell your fathers. Miss Harmer, what's the matter with *you*?'

'Dark Queen is gone!' wailed Miss Harmer, who seemed just as much afraid of Mr. Tupping as Luke.

'Serves you right if you lose your job,' said

Mr. Tupping. 'What use are them cats, I'd like to know? Just rubbish, that's all they are. Good riddance if one *is* gone!'

'Shall we stay and help you to look for Dark Queen?' said Daisy to the kennel-girl.

'You get out,' said Mr. Tupping, and his big hooky nose got very red. His stone-coloured eyes glared at Daisy. He was an ugly, bad-tempered-looking fellow, with straw-coloured hair streaked with grey. Dirt was in all his wrinkles, and the children didn't like the look of him at all.

They decided to go. Tupping looked as if he might hit them at any moment. They made their way to the wall. They saw that Bets was not with them, but they thought she must have run back and climbed over the wall in her fear of the surly gardener. Fatty called Buster.

'No; you leave that dog with me,' said Tupping. 'A good hiding will do him good. I'll give him one, then he won't come interfering in *my* garden again.'

'Don't you dare to touch my dog!' cried Fatty at once. 'He'll bite you.'

Tupping made a grab for Buster and got him by the collar. He held him firmly by the back of the neck so that he couldn't even snap. He jerked him off his feet into the air, and then, carrying him by the back of the neck, marched off with him. Fatty was almost beside himself with anger.

He ran after the gardener and pulled at his arm. The man hit out at the boy, and Fatty gasped. Tupping threw the dog into a shed, shut the door, turned the key and put it into his pocket. Then he turned to Fatty with such an ugly look on his face that the boy turned and ran.

Tupping made a grab for Buster

Soon all four were over the wall, lying on the grass, panting and angry. They had left poor frightened Luke behind, and poor scared Miss Harmer. They had left Bets behind too, though they didn't know it—and Buster was locked in the shed.

' Hateful man ! ' said Daisy, almost in tears.

' The beast ! ' said Fatty between his teeth. ' Look at this bruise already showing on my arm. That's where he hit me.'

' Poor old Buster,' said Pip, hearing an anguished whine in the distance.

' Where's Bets ? ' said Larry, looking all round. ' Bets, Bets ! Where are you ? '

There was no answer. Bets was still over the wall. ' She must have gone indoors,' said Pip. ' I say, what are we going to do about Buster ? Fatty, we've got to rescue him, you know. We can't leave him there. I bet he *will* whip the poor little dog.'

' Poor Buster,' said Daisy. ' And poor Dark Queen. Oh ! I do hope she is found. I wonder how Buster got over the wall.'

' He didn't,' said Fatty. ' He couldn't. He must have thought hard, run down the drive, and up the drive next door and into the garden to find us. You know what brains Buster has got. Oh, golly ! how are we going to rescue him ? How I hate that man Tupping ! How awful for poor Luke to have to work under him ! '

' I'll go and find Bets,' said Pip. ' She must have gone to hide or something—maybe she's scared.'

He went into the house to find her, and soon came out looking puzzled. ' She's not anywhere about,' he said. ' I've called and called. Wherever can she be ? I suppose she *did* come back over the wall ? She can't be in next door's garden still, can she ? '

But she was. Poor little Bets was hiding there, scared stiff. What was she to do ? She couldn't get over the wall by herself—and she didn't dare to run down the drive in case Mr. Tupping saw her !

3   LUKE IS A GOOD FRIEND

WHEN Bets had run to the bushes to see if Dark Queen was there, she had found that it was only a big blackbird that had flown out as soon as she had got there. All the same, she went into the bushes and had a look round, calling, ' Puss, puss, puss ! '

Suddenly she saw two bright blue eyes looking down at her from the tree above. She jumped. Then she gave a cry of delight.

' Oh, it's you, Dark Queen ! Oh, I'm so glad I've found you ! '

She stood and thought. It was no good getting Dark Queen down until Buster was safely out of the garden. The lovely cat was much safer where she was. Bets looked up at Dark Queen and the cat began to purr. She liked the little girl.

Bets saw that the tree would be easy to climb. It wasn't long before she was up on the branch beside the cat, stroking her, and talking to her. Dark Queen simply loved it. She rubbed her dark brown head against the little girl, and purred very loudly.

And then Bets heard Mr. Tupping shouting,

and she was frightened. Oh dear ! the gardener must have come back. He wasn't out after all. She listened to the angry yelling, and trembled. She did not dare to join the others. She sat quietly by the cat and listened.

She could not hear exactly what happened, but after a while she realised that the others must have gone back over the wall and left her. She felt very forlorn and frightened. She was just about to slip down the tree to try and find Hiss Harmer and tell her where Dark Queen was, when footsteps came along the path. The little girl peeped between the leaves of the tree and saw Mr. Tupping dragging poor Luke along by one of his big ears.

' I'll teach you to let children into my garden ! ' said Mr. Tupping, and he gave Luke such a slap that the boy let out a yell. ' You're paid to do work, you are. You'll stay here and work two hours overtime for letting them children in ! '

He gave Luke another blow, pulled his ear hard, then pushed him and sent him flying down the path. Bets was so sorry for Luke that tears ran down her cheeks, and she gave a little sob. Horrid Mr. Tupping !

Mr. Tupping went off down another path. Luke picked up a hoe, and was just setting off in the opposite direction when Bets called softly to him :

' Luke ! '

Luke dropped his hoe with a clatter, and looked all round, startled. He could see no one. ' Luke ! ' called Bets again. ' I'm here, up the tree. And Dark Queen is with me.'

Then Luke saw the little girl up the tree and the Siamese cat beside her. Bets slipped down and stood beside him.

'Help me over the wall, Luke,' she said.

'Well, if Mr. Tupping sees me I'll lose my job,
and my stepfather will belt me black and blue,' said
poor Luke, his big red face as scared as Bets' little one.

'Well, I don't want you to lose your job,' said
Bets. 'I'll try and get over by myself.'

But Luke would not let her do that. Scared as
he was, he felt that he must help the little girl. He
lifted Dark Queen down from the tree, and together
the two of them walked softly up the path, keeping
a sharp look-out for Mr. Tupping.

Luke slipped Dark Queen into her cage and shut
the door. 'Miss Harmer will be glad she's found,'
he whispered to Bets. 'I'll tell her in a minute.
Now, come on—sprint for the wall and I'll get you
over.'

They ran for the wall. Luke gave Bets a leg-up,
and soon she was sitting on the top. 'Buck up!'
called Luke in a low voice. 'Old Tupping is
coming!'

Bets was so frightened that she jumped down at
once, falling on hands and knees and grazing them.
She rushed to the lawn, seeing the others there, and
flung herself down beside them, trembling.

'Bets! Wherever have you been?' cried Pip.

'Were you left behind?' said Fatty. 'Oh, look
at your poor knees!'

'And my hands too,' said Bets in a trembling
voice, holding out bleeding hands. Fatty got out
his hanky and wiped them. 'How did you get
over the wall by yourself?' he asked.

'I didn't. Luke helped me, though he was
terribly, terribly afraid that Mr. Tupping would
come along and catch him. Then he would lose
his job,' said Bets.

186

'Jolly decent of him to help you, then,' said
Larry, and the others agreed.

'I like Luke,' said Bets. 'I think he's very,
very nice. I do wish he hadn't got into trouble
through letting us come over the wall and see the
cats.'

A distant whining came on the air again. Bets
looked puzzled. She looked all round.

'Where's Buster?' she asked. She had not
heard him being dragged away and locked up,
though she had heard the noise of the commotion.
The others told her. The little girl was indignant
and upset.

'Oh, we *must* rescue him ; we must, we must !'
she cried. 'Fatty, do, do go over the wall and get
Buster !'

But Fatty didn't feel at all inclined to run the
risk of meeting the surly Mr. Tupping again. Also
he knew that the gardener had the key of Buster's
shed in his pocket.

'If Lady Candling wasn't away I'd get my
mother to ring her up and ask her to tell that fellow
Tupping to set him free,' said Fatty. He rolled up
his sleeve again and looked at the big bruise on his
arm, now turning red-purple. 'If I showed my
mother that, I bet she'd ring up a dozen Lady
Candlings.'

'It's going to be quite a good bruise,' said Bets,
knowing how proud Fatty always was of his bruises.
'Oh dear, there's poor darling Buster howling
again ! Let's go to the wall and peep over. We
might see Luke and get him to peep in at the shed
window and say a kind word to Buster.'

So they tiptoed cautiously to the wall and Larry
carefully looked over. No one was about. Then

there came the sound of someone whistling. It was Luke. Larry whistled too. The distant whistling stopped, then began again. It stopped, and Larry whistled the same tune.

Presently there came the sound of someone coming through the bushes and Luke's face appeared, full and red, like a round moon. 'What's up?' he whispered. 'I daren't stop. Mr. Tupping's still about.'

'It's Buster,' whispered Larry. 'Can you peep in at the shed window and just say, " Poor fellow," or something like that to him?'

Luke nodded and disappeared. He went towards the shed, keeping a sharp look-out for the gardener. He saw him in the distance, taking off his coat to do a bit of work. He hung it on a nail outside one of the greenhouses. He caught sight of Luke and yelled at him.

'Now then, lazy! Have you finished that bed yet? I want you to come and tie up some tomatoes.'

Luke shouted something back and went into the bushes nearby. He watched Mr. Tupping walk off to the kitchen-garden, unravelling some raffia as he went. The gardener disappeared through a green door let into the wall that ran round the kitchen-garden.

Then Luke did a very brave thing. He ran swiftly and quietly to Mr. Tupping's coat. He slipped his hand into the outer pocket, took the key of the little shed, and raced off with it. He unlocked the shed, and Buster rushed out. Luke tried to catch him in order to bundle him over the wall, but Buster escaped him and tore off down a path.

Luke locked the door quickly, ran back to the

gardener's coat and slipped the key back into the
pocket. Then he went to join Mr. Tupping in the
kitchen-garden, hoping to goodness that Buster had
had the sense to shoot off down the drive.

But Buster had lost his way. He suddenly
appeared in the kitchen-garden and gave a yap of
joy when he saw Luke. Mr. Tupping looked up
at once.

'That dog!' he said in astonishment and anger.
'Blessed if it isn't that dog again! How did he
get out of the shed? Didn't I lock that door?
And isn't the key in my pocket?'

'I saw you lock the door, sir,' said Luke.
'Perhaps it's a different dog.'

Mr. Tupping waved his arms wildly and yelled
at Buster. Buster gambolled into the kitchen-
garden and ran right across a bed of carrots. Luke
felt certain the little dog did it on purpose. Tupping
went purple in the face.

'You get out!' he yelled, and threw a big stone
at Buster. Buster yelped, and began to dig hard
in the middle of the carrots, sending roots flying
into the air.

Tupping went quite mad. He rushed over the
carrot-bed, shouting, and Buster retired a good way
off, and began to dig up some onions.

When a big stone came rather too near him
Buster ran out of the green door in the kitchen-
garden wall, and tore off down the nearest path.
He soon found his way out of the garden, and went
racing up the drive of Pip's house next door.

He flung himself joyfully on the surprised
children. 'Buster! Darling Buster! How did you
get free? Oh, Buster, have you been hurt?'

Everyone spoke to Buster at once. He rolled

over on his back and lay there, all his feet in the air, his tail thumping the ground and his pink tongue out.

'Good dog,' said Fatty, patting his tummy. 'I wish you could tell us how you got free!'

The children lay in wait for Luke that night as he went home. His time for knocking off was usually five, but that day Mr. Tupping kept him at work till seven as a punishment, and the boy, big and strong as he was, was tired out.

'Luke! How did Buster get free? Did you know he was free?' cried Pip. Luke nodded.

'Got the key out of old Tupping's coat meself and let the little dog out,' he said. 'Coo! you should have seen old Tupping's face when Buster came into the kitchen-garden. He nearly had a fit.'

'Luke! Did you *really* let Buster out!' cried Fatty. He gave the big boy a thump on the back. 'I say, thanks an awful lot! We were terribly upset about him. I guess you were scared to do it.'

'Reckon I was,' said Luke, scratching his head, and remembering how scared he had felt. 'But the little dog meant no harm—nice little dog he is. I like dogs. I guessed you'd all be worried about him.'

'Oh, I do think you're nice, Luke,' said little Bets, hanging on to his arm. 'You got me safely over the wall, and you set Buster free. We'll all be your friends!'

'The likes of you can't be friends with the likes of me,' said the big boy shyly, looking very pleased all the same.

'Well, we can,' said Larry. 'And what's more, in return for what you've done for us to-day, we promise to help *you* if ever you want help. See?'

'Don't reckon I'll want no help from kids like you,' said big Luke in a friendly voice. 'But thanks all the same. Don't you come over the wall any more now. You'll make me lose my job if you do.'

'We won't,' said Fatty. 'And don't forget— if you're ever in real trouble, we'll help you, Luke !'

4   MISS TRIMBLE MAKES TROUBLE

LUKE proved to be a most amusing friend to have. Certainly he was a bit 'simple' and could hardly read or write, but he knew all kinds of things that the children didn't know.

He could make whistles out of hollow twigs, and he presented Bets with a wonderful collection. He showed her how to whistle little tunes on them, and she was thrilled.

Then he knew every bird in the countryside, where they nested, what their eggs were like, and the songs they sang. Soon the five children and Buster were going for walks with Luke, hanging on to his words, thinking that he was really marvellous.

'Funny he knows all that and yet can't read or write properly,' said Pip. 'He's terribly clever with his hands too—he can carve animals and birds out of bits of wood in no time. Look at this squirrel he did for me.'

'He's doing a model of Dark Queen for me,' said Bets proudly. 'It's going to be exactly like her, even to the little ring of pale cream hairs in her dark-brown tail. Luke is going to paint the model for me, blue eyes and all.'

Luke finished the wooden carving of Dark Queen, the Siamese cat, two days later. The children heard his now familiar whistle over the wall, and crowded there to see what he wanted. Luke handed over the cat-model.

It was really excellent. Even Fatty, who fancied himself very much at all kinds of art work, was very much impressed.

He handled the little model admiringly. 'Fine, Luke,' he said. 'You've got the colouring marvellously too—dark-brown ears, face, legs, tail—and creamy fur—and brilliant blue eyes—and even the tiny ring of creamy hairs round the middle of Dark Queen's tail. That's where she got bitten by another cat, isn't it?'

'Yes,' said Luke. 'But they will grow dark again all right. Miss Harmer says it won't spoil her for shows.'

'How's old Tupping these days?' asked Pip.

'Awful,' said Luke. 'I wish I hadn't got to work for him. He's that bad-tempered. I'm always afraid of him complaining about me to my step-father too. I'd get a good thrashing if he did. My stepfather doesn't like me.'

The five children were sorry for Luke. He didn't seem to have much of a life. He was a kindly, generous fellow, always ready to do anything he could for them. He loved little Bets, and stuck up for her when Pip teased her, as he often did.

Buster adored Luke. 'He's grateful to you for saving him from Tupping!' said Fatty, watching Buster trying to climb up Luke's legs, panting with delight.

'He's a nice little dog,' said Luke. 'I like

dogs. Always did. I like them cats too. Beautiful things, aren't they ? '

' We saw someone else in your garden to-day,' said Larry. ' A middle-aged lady, very thin, with a rather red nose, glasses that kept falling off, and a funny little bun of hair at the back of her neck. Who is she ? That's not Lady Candling, is it ? '

' Oh no,' said Luke. ' That's her companion, Miss Trimble. Miss *Tremble* I call her, to myself —she's that scared of old Tupping ! She has to do the flowers for the house, you see ; and if she goes out and picks them when Tupping is there, he follows her around like a dog ready to bite her, and says, " If you pick any more of them roses, that'll spoil the tree ! " " If you take them poppies of mine they'll fall to bits—you shouldn't ought to pick them in the sun." Things like that. The poor old thing trembles and shakes, and I feel right-down sorry for her.'

' Everyone seems afraid of Tupping,' said Daisy. ' Horrid fellow. I hope he gets a punishment one day for being so hateful. But I bet he won't.'

' Come and see my little garden, Luke,' said Bets, pulling the big boy up the path. ' It's got some lovely snapdragons out.'

Luke went with her. It was a funny little garden, done by Bets herself. It had one old rose tree in it, a tiny gooseberry bush, some virginian stock, a few red snapdragons, and some Shirley poppies.

' Fine ! ' said Luke. ' Did you have any goose-berries off that little bush ? '

' Not one,' said Bets sadly. ' And Luke, I planted two strawberries last year—nice red ripe ones—and they didn't even grow up in strawberry plants. I was dreadfully disappointed. I did so want to pick strawberries of my own this year.'

Luke laughed his loud, clear laugh. ' Ho, ho, ho, ho ! Strawberries don't grow from strawberries, Bets ! They grow from runners—you know, long stems sent out from the plants. The runners send up little new plants here and there. I'll tell you what I'll do—I'll give you a few of our runners from next door. I'm cleaning up the beds now, and there'll be a lot of runners thrown away on the rubbish-heap. You can have some of those.'

' Will it matter ? ' asked Bets doubtfully. 'Would they really be rubbish ? '

' Yes—all burnt up on the rubbish-heap ! ' said Luke. ' It's Tupping's day off to-morrow. You come on over the wall and I'll show you how the runners grow, and give you some.'

So the next day Pip helped Bets over the wall and Luke helped her down the other side. He took her to the strawberry-bed and showed her the new plants growing from the runners sent out from the old plants.

' It's very clever of the strawberries to grow new plants like that, isn't it ? ' said Bets. She saw a pile of pulled-up runners in Luke's barrow nearby. ' Oh,' she said, ' are these the ones you're going to throw away ? How many can I have ? '

' You take six,' said Luke, and he picked out six good runners, each with little healthy straw-berry plants on them. He gave them to Bets.

' Who's that ? ' said Bets suddenly, as she saw someone coming towards them.

' It's Miss Tremble,' said Luke. ' You needn't be afraid of *her*. She won't hurt you.'

Miss Trimble came up, smiled at Bets. Bets

didn't like her very much, she was so thin and bony. She wore glasses without any rims, pinched on to the sides of her nose. They kept falling off, and dangled on a little chain. Bets watched to see how many times they would fall off.

'Well, and who is *this* little girl?' said Miss Trimble, in a gay, bird-like voice, nodding at Bets. Her glasses at once fell off and she put them on again.

'I'm Bets from next door,' said Bets.

'And what have you got there?' said Miss Trimble, looking at the strawberry plants in Bets's hand. 'Some lovely treasure?'

'No,' said Bets. 'Just some strawberry runners.'

Miss Trimble's glasses fell off again and she put them back.

'Be careful they don't run away from you!' she said, and laughed loudly at her own joke. Bets didn't think it was very funny; but she laughed too, out of politeness. Miss Trimble's glasses fell off again.

'Why don't they keep on?' asked Bets with interest. 'Is your nose too thin to hold them on?'

'Oh, what a funny little girl!' said Miss Trimble, laughing again. 'Well, good-bye my dear, I must away to my little jobs!'

She went off, and Bets was glad. 'Her glasses fell off six times, Luke,' she said.

'You're a caution, you are,' said Luke. 'I only hope she doesn't go and tell Mr. Tupping she saw you here!'

But that is just what Miss Trimble *did* do! She did not mean any harm. She did not even know that Tupping had ordered the children out of the garden some days before. She was picking roses the very next day, when Tupping came along behind her and stood watching her.

Miss Trimble began to feel scared, as she always did when the surly gardener came along. He was so rude. She turned and gave him a frightened smile.

' Lovely morning, Tupping, isn't it ? ' she said. ' Beautiful roses these.'

' Won't be beautiful long when you've finished messing about with them,' said Tupping.

' Oh, I'm not spoiling them ! ' said Miss Trimble. ' I know how to pick roses.'

' You don't know any more than a child ! ' said surly Tupping, enjoying seeing how scared poor Miss Trimble was of him.

The mention of a child made Miss Trimble remember Bets. ' Oh,' she said, trying to turn the conversation away from roses—' oh, there was such a dear little girl with Luke in the garden yesterday ! '

Tupping's face grew as black as thunder. ' A girl here ! ' he shouted. ' Where's that Luke ? I'll skin him if he lets those kids in here whilst my back is turned ! '

He went off to find Luke. Miss Trimble shook with fright, and her glasses fell off and got so entangled in her lace collar that it took quite twenty minutes for her trembling hands to disentangle them.

' A most unpleasant fellow ! ' she kept murmuring to herself. ' Dear, dear ! I hope I haven't got poor Luke into trouble. He's such a pleasant fellow—and only a boy too. I do hope he won't get into trouble.'

Luke *was* in trouble. Tupping strode up to him and glowered, his stone-coloured eyes almost hidden under his shaggy brows.

'Who was that girl in here yesterday?' he demanded. 'One of them kids next door, was it? What was she doing here?'

'Nothing she shouldn't do, Mr. Tupping,' said Luke. 'She's a good little thing.'

'I said "*What was she doing here?*"' shouted Mr. Tupping. 'Taking the peaches, I suppose— or picking the plums!'

'She's the little girl from next door,' said Luke hotly. 'She wouldn't take nothing like that. I just gave her some strawberry runners for her garden, that's all. They'd have been burnt on the rubbish-heap, anyway!'

Mr. Tupping looked as if he was going to have a fit. To think that Luke should give anyone anything out of *his* garden! He really thought it was his garden, and not Lady Candling's. He didn't stop to think that Lady Candling would willingly give a little girl a few strawberry runners, for she was fond of children.

Tupping gave Luke a box on the ears, and went straight to the wall. Luke did not dare to follow him. He felt certain that all the children were out, because he had heard their voices and their bicycle bells some time back on the road. He stooped over his work, his ears red. He felt angry with Miss Trimble. Why had she given Bets away?

The children *had* gone out on their bicycles— all but Bets. The ride they were going was too far for her, so the little girl had been left behind with Buster, much to her annoyance. It was such a nuisance being four or five years younger than the others. They kept on leaving her out!

'Buster, come and sit by me and I'll read you a story about rabbits,' said Bets. At the word 'rabbits' Buster ran to Bets. He thought she was going to take him for a walk. But instead she sat down under a tree and took a book from under her arm. She opened it and began to read.

'Once there was a big, fat rabbit called Woffly. He . . .'

But Buster was bored. He got up and ran to the bottom of the drive waiting for the others to come back. Bets sat there alone. She suddenly heard a noise and looked up—and, oh dear me, there, climbing over the wall, looking as fierce as could be, was that horrid Mr. Tupping !

5 TUPPING—BUSTER—AND MR. GOON

BETS was horrified. She couldn't even get up and run away. She looked round for Buster, but he wasn't there. She stared in fright at Mr. Tupping, who came towards her with a red and angry face.

'You the little girl who came into my garden yesterday ?' he said.

Bets nodded. She couldn't say a word.

'Did you take my strawberry runners ?' asked Mr. Tupping, even more fiercely.

Still Bets couldn't say a word. She nodded again, her face very white. Surely, surely, it hadn't been wrong to have those strawberry runners ! She had planted them carefully in her little garden, and had watered them well. They were hers now. They would only have been thrown away and burnt.

Mr. Tupping put out his hand and jerked the

frightened little girl to her feet. 'You show me where you put them,' he said.

'Let me go,' said Bets, finding her tongue at last. 'I'll tell Mummy about you!'

'You tell her if you like,' said Mr. Tupping. 'And I'll tell Mr. Goon the policeman, see? I'll tell him you took my strawberry runners, and he'll put you and Luke into prison!'

'They don't put little girls into prison,' sobbed Bets. But her heart went cold at the thought of Luke going to prison.

'Where's them strawberry runners?' demanded Mr. Tupping. Bets led him up to her garden. As soon as Mr. Tupping saw the neatly-planted, well-watered little strawberry plants he bent down and wrenched every one of them up. He tore them up into tiny pieces and threw them on to the bonfire that was smouldering nearby. Bets sobbed bitterly. Poor little strawberry plants!

'You're a bad girl,' said Mr. Tupping. 'And I tell you this—if you come into my garden again, I'll go straight to Mr. Goon the policeman. Great friend of mine, he is, and he'll be along to see your father before you can say "Jack Robinson." As for that Luke—well, he'll end up in prison, no doubt about that.'

With that Mr. Tupping began to walk back to the wall; but before he could get there, Buster came running up. He heard Bets sobbing, he smelt Mr. Tupping, and he put two and two together at once. Buster certainly had brains!

He flew straight at Tupping and caught him by the trouser-leg, growling in a most fearsome way Mr. Tupping gave a howl.

'Call your dog off!' he yelled. Bets called Buster.

' Oh, Buster, don't ! Come here, Buster ! '

But Buster was having a lovely time. Here was his enemy ill-treating his beloved little Bets. Grrrrrrrrrr !

Tupping was frightened. He kicked out and picked up a stick. Buster tore a large piece out of Tupping's trouser-leg, and retired under a bush to chew it. Tupping took his chance and shinned up the wall. Buster was out from the bush in a trice, snapping at Tupping's ankles, getting another bit of trouser and a nice piece of woollen sock too. Tupping gave a yell, and fell off on the other side of the wall.

Bets was half-laughing and half-crying by now. ' Oh, Buster, darling Buster, I think you're marvellous ! ' she said.

' Grrrrrrrr ! ' said Buster happily, still chewing a bit of trouser.

Bets sat down and thought. She longed to run in and tell her mother all about everything, and feel her mother's arms round her. The little girl had had a shock. But she was afraid that if she told her mother, Mummy would go and tell Lady Candling, and Lady Candling would scold Tupping, and Tupping would go to the police and say that Luke had stolen things to give to her, Bets.

' And Mr. Goon doesn't like us, ever since we solved the mystery of the burnt cottage before he did ! ' said Bets to herself. ' So he would love to listen to everything that Tupping said and make a fuss about it. And Luke might really and truly be sent to prison. Oh, I do wish the others were here.'

They came back at last. Fatty noticed Bets's tear-stained face at once.

' What's up ? ' he said. ' Got into a row, little Bets ? '

'Oh, an awful thing happened this morning,' said Bets, glad to pour out everything to the others. She told them the whole story. The three boys went red with rage to think that little Bets should have been treated like that. Daisy put her arms round her and gave her a hug.

'Poor old Bets,' she said. 'Go on—what happened next?'

Then Bets told about Buster and how he had torn pieces out of Tupping's trouser-legs. The children roared with laughter, and gave Buster a great petting. 'Good dog, good dog!' said Pip. 'That's the stuff to give to surly old Tupping. Good dog!'

Fatty put his arm round Bets. 'You did quite right not to tell your mother,' he said. 'I mean—it will save Luke a lot of trouble if we keep this quiet, because he would be terribly scared if the policeman came to question him. You know what old Luke is—frightened of all grown-ups simply because most of them have been so beastly to him.'

'Fancy tearing up Bets's plants like that,' said Pip. 'If I was old enough I'd go and shake Tupping till his teeth fell out!'

The others laughed. They all felt like that when they thought of poor frightened little Bets and her precious strawberry plants. Buster barked and wagged his tail.

'He says he did his best to give Tupping a shaking!' said Daisy.

The children did their best to make up to Bets for her fright. They were very kind to her. Larry went straight home, asked his mother if he might dig up a few strawberry plants for Bets, and brought them back. He planted them himself for her, and the little girl was very pleased.

Fatty brought her a book. He spent all his pocket-money on it, and never even said so, which was good for Fatty.

Daisy gave her one of her old dolls, which pleased Bets more than anything. Even Pip, who usually hadn't much time for his ' baby-sister ' as he called her, took her for a ride all round the garden on his big bicycle. So altogether Bets had a good time.

The children wondered if Luke had got into trouble. When they heard his familiar whistle at five o'clock they ran down to the gate to meet him as he went home.

' Luke ! How did Tupping find out about Bets and the strawberry plants ? Did you get into trouble ? Did you know he scared Bets terribly ? '

' Poor little Bets,' said Luke. ' I didn't know she was in, or I'd have gone after old Tupping. I thought you were all out. I heard your bicycle bells, you see. When Tupping came back and told me he'd gone for Bets, and torn up all her plants, I could have knocked him down. But he would only have reported me to Mr. Goon the policeman, so what would have been the good of that ? '

' Did you get into an awful row ? ' asked Bets. ' How did he find out about me ? '

' Miss Tremble must have told him, the silly old thing,' said Luke. ' Yes, I did get into a row. I got my ears boxed, and I had to work harder than ever to-day. I wish I could leave.'

' I wish you could, too,' said Larry. ' Why can't you ? '

' Well, it's my first job you see, and you should

stick in your first job as long as you can,' said Luke.
' And there's another thing—I bet Tupping would
give me a bad name if I gave him notice, and I might
not be able to get another job. Then I'd get into
trouble with my stepfather. I give him half my
money, you see.'

' You have a lot of troubles, Luke,' said Daisy.
' I wish we could help you.'

' Well, you do in a way,' said Luke. ' I tell you
things, don't I ? I don't keep them all bottled up
like I used to. It's nice to tell them to somebody.
Look, there's old Goon, the village bobby ! '

Mr. Goon, burly, red-faced, with bulging frog-
eyes, was walking down the lane towards the
children.

' Do you suppose he is going to see Mr. Tupping?'
asked Bets in alarm.

' Don't know,' said Luke, also looking rather
alarmed. He was afraid of policemen, and Mr.
Goon was not a very nice one.

' I wonder if he'll tell us to clear orf,' whispered
Daisy. ' Do you remember how often he shouted
" Clear orf ! " to us in the Easter holidays ? Horrid
old Clear-Orf ! '

Mr. Goon came slowly towards them. The
children watched him. Buster growled. Mr. Goon
pretended not to notice any of them. He did not
feel at all friendly towards the children since they had
solved a mystery he had been unable to solve himself.

Buster suddenly flew round Mr. Goon and
barked madly at his ankles. He did not attempt to
bite him or snap at him, but he startled Mr. Goon all
the same.

' Clear orf ! ' said Mr. Goon to Buster, in a
threatening tone. ' Do you hear ? Clear orf ! '

'Buster, come here!' said Fatty, but not in a very commanding voice. Buster took no notice. He was having a lovely day. First Mr. Tupping and now Mr. Goon to frighten. Oh, what a treat for a little black Scottie!

'Clear ORF,' said Mr. Goon. Luke gave one of his loud laughs as Buster jumped nimbly out of the way of a kick. The policeman looked at him.

'Ho, you!' he said, 'you'll get into trouble, you will, if you laugh at the Law. What you doing here? You clear orf!'

'He's our friend,' said Fatty. 'Come here, Buster!'

Mr. Tupping, hearing the noise of barking and shouting, appeared at the other gate of the drive. He knew Buster at once.

'You'd better report that there dog,' remarked Mr. Tupping to the policeman. 'Tore a bit out of me trousers to-day—look here! Vicious dog, that's what he is. Right-down vicious.'

He caught sight of Luke. 'What you doing hanging about here instead of going home?' he asked. Luke disappeared at once, going off up the lane quickly. He wanted no more trouble from either Mr. Tupping or Mr. Goon.

Buster returned from the battle and went to Fatty, who picked him up.

'Right-down vicious dog,' said Mr. Tupping again. 'If you want any details, Mr. Goon, I'll give you them.'

Mr. Goon did not want to report Buster, because he knew that any report would go before Inspector Jenks, who was very friendly with the children. Still, he thought there would be no harm in pretending that he *was* going to report Buster for being vicious and out of control, so he pulled out his big black notebook, took his stubby pencil and began to write solemnly and slowly.

The children were rather alarmed. They all went back into Pip's garden at once. Bets gazed at Buster, her eyes wide with fright.

' Would they—would they put Buster in prison ? ' she asked fearfully—and was very much relieved when all the others burst out laughing.

' Of course not,' said Fatty. ' Nobody ever heard of a dogs' prison, Bets. Don't you worry about old Buster ! '

6   DARK QUEEN DISAPPEARS

THINGS began to happen very quickly after this, and, quite suddenly, the Five Find-Outers found that there was a first-class mystery for them to solve.

The children played in Pip's garden that morning, and there was a lot of whooping and screaming, because they were playing Red Indians. It got too lively for Bets after a bit, and she begged to be a squaw in a wigwam. She thought that wouldn't be quite so terrifying as being caught and scalped, or tied to a tree and shot at with bow and arrows !

That afternoon Pip's mother, Mrs. Hilton, went to tea with Lady Candling, who was now back again next door after a short holiday.

' You may all have a picnic tea in the garden,' she told Pip. ' Daisy, see that everyone behaves, please, and if you haven't enough to eat, go and ask

Cook politely—*politely*, remember—for some more bread-and-butter.'

' Yes, Mrs. Hilton. Thank you very much,' said Daisy. The children watched Pip's mother going down the drive at half-past three that afternoon, looking very smart. They were glad that *they* did not have to dress up and go out to tea. It was much more fun to have a picnic tea and wear old shorts and shirts !

They had a lovely tea, and went in twice to ask Cook for some more bread-and-butter. Daisy went, and remembered to ask very politely. There were ripe plums and greengages as well to eat, so it was a good tea.

Soon after tea Mrs. Hilton came back. She went straight to the children, looking rather worried.

' Children,' she said, ' what do you think has happened ? That lovely prize-cat, called Dark Queen, has disappeared ! Lady Candling is very upset, because she is most valuable. And the dreadful thing is—Luke may have stolen her ! '

' *Mother !* ' said Pip indignantly, ' Luke's our friend. He would never, never do a thing like that ! '

' He wouldn't, he wouldn't ! ' cried Bets.

' Oh, Mrs. Hilton,' said Fatty earnestly, ' I really don't think you are right in saying that Luke did that ! '

' I didn't say he *had*,' said Mrs. Hilton. ' I said that he might have. All the evidence points to the fact that he was about the only one who could have done so.'

' But he couldn't, he simply couldn't,' said Daisy. ' He's as honest as the day. It is much more likely to have been that hateful old Tupping.'

' Tupping has been out all the afternoon with Mr. Goon the policeman, who appears to be his friend,' said Mrs. Hilton. ' So it is quite impossible that he could have stolen her.'

The children stared at Mrs. Hilton, feeling upset and puzzled. Fatty took command of the whole affair, and spoke politely to Mrs. Hilton.

' Luke is a very good friend of ours, Mrs. Hilton, and if he is in trouble we must help him. I am quite sure he had nothing to do with Dark Queen disappearing, nothing at all. Could you please give us the whole story ? This looks like something the Five Find-Outers can tackle again.'

' My dear Frederick, don't talk so pompously,' said Mrs. Hilton rather impatiently. ' And don't start interfering in this matter, for goodness' sake. It's nothing to do with you. Just because you solved one mystery quite well is no reason why you should think you can interfere in anything else that crops up.'

Fatty went red. He didn't like being ticked off in public like that.

' Mother, please do tell us all that has happened,' said Pip.

' Well,' said Mrs. Hilton, ' Miss Harmer went off for the day this morning, after feeding all the cats and cleaning out their cages. Dark Queen was in the big cage with the other cats to-day. Miss Harmer went to catch the ten o'clock bus. Miss Trimble went with Lady Candling to see that the cats were all right at just before one o'clock, and Tupping pointed out Dark Queen to them. You know what a beauty she is.'

The children nodded. ' Go on, Mother,' said

Pip. 'Was that the last time that anyone saw Dark Queen?'

'No,' said his mother. 'Miss Trimble went with me to show me the cats at four o'clock, just before tea—and Dark Queen was there then, in the cage with the others.'

'How do you know, Mother?' asked Pip. 'How could you tell which was Dark Queen? They are all exactly alike.'

'I know,' said Mrs. Hilton, 'but apparently Dark Queen has been bitten on the tail, and a few hairs there grew cream instead of dark-brown. Miss Trimble pointed out the cat to me and I remember noticing the ring of creamy hairs—most noticeable. So she was in the cage, quite safe, at four o'clock.'

'Go on,' said Pip.

'Tupping came back at five o'clock and he brought Mr. Goon the village policeman with him,' said Mrs. Hilton. 'He showed Mr. Goon his prize tomatoes, and then he showed him the cats. Then Mr. Tupping suddenly noticed that Dark Queen was missing!'

'Gracious!' said Fatty. 'Then the cat must have disappeared between four and five o'clock, Mrs. Hilton.'

'Yes,' said Pip's mother. 'And as Luke was the only one in the garden, I am afraid that he is suspected. He knew that the cat was worth a lot of money. Tupping says that the boy stole something the other day too—strawberry runners or something silly like that.'

Bets went fiery red. Tears came into her eyes. Those awful strawberry runners! She wondered if she should tell her mother about them, but Fatty frowned at her, warning her not to.

' Well, that's all,' said Mrs. Hilton, pulling off her gloves. ' But I'm afraid your friend Luke is in for trouble now. I wonder where he took the cat. No one seems to have seen Luke between four and five o'clock, so I suppose he could have put her into a basket and taken her off anywhere.'

' Mummy, Luke wouldn't ! ' burst out Bets. ' You don't know how kind and honest he is. He gave me a lot of whistles he made—and this lovely model of Dark Queen too. Look ! '

' I wish you wouldn't make such extraordinary friends,' said her mother, not looking at the model at all. ' You are none of you old enough to know whether anyone is really honest or not. Please don't talk to Luke any more.'

Mrs. Hilton went towards the house and disappeared indoors. The children looked at one another in dismay.

' It's just no good to say, " Don't talk to Luke any more," ' said Fatty. ' We've simply got to. He's our friend, and he's helped us lots of times—and Buster too. We've got to help *him* now.'

All the others agreed. They sat and thought about everything for a little, and then began to talk about it.

' *Some*body must have stolen Dark Queen, there's no doubt about that,' said Fatty. ' It seems as if it could only be old Luke ; but we're all absolutely certain it isn't, so who else could it be ? '

' Let's look for clues ! ' said Bets eagerly, remembering how exciting it had been to look for clues in the last mystery they had solved.

' Let's draw up a list of Suspects ! ' said Daisy. ' We did that before.'

' Now,' said Fatty importantly, ' it seems to me

that the Five Find-Outers can really get to work again. I propose . . .'

'Look here,' said Larry, 'you're forgetting something, Fatty. *I'm* head of the Find-Outers, not you.'

'All right,' said Fatty, looking sulky. 'Go ahead then. Only I've got far more brains than you have. I was top of my form last term, and . . .'

'Shut up, Fatty,' said everyone together, except Bets. Fatty looked as if he was going to get up and go ; but he was too excited and interested to be sulky for long, and soon the five children were eagerly discussing their plans.

'Now, let's think everything out clearly,' said Daisy. 'Dark Queen was with the others until four o'clock, because it was then that Miss Tremble and Pip's mother saw her. She wasn't there when Clear-Orf and Tupping went to see them at five. So, in that hour, somebody must have gone to the cage, unlocked it, taken out the cat, locked the cage again, and gone off with Dark Queen, and either given her to someone else or hidden her away.'

'Right,' said Larry. 'Very clearly put, Daisy.'

'The next thing is : Who could have stolen the cat ? Whom can we suspect ? ' said Pip.

'Well, I suppose Miss Tremble might have slipped down and taken Dark Queen out,' said Fatty. 'Not very likely, of course, because Miss Tremble, poor thing, is the kind of person who would have a fit if she even posted a letter without a stamp. She'd dream about it all night long ! Still, we have to consider everyone who had a *chance* of stealing Dark Queen.'

Larry pulled out a notebook. 'I'll write the

names down,' he said. ' Miss Tremble is one.
What about Lady Candling ? '

' She wouldn't steal her own cat, silly,' said
Daisy.

' She might,' said Larry. ' It might be insured
against theft, you know. She would get a lot of
money. You've got to think of all these things.'
He wrote down Lady Candling's name.

' Tupping ? ' said Bets.

Larry shook his head very regretfully. ' No,
Bets. I'd love to put his name down ; but if he
was with old Clear-Orf all the afternoon it's just
no good suspecting him. What about Miss Harmer ?
Could she possibly have come back quietly and
secretly from her day out and taken the cat ? She
knew how valuable Dark Queen was.'

This was quite a new idea. Everyone thought
of the plump, smiling Miss Harmer. She didn't
seem at all the sort of person who would steal a
valuable cat from her employer. Still—her name
went down on the list of Suspects.

' We'll have to try and find out where Miss
Harmer was between four and five o'clock to-day,'
said Pip.

' Who else is there ? ' said Daisy. ' We've got
Miss Tremble, Lady Candling, and Miss Harmer
down. What about the cook and house-parlourmaid
next door ? They would have had a chance of
going down to the cat-house and taking Dark
Queen, wouldn't they ? '

' I've never seen the cook or parlourmaid,' said
Pip. ' None of us have. We'll have to find out
about them too. Goodness, we've got quite a lot
of suspected people after all ! We'll have a lot of
work to do ! '

'The one person who is horrid enough to have done it is Tupping—and he's just the very one we can't even suspect,' said Bets sadly. 'Well, there aren't any more Suspects, are there?'

'We'll have to put old Luke down,' said Larry. 'I know we *don't* suspect him—but Tupping has accused him of the crime, so we'd better put him down. We can cross him out as soon as we like.'

So Luke's name went down too. Poor old Luke! He always seemed to be in trouble.

'Let's go and whistle to him,' said Larry. 'He hasn't gone home yet, or he'd have whistled to us and told us everything.'

So they went to the wall and whistled the special notes that they and Luke used for signalling to one another. But although they whistled and whistled, nobody came. Whatever could Luke be doing?

7   LUKE GETS INTO TROUBLE

THE five children sat on top of the wall, with Buster scratching at the bricks below. They wondered what to do. Pip looked at his watch.

'Just gone quarter to six,' he said. '*Can* Luke have gone home? No; he surely would have spoken to us first.'

'Perhaps old Clear-Orf is questioning him,' said Fatty. This seemed very likely. The children wished they could find out.

Fatty had a good idea. 'Look here, Pip,' he said, '*you* could find out what's happening if you liked.'

' How ? ' asked Pip.

' Well, your mother has just been to tea next door, hasn't she,' said Fatty. ' You could hop over the wall, and go and see what's happening ; and if anyone sees you and wants to know what you are doing there, you could say your mother has just been to tea, and has she by any chance dropped her hanky in the garden ? '

' But she hasn't,' said Pip. ' Didn't you see her take it out of her bag when she was talking to us ? It had a most lovely smell.'

' Of course I did, idiot,' said Fatty impatiently. ' It's only just an excuse. You don't need to say she *did* drop her hanky, because we know she didn't —but you could easily say, " Had she ? " couldn't you ? '

' It's a good idea of Fatty's,' said Larry. ' It's about the only way any of us could get into the garden without being sent out at once by Clear-Orf or Tupping. Go on, Pip. Jump down and see whether you can find out what's happening. Hurry up. It's really a great bit of luck that your mother has just been there to tea.'

Pip was anxious to go—and yet very much afraid of meeting Tupping or Clear-Orf. He jumped down, waved to the others, and set off through the bushes.

There was no sign of Luke at all. Pip passed by the cat-house, but there was no one there either. He peeped into the cage where Dark Queen should have been with the others. The cats looked at him and mewed. Pip went on down the path, round by the greenhouses, and then stood hidden in the bushes. He could hear voices nearby.

He peeped through the bushes. There was a

little group of people on the lawn. Pip knew most of them.

'There's Lady Candling,' he thought. 'And that's Miss Tremble—doesn't she look upset! And there's Tupping, looking very pleased and important —and that's old Clear-Orf the bobby! And oh, there's poor old Luke!'

Poor Luke was there, in the centre, looking quite bewildered and terribly scared. The policeman was standing opposite to him, big black notebook in hand, and Luke was stammering and stuttering out replies to questions that Mr. Goon was barking out at him.

At the back were two maids, plainly the cook and the parlourmaid, both looking excited. They were whispering together, nudging one another.

Pip crept nearer. He could hear the questions now that were fired at poor frightened Luke.

'What were you doing all the afternoon?'

'I was—I was—digging up the old peas—in the Long Bed,' stammered Luke.

'Is that the bed by the cat-house?' asked Mr. Goon, scribbling something down in his book.

'Y-y-y-yes, sir,' stuttered Luke.

'So you were by the cats the whole afternoon?' said the policeman. 'Did anyone come near them?'

'Miss T-t-tremble came at f-f-four o'clock about, with another l-l-lady,' said Luke, pushing back his untidy hair. 'They stayed a few minutes and went.'

'And what did *you* do between four and five o'clock?' said Mr. Goon in a very threatening sort of voice.

Luke looked as if he was going to fall down in terror. 'N-n-nothing, sir—only d-d-d-dug!' he stammered. 'Just d-d-d-dug—alongside the cat-house. And nobody came near, not a soul, till you and Mr. Tupping came along to see the cats.'

'*And* we found that Dark Queen was gone,' said Mr. Tupping in a fierce voice. 'Well, Mr. Goon—the evidence is as plain as plain, isn't it? Dark Queen was stolen between four and five o'clock —and here's this boy stating that there was no one else near the cats except himself the whole of that time. He took that cat—no doubt about it—and handed her to some friend of his for a bit of pocket-money. He's a bad boy is Luke, and always has been ever since I had him.'

'I'm not bad, Mr. Tupping!' shouted Luke, suddenly finding a little courage. 'I've never took a thing I shouldn't! I've worked hard for you! I've stood things from you I shouldn't stand. You know I'd never steal one of them cats. I'd be too scared to, even if I thought of it!'

'That's enough, now, that's enough,' said Mr. Goon fiercely. 'Don't you go talking to Mr. Tupping like that. What boys like you want is a good hiding.'

'Ah, I'll see he gets it all right,' said Mr. Tupping in a horrid voice. 'I'll have a word with his step-father. *He* knows what this lad's like, right enough.'

'I think, Tupping,' said Lady Candling in her low, clear voice, 'I think there is no need to say anything to Luke's stepfather until we know a little more about this curious happening.'

Tupping looked rather taken aback. He had been enjoying himself so much that he had half-forgotten Lady Candling was there. Luke turned to his mistress.

'Please, Mam,' he said in an urgent voice,

215

'please, Mam, I do beg of you not to believe what Mr. Tupping and Mr. Goon say about me. I didn't take Dark Queen. I don't know where she is. I've never taken a thing I shouldn't take from your garden!'

'And that's a lie!' said Mr. Tupping in a triumphant voice. '*What about them strawberry runners?*'

To Pip's horror, poor Luke, now frightened and upset beyond bearing, burst into enormous sobs that shook his big body in an alarming manner. He put his arm across his face, trying to hide it.

'Let him go home,' said Lady Candling in a gentle voice. 'You have questioned him enough. He's only a fifteen-year-old boy, after all. Mr. Goon, I ask you to go now, please, and Luke, you may go home too.'

Mr. Goon didn't look at all pleased. He was sorry he could not treat Luke as he would have treated a grown man. He knew he would have to let him go home. He didn't like being sent off himself by Lady Candling either. He cleared his throat loudly, gave Lady Candling a scornful look, and shut his notebook.

'I must have a few words with your stepfather,' he said in a pompous tone to Luke, who turned very pale at these words. He was very much afraid of his stepfather.

'I'll walk down with you,' said Mr. Tupping. 'It's possible that the boy's father may tell us something about his friends. He must have given Dark Queen to one of them.'

So poor Luke was marched off between Mr. Goon and Mr. Tupping, still giving enormous sobs now and then. Pip hated the policeman and the

gardener. Poor Luke! What could he do against
two men like that? There just wasn't a chance for
him!

Pip didn't know that the two were taking Luke
down nearby where he was hiding, and he didn't
step back into the thick bushes in time to prevent
himself from being seen. Mr. Tupping suddenly
saw the boy's face peering out from a rhododendron
bush.

He stopped, stepped swiftly into the bushes,
grabbed hold of Pip, and pulled him out on to the
path.

'What are *you* doing here?' he roared. 'It's
one of them kids next door, Mr. Goon,' he said to
the surprised policeman. 'Always poking in here.
I'll march him straight off to her ladyship, and she'll
give him a good talking-to!'

Luke stood staring open-mouthed as Pip was
pushed roughly up the path by the angry gardener.
Lady Candling had heard the noise, and had turned
back to the lawn to see whatever was happening
now!

'Let me go,' said Pip angrily. 'You hateful
thing, let me go! You're hurting my arm!'

Tupping was twisting the boy's arm on purpose,
and Pip knew it. But he couldn't possibly get away.
Soon they were in front of Lady Candling, who
looked extremely surprised.

'Found this boy hiding in the bushes,' said
Tupping. 'Always finding them children in here.
Friends of Luke, they are. Up to no good, I'll be
bound!'

'What were you doing in my garden?' asked
Lady Candling in rather a stern tone.

'My mother has just been to tea with you, Lady

He grabbed Pip and pulled him out

Candling,' said Pip in his most polite voice. 'I suppose you haven't by any chance found a handkerchief of hers left behind, have you ?'

'Dear me ! Are you Mrs. Hilton's son Philip ?' asked Lady Candling, smiling at him. 'She was telling me about you, and you have a little sister, haven't you, called Bets ?'

'Yes, Lady Candling,' said Pip, smiling sweetly too. 'She's a dear little girl. I'd like to bring her in to see you some day if I may.'

'Yes, do,' said Lady Candling. 'Tupping, you have made a stupid mistake. This little boy quite obviously came in to look for his mother's handkerchief. Mrs. Hilton was at tea with me to-day.'

Pip rubbed his arm hard, screwing up his face as if it hurt him. 'Did Tupping hurt you ?' said Lady Candling. 'I'm really very sorry. Tupping, you seem to have been very rough with this child.'

Tupping scowled. Things were not going at all the way he had expected.

'If we find your mother's handkerchief we will certainly send it in,' said Lady Candling to Pip. 'And do remember to bring in your little sister to see me, won't you ? I am very fond of little girls.'

'Tupping will turn us out if we come,' said Pip.

'Indeed he won't !' said Lady Candling at once. 'Tupping, the children are to come in when they wish to. Those are my orders.'

Tupping's face went red, and he looked as if he was going to burst. But he did not dare to say anything to his mistress. He turned rudely, and went back to Mr. Goon and Luke, who were waiting some way off.

Pip shook hands with Lady Candling, thanked her, said good-bye, and went after Tupping.

' Luke ! ' he called. ' Luke ! Don't give up hope ! All your friends will help you ! *We* know you didn't do it ! '

' You clear orf ! ' said Mr. Goon, now really angry. ' None of your sauce ! Always poking your nose in and interfering ! Clear orf, I say ! '

But Pip didn't clear off. Keeping just beyond Mr. Goon's reach he danced along behind the three, shouting encouraging messages to Luke, and annoying the policeman and the gardener beyond measure.

He heard Mr. Goon say to Mr. Tupping that he would return later in the evening to have a ' good look round that cat-house.'

' Oh,' thought Pip, ' he's going to hunt for clues to help him to put the blame on Luke. *We*'d better go hunting for clues first. I'll go and tell the others.'

So, with a last hearty yell to Luke, Pip ran for the wall, climbed it, and rushed to tell the others all that he had heard. Things were getting really exciting !

8   ALL ABOUT CLUES

' WHAT happened, Pip ? You've been simply ages and ages ! ' said Larry, as Pip flung himself down beside the four children and Buster.

' Oh, Clear-Orf and Tupping have quite made up their minds that Luke Did the Deed,' said Pip. ' Poor old Luke ! Fancy, he howled just like Bets does sometimes ! '

It seemed dreadful to think of a big fellow like

Luke howling. 'Why are they so certain he stole Dark Queen?' said Daisy.

'Well—it's most unfortunate—but, you see, the cat was stolen between four and five o'clock this afternoon, and Luke was working beside the cat-house the whole of that time,' said Pip. 'He says he was; and he says, too, that no one else came near all that time.'

'It's funny, isn't it?' said Bets, puzzled. 'We know quite well that Luke didn't do it—and yet it seems as if he simply must have! It's a real, proper mystery.'

'It certainly is,' said Fatty thoughtfully. 'It doesn't really seem much good questioning any of our Suspects, because the chief one, Luke himself, says that only he was by the cat-house that afternoon. And yet—I simply CAN'T believe he stole the cat. He'd never dare to, even if he wanted to— which I'm sure he didn't.'

'I wonder where Dark Queen *is*,' said Bets.

'Yes. If we could find her, we should have a better idea of who stole her,' said Larry. 'I mean, whoever has her now must be a friend of the thief. Golly! this *is* a puzzle, isn't it?'

'Can't we look for clues?' asked Bets, thinking that perhaps this might help to clear Luke.

'Oh, that reminds me,' said Pip at once. 'Old Clear-Orf said he was coming back to-night to have a look round the cat-house. I expect he wants to find some clues himself—clues that will point to poor old Luke, I suppose!'

'Well, I vote we go and have a look first,' said Fatty at once, getting up.

'What, go over the wall now!' said Larry in surprise. 'We'll get into trouble.'

'We shan't,' said Fatty. 'We'll be gone long before Tupping and Clear-Orf get back. They'll be having a fine time telling poor old Luke's step-father all about him.'

'All right. Let's go now then,' said Larry. 'We might be able to find some sort of clue, though goodness knows what! Come on.'

'Bets had better not come,' said Pip. 'She is a bit small to go into possible trouble.'

'Of course I'm coming!' said Bets indignantly. 'Don't be mean, Pip. I only want a bit of help going over the wall. I might quite well find a clue you didn't see. I might be very useful.'

'You might, Bets,' said Fatty, taking her part as usual. 'Let her come, Pip. It's horrid to be left out of anything exciting.'

So Bets came. Buster was left behind; and this time he was put into the shed and locked up there, so that he wouldn't go rushing down Pip's drive and up Lady Candling's to find them!

They all climbed over the wall, Fatty giving Bets a helping hand. There didn't seem to be anyone about. The children made their way cautiously to the cat-house. The cats lay lazily on their benches, their blue eyes blinking at the children.

'Now,' said Larry, 'look for clues.'

'What sort of clues?' whispered Bets.

'Don't know till we see some,' said Larry. 'Look on the ground—and all round about. See! this is where old Luke must have been working this afternoon.'

The boy pointed to where a barrow stood half full of weeds. A spade was stuck in the ground. Luke's coat hung on a tree nearby.

'He was digging over that bed,' said Fatty

thoughtfully. ' He couldn't have been working any nearer to the cat-house than that ! He would have seen anyone coming or going to the cats, wouldn't he ? He couldn't have helped it.'

The children went and stood where Luke had been working. They could see every cat from where they stood. It would surely have been impossible to take a cat out, and lock the door, without being seen by Luke.

And yet a cat had gone, and Luke swore *he* hadn't stolen her—so who in the wide world could have taken Dark Queen ?

' Let's look all round the cat-house and see if the cat could have escaped by herself,' said Larry suddenly.

' Good idea,' said Fatty. So they walked all round the strongly-built wooden houses, which were set high on stout wooden legs, rather like modern hen-houses.

' There's absolutely nowhere that a cat could get out,' said Pip. ' Not a hole the size of a small mouse even ! Dark Queen certainly couldn't have escaped. She was taken out by somebody. That's certain.'

' She was there at four o'clock when your mother and Miss Tremble saw her—but she was gone at five when Tupping and Clear-Orf came here,' said Daisy, ' and all that time Luke was working beside the cats. I simply don't understand what happened. Dark Queen must have disappeared by magic !'

' Perhaps she did,' said Bets seriously. ' Magic is very powerful, isn't it ? Perhaps . . .'

The others laughed at her. Bets went red. ' Well, Dark Queen either disappeared by magic, or she couldn't have been there at all !' she said defiantly.

'Well, she *was* there, because Mother saw her, idiot,' said Pip. 'I say—what's that?'

He pointed to something that lay on the floor of the big cage in which all the cats lived. The children peered through the wire-netting at it.

There was a short silence. Then Fatty pursed up his lips, raised his eyebrows, and scratched his head.

'Blow!' he said. 'I know what that is! It's one of those cunning little whistles that Luke is always making for Bets.'

It was. There it lay on the cage-floor, a most tiresome and shocking clue. How could it have got there? Only one way—Luke must have been inside the cage and dropped the whistle. All the children felt suddenly puzzled and shocked.

'It wasn't Luke; it wasn't, it wasn't,' said Bets, with tears in her voice. 'We all know it wasn't.'

'Yes. We all know it wasn't. And yet there in the cage is a whistle that only Luke could have dropped,' said Fatty. 'This is a very extraordinary mystery, I must say.'

'Fatty, if Mr. Goon sees that whistle, will he say it's a proper proof that Luke was the thief?' asked Bets anxiously.

Fatty nodded. 'Of course. It's a most enormous, unmistakable clue, Bets—to someone like Clear-Orf, who can't see farther than his nose.'

'But it isn't a clue like that to you, is it, Fatty?' went on Bets, clutching his hand. 'Oh, Fatty! you don't think Luke dropped it, do you?'

'I'll tell you what I think,' said Fatty. 'I think that somebody put it there so that Luke might be suspected. That's what I think.'

'Golly! I think you're right!' said Larry.

'This is getting very mysterious. I say, do you think we ought to leave this clue for Clear-Orf to see ? After all, we're pretty certain it's a false clue, aren't we ? '

'You're right,' said Pip. 'I vote we get the clue out, and take it away ! '

The five children stared at the whistle lying on the floor. The cage was locked. The key was gone. How could they get the whistle out ?

'We'll have to be quick,' said Fatty desperately. 'Clear-Orf may be back in a short while. For goodness' sake ! how can we get that whistle out of the cage ? '

Nobody knew. If the whistle had been a little nearer the wire-netting, the children might have got some wire or a stick and worked it near enough to take out. But it was at the back of the cage.

Then Fatty had one of his brain-waves. He picked up a small pebble and shot it into the cage, so that it rolled near the little whistle. One of the cats saw the pebble rolling and jumped down to play with it. She put out a paw and patted the pebble. Her paw touched the whistle and moved it. She began to play with the wooden whistle too.

The children watched breathlessly. The cat sent the pebble rolling away and went after it. Then she came back to the whistle and looked hard at it, as if she expected it to move.

Then out went her paw again and she gave the whistle a push. It rolled over and over and the cat was delighted. She picked the whistle up cleverly in her two front paws, juggled with it a little, then let it drop. She struck it with her paw, and it flew through the air, landing quite near to the wire netting.

'Oh, good, good, good!' said Fatty joyfully. He took a small roll of wire from his pocket. It was wonderful the things that Fatty kept in his pockets. He undid a length of the wire, twisted two pieces together, and made a small loop at one end. Then he pushed the wire through one of the holes in the netting.

Everyone watched eagerly. The wire reached the whistle. Fatty jiggled it about patiently, trying to fit the loop at the end over the whistle. The cat that had played with the whistle watched with great interest. Then suddenly it put out a playful paw and patted the wire, sending the loop neatly over the whistle!

'Oh, thanks, puss!' said Fatty gleefully, and drew the whistle carefully to the wire-netting. He jerked it up, and the whistle flew through one of the holes and landed at Bets' feet. She picked it up.

'Got it!' said Fatty. 'Let's have a look at it. Yes, it's one of Luke's all right. What a good thing we got it out. Now that clue won't be found by old Clear-Orf! Luke won't get into further trouble because of *that*!'

'You really are clever, Fatty,' said Bets, in the greatest admiration.

'Good work, Fatty,' said Pip.

Fatty at once swelled up with pride and importance. 'Oh, that's nothing,' he began. 'I've often had better ideas than this. Why, once . . .'

'Shut up!' said Larry, Daisy, and Pip together. Fatty shut up. He stuffed the whistle into his pocket.

'Look about for any more clues,' said Pip. 'There might be some more in the cage.'

The five of them pressed their noses once more to the cage netting. Bets wrinkled up her nose.

' I don't like the smell in the cage,' she said.

' Well, animals never smell very nice when they are caged,' said Larry.

' No, it's another smell,' said Bets. ' Like petrol or something.'

They all sniffed. ' She means turpentine,' said Fatty. ' I can smell it too—quite faintly. Afraid that's not a clue though, Bets. Still, it's good to notice even a smell. Perhaps Miss Harmer uses turps to clean out the cage. Now—any other clue anybody ? '

But there really did not seem to be anything at all to be found, although the children hunted around the cages and peered inside them time and again.

' Sickening,' said Fatty. ' Nothing to help us at all. Not a thing. Well, it's a jolly good thing we found that whistle before Tupping or Clear-Orf spotted it. I feel certain somebody put it there so that Luke might be suspected of stealing the cat. What a mean trick to play ! '

' I wish *we* could put a whole lot of clues in the cage so that it would muddle up old Clear-Orf,' said Pip.

The others stared at him in delight, the same delicious thought striking them all at the same moment.

' Golly, what a marvellous idea ! ' said Fatty, wishing he had thought of it himself.

' Yes ; let's do it ! ' said Larry excitedly. ' Let's put all kinds of silly clues, that couldn't possibly point to Luke. It will give old Clear-Orf a most frightful headache sorting them all out ! '

They began to giggle. What should they push into the cage ?

' I've got some peppermint drops,' said Pip, with a chuckle. ' I'll chuck one into the cage.'

' And I'll put a piece of my hair-ribbon in,' said Daisy. ' It tore in half to-day and I've got the bits in my pocket. I'll put a half-bit in through the wire ! '

' And I've got some blue buttons off my doll's coat,' said Bets. ' I'll put one of those in ! '

' I believe I've got a new pair of brown shoe-laces somewhere in my pocket,' said Larry, digging about in his shorts pockets. ' Yes, here they are. I'll put one into the cage.'

' What will you put in, Fatty ? ' asked Bets.

Fatty produced a collection of cigar-ends out of his pocket. The others stared at them in amazement.

' What do you want to collect cigar-ends for ? ' asked Larry at last.

' I smoke them,' said Fatty. ' They're the ends of the cigars my father smokes. He leaves them on the ash-tray in his bedroom.'

' You *don't* smoke them ! ' said Pip disbelievingly. ' You're just saying that to swank as usual. You just take them to make yourself smell of grown-up cigar-smoke, that's all. I often wondered why you smelt like that.'

This was rather too near the truth for Fatty's liking. He pretended not to hear what Pip said. ' I shall throw a cigar-end *under* the cage—on the ground,' he said, ' and one inside the cage—though I hope none of the cats will chew it and get ill. *Two* cigar-ends will just about send old Clear-Orf off his head.'

Very solemnly the five children spread their ' clues.' Pip threw a large round peppermint drop into the cage, where the cats eyed it with displeasure They evidently disapproved of the smell.

Daisy stuffed half a bit of rather grubby blue

hair-ribbon into the netting. Bets put in a small blue button. Larry pushed in one of his new brown shoe-laces—and Fatty threw a cigar-end under the cage and one inside as well!

' There,' he said, ' plenty of clues for old Clear-Orf to find! Hope he comes soon.'

9   MR. GOON ON THE JOB

' I SAY,' said Daisy suddenly, watching her hair-ribbon flap on the floor of the cage, in a little draught from under the door. ' I say, I hope no one will think *I*'ve stolen the cat! Mother would know that was a piece of my hair-ribbon if ever she saw it.'

' Oh, crumbs! I never thought of that,' said Pip.

' It's all right,' said Fatty. ' I've got a big envelope here—see? Now then, let's each put into the envelope the same thing that we've already settled for clues. I'll put in two cigar-ends, to match the ones I've left. Daisy, put in your other half of ribbon.'

Daisy did so. Then Bets put in one of the blue doll's buttons, Larry put in the other shoe-lace, and Pip put in a peppermint drop.

Fatty folded up the envelope carefully and put it into his pocket. ' If any of us is accused of the theft, because of the clues we've put in the cage, we've only got to show them what's in this envelope for them to know we did it for a joke,' he said.

A bell rang out in Pip's house, and Bets gave a groan. ' That's my bed-time bell. Blow! I don't want to go.'

'You must,' said Pip. 'You got into a row yesterday for being late. Oh dear, I do wish we could stay here and see old Clear-Orf and Tupping finding the clues we've left!'

'Well, let's,' said Larry.

'Oh, me too!' wailed Bets, afraid of being left out again. Pip gave her a push.

'Bets, you *must* go! There's your bell again.'

'Well, it's your bell too—it means you've got to come in and wash and change into your suit for supper-time,' said Bets. 'You know it does.'

Pip did know it. Larry gave a sigh. He knew that he and Daisy ought to go home too. They had farther to go than Pip and Bets.

'We'll have to go too,' said Larry. 'Fatty, I suppose you couldn't possibly stay and watch, could you? It really would be funny to see. Why don't you stay? Your mother and father don't bother about you much, do they? You seem to go home or go out just whenever you like.'

'All right, I'll stay here and watch,' said Fatty. 'I think I'll climb that tree there. It's easy to climb, and the leaves are nice and thick. I can see everything well from up there, and not be seen myself.'

'Well, come on then, Bets,' said Pip, not at all wanting to go. Fatty was going to have all the fun.

Then there came the sound of men's voices up the garden, and the children looked at one another at once.

'It's Tupping and Clear-Orf coming back,' whispered Larry. 'Over the wall, quick!'

'Good-bye, Fatty, see you to-morrow some-time,' said Pip in a low voice. The four ran quietly to the wall. Pip gave Bets a leg-up, and got her

safely over.   The others were soon safely on the
other side.   Fatty was left by himself.   He shinned
up the tree very quickly, considering his plumpness.

Fatty sat on a broad bough, and carefully parted
the leaves so that he could see what was going on
down below.   He saw Mr. Tupping coming towards
the cat-house with Clear-Orf.

' Well now,' Clear-Orf said, ' we'll just have a
look-round, Mr. Tupping.   You never know when
there's clues about, you know.   Ah, many a clue
I've found that's led me straight to the criminal.'

' Ah ! ' said Mr. Tupping wisely, ' I believe
you, Mr. Goon.   Well, I shouldn't be surprised if
that boy Luke hasn't left something behind.   He
may be clever enough to steal a valuable cat, but
h‍ wouldn't be clever enough to hide his tracks.'

The two men began to hunt carefully round and
about the cat-house.   The Siamese cats watched
them out of brilliant blue eyes.   They could not
imagine why so many people came to their shed that
day.   Fatty looked down at the hunters, carefully
peering between the leaves.

Mr. Goon found the cigar-end under the cat-
house first.   He pounced on it swiftly and held it up.

' What's that ? ' asked Mr. Tupping in astonishment.

' Cigar-end,' said Mr. Goon with great satisfaction.   Then he looked puzzled and tilted back
his helmet to scratch his head.   ' Do that boy Luke
smoke cigars ? ' he asked.

' Don't be silly,' said Mr. Tupping impatiently.
' 'Course not.   That's not a clue.   Somebody who
came with Lady Candling to see her cats must have
chucked his cigar-end away under the house.   That's
all.'

'Hmmm!' said Mr. Goon, not at all wanting to dismiss the cigar-end like that. 'Well, I'll have to think about that.'

Fatty giggled to himself. The two men went on searching. Mr. Tupping straightened himself up at last.

'Don't seem nothing else to be found,' he said. 'I suppose there wouldn't be anything in the cat-house to see, do you think?'

Mr. Goon looked doubtful. 'Shouldn't think so,' he said. 'But we might look. Got the key, Mr. Tupping?'

Mr. Tupping took the key down from a nail at the back of the cat-house. But before he had unlocked the door Mr. Goon gave a loud exclamation. He had looked through the wire-netting of the cat-house and had seen various things on the floor that caused him great excitement. Why, the place seemed to be alive with clues!

'What's up?' asked Mr. Tupping.

'Coo! Look here! See that shoe-lace there?' said Mr. Goon, pointing. 'That's a whopping big clue, that is. Somebody's been in there and lost his shoe-lace!'

Mr. Tupping stared at the shoe-lace in the greatest astonishment. Then he saw the blue button—and the hair-ribbon. He gave a gasp of surprise. He inserted the key in the lock and opened the door.

The two men collected the 'clues' from the cat-house. They brought them out to look at them.

'Whoever went in there wore shoes with brown laces, that's certain,' said Mr. Goon with great satisfaction. 'And look at that there button—that's come off somebody's coat, that has.'

'What's this?' asked Mr. Tupping, showing Mr. Goon Pip's peppermint drop. Mr. Goon sniffed at it.

'Peppermint!' he said. 'Now, does that boy Luke suck peppermints?'

'I expect so,' said Mr. Tupping. 'Most boys eat sweets. But Luke don't wear a hair-ribbon, Mr. Goon. And look, there's another cigar-end—like the one you found under the house.'

Mr. Goon soon lost his excitement over his finds, and became puzzled. He gazed at his clues in silence.

'Judging by these here clues, the thief ought by rights to be someone that smokes cigars, wears blue hair-ribbons and blue buttons, sucks peppermint drops, and has brown laces in his shoes,' he said. 'It don't make sense.'

Fatty was trying his hardest not to giggle out loud. It was so funny seeing Mr. Goon and Mr. Tupping puzzle their heads over all the clues that the children had so carefully left for them to find. Mr. Goon cautiously licked the peppermint drop.

'Yes; it's peppermint right enough,' he said. 'Well, this is a fair puzzler—finding all these clues, and nobody we can fit them to, so to speak. You finding anything else, Mr. Tupping?'

Mr. Tupping had gone into the cat-house, and was looking all round it again very, very carefully.

'Just looking to see if there's any clue we've overlooked,' he said. But he couldn't seem to find anything else, however hard he hunted. He came out again, looking rather untidy and cross.

'Well, there don't seem much else to be found,' he said, sounding very disappointed. 'I'm sure you'll find it's that boy Luke, Mr. Goon, that's the thief. These clues can't be clues—just things that got into the cage by accident.'

'Well, a peppermint drop seems a funny sort of thing to get into the cage by accident,' said Mr. Goon grumpily. 'I'll have to take all these things home and think about them.'

Fatty chuckled deep down in himself as he watched Mr. Goon put his ' clues ' into a clean white envelope, lick it up, write something on it, and put it carefully into his pocket. He turned to Mr. Tupping.

'Well, so long ! ' he said. ' Thanks for your help. It's that boy Luke, no doubt about it. I've told him I'll go along and give him a thorough questioning to-morrow, and if I don't force a confession out of him, my name's not Theophilus Goon ! '

And with that mouthful of a name old Clear-Orf departed majestically down the path, his ' clues ' safely in his pocket, his mind puzzling them over. A hair-ribbon—very strange ! A blue button—most peculiar. A brown shoe-lace, quite new—most extraordinary. A peppermint drop—most bewildering. And *two* cigar-ends, *two*. Mr. Goon felt that if there had just been one, it would have been easier. Why should a thief stand and smoke two cigars whilst stealing a cat ?

Fatty longed to get down the tree, go home, and have some supper. He suddenly felt tremendously hungry. He peered down to see if Mr. Tupping had gone. But he hadn't.

He was in the cat-house again, hunting about very carefully. After a while he came out, looking thoughtful, locked the house, and went off up the path still looking thoughtful. Fatty waited till his footsteps had died away, then slithered down the tree.

He jumped down to the path and looked in at the blue-eyed cats. He was glad he had Luke's whistle in his pocket. That really *would* have been a clue! Fatty chuckled when he thought of Mr. Goon's delight and surprise at finding so many ' clues.'

' Well, we'll see old Luke to-morrow and ask him no end of questions,' thought Fatty as he went home. ' My word—this has been an exciting day ! '

But there were more exciting things to come !

10   PIP AND BETS PAY A CALL

NEXT morning Fatty was down at Pip's house early, longing to tell the others how surprised and puzzled Mr. Goon and the gardener had been when they had found all the ' false ' clues. Larry and Daisy arrived about the same time as Buster and Fatty, and soon the children were giggling over Fatty's story.

' Clear-Orf asked Tupping if Luke smoked cigars,' said Fatty with a chuckle. ' I almost fell out of the tree trying not to laugh ! '

' We've whistled lots of times to Luke this morning,' said Pip, ' but he hasn't answered us, or come to the wall either. Do you think he is too frightened to ? '

' Perhaps he is,' said Fatty. ' Well, we simply must talk to him, and tell him about the whistle we found in the cats' cage, and all the clues we put there ourselves. I'll go and whistle awfully loudly.'

But not even Fatty's loudest and most vigorous whistling brought any answer. So the children decided to wait at the gate about one o'clock. That was the time when Luke went home to his dinner.

So they waited at the gate. But no Luke appeared. The children waited until ten minutes past one, and then had to rush off to their own meal.

' Perhaps he's got the sack,' said Fatty, the idea occurring to him for the first time. ' Perhaps he won't come next door any more.'

' Oh,' said Bets in dismay, ' poor Luke ! Do you think Lady Candling gave him notice then, and said he wasn't to come any more ? '

' How shall we find out ? ' said Larry.

' We could ask Tupping,' said Daisy doubtfully. The others looked at her scornfully.

' As if we'd go and ask Tupping *any*thing ! ' said Larry. They all stood and thought for a moment.

' I know,' said Pip. ' Lady Candling said I could take Bets in to see her. So I will, this afternoon. And I could ask Lady Candling herself about Luke, couldn't I ? '

' Good idea, Pip,' said Fatty. ' I was just thinking the same thing myself. And also you could take the chance of finding out where Lady Candling was between four and five o'clock perhaps. I mean, find out whether she had any chance of slipping off down to the cats herself, to steal her own Dark Queen away.'

' Well, I'm sure she didn't,' said Pip at once. ' You've only got to look at her to know she couldn't even *think* of doing such a thing ! Anyway, I thought we had decided that it wasn't worth while questioning our Suspects, seeing that Luke was by the cat-house all the time during that hour and would have seen anyone there.'

'Well, I suppose it isn't really,' said Fatty. 'I don't see that it's any way possible for the thief to have stolen the cat right under old Luke's nose. He said that he hadn't left the spot for even half a minute.'

'There's our dinner-bell *again*,' said Bets. 'Come on, Pip, we shall get into an awful row. Come back afterwards, you others, and we'll tell you how Pip and I get on this afternoon.'

They parted and went home to their various meals. They were all worried about Luke. Had he lost his job? Lady Candling must have given him notice, or surely he would have been back as usual in the morning. Poor old Luke!

At half-past three Pip and Bets thought they would go and see Lady Candling. Daisy looked at Bets. The little girl had on a very grubby overall, and Pip's shorts were extremely dirty.

'Don't you think you ought to put on a clean frock, Bets?' said Daisy. 'And just *look* at your shorts, Pip. Honestly, you look as if you've been sitting down on a sack of soot or something.'

'Golly! Have we got to go and change?' said Pip in alarm. He hated getting into clean things.

'Well, I think it would be more polite to Lady Candling if you went looking clean,' said Daisy. So poor Pip and Bets went into the house to wash and put on clean clothes.

Their mother saw them going indoors and called out to them. 'What do you want?'

'We're just going to wash and put on clean clothes, Mummy,' said Bets.

'*What?*' said her mother in amazement. 'Whatever has come over you? Where are you going in your clean clothes?'

'To see Lady Candling,' said Bets before Pip could stop her.

'To see Lady Candling!' said Mrs. Hilton, even more astonished. 'But why? She hasn't asked you in. You can't go without being asked.'

By this time Pip had given Bets such a nudge that she nearly fell over. Bets stood looking at her mother, afraid that she had given away something she shouldn't have mentioned.

'Well, Bets seems to have lost her tongue,' said Mrs. Hilton impatiently. 'Pip, what *is* all this about? It isn't like you to go rushing off paying afternoon calls with Bets. What's come over you?'

'Well, Mother,' said Pip, 'I saw Lady Candling yesterday, and she said you had spoken about Bets to her, and would I bring her in to see her as she liked little girls.'

'But when did *you* see Lady Candling?' said his mother, astonished. 'Oh, Pip! I do hope you haven't been going into next door and making a lot of trouble there.'

'Oh *no*, Mother,' said Pip, looking very innocent. 'I wouldn't dream of making trouble. Well—we won't go if you'd rather we didn't—but Bets will be awfully disappointed now.'

He whispered to Bets out of the corner of his mouth. 'Begin to cry, can't you? Then it'll be all right.'

Bets screwed up her voice and gave a most heart-rending howl. 'I want to go, I want to go!' she wailed.

'Well, go then,' said Mrs. Hilton hastily. 'But do behave yourselves.'

'I thought it would be nice to tell Lady Candling we were sorry about her lost cat, and ask her if she had found it yet,' said Pip. His mother stared at him.

'It doesn't seem like you to get so polite and considerate all of a sudden, Pip,' she said. 'I can't help feeling there's something behind all this. Well, if I hear from Lady Candling that you have been making a nuisance of yourself, I shall be very cross.'

The children escaped to change into clean things. Bets was afraid that Pip was going to scold her for saying they were going to see Lady Candling, but he didn't.

'You made up for giving away a bit of our secret by making that lovely howl,' he said. 'I almost thought you were *really* crying, Bets.'

Soon they were walking sedately down the drive, out of the gate, and up Lady Candling's drive. They passed Tupping on the way. He was cutting the hedges there. He scowled at them as they passed.

'Good afternoon, Tupping, what a beautiful day it is!' said Pip, in an imitation of his mother's politeness. 'I really think we shall have a little rain before long, though; don't you? Still, the vegetable garden needs it, I'm sure!'

Tupping gave a growl, and snipped viciously at the hedge. Pip felt sure he would like to have snipped at him and Bets. He grinned and went on his way.

The two children went to the front door and rang the bell. A trim little maid came to the door and smiled at the children.

'Please, is Lady Candling in?' asked Pip.

' I think she's in the garden,' said the maid.
' I'll take you out to the verandah, and you can go
and look for her if you like. She may be picking
roses.'

' Have they found the cat yet ? ' asked Pip as
he and Bets followed the maid out to a sunny
verandah.

' No,' said the maid. ' Miss Harmer's in a great
state about her. It's a funny business, isn't it ?
I'm afraid it must have been Luke. After all, he
was the only one near the cats between four and
five o'clock.'

' Didn't you hear or see anyone strange at all
yesterday afternoon ? ' asked Pip, thinking that he
might as well ask a few questions.

' Nobody,' said the maid. ' You see, Lady
Candling had quite a tea-party yesterday—nine or
ten people altogether—and Cook and I were busy
all the time. We didn't go down the garden at all
between four and five o'clock, we had such a lot
to do. If we *had* slipped down, we might have
seen the thief at his work. Ah ! it was a good day
for the thief—with Miss Harmer out, and Tupping
out, and Cook and me busy, and Lady Candling
up here at the house with her friends ! '

' It was,' said Pip. ' It looks as if the thief
must have known all that too, to arrange his theft
so neatly.'

' That's why we think it must be Luke,' said
the girl. ' Though I always liked Luke. A bit
simple, but always very kind. And that Tupping's
a perfect horror to him.'

' Don't you like Tupping either ? ' said Bets
eagerly.

' He's a rude, bad-tempered old man ! ' said

the girl. ' But don't you say I said so. Cook
and me wish it had been *him* that took the cat.
Well, I mustn't talk to you any more. You go out
and find her ladyship.'

Pip and Bets went into the sunny garden.
' From what that maid says it's quite clear that we
can cross Lady Candling, the parlourmaid, and the
cook off our list of Suspects,' said Pip. ' Hallo!
there's Miss Tremble.'

Miss Trimble advanced to meet them. Bets
spoke to Pip in a whisper.

' Pip! Let's count how many times her glasses
fall off! They keep on doing it.'

' Well, children!' said Miss Trimble in her
bird-like voice, giving them a wide and toothy smile.
' Are you looking for Lady Candling? I think I
have seen this little girl before, haven't I? Aren't
you the little girl that the strawberry runners ran
away with? Oh, what a joke, ha, ha!'

She laughed, and her glasses fell off, dangling
on their little chain. She put them on again.

' Yes, I'm the little girl,' said Bets. ' And we
have come to see Lady Candling.'

' Oh, what a pity! She's just gone out!' said
Miss Trimble. ' I'm afraid you'll have to put up
with poor old me!'

She laughed again, and her glasses fell off.
' Twice,' said Bets, under her breath.

' Do you know where Luke is?' said Pip,
thinking it would be a good idea to go and find him
if he was anywhere about.

' No, I don't,' said Miss Trimble. ' He didn't
turn up to-day. Tupping was very annoyed about it.'

' Did Lady Candling give Luke the sack, Miss
Tremble?' asked Bets.

' My name is Trimble, not Tremble,' said Miss
Trimble. ' No, Lady Candling didn't give him
notice. At least, I don't think so. Wasn't it a pity
about that lovely cat ? I saw her at four o'clock,
you know.'

' Yes, you were with my mother,' said Pip.
' I suppose you didn't see anyone near the cat-
house except Luke ? '

' No, nobody,' said Miss Trimble. ' Luke was
there, of course, digging hard all the time. Your
mother and I were only there a minute or two,
then I had to hurry her back to the tea-table, because
there was a lot for me to do there. I didn't have a
moment to myself until after the party.'

' Then *you* couldn't have stolen the cat ! ' said
Pip, with a laugh. Miss Trimble jumped, and her
glasses fell off. Her nose went even redder than it
already was.

' What a funny joke ! ' she said, and she tried to
disentangle her glasses from her lace collar. ' The
very idea of stealing *any*thing makes me go hot and
cold ! '

' Could we go and see the cats, Miss Tremble ? '
asked Bets.

' I should think so,' said Miss Trimble. ' My
name is Trimble, not Tremble. Do try and remember. Miss Harmer is with the cats. We'll go and
see her. Come along, dears.'

She tripped along in front of them, her glasses
on her nose once more. They fell off going down
a few steps, and Bets counted out loud.

' That's four times.'

' Four times what, dear ? ' said Miss Trimble,
turning round and smiling sweetly. She put up her
hand to stop her glasses from falling.

242

'Don't stop them,' said Bets. '.I'm counting how many times they fall off.'

'Oh, what a funny little girl!' said Miss Trimblc, looking rather cross. She held her glasses on with her hand, and Bets was sorry. She felt that wasn't fair!

They came to the cat-house. Miss Harmer was there, mixing some food. She looked up. Her plump, jolly face looked worried.

'Hallo!' she said. 'Come to see my cats?'

'Yes, please,' said Bets. 'Miss Harmer, wasn't it awful Dark Queen being stolen whilst you were away?'

'Yes,' said the kennel-girl, stirring the food in the pan. 'I wish I hadn't gone. I should only have taken half a day, really; but Mr. Tupping offered to look after the cats for me if I'd like the whole day —so I thanked him and went. But I've reproached myself ever since.'

'Mr. *Tupping* offered to look after the cats, did you say?' said Pip, full of amazement at the thought of Tupping offering to do anyone a kindness. 'Golly! that's not like *him*.'

'No, it isn't,' said the girl, with a laugh. 'But I badly wanted to go home, and I can't unless I have a whole day, because my home is so far away. Do you collect railway tickets? Because the collector didn't take my ticket when I got back to the station last night. You can have it if you like.'

Pip did collect railway tickets. He took the return-half that Miss Harmer held out to him. 'Thanks,' he said, 'I'd like it.' He put it into his pocket, thinking how envious Larry would be, for he collected railway tickets too.

'Do you think Luke stole the cat, Miss Harmer?' said Pip.

'No, I don't,' said Miss Harmer. 'He's a bit silly, but he's honest enough. But I tell you who *might* have taken the cat—that circus friend of Luke's! What's his name, now—Jake, I think it is.'

This was news to the two children. Luke had never told them about Jake. A circus friend! How exciting! Why had Luke never mentioned him?

'Does Jake live near here?' asked Pip.

'Oh no, but the circus he belongs to is performing in the next town—in Farring,' said Miss Harmer. 'So I suppose he's somewhere near. You know, Dark Queen would be marvellous in a circus. I had already taught her to do a few tricks.'

Miss Trimble was getting impatient, for it was near her tea-time. She gave three or four polite little coughs, and her glasses promptly fell off.

'We'd better go,' said Pip. 'Thanks for showing us the cats. You needn't bother to show us out, Miss Tremble. We'll go over the wall.'

'My name is Trimble, not Tremble,' said Miss Trimble, losing her smile for a moment. 'I wish you would try and remember. And surely you should not go over the wall? Let me take you down the drive.'

'Tupping's there,' said Bets. Miss Trimble's glasses fell off at once at the mention of the surly gardener.

'Oh well, if you *really* want to get over the wall, I won't stop you!' she said. 'Good-bye, dear children. I'll tell Lady Candling you came.'

'They fell off eight times,' said Bets in a pleased tone as the two of them climbed over the wall. 'I say, Pip, isn't it funny that Luke never told us about Jake?'

PIP and Bets were to go to tea with Larry and
Daisy that afternoon, so they all went up the lane
together, Fatty and Buster too. Pip had a lot to tell.

' Luke hasn't turned up to-day,' he said. ' It's
funny, isn't it, because Lady Candling hasn't given
him notice. And I say, I wonder why he never told
us about Jake.'

' I suppose—I suppose he couldn't possibly have
told Jake to come to the cat-house yesterday, and he
couldn't possibly have given *him* the cat, could he ? '
said Larry. ' I mean—I know we think Luke didn't
do it—but, well, what do you others think ? '

For the first time a small doubt about Luke
came into the children's minds. He hadn't told
them about Jake. And he was a man they would
have liked to hear about if he lived with a circus.
And after all, Luke had been the only one near the
cat-house during the whole of that hour.

' Well, I still don't believe it was Luke or his
friend Jake,' said Bets stoutly. ' So there ! '

' Nor do I,' said Daisy. ' But I wish everything wasn't so dreadfully puzzling.'

' We were much better find-outers last time,'
said Larry gloomily. ' Think of the clues and things
we found, and all the Suspects we questioned.'

' Well,' said Pip, ' I can tell you this—all the
Suspects on our list can be crossed off now. I was
only about half an hour in next door, but I found
out enough to know that not one of the people on
our list could have stolen Dark Queen.'

' How do you know ? ' asked Fatty.

' Well, Lady Candling had quite a big party,' said Pip, ' and it stands to reason she couldn't leave a big party and go off to steal her own cat in the middle of it. The cook and parlourmaid were very busy all the time during the tea-hour, so that rules them out too. Miss Tremble had to help as well, and I'm sure Lady Candling would have been very suspicious if she'd gone off for ten minutes or so to steal the cat ! '

' Go on, Pip,' said Fatty. ' Where's your list of Suspects, Larry ? Let's cross them off one by one.'

' And you can cross off Miss Harmer,' said Pip, ' because she went home yesterday and her home is at Langston, miles away. And look, here's the return-half she gave me, because the collector didn't take it when she got back. So we can cross her off too.'

' That's all the Suspects crossed off—except Luke,' said Larry. ' Golly ! it does look as if it might have been a friend of Luke's, doesn't it— someone who came slipping up, winked at Luke, took the cat and went off, trusting to Luke not to give him away. I wish we could find Luke and question him about Jake.'

' I know where Luke is—I bet I know ! ' said Pip. ' I bet he's gone to the circus—and he's with his friend Jake ! I bet he'll go off with the circus, too, when it moves away ! '

Everyone felt certain that Pip was right. Of course that was where Luke would be.

' Look here, let's get out our bikes after tea and ride over to Farring,' said Fatty. ' We'll soon find the circus-tents, and if Luke's there we'll find him too ! '

'Good idea!' said everyone, brightening up at the thought of doing something exciting. 'Come on, let's hurry up over tea and go.'

Mrs Daykin (Larry's mother and Daisy's) was astonished to find the children galloping so fast through the lovely tea she had provided for them. She looked at them in astonishment.

'Are you terribly hungry, or just in a hurry?' she asked. 'Didn't any of you have any dinner?'

'We're just in a hurry, Mrs. Daykin, that's all,' said Fatty, as politely as he could with his mouth full. 'We want to go for a bike-ride after tea.'

'To Farring,' put in Bets. She got two hard nudges at once, one from Pip and one from Larry. They were both afraid she would say too much.

'Why to Farring?' said Mrs. Daykin, surprised. She didn't know the circus was there. 'It's not a very pretty place.'

'Well, we thought it would be quite a nice ride there and back,' said Larry. 'We'd better be going now. We'll not be late home, Mother.'

Fatty had to go and get his bicycle, and so had Bets and Pip. To her joy Bets was allowed to come, as Farring was not a great distance away. The children rode off gaily.

Soon, in front of them, they saw another bicyclist —a big burly one, dressed in dark blue.

'Golly! There's old Clear-Orf!' said Pip. 'Don't catch him up, anyone. He may turn off somewhere, and then we can get on quickly on our way to Farring.'

But Clear-Orf took the way to Farring too! 'I say! I hope he isn't going to see Jake as well,' said Fatty in dismay. 'Do you suppose he got out of Luke that he had a circus friend? Blow! We can't let Clear-Orf get ahead of us like this. After all, Jake may be a fine big Clue.'

Then a lovely thing happened. Mr. Goon got a puncture ! He rode over a piece of glass, and his back tyre went flat quite suddenly. The big police-man bumped along the road, gave a loud and angry exclamation, and got off.

He took his bike to the side of the road and got out a puncture-mending outfit. The children, grinning, rode quickly by. Fatty waved to him.

' Evening, Mr. Goon ! Sorry to see you are in trouble ! '

The policeman looked up in surprise that turned to annoyance when he saw the five children cycling quickly on the way to Farring. He began to mend his inner tube. The children simply sped along, knowing that they had at least a quarter of an hour before Clear-Orf could catch them up.

' There's the circus-tents,' said Bets, as they topped a hill and rode down. ' And look at the cages, too—and the gay caravans. Oh, I do think it looks exciting ! '

It was exciting. A big elephant was tethered by a hind leg to a stout tree. Five tigers in a very strong cage roared for their dinner. Seven beautiful black horses were being ridden round the field by the grooms, who were giving them a little exercise.

Smoke rose from the chimneys of the gay caravans, and all kinds of exciting smells rose on the air.

' Kippers,' said Bets, wrinkling up her nose.

' Sausages,' said Daisy.

' Stew ! ' said Fatty. "Oooh ! I had a good tea, but I could do with a good supper as well ! '

' What's our plan ? ' said Larry, jumping off his

bicycle and leaning it against the fence. 'Do we hunt round for Luke, or do we ask for Jake ? '

'We better not *all* go,' said Fatty. 'I think I'd better go by myself and just ask politely for Jake.'

'The tigers will jump out and eat a nice fat morsel like you as soon as they see you,' said Larry. ' *I*'ll go.'

' *I* thought of the circus idea, and that Luke might be here,' said Pip. 'I think *I* ought to go ! '

'Buck up and decide,' said Daisy impatiently. 'Clear-Orf will be here soon.'

'Well, we'll all go, except Bets,' said Larry. 'It can't matter us wandering separately round the field. I can see other children doing it too. But Bets had better stay and look after the bikes.'

' *Well*,' began Bets indignantly, 'I like *that* ! Why should I ? '

'You know you're afraid of tigers,' said Pip. 'And you're afraid of elephants too. You wouldn't ride one when you went to the Zoo. And goodness knows what there might be in that cage over there, look—big brown bears, I expect.'

'Oh,' said Bets. 'Well, I *will* stay here then. But I think it's mean of you *all* to go, all the same.'

The little girl had tears in her eyes. She knew she would not dare to go into the circus camp by herself, but she did think one of the others could have stayed to guard the bikes with her.

The others climbed over the fence and went into the field. They separated and wandered about, waiting to meet someone they could ask about Jake.

It was Pip who found Jake. He had asked a cheeky little circus-girl if she knew where Jake was, and she had first put out her tongue at him, then called him an impolite name, and then pointed to where a big man was giving a pail of water to a horse.

Pip went across to him. The man looked up. ' What do you want ? ' he said.

' I say,' said Pip, ' I'm looking for a boy I know, called Luke. I've got a message for him. Is he here? '

' Nope,' said the man shortly. ' Haven't seen him for weeks.'

Pip was disappointed. ' Oh,' he said. ' I did want to talk to him. You don't know his address, do you ? '

' Nope,' said the man again. ' I don't give addresses to little busybodies. You go away and mind your own business.'

Fatty came up when he saw Pip talking to the man. ' Is this Jake ? ' he said to Pip. Pip nodded.

' But he says he hasn't seen Luke for weeks,' said Pip.

' We're his friends,' said Fatty earnestly. ' Please believe us. We just want to talk to him.'

' I've told you I don't know where he is,' said the man. ' Now you get out of this field ; and just remember what I say, I haven't seen Luke for weeks.'

Bets stood by the bicycles, watching the others wandering about the camp. She kept an eye open for old Clear-Orf, and hoped he wouldn't stop and ask her what she was doing there if he came by. She decided to creep through to the other side of the hedge, where she would be hidden from any passer-by.

So she crept through and settled herself comfortably there. She was near a bright-red caravan. She looked up at it, and saw something that gave her an enormous surprise. Somebody was peeping at her from behind the little lace curtain—and that somebody was Luke !

BETS sat quite still, holding her breath. The curtain was then drawn a little farther, and the window was quietly opened. Luke put his head out.

' Hallo, little Bets ! ' he said in a cautious voice. ' Why are you here ? Have you come to see the circus ? '

' No,' said Bets, standing up and speaking in a low voice too. ' We heard you had a friend here, Luke, and we wanted to find you and talk to you— so we thought perhaps you had gone to your friend.'

' He's my uncle,' said Luke. ' I don't like him much, but I couldn't think of anyone else to go to. You see, I was afraid they'd put me into prison for stealing Dark Queen. So I ran away.'

' But you didn't steal her, did you ? ' said Bets.

' 'Course not,' said Luke. ' As if I'd go stealing anything ! I'd be too scared, let alone it's wrong. Are you alone ? '

' No ; the others are here too,' said Bets. ' They have gone to find Jake to ask if you are here.'

' Oh,' said Luke. ' Well, I didn't tell him any-thing about the trouble I'm in—nothing about Dark Queen, I mean. I was afraid if I told him that he'd not hide me here. I just told him I'd got into trouble with my stepfather and wanted to run away with the circus. I showed him the bruises where my stepfather hit me last night, and he said he'd hide me till the circus went away and take me with him. He can do with a strong lad like me to help.'

' Did your stepfather beat you ? ' said Bets, with great sympathy. ' Oh, Luke, you do have a bad time, don't you ? I hope the others don't say anything to Jake about the stolen cat ; but I don't think they will. They were only going to say that they wanted to give you a message.'

' Well, if they tell him I'm suspected of stealing anything, he'll not keep me here, that's certain,' said Luke. ' No circus-folk like to be mixed up with the police. Don't you go and tell anyone I'm here, will you, Bets ? I've got to keep hidden in this caravan till the circus moves off.'

' I won't tell a soul—except the boys and Daisy,' said Bets. ' You can depend on that. Oh, Luke, whoever do you think can have stolen the cat ? It went between four and five o'clock, you know— and you were there all the time. Didn't you see *any*one ? '

' No, no one,' said Luke. ' It's a real puzzler, that's what it is.'

' Oh, and Luke—I must tell you something queer,' said Bets, remembering the finding of the whistle. But before she could say any more, there came the sound of voices nearby. Luke shut the window hastily, and drew the curtain.

It was only the boys and Daisy coming back to Bets, bitterly disappointed.

' Nothing doing, Bets,' said Fatty. ' We found Jake, and he wouldn't open his mouth about Luke at all. Said he hadn't seen him for weeks.'

' But all the same I can't help feeling that he *has* seen him and that he knows where he is,' said Pip. ' It's sickening—coming all this way for nothing.'

' What's the matter with Bets ? ' said Fatty,

looking at her suddenly. ' She's all red, and bursting to tell us something. What's up, Bets ? '

' Nothing,' said Bets. ' Except that I know where Luke is, that's all.'

The four children stared at Bets as if she had suddenly gone mad. ' What do you mean ? ' said Pip at last. ' Where is he ? '

Bets dropped her voice. ' See that red caravan over there ? Well—he's hiding in there. I saw him. He was peeping out at me. And I talked to him.'

' Crumbs ! ' said Larry. ' Here we go wandering all over the field, finding Jake and not getting a word out of him—and all the time little Bets is talking to Luke ! Whatever will she do next ? '

Bets glowed. It was just a bit of luck that she had crept through the hedge and sat down beside the red caravan. She knew that — but all the same she couldn't help feeling rather clever and important.

' Did you say anything to Jake about the stolen cat ? ' asked Bets. ' Because Luke said he didn't say a word to him about that in case Jake wouldn't hide him. He just told Jake that he was running away from his stepfather, and he showed him his bruises.'

' We didn't say a word about the cat, silly, of course not,' said Pip. ' I wonder if we can speak to Luke. Which window did he look out of, did you say ? '

Bets showed him. Pip whistled the little tune that Luke always used as a signal. The curtain moved slightly, and the children could see the outline of Luke's head behind. The window softly opened.

'Hallo there, Luke!' said Fatty in a low voice. 'We haven't said anything to Jake about the cat. I say, are you really running away with the circus?'

'Yes,' said Luke.

'But don't you think that everyone will feel certain you stole Dark Queen if you run away?' said Larry. 'You know, it's not a very good plan to run away from things.'

There came the sound of somebody jumping off a bicycle the other side of the hedge—somebody heavy and panting. The children looked at one another, and then looked over the hedge. Yes, just as they had feared—it was Mr. Goon. His puncture was mended and he had caught them up.

'These your bikes?' said Mr. Goon. 'What you doing here?'

'Having a look round the circus,' said Fatty politely. 'Lovely tigers here, Mr. Goon. You'll have to be careful they don't eat you. They like a nice big dinner.'

Mr. Goon snorted. 'You'd better clear orf,' he said. 'You're up to no good here, I'll be bound. Have you seen your friend Luke?'

'Luke?' said Fatty, staring with wide eyes at Mr. Goon. 'Why, where *is* Luke? Isn't he at Lady Candling's? We'd like to talk to him, if only you'll tell us where he is.'

Mr. Goon snorted again. He had a very good snort. Fatty wished he could snort like Mr. Goon. He was sure the boys at his school would love to hear a snort like that.

'You clear orf,' said Mr. Goon again, getting on his bicycle. 'Butting in where you're not wanted. Interfering with the Law.'

He rode off to the gate that led into the field.

The children did not dare to speak to Luke again.
They slipped through the hedge and got their bikes.
They saw Mr. Goon speak to someone and then go
off to where Jake was still watering his horses.

'There, just what we thought!' said Fatty.
'He's heard about Jake too. I only hope Jake
won't give away Luke's hiding-place when he knows
he's suspected of stealing Dark Queen!'

'We'd better get away from this caravan,' said
Pip. 'It might look funny, being so near it. Old
Clear-Orf is terribly stupid, but it might occur to
him that we are interested in this caravan for some
special reason!'

So they all rode off, leaving poor Luke behind
in the red caravan. How they wished they could
do something for him. But they couldn't. They
must just hope he could get away safely with Jake
and that nobody would find him.

'All the same, I think he's jumped out of the
frying-pan into the fire,' said Larry as they cycled
home together. 'I don't think he's going to be any
happier with that surly Jake than with Tupping or
his stepfather.'

It was late when they got back, almost Bets'
bed-time. 'We'd better say good-night,' said
Larry, stopping at the corner of the road where he
lived. 'See you all to-morrow!'

'Good-night,' called the others, and rode on,
leaving Daisy and Larry behind.

'We'll drop you next, Fatty,' said Pip. 'I say,
isn't it a pity that this new mystery doesn't seem to
be coming to anything? Luke's run away, and now
we shall never know who stole Dark Queen.'

'Yes; this mystery is at an end, I suppose, as
far as we are concerned,' said Fatty, jumping off his

bike as he came to his house. 'With Luke gone away, old Goon will have to drop his enquiries, and I don't expect we shall ever find out any more. It's a pity.'

'Good-bye,' said Bets, 'see you to-morrow.' She and Pip rode home down the lane. Bets' bed-time bell was ringing as she rode up the drive.

'Just in time,' said Pip. 'You won't get into a row to-night, that's certain ! Happy dreams, Bets ! '

Bets went off to the bathroom to have her bath. Pip went to clean up and change into a decent suit. He whistled as he changed. He found that he was whistling the tune Luke always used.

'Poor old Luke,' thought Pip, scrubbing his nails. 'I suppose we'll never hear of him again. Well, I shall always remember him because of those lovely whistles he made.'

Pip had his meal, and then went out to clean his bike. He did not go to bed until half-past eight, so he had plenty of time. He cleaned his bike and then went down to the end of the garden. There was an old summer-house. Pip took a book and sat there reading.

He thought he heard a rustling noise once or twice and he looked up, wondering if there was a bird in the bushes outside. But there seemed to be nothing, and Pip went on reading. Then he heard the clock in the village nearby strike the half-hour, and he shut his book. He went to find his mother and father to say good-night to them.

Pip was tired. He soon fell asleep. He dreamt all kinds of things. He dreamt that old Clear-Orf was chasing him, riding on Buster's back. He dreamt that Jake joined in, riding on a tiger. Then he dreamt that Luke was in front of them, running away in fright. He heard the tuneful whistle that Luke used as a signal.

Pip turned in his sleep. The dream went on. Luke was in it all the time. The whistle kept there too, insistent and clear.

Then someone clutched Pip, and he awoke with a terrible jump. He sat up, trembling, still thinking of his dream. He gave a little yelp.

'Sh! It's me, Pip,' said Bets' voice. 'Don't make a noise.'

'Bets!' said Pip in anger. 'What do you mean by giving me a fright like this? You nearly made me jump out of my skin.'

'Pip, listen! There's someone whistling in the garden,' whispered Bets. 'And it's Luke's little tune. You know, the one we always use to whistle to one another. Do you think it's Luke out there? Does he want us?'

Pip was now wide awake. He was just about to answer Bets when he heard the whistle again, the noise he had heard in his dreams. He now knew it had been a real whistle, not a dream one. He jumped out of bed.

'Good for you, Bets!' he said. 'It must be Luke. He's left the circus for some reason and come back here. We'd better see what he wants. At least—*I'll* go and see what he wants. You stay here.'

'I'm coming too,' said Bets in an obstinate voice. 'I heard him, and you didn't. I'm coming too.'

'You'll only fall down the stairs or something and make a row,' said Pip.

'I shan't,' said Bets crossly, raising her voice. Pip nudged her.

'Shut up! You'll wake everyone. All right—

come if you want to, but for goodness' sake be quiet.'

They did not bother to put on dressing-gowns, for the night was so warm. They padded down the passage and on to the landing. Pip fell over something, and rolled down a few stairs before he was able to catch hold of the banisters and stop himself from falling any farther.

'What's the matter, Pip?' said Bets in alarm.

'Fell over the silly kitchen cat,' whispered back Pip. 'Golly, I hope no one heard me.'

The two sat on the stairs holding their breath for a minute or two, expecting to hear a movement in their parents' room. But nobody stirred. The cat sat at the bottom of the stairs, her green eyes gleaming in the darkness.

'I believe she tripped me up on purpose,' said Pip. 'She's been awfully cross ever since we let Buster into the house. Get away, Puss.'

The cat mewed and fled. The children went groping their way down the dark passage to the garden door. Pip unlocked it, and they stepped out into the silent garden. Bets clung to Pip's hand. She didn't very much like the dark.

The whistle sounded again. 'It's somewhere at the top of the garden,' said Pip. 'Come on! Keep on the grass, Bets. The gravel makes a noise.'

The two crept over the lawn, up the kitchen-garden, and round past the big rubbish-heap. A shadow moved by the old summer-house.

It was Luke! They heard his voice in the darkness. So Luke had come back after all!

13 LUKE FINDS SOME GOOD FRIENDS

'LUKE! Is that you?' whispered Pip. 'What's the matter? Why did you leave the circus?'

Pip drew Luke into the summer-house. Bets sat on one side of him and Pip on the other. Bets slipped her little hand into Luke's big rough paw. The big boy held it there gently.

'Yes. I left the circus camp,' he said. 'That policeman went to my Uncle Jake, and he told him all about the stolen cat and that he thought I'd taken it—and he said did my uncle know anything about the cat.'

'And I suppose your uncle sent you off when he heard all that,' said Pip.

'He didn't give me away to the policeman,' said Luke. 'He said he hadn't heard of no stolen cat, and he hadn't seen me for weeks and didn't want to. I reckon a search will be made of the circus, though, because that bobby is quite certain Dark Queen is somewhere there.'

'I suppose they'd make a search for you too,' said Bets.

'Yes,' said Luke. 'Well, my uncle waited till the bobby was safely out of sight, then he came to me and told me to go. Said he didn't mind me running away from my stepfather, but he wasn't going to help me run away from the police.'

'But you can't go back to your stepfather!' said Pip. 'He's awful to you.'

''Course I can't,' said Luke. 'Don't want to be half killed, do I? Thing is—what am I going to do ? I came here to-night because I thought you might be able to give me something to eat. I've had nothing since twelve o'clock and I'm fair starved.'

'Oh, *poor* Luke ! ' said Bets. ' I'll go and get you something at once. There's a steak-pie in the larder and a plum-tart. I saw them both.'

' Here, Bets, don't be an idiot,' said Pip, pulling her back. ' What do you suppose Mother will say in the morning if she finds both pie and tart gone ? You can't tell a lie and say you don't know anything about it. Then, if you have to own up, people will ask you whom you gave the stuff to and they'll guess it's Luke.'

' Well, what shall we give him then ? ' asked Bets.

' Bread and butter,' said Pip. ' That won't be missed. And we could take a small bun or two out of the tin. And there's lots of plums and green-gages.'

' That'll do fine,' said Luke gratefully. Bets sped off at once to the kitchen. She fell over the cat, but did not hurt herself. Soon she had collected the food and was back with Luke and Pip. Luke began to munch hungrily.

' I'm feeling better now,' he said. ' Nothing like hunger to make you feel miserable, I always say.'

' Where are you going to sleep to-night ? ' asked Pip.

' Don't know,' said Luke. ' Under a hedge somewhere. Reckon I'd better go tramping.'

' Don't do that,' said Bets. ' You stay with us for a little while. You can sleep in this old summer-house. We can put the mattress from the swing-seat on the bench here and you can sleep on that.'

'And we'll bring you food each day till we think of some plan for you,' said Pip, feeling rather excited. 'It will be fun.'

'I don't want to get you into no trouble,' said Luke.

'Well, Luke, you won't,' said Pip. 'You stay in our garden, and maybe we'll be able to solve the mystery of Dark Queen, and then you can go back to your job and everything will be all right.'

'I'll get the mattress off the swing-seat now, said Bets, and she ran to get it in the dark. She was more used to the dark now, and she found the swing-seat without difficulty. Pip went to help her. Together the two dragged the mattress up the garden to where Luke sat in the summer-house.

They made a bed on the bench with the mattress and then Pip fetched an old rug from the garage.

'It's a warm night,' he said to Luke. 'You won't be too cold. We'll bring you some breakfast to-morrow morning.'

'What about your gardener?' said Luke fearfully. 'What time does he come? Will he be up here at all?'

'He's ill,' said Pip. 'He won't be back for a few days. Mother's fed up because of the vegetables. She says they want weeding, and she keeps on trying to make me and Bets do it. But I hate weeding.'

'Oh,' said Luke, relieved. 'Well, I'll be pretty safe up here then. Good-night—and thanks.'

The others slipped back to bed, excited. It was good to think of the surprise of the others next day when they heard Luke was in the garden, sleeping there. Bets snuggled into bed happily. She was glad to have helped Luke. She did like him so much.

It was exciting to wake the next morning and think of Luke in the summer-house. Pip sat up in bed and wondered what there was for breakfast. If it was sausages he could secrete one somehow and take it to Luke. If it was boiled eggs he couldn't. Anyway, he could take bread and butter.

Bets was thinking the same thing. She dressed quickly and went downstairs, wondering if she could cut some bread and butter before anyone came into the dining-room. She thought she could.

But just as she was cutting a big thick slice of bread, her mother came in. She stared in surprise at Bets.

'Whatever are you doing?' she said. 'Are you so hungry that you can't wait for breakfast? And what an enormously thick slice, Bets!'

Poor Bets had to put the slice on her own plate and eat it. The porridge was brought in and she and Pip ate theirs. Then—hurrah!—a dish of sausages came in! The children's eyes gleamed. Now they would be able to take one or two to Luke.

'Please can I have two sausages to-day?' asked Pip.

'Me too,' said Bets.

'Gracious, you must be hungry, Bets!' said her mother. She gave them each two. Their father was hidden behind his newspaper, so he would not be able to see what they were doing. But their mother could see quite well. How could they manage to hide away a sausage each? It was going to be difficult.

But just then Annie the maid came into the room. 'Would you care to buy a flag for our local hospital, Madam?' she said. 'Miss Lacy is at the front door.'

'Oh, of course,' said Mrs. Hilton, and got up to get her bag, which she had left upstairs. The two children winked at one another. Pip got out a clean hanky and wrapped a sausage up quickly. Bets did the same—but her hanky was not so clean! They pushed the wrapped-up sausages into their pockets with slices of bread, just as their mother came back. She stared at their plates in surprise.

'Pip! Bets! How you *have* gobbled your breakfasts! You shouldn't stuff like that—you had two sausages each too! And a plate of porridge!'

Bets gave a little giggle, and Pip kicked her under the table. Neither of them liked to try and smuggle any more food into their pockets that meal, for they couldn't help feeling that their mother was watching them, puzzled and surprised.

Luke was glad of the bread and sausages. They took him some water to drink too. He sat in the summer-house eating, and they talked in low voices. 'We'll bring you something at dinner-time too,' said Pip. 'And you can pick yourself plums and greengages from the trees, can't you, Luke?'

Luke nodded. He drank the water and handed back the cup. Then there came the sound of someone calling 'Coo-ee' and Bets jumped up.

'It's Fatty—and Buster! Hie, Fatty, here we are in the summer-house.'

Fatty came up the garden with Buster. The little Scottie darted into the summer-house, barking with delight to see his friend there. Luke patted him.

Fatty stopped at the entrance to the summer-house, his mouth falling open in the greatest amazement when he saw Luke there. Bets laughed at his surprise.

Luke sat in the summerhouse, eating

'We're going to hide him here,' she explained to Fatty. 'And we're going to bring him food. It's exciting. Oh, Fatty, can't we solve the mystery so that Luke isn't afraid any more ? Do let's hurry up and solve the mystery ! '

Fatty had to hear all about the night's happenings. Then Daisy and Larry came, and added their surprise and delight to the little company. Altogether it was a very pleasant morning.

'Where's that whistle we found in the cats' cage ? ' said Pip. It was produced and held up for Luke to see.

'We found it in the cage,' said Fatty. 'And as we thought Mr. Goon would be sure to find it, and Mr. Tupping would tell him it was yours, we took it out and kept it. And we put a lot of false clues in the cage. You'd have laughed to see them. I put a cigar-end in the cage and one under it ! '

Luke whistled. 'Oho ! ' he said, ' so that's why Mr. Goon got all excited when he found my uncle smoking a cigar ! I couldn't think why he did. My uncle said he went quite purple in the face when he took out a cigar and lighted it. He had a box given to him once, and when he wants to be careful what he says to anyone, he lights one of those cigars and smokes it. He says it helps him to think.'

The children giggled to think that Fatty's cigar-ends had made Mr. Goon get all excited when he saw Jake smoking a cigar. Then Luke looked at the whistle that Fatty held.

'Yes ; that's one I made,' he said. 'I lost it somewhere in the garden. How could it have got into the cats' cage ? I made that whistle months ago.'

They all talked over the mystery again, but somehow they could not make head or tail of it. Luke insisted that no one had come near the cage whilst he had been at work there—and that being so, how was it that Dark Queen had disappeared then ?

All the children saved bits of their dinner for Luke. Daisy nearly got into trouble for putting a jam tart into her pocket. Her mother saw her and was very cross.

' Daisy ! What are you doing with that tart ? Surely you are not putting it into your pocket ? '

' Oh, how silly of me,' said Daisy, taking it out again and looking at the tart as if she had thought it was her handkerchief.

' If you are trying to take food away for that dog of Frederick's, I must certainly forbid it,' said her mother. ' The dog is too fat already.'

' Oh, Mother, I certainly won't give food away to Buster,' said Daisy earnestly. ' I wouldn't dream of it.'

Between them the children managed to supply Luke with plenty of food. They gave him a pail of water and soap and an old towel. They made up a bed for him each night in the summer-house. And, in return, Luke worked in the vegetable garden whenever Pip's mother was out, weeding it carefully and doing all he could to make it nice. The kitchen-garden was far away from the house and he could not be seen.

' Must do something in return for your kindness,' he said to the children. And they liked him all the better for it. For three days Luke stayed in Pip's garden, and then things began to happen again.

MRS. HILTON, Pip's mother, walked up the garden one day and was filled with astonishment to see the vegetables looking so neat and so well-weeded.

She stood and gazed at them in amazement, and then she called Pip and Bets. She smiled lovingly at them.

'Pip! Bets! What good, kind children you are! You have been weeding the vegetable-garden for me whilst the gardener is ill, and you haven't told me a word about it. I am very, very pleased with you!'

Bets opened her mouth to say at once that she and Pip had had nothing to do with it, but Pip gave her such an alarming frown that she shut it again. She went very red.

Pip was red too. Neither of them liked being praised for something they hadn't done ; but how could they say they hadn't done it without giving Luke away ?

' It's almost as bad being praised for something we oughtn't to get praise for, as being blamed for something we haven't done ! ' thought Pip. ' Oh, golly ! I suppose Bets and I had better set to work and *do* a little weeding—then we can safely admit to having worked in the garden even though old Luke has done most of it.'

So, much to the others' surprise, Pip and Bets actually did some weeding, and felt very virtuous indeed. Luke laughed to see them.

'Little Bets has pulled up half the lettuce seedlings,' he said. 'She thought they were weeds. Never mind, Bets, there are plenty more lettuces!'

One afternoon Mr. Goon met Fatty and Buster, and he stopped them.

'I want a word with you, Master Frederick,' he said in his pompous voice. He took out his big black notebook. He flicked over the pages.

'I'm afraid I can't stop,' said Fatty in a polite voice. 'I'm taking Buster for a walk.'

'You just stop where you are,' said Clear-Orf angrily. 'I tell you I've got something to say to you.'

'Well, what you say to me is usually " clear orf,"' said Fatty. 'Are you sure that isn't what you want to say?'

'One of these days, young man—*one* of these days you'll be had up for Contempt of the Police,'. said Mr. Goon in an awful voice.

'Shall I really?' said Fatty with great interest.

'Ah, here we are,' said Mr. Goon, apparently finding the page he wanted in his notebook. 'Here we are. On the fifth of this month, Master Frederick, you and the other four children were wandering around the circus camp, and you spoke to a man called Jake.'

'Right first time,' said Fatty, wondering what was coming.

'You be civil, young man,' said Mr. Goon angrily. Fatty looked very innocently at him, and Mr. Goon wished he could box his ears. Fatty could be intensely annoying in a most polite way.

'Well, tell me what you want,' said Fatty. 'I really must go. Buster is getting most impatient!'

'Woof,' said Buster, playing up well.

'Now then, said Mr. Goon, putting his face

near to Fatty's, who drew back at once, ' now then, what I want to know is this—that Luke was in the camp, wasn't he ? '

' Was he ? ' said Fatty. ' Well, why ask me if you know where he was. Go and find him there.'

' Ah,' said Mr. Goon, ' that's the point. He's not there now. One of them circus children let the cat out of the bag and——'

' Let the cat out of the bag ! ' said Fatty, purposely misunderstanding. ' What ? Dark Queen, do you mean ? Had they put her into a bag ? Did you see her ? Where is she now ? Why did they put her into a bag ? What——'

' Hold your tongue,' said Mr. Goon. ' I said " let the cat out of the bag," not meaning anything about Dark Queen, as you very well know. I meant that this circus-kid told me she had seen Luke there. But when I searched the camp he'd gone.'

' Bad luck,' said Fatty sympathetically.

Mr. Goon glared at him. ' Well, what's the matter with saying " bad luck," Mr. Goon ? ' said Fatty in an aggrieved voice. ' You told me to be civil.'

' Now, look here,' said Mr. Goon, coming to the point at last, ' I think you and them other children knows where Luke is. See ? And I'm just warning you. If you hide him or know where he's hiding and don't inform the police, you'll get into Serious Trouble. Very Serious Trouble.'

Fatty was startled. Why did Mr. Goon suspect that they knew where Luke was, or were hiding him ?

' What makes you think we'd try to hide Luke ? ' he said. ' As if we could hide him without *you* knowing, Mr. Goon ! Why, a clever policeman like you knows everything ! '

'Ah,' said Mr. Goon. 'I know a lot more than you think.'

That apparently was the end of the talk. Mr. Goon shut his notebook with a snap and went on his way. Fatty went down the lane, thinking hard.

'Old Tupping must have popped his head over the wall, and either spotted Luke or thought he did,' thought Fatty. 'Blow! We don't want to get into trouble. But what are we to do with poor old Luke? Perhaps we had better give him some money and get him away.'

The others listened to what Fatty told them. Bets was upset. 'Don't send Luke away,' she said. 'We might solve the mystery any time, and then he could go back to Lady Candling's.'

'We shan't solve this mystery,' said Fatty gloomily. 'We aren't so clever as we thought we were. I bet even Inspector Jenks wouldn't be able to solve the mystery of Dark Queen.'

'Oooh!' said Daisy at once, remembering how nice and friendly the Inspector had been in the Easter holidays when they had solved another mystery. 'Inspector Jenks! I'd forgotten about him. Can't we get into touch with him and tell him about poor old Luke? I'm sure he wouldn't want to put him into prison or anything. He'd keep our secret all right.'

'Do you think he would?' said Larry. 'Well, I'm blessed if I can see any way out of this. If old Clear-Orf starts searching Pip's garden he'll find Luke, and then maybe it will be worse for him, and bad for us. Let's tell the Inspector. He always said he would help us and be a friend to us if he could.'

'I like him,' said Bets.

'Oh, you like nearly everyone,' said Pip.

'Not Tupping or Clear-Orf,' said Bets. 'Oh, do let's tell the Inspector everything. I'm sure he'll understand.'

'I'll telephone,' said Fatty. The others looked at him respectfully. They thought it was rather marvellous of Fatty to offer to telephone to what Bets called 'a very, very high-up policeman.'

Fatty kept his word. He went back home, waited until no one was about to hear him, and then put a call through to the police-station in the nearest big town, where the Inspector lived.

Very luckily for him, Inspector Jenks happened to be there. He came to the telephone and spoke pleasantly to Fatty.

'Ah, Master Frederick Trotteville? I hope you are well. Yes, yes; I well remember the most interesting time we had together in the Easter holidays, when you so kindly solved the mystery of the burnt cottage—very clever piece of work, if I may say so. And have you solved any other mysteries since?'

'Well, sir, there *is* a mystery here we can't solve,' said Fatty, relieved to find the Inspector so very friendly. 'We simply can't. I don't know if you've heard of it. A very valuable cat disappeared.'

The Inspector appeared to think hard for a minute. Then his voice came again over the phone.

'Yes; the report came in to me. I remember it. I believe our friend Mr. Goon is in charge of that particular puzzle.'

'Well, he isn't exactly a friend of *ours*,' said Fatty honestly. 'But the person who is supposed to have done the crime *is* a friend of ours. And that's what I'm really ringing you up about. We're in a bit of a muddle about him. I was just wondering if by any chance you could give us a little advice.'

' Very nice of you to ask me,' said the Inspector. ' It so happens I am coming through your village to-morrow. I suppose you couldn't invite me to tea—say a picnic tea by the river ? '

' Oh, *yes*,' said Fatty joyfully. ' That would be simply fine. We could tell you everything then.'

' Then that's settled,' said the Inspector. ' I'll be along your lane about four o'clock. It will be most pleasant for us all to meet again. I hope you agree with me.'

' Oh, I do,' said Fatty. ' Good-bye, sir, and thank you very much.'

Fatty put down the receiver and sped down the lane to Pip's house, full of excitement. He ran up the drive and found the others in the garden.

' Well,' said Fatty, ' that's all settled. The Inspector is coming to tea with us to-morrow—a picnic tea down by the river. We'll tell him everything.'

' Fatty ! Is he really coming ? Did you ask him to tea ? Oh, Fatty, how marvellous ! ' cried the others. Fatty swelled up, full of pride and importance.

' You want a fellow like me to arrange these things,' he said. ' It's nothing to me to get things like this done. You'd better leave everything to me.'

' Shut up ! ' said Larry and Pip at once. But they could not be annoyed with Fatty's boasting for long, because they were all so excited at the thought of seeing the big, kindly Inspector once more. Bets was really thrilled. She had liked him so much, and he had put everything right at once last time. Perhaps he could this time.

'We'll plan a fine tea,' said Daisy. 'We'll tell our mothers who is coming with us, and they are sure to let us have anything we want. Even grown-ups seem to think that Inspectors are somebody to make a fuss about!'

Daisy was right. As soon as the children's mothers knew that the great Inspector Jenks had condescended to have a picnic tea with the children, they provided a very fine meal.

'Chocolate buns!' said Daisy joyfully. 'And cucumber sandwiches.'

'Ginger biscuits and a big currant cake!' said Pip. 'What a pity old Luke can't come too. Well, we'll save some for him.'

'Tomato and paste sandwiches and a jam sponge,' said Fatty. 'Golly! aren't we lucky?'

The children packed up the food, and went to stand at the front gate to watch for the Inspector. Mr. Goon came riding down on his bicycle. He jumped off when he saw them.

'I'd like a word with you,' he said in his pompous voice.

'Sorry,' said Larry, 'but we're on our way to a picnic. I bet you'd like to come—it's going to be a gorgeous one.'

'We've got chocolate buns and currant cake and a jam sponge, and . . . ' began Bets.

Mr. Goon looked in astonishment at all the food. 'You going to eat all that yourselves?' he said suspiciously. Fatty guessed that he thought they were going to take some to Luke. He grinned.

'Oh, no,' said Fatty. 'The food is for somebody else besides ourselves, Mr. Goon. We shan't tell you who. That would be giving away a secret.'

' Hmmmm ! ' said Mr. Goon, feeling more and more suspicious. ' Where are you going for your picnic ? '

' Down by the river,' said Bets. Mr. Goon got on his bicycle and rode away, thinking hard. Fatty chuckled.

' He thinks we're taking this food to Luke in some hiding-place somewhere,' he said. ' He doesn't know we're having a picnic with the Inspector. I say, wouldn't it be perfectly marvellous if he tried to follow us and pounced on us to see if we really had got Luke with us—and all the time it was Inspector Jenks ? '

' Yes, marvellous,' said Daisy. ' Oh, look, here's the Inspector ! '

It was. He drove up in a very smart black police car, parked it in Pip's garage, and then shook hands solemnly all round.

' Very, very pleased to meet you all again,' he said, with his beaming smile. ' Let me see, what did you call yourselves—the Five Find-Outers and Dog. Ah yes ! and here's the dog. A very, very nice little fellow, if I may say so.'

They all went down the lane to the river, Bets hanging on to his arm. The Inspector was a tall, burly man, with twinkling eyes, a smiling mouth, and a very clever face. He looked very fine indeed in his uniform. Bets chattered to him, telling him all the good things they had got for tea.

' We'll have our meal straight away, shall we ? ' said the Inspector. ' You are making my mouth water. Now, where shall we sit ? '

15   MR. GOON HAS A BAD TIME

THEY found a nice sheltered place close to the water. Behind them rose an overhanging bank with trees. No one could see them there. It was a good place to talk.

They said nothing about their difficulties at first. They all ate hungrily, and the Inspector enjoyed his tea just as much as anyone else. Buster adored him, lay on his knee and licked up every crumb that fell from his fingers. It was a very happy party.

' Well, now,' said the Inspector, when the meal was finished and there was very little left—' Well, now, what about a little business ? I've looked up the report of the case you told me about, so I know all the details. But I should very much like to hear what you have to say. You tell me that this boy, Luke, is a friend of yours ? '

The children began to talk eagerly, telling Inspector Jenks all that they knew, but they did not tell him about the false clues they had laid for Tupping and Clear-Orf. Nobody quite liked to tell him that.

Then they came to where they had talked to Luke at the circus, and how he had come to them one night.

' And ever since then we've fed Luke and let him sleep in the summer-house,' said Pip. ' But now we think Clear-Orf—Mr. Goon, I mean— has guessed we're hiding him, and we're afraid if we go on doing it we may get him and ourselves into trouble.'

'Very wise of you to come to me,' said the Inspector. 'Yes ; you mustn't hide Luke, that is certain. For one thing it tells against Luke if he runs away and hides. That is never a good thing to do. But he won't be put into prison, don't be afraid of that. For one thing, he is only fifteen— and for another thing, we don't put people into prison unless it is really proved that they have committed a crime. And it is by no means proved that Luke stole the cat, although I admit that things do look very black against him. I am sure you agree with me ? '

'Yes. We think they do too,' said Fatty. 'It has puzzled us very much. Because, you see, Inspector, we know and like Luke, and we don't see how a boy like him *could* have done such a thing. He's a bit simple, and always scared of grown-ups and what they'll do to him. And he's very kind. But Mr. Goon and Mr. Tupping are both quite sure he did it.'

'Well, I would advise Luke to come out of hiding and go back to his job,' said the Inspector. 'Er—I don't see that he need say anything about *where* he has been, or *who* has hidden him. No need for that at all.'

'He'll have to go back to his stepfather,' said Bets, 'and oh, Inspector Jenks, he's got such a *cruel* stepfather. He'll beat him.'

'No, he won't,' said the Inspector. 'I shall have a word with him. I think you'll find that he'll let Luke severely alone. In the meantime, I will look more carefully into this mystery and see if I can get a little light shed on it. It certainly sounds most interesting now that I have heard all you have told me.'

'You *are* a nice Inspector,' said Bets, putting her hand into his. 'I hope, if ever I do anything very wrong, that it will be *you* who catches me and no one else!'

Everyone laughed. 'I don't expect you will ever do anything wrong, Bets,' said the Inspector, smiling down into Bets' earnest little face. 'I shall be most astonished if you do.'

'What's up with Buster?' said Fatty at that moment. Buster had left the little company and could be heard barking madly at the top of the bank. Then a voice came to their ears.

'Call this dog orf! Get him under control, or I'll report him!'

'It's old Clear-Orf!' whispered Daisy gleefully. 'He's tracked us after all! I bet he thinks we've got Luke down here! Old Buster must have heard him creeping up and gone and barked at him!'

'Hie you! Will you call this dog orf of me!' came Mr. Goon's angry voice. Fatty went up the bank and through the overhanging bushes, and stood on the top, looking at a very angry Mr. Goon.

'Ho! I knew you were down there,' said Mr. Goon. 'Yes, and I know who you've got with you too!'

'Then I wonder you're not a bit more polite about it,' said Fatty in a smooth voice.

'Polite about it! Why should I be?' said Mr. Goon. 'Ah, I've caught you properly, I have —harbouring someone who's done a crime! You've gone too far this time, you have. You call this dog orf, and let me go down the bank and get my hands on you-know-who.'

Fatty gave a chuckle. He called Buster off and held him by the collar standing politely aside whilst

Mr. Goon pushed his way through the bushes, and then jumped down beside the water, expecting to find four frightened children and a very scared Luke.

Instead, to his awful horror and amazement, he found his Inspector ! Mr. Goon simply could not believe his eyes. They always bulged out, but now they looked as if they were going to drop out. He stood and stared at Inspector Jenks and could not utter a word.

' Good afternoon, Goon,' said the Inspector.

' G-g-g-g-g-g,' began Goon, and then swallowed hastily. ' G-g-g-g-good afternoon, sir, I d-d-d-didn't expect to see you here.'

' I thought I heard you say you wanted to get your hands on me,' said the Inspector. Goon swallowed hard again, loosened his collar with his finger, and then tried to smile.

' You will have your joke, sir,' he said in a rather trembling voice. ' I—er—I—expected to find somebody else. It's—it's a great surprise to see you here, sir.'

' Well, these children have paid me the honour of consulting me about this little affair of the stolen cat,' said the Inspector. ' Sit down, Goon. It would be good to hear your version of the business. I suppose you haven't got very far with the case ? '

' Well, sir—I've got a lot of clues, sir,' said Mr. Goon eagerly, hoping to alter the Inspector's opinion of him. ' I'd like your advice on them, sir, now you're here, sir.'

He took a white envelope from his pocket and opened it. Out came the two cigar-ends, the blue button, the half hair-ribbon, the peppermint drop, and the brown shoe-lace. The Inspector stared at them in considerable astonishment.

'Are all these clues?' he asked at last.

'Yes, sir,' said Goon. 'Found in the place where the crime was committed, sir. In the cat-house itself.'

'Did you *really* find all these things in the cat-house?' said the Inspector, looking at everything as if he really could not believe they were there. 'Was this peppermint drop there, Goon?'

'Yes, sir, everything. Never found so many clues in my life before, sir,' said Goon, pleased to see the Inspector's surprise.

'Neither have I,' said the Inspector. He glanced round at the five children. They were horrified at seeing Goon show the false clues to Inspector Jenks. A very small twinkle came into the Inspector's eyes.

'Well, Goon,' said the Inspector, 'you are much to be congratulated on discovering so many clues. Er—I suppose you children haven't discovered any too?'

Fatty pulled out the envelope in which he had put duplicates of the same things that Goon had found. He undid the envelope solemnly and slowly. Bets wanted to giggle, but she didn't dare to.

'I don't know if you'd call these clues, sir,' said Fatty. 'Probably not. We don't think they are, sir, either.'

To Goon's open-mouthed astonishment Fatty proceeded to take from the envelope complete duplicates of the clues that Goon had taken out of his own envelope.

First came the peppermint drop. 'One peppermint drop,' said Fatty solemnly. Then came the hair-ribbon.

'Half of somebody's hair-ribbon,' said Fatty. Daisy gave a squeal of laughter.

279

'One brown shoe-lace,' said Fatty, and pulled that out too. Then came the blue button. 'One blue button—and—er—*two* cigar-ends!'

'Two!' said Goon faintly. 'What's all this? There's somethink funny about all this.'

'It is certainly peculiar, to say the least of it,' said the Inspector. 'I am sure you children all agree with me?'

The children said nothing. They really did not know what to say. Even Fatty said nothing, though in his heart he applauded Inspector Jenks very loudly for guessing everything and giving away nothing!

'Well,' said Inspector Jenks, 'suppose you replace all these various clues in their envelopes. I hardly feel they are going to help us a great deal, but perhaps you think otherwise, Goon?'

'No, sir,' said poor Goon, his face purple with rage, astonishment, and shock. To think that his wonderful clues were the same as the children's— whatever did it mean? Poor Goon! The meaning did eventually dawn on him, but not until he was in bed that night. Then he could do nothing about it; for he knew he would never dare to reopen the matter of his clues again, with Inspector Jenks on the children's side.

'And now, Goon,' said the Inspector, in a businesslike tone, 'I propose that we go to this boy Luke and tell him to come out of his hiding-place and face up to things. We can't have him hiding away for weeks.'

Mr. Goon's mouth fell open for the third or fourth time that afternoon. Find Luke? Go to his hiding-place? What in the world did the Inspector know about all that? He gave the children a glare. Interfering busybodies! Now, with the Inspector at his elbow he wouldn't even be able to scare the life out of that boy Luke when he found him, as he would dearly like to do.

' Just as you say, sir,' he said to the Inspector, and rose ponderously from the ground.

' Come along,' said Inspector Jenks to the children. ' We'll go and have a word—a kind word —with poor old hunted Luke.'

16   A GREAT SURPRISE

THE Inspector led the way over the field and up the lane, with Bets hanging on to his arm. Goon came last of all, with Buster hopefully sniffing round his heels. Poor Goon did not even like to say ' Clear orf ! ' to Buster, he was so subdued.

Somehow the children had not thought that the Inspector would have insisted on Luke's coming out from his hiding-place and going back to his job. They wondered what Luke himself would have to say about it.

They all went up the lane. Fatty tried to hold a cheerful conversation with Mr. Goon, but the policeman only scowled at him behind Inspector Jenks' broad back.

' The river's a very nice place for a picnic, don't you think so, Mr. Goon ? ' asked Fatty cheerfully. ' I wonder you don't go there sometimes on your days off. Or don't you ever have a day off ? '

Mr. Goon made some sort of answering noise, giving Fatty a look that should have burnt him up, but didn't.

' It's funny we found the same clues as you did, isn't it, Mr. Goon ? ' said Fatty, still in the same innocent voice. Daisy exploded into a laugh. Mr. Goon made another noise, and his eyes bulged out a little more.

' He'll have a heart attack or a fit or something if you say any more, Fatty,' said Larry in a low voice.

Fatty grinned. He said no more, but watched Buster with great approval. The little Scottie was getting under poor Mr. Goon's feet in a most annoying manner.

' In here,' said Pip, when they reached his gate. They all went up the drive and into the garden. Then Pip stopped and looked at the Inspector.

' Should I just go up and explain to Luke that you say he's to come out and go back to his job ? ' he said. ' You can't think how scared he is.'

' I think that's a good idea,' said Inspector Jenks, ' but I think the one to see him and talk to him should be me. Now, don't you worry. I know how to treat boys like Luke.'

Mr. Goon scowled again. *He* knew best how to handle young scoundrels like Luke. The Inspector was too soft for words. Always giving people a chance ! Never believing things till they were proved ! Why, it stuck out a mile that Luke had stolen that cat.

But Goon could not say what he thought. So he sat down on a nearby seat and began to write in his notebook, taking no notice of the children at all. Inspector Jenks went with Pip up the garden to the summer-house. But Luke was not there.

' Oh, there he is, look,' said Pip, pointing to where Luke was busy hoeing the kitchen-garden. ' He says he just can't sit and do nothing, Inspector, and he thinks if he does a bit of weeding for us, it is a small way of returning a kindness.'

'A nice thought, if I may say so,' murmured the Inspector, watching Luke at his work, taking in the boy from head to foot. He turned to Pip.

'Just give him a call, tell him I'm a friend, and then leave us, please,' he said.

'Hey, Luke!' yelled Pip. 'I've brought a good friend of ours to see you. Come and talk to him.'

Luke turned—and saw the big Inspector in his blue uniform. He went white, and seemed as if he was rooted to the ground.

'I didn't steal no cat,' he said at last, staring at the Inspector.

'Well, suppose you tell me all about it,' said Inspector Jenks. 'We'll go and sit in the summer-house.'

He took Luke firmly by the arm and led him to the summer-house, where the children had so often talked over the mystery of Dark Queen's disappearance. Luke was trembling. Pip gave him a comforting grin, and then ran back down the garden to the others.

Mr. Goon looked up from his notebook. 'Ho!' he said, 'so that's where you hid him—up at the top of your garden, is it? And why didn't you tell *me* that, instead of the Inspector? Always trying to put me in the wrong, you are!'

'Oh, Mr. Goon! We couldn't do that, could we?' said Fatty. 'I shouldn't ever have thought *you* could have been put into the wrong. Not a clever policeman like *you*.'

'I've had enough of you this afternoon, I have,' said Mr. Goon in a threatening voice. 'Always

cheeking me ! Right-down bad boy you are. I
know what I'd do with you if I were your father ! '

' Have a peppermint drop, Mr. Goon ? ' said
Fatty, holding out the peppermint drop from his
white envelope. ' We shan't want these clues any
more, I suppose. So we might as well eat the
peppermints.'

Mr. Goon made a disgusted noise and said no
more. It simply wasn't any use at all talking to
Fatty. He could always go one better than anyone
else ! Larry thought he must be very trying indeed
to his teachers at school.

The children all wondered how Luke was getting
on with the Inspector. They seemed to be a very
long time together. But at last footsteps were
heard coming down the gravel path.

Mr. Goon shut his notebook and stood up. All
the children looked to see if Luke was with the
Inspector.

He was, and he looked quite cheerful too !
The Inspector was smiling his usual twinkling
smile. Bets ran to him.

' Is Luke going to come out of hiding ? What
is he going to do ? '

' Well, I am pleased to say that Luke agrees
with me that it would be better to go back to his
job than to hide here any longer,' said the Inspector.

' But what about his unkind stepfather ? ' said
Daisy, who couldn't bear the thought of Luke
being beaten any more.

' Ah ! ' said the Inspector, ' I must arrange about
that. I had meant to have a word with him myself
—but the time is getting on.' He looked at his
watch. ' Hm, yes, I must be getting back. Goon,
you must go down to Luke's stepfather at once, and

284

inform him that the boy is not to be ill-treated.
You must also go to Mr. Tupping, who, I understand, is the gardener next door, and inform him
that Luke is to be taken back, with Lady Candling's
permission, and is to be given a chance in the garden
again.'

Mr. Goon looked very taken aback. After
encouraging both the boy's stepfather and Mr.
Tupping to treat the boy sternly and hardly, it
was scarcely a pleasant job for him to do. Fatty
looked sharply at the Inspector.

'I bet he's making Goon do that to punish
him for frightening a young boy,' thought Fatty.
Inspector Jenks fastened his eyes on Mr. Goon.

'You have understood my orders, Goon?' he
said in a voice that sounded quite pleasant and yet
had a very hard note in it. Mr. Goon nodded hastily.

'Yes, sir, perfectly, sir,' he said. 'I'll go to
the boy's stepfather now, sir. Name of Brown.
And I'll make it my business to see Mr. Tupping
too, sir.'

'Naturally, if any complaints are made to me of
ill-treatment, I shall hold you responsible, Goon,'
said Inspector Jenks. 'But I imagine you will
impress it carefully on these two men that the orders
are mine, and that one of your duties is to see that
my orders are carefully carried out. I am sure you
agree with me in this, Goon?'

'Oh yes, sir, of course, sir,' said Mr. Goon.
'And—er—about the stolen cat, sir. About the
case, I mean. Are we to drop the case, sir—not
make any more enquiries, I mean.'

'Well, you might study those clues of yours and
see if they shed any light on the case,' said the
Inspector gravely, with a wicked twinkle in his eye.

Mr. Goon did not answer. The Inspector turned to the children, and gravely shook hands with them all.

' It's been splendid to see the Five Find-Outers —and Dog—again,' he said. ' Good-bye—and thanks for a wonderful tea—the nicest I've had for weeks, if I may say so.'

The Inspector got out his shiny black car. He roared down the drive, waving to the children. He was gone.

' I'm going to see Mr. Tupping,' said Mr. Goon, with a scowl at the children and Luke. ' But don't you think this case is all closed and forgotten. It isn't. I'm still working on it, even if the Inspector don't pay much attention to it. And I'll get the thief all right in the end—you see if I don't ! '

He gave Luke such a nasty look that the boy knew quite well he was still suspected. He watched Mr. Goon go down the drive on his way to see Tupping.

The children crowded round him. ' Luke, did you like our Inspector ? Luke, what did he say to you ? Tell us everything ! '

' He was mighty nice,' said Luke. ' Not a bit like that Mr. Goon—all threats and shouts. But how did I ever come to promise I would go back to my job—and go back to live with my stepfather, too ? I wish I hadn't promised that. I'm frit.'

This was a new word to the children. Bets stared at Luke.

' What's " frit " ? ' she asked.

' Well—I'm frit,' repeated Luke. ' Real frit. Frit of Mr. Tupping and Mr. Goon, and my step-father too.'

' He means he's frightened,' said Fatty. ' What

a lovely word—frit ! I shall always say that now. Frit ! '

' I'm often frit,' said Bets. ' I was frit the other night when I had a bad dream. I was frit to-day when old Clear-Orf stopped to speak to us.'

' And poor Luke is frit, too,' said Daisy, looking at the big boy, with his untidy hair hanging over his brown forehead. ' What are we to do about it ? How can we stop him being frit ? '

' If only we could find that cat,' said Pip. ' Then Luke wouldn't need to be frit of anyone. He's only frit because he thinks they all suspect him of stealing it. I'd be frit, too, if I thought something like that.'

There came a sound from the bushes nearby. Buster pricked up his ears, gave a loud bark and flung himself into the bushes. There was a terrific scrimmage, and then something leapt wildly up a tree. The children went to see what the matter was.

They all had a tremendous surprise. Staring down at them from the tree was a beautiful Siamese cat ! There was no mistaking its brilliant blue eyes and chocolate-and-cream colouring. But it was Luke who gave them the biggest surprise of all.

' It's Dark Queen ! ' he shouted. ' Can't you see the ring of creamy hairs in her tail ? I tell you, it's Dark Queen come back ! Oh, what a queer thing ! '

All the children at once saw the ring of light hairs in Dark Queen's swinging tail. The lovely Siamese swung it to and fro in anger as she watched Buster jumping up and down below.

' Take Buster away, Fatty,' said Larry in excitement. ' Shut him up in a shed, or something. He'll scare Dark Queen and she'll run away—and poor old Luke will probably get the blame again, if old Goon has anything to do with it ! '

Buster was shut up in a shed, much to his indignation. He nearly tore the door down in his eagerness to escape. Dark Queen quietened down when Fatty led the dog away. She sat up there in the tree, purring.

' She's thin,' said Daisy.

' And look how muddy she is,' said Larry. ' Her coat is dirty and tangled. Let's take her to Miss Harmer. What a surprise she will have ! '

17   LUKE HAS A BETTER TIME

DARK QUEEN allowed Daisy to lift her gently down from the tree. Then the five of them made their way with Luke down the drive, and into the garden next door.

They went to the cat-house, and on the way they met Lady Candling. She cried out in surprise when she saw a cat in Daisy's arms.

' You mustn't take my cats out of their house ! Did Miss Harmer let you ? '

' It's Dark Queen ! ' said Larry. ' She suddenly appeared in Pip's garden just now, Lady Candling ! Isn't it marvellous ! Won't Miss Harmer be pleased ? '

' Good gracious ! ' said Lady Candling, most astonished. She glanced at Dark Queen's tail and saw the little ring of light hairs that grew there. ' Yes—it's my beautiful Dark Queen. Wherever has she been ? She looks thin and half-starved.'

' Isn't it a pity she can't talk, then she could tell us,' said Bets, stroking the purring cat. ' Lady

Candling, here's Luke, too. We've been hiding him, because we were sorry for him. You'll take him back, won't you ? '

' Of course,' said Lady Candling. ' Inspector Jenks has just been telephoning to me. Well, Luke, you can certainly come back freely now, can't you—for here is Dark Queen, returned in safety ! '

' We're just taking her to Miss Harmer,' said Larry. ' Won't she be pleased ? '

' I'll come with you,' said Lady Candling. ' Oh, there is Miss Trimble. Miss Trimble, what do you think has happened ? Dark Queen has come back ! '

' Good gracious me ! ' said Miss Trimble, trotting up in excitement, her glasses falling off at once. ' Where did she come from ? Who brought her ? '

The children told her, and Miss Trimble listened in surprise, putting on her glasses again. Bets began to count how many times they fell off.

They all went to the cat-house. Miss Harmer was there, petting one or two of the cats, for she was very fond of them. When she saw Dark Queen in Daisy's arms she was so astonished that she couldn't say a word. She held out her arms and Dark Queen, with one graceful bound, was into them. The cat snuggled up to Miss Harmer, butting her with its head, and purring deeply and loudly.

' *Well !* ' said Miss Harmer in delight. ' Where did *you* come from, Dark Queen ? Oh, how glad I am to have you back ! '

Everyone told her at once how Dark Queen had suddenly appeared. Miss Harmer took a good look at the cat.

' She's thin,' she said. ' And her coat is rough and full of those little burrs you find stuck to your stockings when you go out in the fields now. I think she must have escaped from whoever had her, and made her way home—for miles probably—through the fields and woods.'

' Cats are clever in that way, aren't they ? ' said Fatty. ' Poor old Dark Queen—I guess you are glad to be back again.'

At that moment Mr. Tupping came into sight with Mr. Goon. The policeman had evidently been telling him about the Inspector and his orders, and Tupping's voice was very sour. He gave Luke a scowl, and then saw Dark Queen.

' It's Dark Queen ! ' said Bets. ' She's come back. Aren't you glad, Mr. Tupping ? Now she's not stolen any more ! '

Mr. Tupping seemed as if he could not believe his eyes. He kept looking at Dark Queen in amazement, and he twisted her tail round to make sure she had the little ring of creamy hairs there. As for Goon, his mouth fell open, and his eyes bulged more than ever.

His notebook came out, and the policeman began to write slowly in it. ' Have to make a report of this here re-appearance to the Inspector,' he said importantly. ' I'd like some details. Were you here, Lady Candling, when the cat returned ? '

Once more the children retold the story of Dark Queen's re-appearance, and Goon wrote busily in his black notebook. Tupping was the only person who showed no signs at all of being pleased about the cat coming back. He glared at the cat as if it had thoroughly displeased him.

' Oh, Tupping, before you go, I want to say

that Inspector Jenks and I have had a talk about Luke,' said Lady Candling in her low, clear voice. ' And he is to start work here again to-morrow. Those are my wishes as, no doubt, Mr. Goon too has told you. I hope that I shall have no fault to find with your treatment of Luke.'

' Well, your Ladyship, if you and the Inspector want to have a boy like that in your employ . . .' began Tupping in an uncivil tone. Lady Candling cut him short.

' I don't want to discuss the matter with you, Tupping. I have told you my wishes. That should be enough.'

Lady Candling walked off, and Miss Trimble followed her, her glasses falling off with the thrill of hearing Tupping ticked off.

' I wish *I* could speak to people like that,' said Fatty, with a side glance at Tupping. ' People who deserved it, I mean, of course.'

' Now, you clear orf,' said Mr. Goon, seeing that Tupping was rapidly going purple in the face.

' I want to look for more clues,' said Fatty wickedly. ' You know, there might be a pear-drop left about, or a toffee, or something. By the way, Mr. Goon, have you eaten your peppermint drop yet ? '

Now it was Mr. Goon's turn to go purple in the face. The children squealed with laughter and ran for the wall. They didn't know how Fatty thought of such things to say, or how he dared to say them.

They clambered over the wall and dropped down to the other side. Fatty went to let a very angry Buster out of the shed.

Then Bets' bed-time bell rang. The little girl gave a groan. ' Oh, blow ! That bell always rings just when I don't want it to. Haven't we had an exciting time to-day ? '

' I should jolly well think so,' said Pip. ' Tea with the Inspector—Luke made to come out of his hiding-place—Dark Queen coming back—goodness, there's no mystery left to solve now, is there ? '

' Well, we still don't know who did steal Dark Queen,' said Larry. ' I wonder if she *could* have escaped by herself, somehow—and Luke didn't notice that she slipped off. Maybe the cage-door wasn't locked, and she pushed it open—or something like that.'

' I don't think that's at all possible,' said Fatty. ' But we may as well think that. Anyway, we've been a failure at solving the mystery, so we'll pretend there wasn't one ! Dark Queen just escaped by herself, and then came back when she was tired of being loose.'

But nobody really believed that, of course. They were all very disappointed that they, the Five Find-Outers, hadn't been able to solve the next-door mystery.

Luke went back to his stepfather that night. He was not beaten, nor was he grumbled at. Evidently Mr. Goon had made it quite clear that Luke was not to be molested in any way. The stepfather said nothing to the boy at all. His meal was placed before him, and he ate it, washing up the dishes afterwards.

Luke went back to his work the next morning. He still felt very much afraid of Mr. Tupping, but that gentleman did not go for him as he usually did. Plainly, what the Inspector said had to be taken notice of ! Lady Candling's orders could not. lightly be disobeyed either. Tupping had a very good job, and he knew it. He did not want to lose it in a hurry.

Luke was very glad that Dark Queen had come back. Now he felt somehow that things were all right again. He worked very hard, and the children heard his cheerful whistle every now and again as he wheeled his barrow up and down the garden.

They climbed over the wall to see him as he worked. He was forking over a bed.

'Hallo, Luke,' said Bets. 'Is it nice to be back at work ?'

Luke nodded. 'It is that,' he said. 'I'm not one for lazing around. Well, I never thanked you children properly for hiding me and feeding me like you did ; but you know I'm grateful, though I can't talk easily, like you do.'

'That's all right, Luke,' said Larry. 'We were glad to help you.'

'I'll make you all whistles, if you like,' said Luke. 'Fine ones. Not tiddley little ones like I made for Bets. Proper big ones, and I'll paint them up for you, see ?'

'Oh, thanks very much,' said Pip, pleased. 'I think your whistles are lovely. You will be busy if you make us each one !'

Luke *was* busy, and very happy too. It was good to carve out whistles for his five faithful friends. He wished he could make something for Buster too.

He was much happier now. His stepfather did not beat him, and Mr. Tupping no longer boxed his ears, though he still shouted at him. Sometimes Lady Candling gave him a kind word, and the children were always ready to talk to him, or go out with him when he was off-duty.

Things went on very peacefully and happily The days slipped by. The children played together in each other's gardens, and Buster hunted rabbits in both. They went for picnics, they went for bike-rides, they bathed in the river.

'It seems quite a time ago now since we thought we had another mystery to solve,' said Fatty one day. 'We were silly to think it was a mystery, I suppose—just a cat that disappeared, and we didn't know how. There was probably quite a simple explanation of it really.'

'All the same, I wish we *could* solve a mystery these hols,' said Bets. 'It's not much good being a Find-Outer if you don't find out something. I wish something else would happen.'

'Things never do, when you wish them to,' said Fatty wisely.

But for once he was wrong. Something did happen, something that made the Five Find-Outers sit up and take notice at once. Dark Queen disappeared all over again !

18   THE SECOND DISAPPEARANCE

IT was Luke who told the children. He came over the wall about half-past five in the afternoon, looking so white and scared that the children thought he must have had a beating from Tupping or something.

'What's the matter ? ' said Daisy.

'Dark Queen's gone again,' said Luke. 'Yes; and gone under my very nose too, just like the last time ! '

' Whatever do you mean ? ' said Fatty, surprised.
' Sit down. Tell us properly. This is extraordinary.'

' Well,' said Luke, sitting down on the grass
beside the children, ' just listen to this. I was
rolling the paths round and about the cat-house
this afternoon—you know what a lot of rain we had
last night, and I always roll the paths after rain.
Well, I rolled them paths up and down, up and down,
and whilst I was doing that someone stole Dark
Queen, like I told you, under my very nose. And I
never saw no one ! '

' How do you know she's gone ? ' said Larry.

' Well, Miss Harmer had the day off,' said
Luke. ' She went at ten, and she came back about
ten minutes ago. And as soon as she went into the
cage she gave a squeal, and said Dark Queen wasn't
there ! '

' Gracious ! ' said everyone. ' Did you look
and see too, Luke ? '

' That I did,' said Luke. ' But there were only
the other cats. No Dark Queen. Under my very
nose she went ! '

' How do you know she went whilst you were
at work on the paths nearby ? ' said Fatty. ' She
might have gone before.'

' No, she didn't,' said Luke. ' You see, Lady
Candling always visits the cages now, just before
three o'clock, and she and Miss Harmer talk about
the cats together. Well, Lady Candling saw the
cats as usual at three o'clock, and Dark Queen was
there.'

' You said Miss Harmer was out for the day,'
said Fatty. ' So *she* didn't see Dark Queen.'

' No, she didn't, of course,' said Luke. ' Tupping took her ladyship to the cats to-day. He

always does when Miss Harmer is out now, and she gives him any orders to pass on to Miss Harmer. I was there when Lady Candling and Tupping were looking at the cats, and I heard Tupping say, " There's Dark Queen at the back, your Ladyship— you can see the light hairs in her tail." So she was there, then, at three o'clock.'

' And do you mean to say that since three o'clock you have been near the cages, and never left them— till Miss Harmer came back just now and found Dark Queen gone ? ' said Larry. Luke nodded.

' And you know what's going to be said,' he muttered. ' I'll be accused again. I was the only one there last time, and I was the only one there this time. But I didn't touch Dark Queen.'

' How did Miss Harmer find out that Dark Queen was gone ? ' asked Fatty, who was taking a very close interest in all that Luke said.

' Well, she came back, and Tupping met her and said he thought one of the cats wasn't very well,' said Luke. ' So, under my very eyes, he went into the cage, whilst Miss Harmer was coming along, and got the cat he said wasn't well ; and then Miss Harmer joined him, and almost at once squealed out that Dark Queen was gone.'

' Could Tupping have let her loose just in that moment ? ' asked Larry.

' No,' said Luke. ' I couldn't see Tupping in the cage, but I could see the door quite well, and nothing came out. In fact, it was shut tight.'

Everyone was silent. It did seem a most extraordinary thing that Dark Queen should have gone again, under Luke's very nose. How unlucky for Luke that he should have been the only one working near the cages again !

'Was it your own idea to roll the paths near the cat-house?' asked Fatty.

'Oh no,' said Luke. 'I don't do things on my own. Tupping gives me his orders every day. And he told me to spend the afternoon rolling the paths there.'

'Last time you were on the spot all the time,' said Pip. 'And this time you were too. And last time Miss Harmer was out for the day. And this time she was too. And last time it was Tupping who went into the cage with the cats, and this time it was too—when it was found that Dark Queen had disappeared, I mean. Last time he went in with Goon—this time he went in with Miss Harmer. There are a lot of things exactly the same. It's all very, very odd.'

'Well, I didn't take the cat last time, and I didn't this time either,' said Luke. 'I know I didn't. I'd have remembered it if I had, wouldn't I? I mean, I'm not going daft, am I? I couldn't have let the cat out, and not remembered it afterwards, could I?'

'We never thought of that,' said Daisy. 'People do do things like that sometimes, of course, and forget all about them afterwards. But I shouldn't think for a moment that you do, Luke.'

'This is more of a mystery than ever,' said Fatty, and he got up. 'I'm off over the wall to snoop round a bit. Do you remember what we found in the cage last time? One of Luke's whistles. Well, as everything seems to be more or less the same this time, I bet there'll be one of Luke's whistles there again!'

'Don't be silly!' said Daisy. 'It's just an accident that some of the things are the same.'

'All right,' said Fatty. 'But look here, if I *do* find one of Luke's whistles in the cage, we've got to realize that *that* won't be an accident. That will be put there on purpose! Well—I'll go and see.'

Everyone wanted to come, of course. So they all clambered over the wall, Luke too. The boy was upset and 'frit,' and he did not want to be left alone. Only Buster was left on the wrong side of the wall, tied up to a tree. He barked frantically and almost strangled himself trying to get free, but he couldn't.

The five children came to the cat-house. No one was there. Tupping and Miss Harmer had gone to report the matter to Lady Candling. Only the cats looked at the children, their blue eyes gleaming. Bets counted them. There were seven.

'Look,' said Fatty, pointing into the cage. 'One of Luke's whistles again!'

It was quite true—there was one of Luke's beautifully-made whistles lying on the floor. Luke stared at it in amazement. Then he went to feel in his coat, which was hanging on a tree nearby.

'It must have been taken from my pocket,' he said. 'I had it in there, ready to finish. It was for Pip. And someone must have taken it.'

'And put it on the floor of the cage so that you'd be suspected again!' said Fatty grimly. He stared at the whistle on the floor.

'Can't we get it out again,' said Daisy. 'Like we did last time?'

'I don't expect there would be time,' said Fatty. 'Look around for some other clues—quick.'

The children began to hunt around. Bets put her nose to the cage and sniffed hard.

'There's the same smell as I smelt last time,'

she said. 'What did you say it was, Fatty? Oh yes, you said turpentine.'

Fatty pressed his nose to the wire and sniffed. 'Yes, it's turps,' he said, puzzled. 'Golly! this is very queer. Everything seems to be repeating itself, doesn't it—the whistle on the floor—the smell of turps. I do think this is the strangest mystery I've ever come across.'

'Fatty, I suppose this isn't a clue, is it?' said Daisy, pointing to a little round blob of paint on a stone beside the path. Fatty looked at it.

'Shouldn't think so,' he said. He picked up the stone and looked at the blob of paint.

'Luke paints our whistles,' he said. 'Probably this is a drop of paint he spilt. Have you ever painted our whistles here, Luke?'

'No, never,' said Luke at once. 'I always do them in the shed where the pots of paint are kept. Anyway, I don't use that light-brown colour. I always use bright colours—red and blue and green.'

'It can't be a clue,' said Fatty. But he put the stone into his pocket in case.

Just then there came the sound of footsteps, and down the path came Lady Candling, Miss Trimble, Tupping, and Miss Harmer. Tupping looked important. The others looked upset, and Miss Trimble could not keep her glasses on for more than two seconds at a time.

They all looked into the cage, apparently in the vain hope that Dark Queen might possibly be there after all. Miss Harmer gave a squeal.

'What's the matter?' said Lady Candling. Miss Harmer pointed to the floor of the cage.

'What's that?' she said. They all looked in.

'Ho!' said Tupping in a ferocious voice.

' That's one of them whistles Luke is always making, that is ! I'd just like to know how *that* got there ! '

Miss Harmer took the key of the cat-cage and opened the door. Tupping picked up the whistle. He showed it to Lady Candling.

' Is this one of the whistles you make, Luke ? ' asked Lady Candling.

Luke nodded. He looked very pale. He could not understand how Dark Queen could have gone again, nor how his whistle could have been found in the cage.

' Luke has been making whistles for all of us,' said Fatty. He pulled his own out from his pocket. ' I expect it's one of our whistles, Lady Candling. It could just as well have been one of ours, couldn't it ? '

' But how could it have got into the cage ? ' said Lady Candling, puzzled.

' Your ladyship, it's quite plain,' said Tupping. ' That boy went in to take the cat, like he did before —and he dropped this whistle by accident and never saw it. He went out of the cage, locked it, put the key back in its place, and went off with Dark Queen.'

' I don't even know where the key's kept now,' said Luke.

' I usually have it in my pocket, except on the days when I go out,' said Miss Harmer. ' Then I give the key to Tupping. What do you do with it, Tupping ? '

' I keep it in *my* pocket, too,' said Tupping. ' But I left my coat along here somewhere this afternoon, so Luke could easily have got at the key. Mark my words, Dark Queen is hidden somewhere about, ready for somebody to fetch away ! I knew you'd be sorry, Madam, if you took that boy back again. Stands to reason something of this sort will happen if you do that. I said many a time to Mr. Goon——'

'I am not interested in what you say to Mr. Goon,' said Lady Candling. 'I think we will go over Mr. Goon's head this time and get in touch with Inspector Jenks immediately.'

The children were simply delighted to hear this ; but, alas, the good Inspector was away, so Mr. Goon had to be notified, and arrived, full of importance, to look for clues and to hear what everyone had to say.

He looked suspiciously at the five children. Then he looked at the cages as if he expected to find a whole lot of clues there again. But there was nothing to see except the whistle which Lady Candling had given him.

' You found any clues this time ? ' said Clear-Orf to Fatty.

' We've only found a smell and a stone with paint on it,' said Bets. The others frowned at her so suddenly and severely that she nearly ran away. Oh dear, she shouldn't have told Mr. Goon that, of course ! Whatever could she have been thinking of ?

' A smell ? ' said Mr. Goon disbelievingly. ' And a stone with paint on ? Ho ! so you think you can trick me again, do you—with smells and stones this time ! Well, let me tell you that I'm not believing in any peppermint drops, shoe-laces, hair-ribbons, smells, *or* painted stones this time ! You can keep all your clues to yourself. And you just remember what I said to you before—if you go interfering with the Law, you'll get into Very Serious Trouble one of these days ! '

With that Mr. Goon turned his back on the children, who at once went to the wall, climbed over it, and sat down to talk about this new happening.

'Bets! Of all the IDIOTS!' said Pip. 'You deserve to be spanked. Fancy telling Clear-Orf our own clues! Are you quite mad?'

'I must be,' said Bets, almost in tears. 'I can't think why I said it.'

'Never mind, Bets,' said Fatty comfortingly. 'Just *because* you told him, he won't believe you—so if they *are* clues, it won't matter. Cheer up!'

'It really is a most extraordinary mystery,' said Daisy. 'The Mystery of the Disappearing Cat! Where does she disappear to—and *how* does she disappear! How I wish I knew!'

19 BUSTER REALLY HAS GOT BRAINS!

'WHAT is the most puzzling thing of all,' said Fatty, 'is the fact that nearly everything is the same as last time. I mean, Luke was there, and only Luke, both times—and Miss Harmer was away—and the whistle was in the cage.'

'It looks as if all those things had to be like that before the cat could be stolen,' said Daisy. 'It looks as if Miss Harmer must be away, and Luke must be there—and so on.'

'It's no good suspecting anyone but Luke this time,' said Larry. 'The cat was there at three o'clock, because both Tupping and Lady Candling saw it; and Luke was by the cat-house from three until Miss Harmer returned, and then she and Tupping go into the cage and find Dark Queen missing.'

' And Luke says, as he said last time, that no one went near the cage except himself, all that time,' said Pip. ' Well, I simply do *not* see how Dark Queen could have been stolen.'

Everyone was silent. Again it seemed an absolutely mystifying problem with no solution at all— except that Luke was a very stupid and untruthful thief. But not one of the children could believe that.

The children stayed talking until it was Bets' bed-time. Then they said good-bye and got up to go home.

' Meet here again to-morrow,' said Fatty in a gloomy voice. ' Not that we can do much. We'll all think hard in bed to-night and see if we can possibly find some way out of this problem.'

' If only we had a few good clues and a few good Suspects like we had in our other mystery,' said Pip. ' But you can't call a smell and a blob of paint on a stone clues, can you ? '

' Even old Clear-Orf jeered at those,' said Fatty, getting up. ' Well, so long. See you all to-morrow. And for goodness' sake, let's get an idea of some sort. Luke will be absolutely done for this time if we don't.'

The children did not go to sleep easily that night. They all lay and thought about the Mystery of the Disappearing Cat. Nobody had got any good idea when they met the next morning—except Bets. And she hardly liked to mention her idea, because she thought the others would laugh at it.

' Anyone got anything to say ? ' asked Fatty.

'Well,' said Bets, 'I did get a sort of an idea about one of our clues.'

'What?' said Fatty.

'You know that smell we smelt—turpentine,' said Bets. 'It was in the cage this time, and last time too. It must *mean* something—it must belong to the mystery somehow, mustn't it? So it must be a real clue, and we ought to follow it up.'

'How?' said Pip, rather scornfully.

'Well, we could go and hunt about next door to find where the bottle of turps is kept or something like that,' said Bets. 'I don't say it will help; but after all, if it's a clue, we might find out something.'

'Bets is right,' said Fatty. 'She really is. We did smell turps both times—and of course we ought to go and look to see if we can find where it's kept. Who knows, we might find other clues then!'

'Let's go now, then,' said Pip. 'No time like the present! Come on. Look out for Tupping though. He won't like us snooping about.'

They all went over the wall again, leaving poor Buster in the shed. They sent Pip into the garden to see whereabouts Tupping was.

Pip came back and reported that he was tying up something near the house. 'So we're safe for a bit,' he said. 'Come on. Let's sniff in the cage again, and see if the smell is still there. Then we'll go hunting for the stuff.'

They all sniffed in the cage. The faint smell of turps still hung there. Miss Harmer came up as the children were sniffing. She did not seem very pleased to see them.

'I don't want anyone near the cat-house now,' she said. 'This disappearing of Dark Queen twice running is getting on my nerves. I'd rather you kept away, children.'

'Miss Harmer, do you use turps to clean out the cages at all ? ' asked Fatty.

Miss Harmer looked surprised. 'Of course not,' she said. 'I use an ordinary disinfectant. Cats hate the smell of turpentine.'

'Well, how did the smell of turps get into the cage then ? ' said Larry. 'You sniff, Miss Harmer, and see if you can smell it.'

But Miss Harmer had not got a very good nose for smelling, and she did not think she could smell anything like turps in the cage.

'Didn't you yesterday when you went in and found Dark Queen was gone ? ' said Larry.

'Well, perhaps I did,' said Miss Harmer, trying to remember. 'But I couldn't swear to it. I was so upset at Dark Queen disappearing again.'

The children peered into the cage, still sniffing. Miss Harmer sent them off. 'Do go,' she said. 'I really feel nervous now when anyone comes near the cats.'

'Let's go to the shed and see if we can find any turps there,' said Fatty. So they left the cat-house and went off to the two sheds that leaned back to back, not far from the greenhouses. One shed was full of tools, the other was full of pots, boxes, and odds and ends.

'You girls take one shed and search it and we boys will take the other,' said Fatty.

So they all began to hunt hard in the two sheds, moving pots and tools and boxes, trying to find a bottle of turpentine. What help it would be to them if they did, they didn't really know !

But there was no turps to be found anywhere.

Larry saw Luke passing by, looking very gloomy indeed. He whistled to him.

'Hie, Luke! You look as if you had lost a shilling and found sixpence. Cheer up!'

'You wouldn't feel very cheerful if you felt as frit as I do,' said poor Luke.

'Don't be frit,' said Larry, grinning. 'I do think that's a lovely word of yours, Luke.'

But nothing would make Luke smile that morning. He felt as if at any moment Mr. Goon would come along and take him off to the police-station.

'What you doing in them sheds?' he said. 'You'll catch it if Mr. Tupping comes along and sees you messing about there.'

'We're looking for the turpentine,' said Fatty, poking his round face out of the shed. Luke looked astonished.

'Turps?' he said. 'What do you want turps for? It's kept in the other shed—on the shelf—I'll show you. But what do you want it for?'

Luke led the boys into the other shed, where Daisy and Bets were. He pointed to a shelf on which various bottles and tins stood. 'It's there some-where,' he said.

The children looked. They picked up one bottle after another and sniffed it. But there was no turpentine at all.

'We've already looked, anyway,' said Daisy.

Luke was puzzled. 'It *was* there,' he said. 'I saw it myself yesterday. Where's it gone?'

Fatty began to feel excited, though he didn't quite know why. 'Mystery of Disappearing Turps Bottle,' he murmured. The others giggled.

'We've got to find that bottle,' said Fatty.

'Why ? ' asked Daisy.

'Don't know,' said Fatty. 'But we've got to. It's gone. Maybe it's been hidden away. We've got to find it.'

'Well, we can't go sniffing all over the garden to find a bottle of turps,' said Larry reasonably. 'We're not dogs ! '

'But Buster is ! ' said Fatty. 'I bet old Buster could find it for us.'

'Oooh ! yes,' said Bets. 'Buster has a lot of brains. I *know* he'd find it.'

'How ? ' said Larry. 'You can't say to Buster " Go and find where a bottle of turps is hidden." He may be a brainy dog, but he's not brainy enough to understand *that* ! '

'I'll manage it all right,' said Fatty importantly. 'Have you got any turps in your garden shed, Pip ? '

'Sure to have,' said Pip.

'Well, go and get it,' said Fatty. 'And I'll get Buster. Go back to the wall everyone, in case Tupping comes along and wants to know what we're up to.'

Luke went off to his work, still looking extremely gloomy. The others went to the wall. Pip and Fatty climbed over it and dropped down to the other side. Pip went to the garden-shed at the top of the garden, and found a small jar of turps.

Fatty opened the bicycle shed and let out Buster, who tore round and round him, barking as if he had not seen Fatty for at least five years.

'Come on, Buster,' said Fatty, picking him up. 'You've got to do a little work. You've got to show us your doggy brains.'

In a short time Fatty, Buster, and Pip were over the wall with the others.

'Where's Tupping ? Still up by the house ? ' asked Fatty.

'Yes,' said Larry. 'I peeped to see. The coast is all clear at the moment.'

'What is Buster going to do ? ' asked Bets in excitement. ' Is he going to be a Find-Outer too ? '

' I hope so,' said Fatty. He shook some turps on to his rather grubby hanky, and held it to Buster's nose. ' Smell that, old fellow. Smell it good and hard. That's turps. Now, you just run all over the place and see if you can find the same smell again. Good old bloodhound, aren't you ? '

' He's a turp-hound not a blood-hound,' said Bets in delight. ' Oh, Buster, aren't you a clever dog ? Go and find it ; go and find it ! '

Buster did not like the smell of the turps at all. He looked away from the hanky with a face showing intense disgust. Then he sneezed violently three times.

' Go on, Buster dog, find it, find it ! ' said Fatty, flapping the hanky at him. Buster looked up at Fatty. He knew quite well what ' find it ' meant. He was always finding things for Fatty. He trotted off, his pink tongue hanging out, his tail in the air.

' I shouldn't think he could smell anything but turps wherever he goes,' said Daisy, watching him. ' You simply stuffed that hanky up his nose, Fatty.'

Buster rushed about in the bushes. He ran round the sheds. He trotted round the cat-house. He scurried down the paths.

' He's looking for rabbits, not turps,' said Larry in disgust. ' Look—he's found a rabbit-hole—and now we shan't be able to make him see sense for ages ! '

Buster *had* found a hole. It was in a bank. He

stuck his nose into it, gave a whine, and began to dig hard in his usual way, sending the earth flying out behind him.

'Come out, idiot,' said Fatty. 'I didn't say rabbits, I said turps.'

Fatty pulled Buster out by his hind legs. Something rolled out behind the little dog. All the children stared at it. It was a cork. Fatty picked it up and smelt it.

'It smells of turps!' he said in excitement, and the others crowded round to smell it. It did. There was no doubt about it at all.

In a trice Fatty was down on his hands and knees, feeling in the hole.

He pulled out a bottle. On it was an old label, half-torn, but the letters 'turp' could still be faintly seen. There was still a little turpentine in the bottle, too.

'Here's what we were looking for,' said Fatty triumphantly. He showed the bottle to the others. Bets went to the hole and peered in out of curiosity. She saw something else there.

'There's something else, Fatty,' she cried in excitement, and put in her hand. She pulled out a tin. The others crowded round again to look, feeling very thrilled.

'What is it?' said Larry eagerly. 'A tin of paint. Here's a knife. Let me prise off the lid.'

He did so—and the children saw that the tin was nearly full of a light-brown paint.

'How queer!' said Fatty. 'It's the colour of that blob of paint on the stone we found. Look!'

He compared the stone with the paint in the tin. It exactly matched. Larry went down on hands and knees and scraped in the hole again, but there was nothing more to be found.

'Now,' said Fatty, in glee, looking at the turps and the tin of paint, ' *now*—who put the paint and the turps down that hole—and WHY ? '

20   A HUNT FOR A SMELL!

THE children were terribly excited. They had two really big clues, though quite how to fit them to the stolen cat they didn't know.

'What is turps used for ? ' asked Bets.

'Oh, to clean paint-brushes—to get paint-marks off things,' said Larry. 'It's quite clear that this paint and the turps are connected in some way. Funny there's no brush. I mean—you have to use a brush to paint with, don't you ? '

'I bet it's down the hole somewhere too ! ' said Daisy. But before she could look, Buster had stuffed his blunt nose into the hole, and a shower of earth covered everyone. The little dog at last came out backwards, and in his mouth he held a small paint-brush !

'Isn't he awfully clever ? ' said Bets in the greatest admiration.

'We'd better look and see if there's anything else down that hole,' said Fatty. But there wasn't. Fatty lay down at full-length, and put his arm right in up to the shoulder—but there was absolutely nothing more to be found.

'Listen, there's Tupping yelling to Luke,' said Fatty. 'We'd better get over the wall, quick. Here,

Larry, just help me to clear up round this hole. We don't want whoever hid these things to see that we've found them. It would warn him—or her —that we were after them.'

The boys cleared up the mess quickly, whilst the two girls ran for the wall, and Daisy helped Bets over. Then the others came, with Buster. They got over just in time, for Tupping came along that way half a minute later, grumbling away to himself.

The children retired to their old summer-house with their Clues, and looked at them closely.

' One small bottle of turps, one small tin of light-brown paint, and one small, very old paint-brush,' said Fatty. ' And if we only knew how they had been used, why they had been used, and who had used them, we should have solved the unsolvable Mystery of the Disappearing Cat ! '

' I must say I think it was clever of old Bets to think of hunting for the turps,' said Larry.

' It certainly was,' said Fatty generously. ' Can't you think of any other good idea, Bets ? '

Bets tried very hard. She thought of the cat-house and the smell she had smelt there. She thought of the cats there, who all hated the smell of turpentine. She wondered whereabouts exactly in the cage the turps had been put, or spilt, or used.

' Fatty,' said the little girl earnestly, ' do you think it would be any good going into the cage and sniffing about to see exactly what place had got the turps on it ? I mean—if it was the benches, or the floor, or the ceiling, or the wire-netting ? I can't see how it would help us even if we *did* find the place that smelt of turps, but it just might.'

' Seems rather a silly idea to me,' said Pip.

' Well, I can't say I can see what good that would

do,' said Larry. 'And anyway, how could we get into the cage ? Miss Harmer has the key.'

'Well, you know—I think there *is* something in Bets' idea,' said Fatty. 'Like Larry, I can't see how it would help us if we found out the exact place where the turps had been used, but I've a sort of hunch we'd better go and try. Bets, you're a good one at ideas just now.'

Bets was thrilled. She did love a word of praise, because she got plenty of teasing, and praise from Fatty made up for a lot.

'Well, how could we get the key ? ' said Daisy. 'Miss Harmer keeps it in her pocket.'

Fatty thought hard for a while. 'It's a very hot day,' he said. 'I should think Miss Harmer will have taken her coat off and hung it up somewhere. She won't be doing the cats just now—I expect she'll be at work in the greenhouses. It's part of her job to help there too, you know. I bet she won't be wearing more than she can help in those hot green-houses. So perhaps we could borrow the key, without her knowing, for a while.'

'I guess she'll have her coat under her eye, with all these disappearing acts going on,' said Larry.

'Let's go and see,' said Pip, getting up. He moved the loose board at the back of the summer-house and tucked the three clues there. He put the loose board over them. 'There ! No one will find those clues but us. Come on, let's go and see what Miss Harmer is doing.'

They all went over the wall again, having first shut Buster into the shed. They couldn't have him rushing round the cat-house if they were going inside.

Fatty went to scout about and find out where

Miss Harmer was. She was, as he had guessed, in one of the greenhouses tying up peach-tree branches. She had on her usual breeches and a cool cotton jumper. Fatty looked about for her coat.

It was hung on a nail inside the greenhouse where she was working. Blow! No one could possibly look for a key in the pockets without being seen by Miss Harmer! Fatty went back to the others and told them.

'We must get Miss Harmer out of the greenhouse for a minute, somehow,' said Pip. They all thought hard, and some very complicated plans were talked of. It was Daisy who thought of a very simple one that could be done without anyone being seen at all.

'*I* know!' she said. 'I'll slip along to the end of the greenhouse farthest from the coat—there are doors each end, aren't there? I'll hide in a thick bush in one of the beds, and then I'll call loudly, "Miss Harmer! Miss Harmer!" And I bet Miss Harmer will walk out of the door of the greenhouse to see who's calling her, and that will just give one of you time to slip in at the other door and get the key!'

'We'd get into an awful row if anyone saw us taking the key,' said Larry. 'But after all, we *are* the Find-Outers, and we've got to take a few risks in our work, haven't we? Who's going to get the key?'

'I will,' said Pip. 'Let me do it. I'm very nippy.'

'Yes, you are,' said Fatty. 'All right, you do it, Pip. Now, here's our plan, then. Daisy is to go and hide in a bush at the farther end of the big greenhouse where Miss Harmer is working. Pip had better hide in a bush near the other end. Daisy will call Miss Harmer, and as soon as she pops out of one door, you pop in at the other, Pip, and get the key. See ? '

' It sounds easy,' said Pip, ' but I bet it won't be as easy as it sounds ! Are you and Larry and Bets going to wait for me by the cat-house ? '

' Yes,' said Fatty. ' Come on, let's get going, or Miss Harmer will put on her coat again ! '

Daisy and Pip left the others and crept through the bushes to the greenhouses. Miss Harmer was still at work near the other end. Daisy settled herself in a thick bush near the farther end. She waited until she saw that Pip was safely in another bush near the door inside which Miss Harmer's coat was hanging.

Then the whole plan worked as if it had been oiled ! ' Miss Harmer ! MISS HARMER ! ' called Daisy.

Miss Harmer heard. She turned her head and listened. Daisy called again, ' MISS HARMER ! '

Miss Harmer opened the greenhouse door and stepped out. ' Who's calling me ? ' she cried. And at that very moment Miss Trimble appeared, trotting down the path, her glasses set crooked on her nose.

' Oh, Miss Trimble ! Did you call me ? What did you want me for ? ' asked Miss Harmer. Daisy giggled to herself. Now there would be a nice little conversation between Miss Trimble and Miss Harmer.

' No, I didn't call you,' said Miss Trimble, her glasses falling off. ' But I certainly heard someone shouting for you. Would it be Lady Candling ? '

'Why does she want me ?' said Miss Harmer, going up the path. 'Where is she ?'

'She's over by the lawn,' said Miss Trimble. 'I'll show you.'

The two went up the path together and were soon out of sight of the greenhouse. Pip at once saw his chance, slipped in at the other door, went to Miss Harmer's coat and ran his hand quickly through the big pockets. He found the key at once !

Then he and Daisy made their way joyfully through the bushes to the cat-house, where the others were waiting most impatiently for them. 'Here's the key,' said Pip proudly. 'Now, come on, let's hurry up and sniff round the cage.'

'I'll go in with Bets,' said Fatty. 'Not you others, or the cats will have a fit. I've got a very good nose for smelling, and as it was Bets' idea I think she ought to come in too.'

So the two of them went in together, shutting the door carefully behind them. Then they began to sniff round the cage. It smelt of disinfectant. But there was still a distinct smell of turps somewhere.

The children sniffed along the benches. The cats lay peacefully and watched them. One cat put out a playful paw and patted Fatty.

'The smell seems to be on this bench, I think,' said Fatty, after he had sniffed at the floor, the ceiling, the wire-netting, and the benches. 'Here, Bets, sniff just there—don't you think there's a smell of turps there ?'

A big cat was lying on the bench. Bets pushed her gently away so that she could smell. 'No,' said the little girl. 'I can't smell turps on this bench, Fatty.'

315

Fatty sniffed again and looked astonished. 'The smell isn't there now,' he said. 'But it was, a minute ago !'

Bets lifted back the cat she had moved. 'There, Puss,' she said, 'take your place again.'

'Golly ! the smell's come back,' said Fatty, wrinkling up his nose. 'Smell, Bets.'

'Why !' said Bets in surprise, 'it can't be on the bench. It must be on the cat. *I* can smell it now I've put the cat back. But I couldn't before.'

Then, to the amazement and delight of the big Siamese cat, the two children solemnly and carefully sniffed her all over, from head to tail. The cat purred happily. She loved being stroked, she loved being petted ; but being sniffed at was something quite new, and she liked that too.

'Does the cat smell of turps ?' enquired Pip eagerly. Fatty nodded. His face was scarlet with excitement.

'Bets,' he said, 'where do *you* smell the turps on the cat ?'

'Just here,' said Bets, and she bent her small nose down to the middle of the cat's dark tail.

'So do I,' said Fatty. He looked very carefully indeed at the long tail, which the cat was now trying to swing from side to side.

'Fatty ! Bets ! There's someone coming !' cried Larry in a low voice. 'Come out, quick !'

But, alas for Fatty and Bets, Mr. Tupping appeared on the scene before they could get out of the cage ! And *then* there was a storm !

Mr. Tupping stared as if he could not believe his eyes. Fatty and Bets got out of the cage and shut the door, turning the key in the lock. Bets was trembling. Fatty did not feel at all comfortable himself. The other children had disappeared into the friendly shelter of the bushes.

'What you doing in there?' demanded Tupping. 'How did you get the key? I believe it's you children that have been tinkering about with them cats, making them disappear! Ho! yes, that's what it is! You're the thieves, you are! I'm going straight off to Mr. Goon to tell him about you—then you'll be in a pretty pickle I can tell you. And serve you right too!'

21   SOLVING THE MYSTERY

MR. TUPPING went off, and his face was not pleasant to see. Bets was terrified. She clutched Fatty, and her face turned very pale. Fatty himself looked a bit shaken.

In silence the five got over the wall and made their way to the summer-house.

'Golly! That was a bit of bad luck,' said Larry. Bets began to cry.

'Shall we be put into prison now?' she sobbed. 'Oh, I do feel frightened.'

'Frit, you mean,' said Larry, trying to make her smile. But Bets was beyond smiling. 'Don't be frit, Bets. It's all right. We'll have to tell Inspector Jenks about it : how we took the key, and how you and Fatty sniffed all round the cat-house. Then he won't believe old Clear-Orf if he puts in a report to say he and Tupping suspect *us* of taking Dark Queen!'

Fatty was very silent. The others looked at him.

'Are you frit too, Fatty?' said Daisy. It was not like Fatty to be shaken for long. Fatty shook his head and looked very thoughtful.

'Let's think about the smell of turps on that cat's tail,' he said. 'That's more important than being scared of having been found in the cage. It's a queer clue that—the smell of turps on a cat's tail. Why should it be there? And why was it there before, when Dark Queen disappeared?'

'You said turps was used to get paint-brushes clean, or to get smears of paint off anything,' said Bets, drying her eyes. 'Do you suppose the cat had got against some wet paint or something, and the paint was cleaned off with turps?'

Fatty stared at her. Then he leapt to his feet with a yell, and smacked the summer-house table hard with his hand. His face went very red.

'What's up?' said Larry in alarm. 'Have you sat on a wasp or something?'

'Listen,' said Fatty, sitting down again, looking terribly excited. 'Young Bets has got hold of the right idea. Turps *was* used to get paint off that cat's tail. And how did the paint get there, and what colour was it? Well, we know the colour, because we've got the tin of paint that was used, and we've got a stone with a blob of that same paint on it—it was creamy-brown.'

The others stared at him. Fatty got the tin out from behind the loose board and opened it. He dipped the brush into the tin and then dabbed it on the dark-brown summer-house table.

'Look at that,' he said. 'See that creamy patch? Well, that's what must have been on the cat's tail—in the middle of it—creamy-brown paint ! And now, I ask you, what other cat has a patch of creamy-brown hairs on her tail ? '

' Dark Queen ! ' said everyone at once. Eyes gleamed, and faces grew red with excitement as the five children worked out all that the turps and the paint meant.

' Yes,' said Fatty. ' And that cat whose tail smelt of turps must have had a ring of hairs in her dark tail painted a light colour, so that she might be mistaken for Dark Queen, and then the paint on her tail was rubbed off with strong turps—that's why the cage smelt of turps both times. It was done both times.'

' Golly ! ' said Larry. ' This is frightfully exciting. Somebody made a very clever plan. Let me see ! I suppose Dark Queen was stolen away in the morning, and the other cat's tail painted to make her seem as if she was Dark Queen—everyone knew Dark Queen had a ring of paler hairs in her tail where she had been bitten.'

' Yes ; and then people came and had a look at the cats—like your mother did, Pip, with Lady Candling—and they thought the painted cat was Dark Queen ; and then later on Tupping managed to get into the cage and wipe off the paint before anyone noticed it, and said Dark Queen was gone ! '

' *Tupping !* ' said Bets, her eyes getting large and round. ' *Tupping*, did you say ? But if Tupping took *off* the paint—then Tupping must have put it *on*—and he must have been the one who stole Dark Queen, and——'

' Yes. It was Tupping. It simply must have been,' said Fatty, almost beside himself with excitement. ' Would you believe it ? And he put the blame on Luke all the time.'

'And made old Luke work beside the cages the whole time the painted cat was there till the time when he wiped off the paint and said Dark Queen was gone!' said Pip. 'So that it seemed as if no one but Luke could possibly have stolen her! What a clever plan.'

'Then, when he heard Bets tell Clear-Orf we had got clues of a smell and a smear of paint, he got the wind up and hid them both,' said Fatty. 'Afraid of finger-prints on them or something, perhaps. And old Buster found them.'

'Let's get it all quite clear,' said Daisy. 'Tupping wants to steal Dark Queen and put the blame on Luke. He waits till Miss Harmer is out for the day—because, I suppose, he guesses she knows each cat so well that she wouldn't be deceived by painted hairs in a tail—she'd know it wasn't Dark Queen.'

'Yes; so he waits till she's out, and then he steals Dark Queen, hands her over to someone, goes back to the cage, paints the other cat's tail to make it seem like Dark Queen's, sees that somebody has a look at the cats and says that Dark Queen is there —like Lady Candling did at four o'clock the first time, with your mother, Pip; and Lady Candling again, with Tupping, the second time, at three o'clock.' Fatty paused and Larry went on.

'Yes; and the first time he's very, very clever. He brings back the village policeman himself to see the cats, manages to rub off the paint with a turpy rag, and then announces to Clear-Orf that Dark Queen is stolen! I must say Tupping is very cunning,' said Larry. 'What a nerve he must have, taking the bobby himself into the cage after he'd stolen the cat that morning.'

'He managed to trick Miss Harmer herself

nicely, too, the second time,' said Pip. 'You remember he slipped into the cage when she came back that second time, and he must have again rubbed off the paint, and then said Dark Queen was gone. That's how it was he managed to deceive everyone. They all thought, including Luke, that Dark Queen was there all the time Luke was beside the cage—but she wasn't. She had gone in the morning. So no wonder it was difficult to clear Luke of blame.'

'I suppose Dark Queen must have escaped from whoever had her, and wandered back, that first time,' said Daisy. 'I wonder where she is now.'

'Tupping will have to explain a good deal, I think,' said Fatty. 'Golly! I'm glad he's the thief! I couldn't bear to think it might be old Luke. Wasn't he awful the way he put Luke's whistles into the cage to make everyone think it was Luke?'

'Will Tupping go to prison?' asked Bets.

'Of course!' said Fatty.

'Oooh! then Luke won't have to work under him any more,' said Bets, pleased.

'It's funny to think Tupping has gone off to old Clear-Orf to report Bets and me for being in the cat-house this morning,' said Fatty. 'I wonder what we ought to do.'

'Let's telephone to Inspector Jenks again,' said Pip. 'Now that we have solved the mystery we ought to let him know. And anyway, I don't want Clear-Orf coming and arresting Bets or anything like that!'

Bets gave a little scream. Fatty put his arm round her, laughing.

'It's all right, Bets. No one can harm you. You haven't done anything wrong. I think it's a good idea of Pip's to telephone to the Inspector.'

'What about the key of the cat-house?' said Larry. 'Oughtn't we to put that back in Miss Harmer's pocket?'

'Yes. We'll go and do that now,' said Fatty. 'At least I don't see why we shouldn't just hand it to her and say we borrowed it. She'll be surprised and cross, but after all, it's got to come out that we took it, so we might as well own up to it now.'

The five children and Buster went over the wall. They hunted about for Miss Harmer but could not see her. 'Perhaps she's in one of the sheds,' said Fatty. They went towards a shed near the greenhouses, one they had not been into before. Fatty put his head inside.

'Hallo!' he said, 'this is where Tupping keeps his things. Look! there are his rubber boots and his mack.'

'What a smell of turps again,' said Bets, sniffing.

'You're right,' said Fatty, and he sniffed too.

The boy suddenly pulled a dirty handkerchief out of the old mack hanging up. It was marked with Tupping's name, and smelt strongly of turps.

'He soaked this hanky with turps and used it to rub off the paint he had put on that cat's tail!' said Fatty. 'Another clue! Let me see! It had been raining, hadn't it, the night before, and that morning too—so Tupping would have been wearing a mack—and rubber boots too. I say, look there!'

The children looked, and there, splashed on the toes of the rubber boots, were drops of the creamy-brown paint! Tupping must have worn the boots when he painted the cat's tail ! And it was he, of course, who must have dropped a blob of the paint on to the stone that Fatty had in his pocket. Probably off the paint-brush.

' We'll take these boots, and the hanky too,' said Fatty importantly. ' Come on, Buster. We've got some mighty good clues and bits of evidence, I must say. What a shock dear Mr. Tupping is going to get when he hears all we have to say.'

They went out of the shed and came face to face with Luke, who still looked very gloomy. ' You're going to get into trouble,' he said to Fatty. ' Tupping's gone down to get Goon, because he says he found you in the cat-house, and he says it must have been you children who took that cat. I suppose he's going to make out that you did it when I was there, and I didn't let on, so as to shield you. You're going to get into trouble ! '

22   THE END OF IT ALL

FATTY went off to telephone to Inspector Jenks. He was lucky enough to get him straight away.

' Please, Inspector Jenks,' said Fatty, ' we've solved the Mystery of the Disappearing Cat. Could you possibly come over and let us tell you ? '

' Well,' said the Inspector, ' I've just had a most mysterious message from Goon—something about finding you children in the cat-house, and saying he thought you had something to do with the disappearance of the cat—and I was thinking of coming over anyway.'

'Oh, good!' said Fatty joyfully. 'Are you coming to Lady Candling's?'

'Yes, that would be best,' said the Inspector. 'Meet me there in an hour's time, will you?'

Fatty went back to tell the others—to find them all in a state of great indignation. Mr. Goon had been to Bets' mother and complained to her that the little girl had been caught trespassing in the cat-house. He had now gone to tell Fatty's mother that Fatty had been caught there too.

'Mummy is frightfully cross with me,' said Bets, with tear-stained eyes. 'You weren't here, Fatty, so I didn't like to say anything in case I gave away something you didn't want me to give away. So I said nothing at all, and Mummy scolded me dreadfully.'

'Never mind, Bets,' said Fatty. 'The Inspector will soon be here, and once he hears our story he will soon put things right. We've got to meet him at Lady Candling's in an hour's time. We must take all our clues with us.'

So, carrying one bottle of turps, one tin of paint, one old paint-brush, one stone smeared with paint, one hanky smelling of turps, and one pair of rubber boots spotted with paint, the children set off down Pip's drive and up Lady Candling's drive in an hour's time.

'The only clue we *couldn't* bring was the smell on the cat's tail,' said Bets. 'And that was really the most important clue of all.'

'And it was you who smelt it,' said Fatty. 'I must say I think you've been a very good Find-Outer this time, little Bets.'

'Look! there's Mr. Goon going into the house,' said Daisy. 'And that's Tupping with him. And

324

here comes Luke. Hallo, Luke! Where are you going ? '

' Been told to wash myself and go up to the house,' said Luke, who looked both gloomy and scared.

' Are you frit ? ' asked Fatty.

' Yes, I'm frit,' said Luke

' Well, don't be,' said Fatty. ' Everything is going to be all right. You'll see. Cheer up."

But Luke could not cheer up. He walked off to wash and clean himself, looking very downcast, just as the Inspector's black car drove smartly up the drive and came to a stop. The big Inspector got out and smiled at the children. He beckoned to them.

' Who's the guilty person ? ' he said.

' Tupping,' said Fatty with a grin. ' I bet you guessed it, Inspector, though you didn't have any clues or anything.'

' Well, I didn't think it was Luke, and I did think Mr. Tupping was the type,' said the Inspector. ' Also I happened to know what neither you nor Mr. Goon knew, that he has been mixed up in a thieving case before—dogs, it was, as far as I remember. Well, you go on in. I'm just coming.'

Everyone was gathered together in Lady Candling's big drawing-room. Lady Candling was there, Miss Harmer, and Miss Trimble too, her glasses falling off almost every second. To look at her anyone would think she had been the thief, for she was so nervous, and her hands were trembling and shaking.

' Sit down, children,' said Lady Candling. Fatty had left outside the door some of their clues, feeling that it would not do to let Tupping see his rubber boots, the tin of paint, or the bottle of turps. The boy did not want the surly gardener put on his guard if he could help it. The children sat down, and Fatty took Buster on his knee to stop him from sniffing round Mr. Goon's ankles.

The Inspector came in and shook hands with Lady Candling. He smiled at the children, and nodded to Mr. Goon.

'I think we'd better all sit down,' he said. Everyone sat down. Mr. Goon looked important and stern. He gave Bets and Fatty a severe glance. Aha! those interfering children were going to get into Very Serious Trouble now! Tupping had reported to him that they had actually taken the key and been found inside the cat-house.

'Well, Goon,' said the Inspector, 'I got a rather mysterious message from you this morning—sufficiently serious for me to think of coming over.'

'Yes, sir. It *is* serious, sir,' said Mr. Goon, swelling up with importance. 'I have reason to believe, sir, that these here interfering children know more about the disappearance of that valuable cat than we think. I think, sir, they're in for Very Serious Trouble, and a good warning from you will do them a World of Good.'

'Well, I think it *is* quite possible that these children do know more about this mystery than you think, Goon,' said Inspector Jenks. 'We'll ask them, shall we?'

He turned to Fatty. 'Perhaps you, Frederick Trotteville, would like to say a few words?'

There was nothing that Fatty wanted more. He swelled up almost as importantly as Goon had done.

326

'I should like to say, Inspector, that we Five Find-Outers know who stole Dark Queen,' said Fatty, very loudly and clearly. Tupping gave one of his snorts, and so did Goon. Luke looked thoroughly scared. Miss Trimble's glasses fell off, much to Bets' delight.

'Go on, Frederick,' said the Inspector.

'I should like to explain, sir, exactly how the theft was committed,' said Fatty. The others looked at him admiringly. Fatty always knew the right words to use!

'We should like to hear you, if I may say so,' said the Inspector gravely, with a little twinkle in his eyes.

'Well, Inspector, Dark Queen was stolen twice, as you know,' said Fatty. 'Both times Miss Harmer was out, and Mr. Tupping was in charge of the cats. Well, sir, Dark Queen was *not* stolen in the afternoon each time—but in the *morning*.'

Everyone but the children appeared to be greatly surprised. Mr. Goon's mouth fell open, and he stared at Fatty in astonishment.

'Now that . . .' he began—but Inspector Jenks stopped him.

'Don't interrupt, Goon,' he said. And old Clear-Orf dared say no more.

'I'll tell you how it was all done,' said Fatty, enjoying himself immensely. 'The thief stole Dark Queen out of the cage in the morning; but he cleverly painted a ring of hairs a creamy colour in another cat's tail, so that to anyone not knowing the cats extremely well that other cat seemed to be Dark Queen!'

There was a chorus of exclamations. Miss Trimble's glasses fell off immediately.

'Well,' went on Fatty, 'you can see that any-one coming to see the cats in the afternoon would think Dark Queen was there—but she wasn't. Then, when the right moment came, the thief hopped into the cage, rubbed the paint off the cat's tail with a rag soaked in turps, and then announced that Dark Queen was missing! So, of course, everyone thought the cat must have been stolen in the afternoon, whereas she had been taken in the morning.'

'And that's why everyone thought it was *me* that took the cat,' broke in Luke. 'Because I was the only one near the cage in the afternoons, and no one came near but me.'

'Yes,' said Fatty. 'That was part of the plan, Luke. The blame was to be put on to you. That was why you were set to work near the cat-house each time, and that was why a whistle of yours was dropped into the cage each time too.'

'Who was it?' demanded Luke, his face going scarlet with rage. 'Just let me get my hands on him, that's all!'

The Inspector sent a glance at Luke and the boy sat back, saying no more.

'How do you know all this?' asked Mr. Goon, his face a mixture of amazement, disbelief, and scorn. 'It's just a silly make-up. You got to have proof of these things before you can say them.'

'We *have* got proof,' said Fatty triumphantly. He put his hand into his pocket. 'Look! here is the bottle of turps. It was hidden down a rabbit-hole, with a tin of light-brown paint, used for the cat's tail, and an old paint-brush. Larry, get the other things. They're outside the door.'

Fatty brandished the bottle of turps and the paint-brush for everyone to see. Miss Trimble's glasses fell off again, and she was too nervous to replace them. She stared at the clues with short-sighted eyes, and looked at Fatty as if he was the greatest detective in the world.

Larry brought in the rubber boots and the tin of paint. He set them down before Fatty. Tupping's eyes nearly fell out of his head when he saw his own boots there.

'Now,' said Fatty, picking up the tin of paint, 'here's the paint that was used. Buster found the rabbit-hole in which it was hidden. Didn't you, Buster?'

'Woof,' said Buster, pleased.

'These boots were worn by the thief, the man who painted the cat's tail,' said Fatty, and he pointed to the drops of light-brown paint on them. 'And this is the handkerchief he soaked with turps, and used to wipe off the paint as quickly as possible from the cat's tail when he went into the cage—first time with Mr. Goon, second time with Miss Harmer.'

'May I see that handkerchief?' said the Inspector with great interest. He took it and smelt it. The smell of turps was still very strong on it. Fatty took the stone from his pocket, the one with the smear of light-brown paint on it. He handed it to the Inspector too.

'We found that just outside the cage, sir,' he said. 'That was one of our clues. The other clue was the smell of turps in the cat-house. Little Bets spotted that. She was a splendid Find-Outer.'

Bets went red with joy. The Inspector beamed at her. He looked again at the handkerchief.

'This handkerchief has someone's name on it,'
he said. 'I imagine it is the name of the thief?'

Fatty nodded. Luke leaned forward.

'Who is it?' he said. 'Go on! you tell me
who it is.'

'Yes, whoever is it?' said Miss Harmer.

The Inspector looked gravely round the little
company. Tupping had gone pale, and he kept
swallowing hard. All his insolence and conceit had
gone—he was more 'frit' than Luke had ever been.
One by one the others looked at Tupping and knew
who was the thief.

'Tupping, what have you to say about all this?'
said the Inspector in a voice gone hard as iron.

'What, it's *Tupping*!' said Mr. Goon in a
half-choked voice, and he glared at the gardener with
hatred and scorn. '*You!* Sucking up to me:
taking me into the cage with you; telling me a pack
of lies and making me look foolish like this!'

'Well, Bets told you we had two clues, a smell
and a stone with paint on,' said Fatty. 'And you
only laughed.'

'Tupping, where is the cat?' said the Inspector,
still in the same hard voice. 'You understand that
there is no possibility of the charge made against
you being false. There are other things, in your
past, which fit in very well with this.'

Tupping crumpled up completely. From a
harsh, cruel, bad-tempered man he turned into
a weeping coward, and it was not a pleasant
sight.

'Bullies are always cowards,' Fatty whispered
to Larry. 'Now you can see what he's really like
underneath!'

'You're frit,' said Luke to Tupping, in the

deepest scorn. ' More frit than ever I was. Serves you right.'

This was what everyone was thinking. Suddenly Tupping began to pour out a confession. Yes, he had stolen Dark Queen. He had owed money to someone, and he had thought of taking the cat. He'd tell who had got it and the police could get it back. He *had* tried to put the blame on Luke. He *had* painted the other cat's tail, and he *had* used turps to get off the paint quickly. He'd done it twice, because the first time the cat had escaped and come back. He was sorry now. He'd never do a thing like that again.

' You certainly won't, for some time at least,' said Inspector Jenks grimly. ' You will be in a safe place, out of harm's way, and I don't think anyone will be sorry. Goon, take him away.'

Goon put a heavy hand on Tupping's shoulder and jerked him to his feet. He looked with great scorn at his prisoner.

' You come-alonga-me,' he said in a fierce tone. The Inspector spoke to Goon in an icy voice.

' You do not seem to have shone at all in this case, Goon,' he said. ' You appear to have made enemies of those who were on the right track, and to have actually made friends with the thief himself. I hope in future you will be a little more careful. I trust you agree with me ? '

' Er—yes, sir ; certainly, sir,' said poor Goon, looking very woeful all of a sudden. ' Did my best, sir.'

' Well, very fortunately these children did better than your best, Goon,' said the Inspector. ' I think we can be very grateful to them for their work in solving the Mystery of the Disappearing Cat. I hope that is your opinion too, Goon ? '

' Oh yes, sir,' said Goon, purple in the face now. ' Very clever children, sir. Pleasure to know them, sir.'

' Ah ! I'm glad you agree with me,' said Inspector Jenks in a more amiable voice. ' Now, please remove that man.'

Goon removed Tupping. The children heaved a sigh of relief. ' Well, he's gone ! ' said Daisy. ' And I hope he never comes back.'

' He will certainly not come back here,' said Lady Candling, who had listened to everything in the greatest astonishment. ' As for poor Luke, I hate to think of all he has gone through because of that wicked Tupping.'

' That's all right, your Ladyship,' said Luke, beaming all over his face, forgetting his anger with Tupping because of the kindness in Lady Candling's voice. ' If you'll keep me on, Madam, I'll work hard for you till you get a new gardener. And I'll never forget these here clever children—it fair beats me how they solved that mystery.'

' It was really Bets who put us on the right track,' said Fatty. ' Good old Bets ! '

' Oh, we all did it together,' said Bets. ' Buster too. Well, I *am* glad everything's turned out all right, and I expect you'll get your cat back, won't you, Lady Candling ? '

' We'll see to that,' said Inspector Jenks, getting up. ' Well, I must go ; and once more, allow me to say that I am very pleased to have had the help of the Five Find-Outers—and Dog ! I trust I may have your help again in the future. I hope you agree with me ? '

332

'Oh *yes*!' said all the Find-Outers, going out to the car with the big Inspector. 'We'll let you know at once if we've got another Mystery to Solve!'

Another Mystery? Well, I expect they'll have one all right. I must tell you about that another time!

THE MYSTERY OF
THE SECRET ROOM

CONTENTS

HOME FROM SCHOOL

PIP set out his painting things, poked the playroom fire, and sat down to finish his Christmas cards.

' You do them nicely, Pip,' said Bets, looking over his shoulder. ' I wish I could keep inside the lines like you do.'

' You're only little yet,' said Pip, beginning to paint red berries on his card.

' Well, I've had another birthday, and I'm nine now,' said Bets. ' I'm getting bigger. You're still twelve, Pip, so I'm only three years behind you now.'

' When are the others coming ? ' asked Pip, looking at the clock. ' I told them to come early. It's fun to do our Christmas presents together.'

Bets went to the window of their big playroom. ' Here come Larry and Daisy,' she said. ' Oh, Pip, isn't it fun to be altogether again ? '

Bets didn't go to boarding-school as the others did, and she often felt lonely in term-time, when her brother Pip was away, and their three friends, Larry and Daisy Daykin, and Fatty Trotteville.

But now it was Christmas holidays and they were all home. Bets felt very happy. She had her brother again, and Christmas was coming—and darling Buster, Fatty's dog, would come to see her every single day.

Larry and Daisy came up the stairs to the playroom. ' Hallo ! ' said Larry. ' Finished your cards yet ? I've still got three to do, and Daisy's got a present to finish. We brought them along.'

' Good,' said Pip, putting his paintbrush into his

mouth to give it a nice point. 'There's plenty of room at the table. Fatty's not here yet.'

A loud barking outside sent Bets to the window again. 'It's Buster—and Fatty,' she said. 'Oh, good! Fatty looks plumper than ever!'

In half a minute Fatty and Buster were in the playroom, Fatty looking very sleek and pleased with himself, and Buster bursting with excitement. He flew at every one and licked them thoroughly.

'Hallo, Buster dear!' said Bets. 'Oh, Fatty, Buster's got thin and you've got fat.'

'Well, Fatty won't be any thinner after Christmas,' said Larry, settling down at the table. 'Brought some cards to finish, Fatty? I've just about worked down my list?'

Larry and Daisy were brother and sister. Fatty was an only child, always rather pleased with himself, and Buster was his faithful companion. The five and Buster were firm friends.

Fatty put down a fat book on the table, and a very fine Christmas card, which he had done himself. Bets pounced on it at once.

'Fatty! What a beauty! Surely you didn't do this yourself? Gracious, it's as good as any you can find in a shop.'

'Oh, well,' said Fatty, looking pleased, 'I'm not bad at art, you know. I was top again this term, and the art master said——'

'Shut up,' said Pip, Larry, and Daisy together. Fatty did so love to boast about his cleverness. They wouldn't let him if they could help it.

'All right, all right,' said Fatty, looking injured. 'Always biting my head off! I've a good mind not to tell you who the card is for?'

'For your flattering art master, I suppose,' said Pip, painting a holly leaf carefully.

Fatty kept silence. Bets looked at him. 'Tell me who it's for,' she said. 'I want to know. I think it's lovely.'

'Well, as a matter of fact, I meant this card and this book to go to a friend of ours from *all* of us !' said Fatty. 'But seeing that only Bets admires the card, I'll just send it from myself.'

The others looked up. 'Who's it for then ?' asked Daisy. She picked it up. 'It's jolly good. Are these five children meant to be us ? And is this Buster ? '

'Yes,' said Fatty. 'Can't you guess who the card is for ? It's for Inspector Jenks.'

'Oh ! What a good idea !' said Bets. 'Is the book for him, too ? What is it ? '

She picked it up and opened it. It was a book about fishing.

'That's a fine idea, Fatty,' said Larry. 'The Inspector is mad on fishing. He'll be thrilled with the book and the card. Do send them from all of us. They're fine.'

'I meant to,' said Fatty. 'We can share the price of the book between us, and we can each write our name on the card. See what I've put inside it.'

He flicked it open, and the children bent to see what he had printed there, in beautiful, neat letters :

'BEST CHRISTMAS WISHES FROM THE FIVE FIND-OUTERS—AND DOG.'

'That's fine,' said Pip. 'Golly, we've had some fun, haven't we, being the Find-Outers ? I hope we'll have some more mysteries to solve.'

'We've solved the Mystery of the Burnt Cottage and the Mystery of the Disappearing Cat,' said Daisy. 'I wonder what our next mystery will be. Do you think we shall have a mystery these hols ? '

' Shouldn't be surprised,' said Fatty. ' Any one seen old Clear-Orf yet ? '

Clear-Orf was the village policeman, Mr. Goon, detested by the children. He in turn detested them, especially as twice they had managed to solve problems before he himself had.

No one had seen Mr. Goon. Nobody particularly wanted to. He was not an amiable person at all, with his fat red face and bulging frog-eyes.

' We'd better all sign this card,' said Fatty, producing a very fine fountain pen. Fatty always had the best of everything, and far too much pocket-money. However, he was always willing to share this, so nobody minded.

' Eldest first,' said Pip, so Larry took the pen. He was thirteen. He signed his name neatly, ' Laurence Daykin.'

' I'm next,' said Fatty. ' I'm thirteen next week. You're not thirteen till the New Year, Pip.'

He signed his name, ' Frederick Algernon Trotteville.'

' I bet you never sign your full initials, Fatty,' said Pip, taking the pen next—' " F. A. T." '

' Well, I don't,' said Fatty. ' You wouldn't either, if you had my initials and were fat. It would be just asking for trouble.'

Pip signed his name, 'Philip Hilton.' Then Daisy signed hers, ' Margaret Daykin.'

' Now you, little Bets,' said Fatty, handing her the pen. ' Best writing, please.'

Sticking her tongue well out, Bets signed her full name in rather straggling writing, ' Elizabeth Hilton,' but after it she wrote, ' Bets.'

' Just in case he forgets that Elizabeth is me,' she explained.

' He wouldn't,' said Fatty. ' I bet he never

forgets a thing. He's very clever. You aren't made an inspector of police unless you've got brains. We're lucky to have him for our friend.'

They were—but the Inspector liked and admired the Five Find-Outers too. They had been of great help to him in two difficult cases.

' I hope we can be Find-Outers again,' said Bets.

' I think we ought to find a better name,' said Fatty, putting the cap back on his fountain-pen. 'It's a silly name, I think — the Find-Outers. Nobody would know we were first-class detectives.'

' Well, we're not,' said Larry. ' We're not really detectives at all, though we like to think we are. The name we have is just right—we're only children who find out things.'

Fatty didn't like that. ' We're more than that,' he said, settling down at the table. ' Didn't we beat old Goon twice ? I don't mind telling you I'm going to be a famous detective when I'm grown up, I think I've got just the mind for it.'

' The conceit to think so, you mean,' said Pip, grinning. ' You don't really know much about detectives and the way they work, Fatty.'

' Oh, don't I ! ' said Fatty, beginning to wrap up the book on fishing together with the Christmas card. ' That's all *you* know, see ? I've been studying hard. I've been reading spy books and detective books all the term.'

' Well, I bet you were bottom of the form then,' said Larry. ' You can't do that sort of thing and work, too.'

' *I* can,' said Fatty. ' I was top of the form in everything. I always am. You won't believe my maths marks—I only lost——'

' He's off again,' said Pip to Larry. ' He's like a gramophone record, isn't he ? '

Fatty subsided and glared at Pip. 'All right,' he said. 'Say what you like—but I bet you don't know how to do invisible writing, or get out of a locked room when the key isn't your side!'

The others stared at him. 'You don't know either,' said Pip disbelievingly.

'Well, I do then,' said Fatty. 'Those are two of the things I've learnt already. And I could teach you a simple code, too, a secret code.'

This sounded exciting. Bets stared at Fatty with eyes wide.

'Teach us all those things,' she begged. 'Oh, Fatty, I would so like to do invisible writing.'

'You have to learn the art of disguising yourself too,' said Fatty, enjoying the rapt attention of the others.

'What's disguising?' asked Bets.

'Oh, dressing yourself up in such a way that people don't know it's you,' said Fatty. 'Putting a wig on and perhaps a moustache or different eyebrows, wearing different clothes. For instance, I could disguise myself quite well as a butcher's boy if I had a striped apron, and a knife or something hung down from my belt. If I wore an untidy black wig too, I bet none of you would know me.'

This was really too exciting for words. All the children loved dressing up and pretending. This business of 'disguising' seemed a glorified dressing-up.

'Are you going to practise disguising yourself next term?' asked Bets.

'Well—no, not in term-time,' said Fatty, thinking that his form master would soon see through any disguise. 'But I thought I might these hols.'

'Oh, Fatty! Can we too?' said Daisy. 'Let's *all* practise being proper detectives, in case another mystery crops up. We could do it much better then.'

'And if another mystery *doesn't* crop up, we'll have the fun of practising for it anyway,' said Bets.

'Right,' said Fatty, 'but I think if I am going to teach you all these things I ought to be head of the Find-Outers, not Larry. I know Larry's the oldest —but I think I know more about these things now.'

There was a silence. Larry didn't want to give up being head, though in fairness he had to admit that Fatty was really the cleverest at spotting things when they had a mystery to solve.

'Well, what about it?' said Fatty. 'I shan't give away my secrets if you don't make me head.'

'Let him be head, Larry,' said Bets, who admired Fatty tremendously. 'Head of the next mystery anyway, whatever it is. If he isn't as clever as you at solving it, then we could make you head again.'

'All right,' said Larry. 'I do think Fatty would make a good head, really. But if you get conceited about it, Fatty, we'll sit on you hard.'

'You needn't tell me that,' said Fatty, with a grin. 'Right-o! I'll be head. Thanks, Larry, that was sporting of you. Now I can teach you some of the things I know. After all, you simply never know when they might come in useful.'

'It might be very, very important to be able to write a letter in invisible ink,' said Bets. 'Oh, Fatty, do teach us something now.'

But Bets' mother just then put her head in at the playroom.

'I've got tea ready for you downstairs. Wash your hands and come along, will you? Don't be too long, because the scones are nice and hot.'

Five hungry children and an equally hungry dog

shot off downstairs, forgetting everything for the moment but hot scones, strawberry jam, and cake. But they wouldn't forget for long—things sounded too exciting !

2   FATTY HAS SOME IDEAS

CHRISTMAS came so quickly, and there was so much to do that Fatty had no time to teach the Find-Outers any of the things he had learnt.   The postman came continually to the three homes, and cards soon stood everywhere.   Parcels were hidden away. Mince-pies were made.   Large turkeys hung in the larders.

' I do love Christmas,' said Bets a hundred times a day.   ' I wonder what I shall get on Christmas morning.   I do hope I get a new doll.   I'd like one that opens and shuts its eyes properly.   I've only got one doll that does that, and her eyes always stick shut.   Then I have to shake her hard, and I'm sure she thinks I'm cross with her.'

' Baby ! ' said Pip.   ' Fancy still wanting dolls ! I bet you won't get one.'

To Bets' great disappointment there was no doll for her in her Christmas parcels.   Every one thought that as she was now nine, and liked to say she was getting big, she wouldn't want a doll.   So her mother had given her a work-basket and her father a difficult jigsaw which she knew Pip would like much better than she would !

She was rather sad—but Fatty put everything right by coming round on Christmas morning with a big box for Bets—and inside was the doll she had wanted ! It opened and shut its eyes without any shaking at all, and had such a smiling face that Bets lost her heart to it at once. She flung herself on Fatty and hugged him like a small bear.

He was pleased. He liked Bets. Mrs. Hilton was surprised at the beautiful doll.

' That is very kind of you, Frederick,' she said. ' You shouldn't have spent so much money on Bets, though.'

' I shall have plenty for my birthday,' said Fatty politely, ' and I've had heaps for Christmas, Mrs. Hilton. I asked for money this Christmas instead of toys or books.'

' I should have thought you had plenty without asking for any more,' said Mrs. Hilton, who privately thought that Fatty always had far too much money to spend. ' Why did you want so much money ? '

' Well—to spend on something I didn't think people would give me,' said Fatty, looking rather uncomfortable. ' It's a bit of a secret, really, Mrs. Hilton.'

' Oh,' said Bets' mother. ' Well, I hope it's nothing that will get you into trouble. I don't want Mr. Goon, the policeman, round here complaining about you children any more.'

' Oh *no*, Mrs. Hilton,' Fatty assured her. ' Mr. Goon doesn't come into this at all."

As soon as her mother had gone Bets turned to Fatty with sparkling eyes. ' What's the secret ? What are you going to buy ? '

' Disguises ! ' said Fatty, dropping his voice to a whisper. ' Wigs ! Eyebrows ! Teeth ! '

' Oooh—*teeth* ! ' said Bets, in wonder. ' But how can you wear false teeth without having your real teeth out, Fatty ? '

' You wait and see,' said Fatty mysteriously.

'Do come after Christmas as soon as you can and teach us how to write invisibly and how to get out of locked rooms,' begged Bets. 'I say—I wonder if old Clear-Orf knows those things?'

'Course not!' said Fatty scornfully. 'And if Clear-Orf tried to disguise himself it wouldn't be a bit of good. We'd always know his frog's eyes and big fat nose.'

Bets giggled. She hugged her doll, and thought how clever and kind Fatty was. She said so.

'Oh, well,' said Fatty, swelling up a little, prepared to boast to his heart's content, 'I'm——

But just then Pip came into the room and Fatty stopped. Pip didn't take kindly to Fatty's boasting. Fatty had a few words with Pip and then went.

'I'll come along after Christmas and give you all some Find-Outer lessons,' he promised. 'Give my love to Daisy and Larry if you see them to-day. I've got to go over to my grandmother's for Christmas with my mother and father.'

Bets told Pip what Fatty had said about spending his money on disguises. 'He said he would buy wigs—and eyebrows—and teeth!' said Bets. 'Oh, Pip, do you think he will? What shop sells things like that? I've never seen any.'

'Oh, I suppose they are shops that actors go to,' said Pip. 'They have to buy things like that. Well, we'll see what Fatty gets. We ought to have some fun.'

When the excitement of Christmas was over, the Christmas trees taken down and re-planted in the garden, and the cards sent away to a children's hospital, the children felt rather flat. Fatty apparently was staying at his grandmother's, for they saw nothing of him, and had a post-card saying, 'Back soon. Fatty.'

'I wish he'd come back,' said Bets. 'Suppose a mystery cropped up? We'd have to be Find-Outers again—and our chief wouldn't be here.'

'Well, there isn't any mystery,' said Pip.

'How do you know?' said Bets. 'Old Clear-Orf might be trying to solve one we don't know about.'

'Well, ask him then,' said Pip impatiently, for he was trying to read, and Bets kept interrupting him. He didn't really mean Bets to go and ask the policeman, of course. But she couldn't help thinking it was rather a good idea.

'Then we should know if there *was* going to be something for us to solve these hols,' thought the little girl. 'I'm longing to hunt for clues again—and suspects—and track down things.'

So next time she met the policeman she went up to him. 'Mr. Goon, have you got a mystery to solve these holidays?' she asked.

The policeman frowned. He wondered if Bets and the others were on the track of something he didn't know about—else why should Bets want to know if *he* was solving one?

'Are you interfering in anything again?' he asked sternly. 'If you are, you stop it. See? I won't have you children messing about in jobs that properly belong to me. Interfering with the Law!'

'We're not interfering or messing about,' said Bets, rather alarmed.

'Well, you clear orf,' said Mr. Goon. 'You've put a spoke into my wheel before now, and I'm not having it again!'

'What wheel?' said Bets, puzzled. Mr. Goon did one of his snorts and walked off. He couldn't bear any children, but he particularly detested the Five Find-Outers and Dog. Bets stared after him.

' Well, I didn't get much out of him,' she thought. ' What did he mean about wheels ? '

It was lovely when Fatty came back again. He brought Buster with him, of course, and the little Scottie went mad with joy when he saw all his friends.

' He didn't have too good a time at my grand-mother's,' said Fatty. ' There was an enormous ginger cat there that would keep chasing him, and my grandmother insisted on his having a bath every single day. He was awfully miserable really. He would have chased the cat, of course ; but he was too much of a gentleman to go after a cat belonging to his hostess.'

' Have you bought any disguises yet ? ' asked Bets excitedly.

' Just waiting for my birthday,' said Fatty. ' It's to-morrow, as you know. Then, when I've got enough money, I'm going up to London to do a spot of shopping.'

' By yourself ? ' said Larry.

' You bet,' said Fatty. ' What grown-up would let me spend my money on disguises ? Although we've solved two frightfully difficult mysteries, no grown-up would think it was necessary to buy wigs and eyebrows—now would they ? Even though at any moment we might have to solve a third mystery.'

Put like that, it seemed a really urgent matter to buy disguises of all sorts. Fatty was so very serious about it. Bets felt that the third mystery might be just round the corner.

' Fatty, can we try out the disguises when you buy them ? ' she said.

' Of course,' said Fatty. ' We'll have to practise wearing them. It will be fun.'

' Have you brought the invisible ink with you

348

this afternoon ? ' asked Pip. ' That's what I want to see ! '

' Can you see invisible ink ? ' asked Bets. ' I shouldn't have thought you could.'

The others laughed. ' Silly ! The ink isn't invisible—it's only the writing you do with it that is.'

' I've got a bottle,' said Fatty. ' It's very expensive.'

He took a bottle from his pocket. It was quite small, and contained a colourless liquid which, to Bets, looked like water.

Fatty took out his note-book and a pen with a clean new nib. He put the bottle on the table, and undid the screw-top.

' Now I'll write a secret letter,' he said, ' and my writing will be invisible.'

Bets leaned over him to see. She lost her balance and jerked hard against the table. The bottle of invisible ink was jolted over, rolled to the edge of the table, and neatly emptied its contents on the floor in a small round puddle, near Buster.

' Woof ! ' said Buster in surprise, and began to lick it up. But the taste was horrid. He stopped and looked up at the alarmed children, his pink tongue hanging out.

' Oh, Buster ! Buster, you've drunk invisible ink ! ' cried Bets, almost in tears. ' Fatty, will he become invisible ? '

' No, idiot,' said Fatty. ' Well, that's the end of the ink. What a clumsy you are, Bets ! '

' I'm terribly, terribly sorry,' said poor Bets. ' I just sort of slipped. Oh, Fatty, now we can't write in invisible writing.'

Daisy mopped up the rest of the ink. All the children were disappointed. Buster still hung out his tongue, and had such a disgusted look on his face that Larry fetched him some water to take the nasty taste out of his mouth.

'Well, I know one or two more ways of writing invisibly,' said Fatty, much to Bets' relief. 'Any one got an orange? Now, watch out for a little magic!'

3 TWO THRILLING LESSONS

THERE was a dish of oranges in the room. Bets fetched them. She watched with great interest as Fatty made a hole in one, and squeezed the yellow juice into a cup.

'There!' he said; 'orange or lemon juice makes quite good invisible ink, you know.'

The others didn't know. They thought Fatty was very clever immediately to think of some more invisible ink when Bets had upset his bottle.

He took a clean sheet of paper, dipped his pen in the orange juice, and wrote what looked like a letter. He said out loud what he was writing, and it made the children giggle :

'DEAR CLEAR-ORF,—I suppose you think you will solve the next mystery first. Well, you won't. Your brains want oiling a bit. They creak too much. Hugs and kisses from
            'THE FIVE FIND-OUTERS AND DOG.'

The children giggled, especially at the last bit. 'You are an idiot, Fatty,' said Pip. 'It's a good thing old Clear-Orf won't get the letter.'

'Oh, we'll send it all right,' said Fatty, 'but as it's written in invisible ink he won't be able to read it, poor mutt!'

There was nothing to be seen on the sheet of notepaper. The orange-juice ink was certainly invisible!

'But, Fatty, how can any one read invisible writing?' said Daisy.

'Easy,' said Fatty. 'I'll show you how to read *this* kind. Got an electric iron anywhere?'

'Yes,' said Pip. 'But I don't expect Mother would let us have it. She seems to think that anything she lends us is bound to get broken. Anyway, whatever do you want an iron for?'

'Wait and see,' said Fatty. 'Haven't you got an ordinary flat-iron, Pip, if we can't borrow the electric one? There must be one in the kitchen.'

There was. The cook said Pip might have it. 'If you break that, I'll be surprised!' she said, and Pip sped upstairs carrying the heavy old iron.

'Heat it on the fire,' said Fatty. So it was put on the fire, and well heated. When Fatty judged that it was warm enough, he took it off the fire, being careful to hold it with an iron-holder.

'Now watch,' he said, and in excitement they all watched. Fatty ran the iron lightly over the sheet on which he had written his invisible letter.

'There it is! It's all coming up in faint brown letters!' cried Bets, thrilled. 'Look! "My dear Clear-Orf——"'

'"I suppose you will think . . ."' read Pip, in delight. 'Yes, it's visible now. Golly, that's clever, Fatty. I would never have thought that ordinary orange juice could be used as invisible ink!'

'It's better to know that than to know about the proper invisible ink,' said Larry. 'That's expensive, but you only want an orange for this. It's marvellous, Fatty. Let's all write letters.'

So they all took sheets of notepaper and wrote letters in orange-juice ink. They wrote rather cheeky letters to people they didn't like, and squealed with joy when the iron made the writing visible and they each read what the others had written.

' Did you really mean to send old Clear-Orf a letter in invisible ink ? ' asked Daisy, remembering what Fatty had said. ' But what's the point if he can't read it ? '

' Just the fun of the thing,' said Fatty. ' He'll be so wild to get a letter with no writing on it, and he won't know how to read it. We shan't tell him either ! '

Fatty wrote out his first letter to Clear-Orf again, sealed up the apparently blank sheet of paper in an envelope and printed Clear-Orf's name on it.

' It's rather a silly thing to do, I suppose, but it'll puzzle old Clear-Orf,' said Fatty, blotting the envelope. ' Well, now I've taught you to write in invisible ink. Simple, isn't it ? '

' Awfully,' agreed Pip. ' But I don't quite see what use it will be to us, Fatty.'

' You never know,' said Fatty. ' One of us might be captured in one mystery we solve, and we might want to get a message out to the others. If we wrote it in invisible ink our enemies wouldn't be able to read the message.'

Bets thought this sounded rather thrilling, though she didn't very much want to be captured. Then a thought struck her.

' We'll all have to carry an orange about with us, if ever we have enemies,' she said. ' Won't we ? We'd better not take very juicy ones, or they'll get squashed.'

'And we'd have to take a pen,' said Pip. 'Well, I shan't bother till we have enemies.'

'I shall,' said Fatty seriously. 'You never know when you might need to write an invisible message. I take tons of things about with me in my pockets, just in *case* I might need them.'

This was quite true. The others were often amazed at the things Fatty carried about with him. As a rule he had practically anything needed in an emergency from a lemonade-bottle opener to a pocket-knife that contained twelve different kinds of tools.

'My mother goes through my pockets each night and won't let me keep half what I want to,' said Pip.

'My mother never does things like that,' said Fatty. 'She never bothers about my pockets.'

The others thought that it wasn't only Fatty's pockets his mother didn't bother about—it was Fatty himself! He seemed to come and go as he pleased, missed his meals if he didn't want them, went to bed what time he liked, and did more or less as he wanted to.

'Fatty, you said you'd show us how to get out of a locked room if the key wasn't on your side,' said Bets, suddenly remembering. 'There's time to do that, too. Will you?'

'All right,' said Fatty. 'Take me up to one of your boxrooms, where I shall be out of the way. Lock me up, and leave me there. Come down here, and I'll join you in a few minutes.'

'Fibber,' said Larry and Pip together. It really did sound quite impossible.

'Well, try me and see,' said Fatty. 'I don't usually say I can do things if I can't, do I?'

In excitement the children took Fatty upstairs to a big boxroom, with bare boards inside it, and on

353

the landing as well. They put him inside, then turned the key in the lock. Larry tried the door. Yes, it was well and truly locked.

'You're locked in, Fatty,' said Pip. 'We're going down now. If you can get out of here, you're clever ! You can't get out of the window. There's a sheer drop to the ground.'

'I'm not going to try the window,' said Fatty. 'I shall walk out of the door.'

The others went down, feeling rather disbelieving. Fatty surely couldn't be as clever as all that ! Why, it would be like magic if he could go through a locked door !

Only Bets really believed he could. She sat with her eyes on the playroom door, waiting for him to come. Pip got out the ludo board.

'Let's have a game,' he said. 'Old Fatty won't be down for ages, I expect. We shall hear him yelling to be let out in about ten minutes' time ! '

They set the counters in their places. They found the die, and put it in the thrower. Daisy threw first—but before she could move her counter, the door opened and in walked Fatty, grinning all over his plump face.

'Golly ! How *did* you do it ? ' asked Larry, in the greatest surprise.

'I knew you would ! ' squealed Bets.

'*How* did you do it ? ' asked Pip and Daisy, burning with curiosity. 'Go on—tell us.'

'It's easy,' said Fatty, smoothing back his tidy hair. 'Too easy for words.'

'Don't keep on saying that ! Tell us how you did it ! ' said Larry. 'It's extraordinary.'

'Well, come up and I'll show you,' said Fatty. 'As a matter of fact, it's a thing all detectives ought to jolly well know. Elementary.'

'What's elementary?' asked Bets, climbing the stairs behind Fatty.

'What I've just said—too easy for words,' said Fatty. 'Well, here we are. Now, Larry, you lock us all four into the room—Buster too, if you like, or he'll scratch the door down—and then you can all watch what I do. I tell you, it's elementary!'

The three who were locked in with Fatty watched in excitement. They saw the door shut. They heard Larry turn the key in the lock. They each tried the door. Yes, it was locked all right.

'Now watch,' said Fatty. He took a folded newspaper from his pocket and unfolded it. He flattened the big, wide double-sheet. Then, to the children's surprise, he slid the newspaper under the bottom of the door until only a small piece was left his side.

'What have you done that for? That won't open the door!' said Bets. Fatty didn't answer.

He took a piece of wire from his pocket and inserted it into the keyhole. The key was in the other side, where Larry had left it. Fatty jiggled about with the piece of wire, and then suddenly gave a slight push.

There was a thud on the other side of the door. 'I've pushed the key out,' said Fatty. 'Did you hear it fall? Well, the rest is easy! It's fallen on to the newspaper outside—and all I have to do is to pull the paper carefully back—oh, very carefully, —and the key will come with it!'

Holding their breath, the children watched the newspaper being pulled under the door. There was a fair space between door and boards, and the key slid easily under the bottom of the door, appearing inside the room!

Fatty took it, slid it into the lock, turned it—and opened the door!

'There you are!' he said. 'Very simple. Too easy for words! How to get out of a locked room in one minute!'

'Fatty! It's marvellous! I'd never, never have thought of that!' cried Daisy. 'Did you make up the trick yourself?'

Much as Fatty liked the others to think he was marvellous, he was too honest not to admit it wasn't really *his* brain-wave. 'Well, I read it in one of my spy books,' he said, 'and I tried it out when I got locked in for a punishment one afternoon last term. It gave the master a turn, I can tell you, seeing me walk past him after he'd locked me up.'

'It's wonderful,' said Bets. 'So easy, too. There's only one thing, Fatty, though—it wouldn't work if you were locked up in a room that had a carpet going under the door, because there wouldn't be room to pull in the key.'

'You're right, Bets. That's a good point,' said Fatty. 'That's why I wanted to be locked into a boxroom, and not in the playroom downstairs.'

The others were so thrilled with this new trick that they wanted to try it themselves.

'All right,' said Fatty. 'It will be good practice. You simply never know when you might be locked up somewhere. Each of you do it in turn.'

So, much to Mrs. Hilton's surprise, the five children and Buster spent the whole afternoon apparently doing nothing but walk in and out of the cold boxroom, to the accompaniment of squeals and giggles.

'Jolly good, Find-Outers,' said Fatty, when even Bets could escape from the locked room quite easily. 'Jolly good. Now to-morrow I'll go up to London and get some disguises. Look out for some fun the day after!'

NEXT day was Fatty's birthday. He was always sorry it came so near Christmas, because it meant that many people gave him a Christmas and birthday present in one.

'It's bad luck, Fatty,' said Daisy. 'But never mind, *we* won't do that. We'll give you proper birthday presents as well as Christmas presents.'

So, early after breakfast, Pip, Bets, Daisy, and Larry walked up to Fatty's house to give him the presents they had got for him.

'We'd better go early, because Fatty said he was going up to London to buy those disguises,' said Daisy.

'Yes, by himself,' said Bets. 'He's awfully grown-up, isn't he ? '

'I bet he won't be allowed to go up by himself,' said Pip.

Fatty and Buster were delighted to see them. 'I'm so glad you've come,' said Fatty, 'because I wanted to ask you if you'd mind looking after Buster for me whilst I go to London. I'm catching the eleven forty-three.'

'Are you really ? ' said Pip. 'All alone ? '

'Well, as a matter of fact, Mother is coming with me,' said Fatty. 'She's got it into her head that as I don't want a party I'd better have some sort of treat. So we're going to some show or other. But I shall slip off and buy the things I want all right ! '

'I'm sorry you won't be with us on your birthday, Fatty,' said Bets. 'But I hope you'll have a lovely

time. Will you come and see us to-morrow and
show us all you've got ? '

' I may not be able to come down to-morrow,'
said Fatty. ' I may have two or three friends here
—people you don't know. But I'll come as soon as
I can.'

He was very pleased with his presents, especially
with Bets' gift. She had actually managed to knit
him a brown and red tie, and Fatty at once put it
on. Bets felt proud to think he was going up to
London wearing her tie.

' Freddie ! Are you ready ? ' called his mother.
' We mustn't miss the train ! '

' Coming, Mother ! ' sang out Fatty. He took
down his money-box and hurriedly emptied all his
money into his pockets. The others gaped to see
so much—there seemed to be sheaves of ten-shilling
or pound notes !

' My aunts and uncles were only too glad to give
me money instead of having the bother of buying
me presents,' said Fatty, with a grin. ' Don't tell
Mother I've got so much on me. She'd have a
blue fit.'

' Would she really ? ' said Bets, wishing she
could see Mrs. Trotteville in a blue fit. ' Oh, Fatty
—don't get your money stolen, will you ? '

' No detective would be such an idiot as that,'
said Fatty scornfully. ' Don't you worry—the only
person to take money out of my pocket is myself !
Now, Buster, do be a good dog to-day. Come home
to-night by yourself.'

' Woof ! ' said Buster politely. He always seemed
to understand what was said to him.

' Have you left that invisibly written letter at
Mr. Goon's house yet ? ' asked Bets, with a giggle.

' No. I thought I'd send one of my friends down

to-morrow with it,' said Fatty, grinning. 'I didn't want old Goon to see me. All right, all right, Mother. I'm just coming. I don't mind if I *do* have to run all the way ! Good-bye, Buster. Hold him, Bets, or he'll tear after me all down the road to the station.'

Bets held Buster, who wriggled and struggled wildly, barking desperately. He couldn't bear Fatty to go anywhere without him. Fatty disappeared after his mother, trotting down the drive like a fast pony.

'I hope Fatty will be able to get the things he wants,' said Pip. 'It would be such fun to wear disguises.'

They went home with Buster, who at first looked very aggrieved and kept his tail down. But on being presented with a perfect giant of a bone by Bets he decided to get his wag back. After all, when Fatty went away he always came back again. It was just a question of waiting for him. Buster was prepared to wait, if he could while away the time with such a marvellous bone.

'It's a pity old Fatty won't be down for a day or two,' said Larry. 'I hope his friends don't stay long. He didn't tell us who they were.'

'Some of his school friends, I expect,' said Pip. 'Well, he'll be down in two or three days' time, and then we'll have gorgeous fun looking at his disguises.'

Buster went home by himself that night, trotting down the drive like a good little dog. He took the remains of the bone with him. He wasn't going to leave it for Pip's kitchen cat to finish !

Next day Larry and Daisy came down to play with Pip and Bets. Their playroom was so big and cheerful that it made a nice meeting-place. Bets sat on the window-seat, reading.

She heard the click of the gate down the drive and waited to see who was coming. Perhaps it was Fatty after all. But it wasn't. It was a queer-looking boy with a limp, a pale, sallow face, and curly hair that stuck out from under a rather foreign-looking cap.

He carried a note in his hand. Bets supposed it must be for her mother. She wondered who the boy was.

She heard the front door open below. Then evidently the maid showed the boy into the sitting-room, where Mrs. Hilton was. Bets waited for him to come out into the drive again.

'There's a funny-looking boy come with a note,' she said to the others. 'He must be seeing Mother. Do watch him come out again.'

They went to the window to watch. But suddenly the playroom door was opened, and in came Mrs. Hilton, followed by the boy, who appeared to be very shy.

He hung back, and twisted his cap round and round in his hands and hung his head. His hair was as curly as Bets' was, but his face was very pale. He had jutting-out teeth like a rabbit, and they stuck out over his lower lip.

'Children, this is a friend of Frederick's,' said Mrs. Hilton. 'He brought me a note from Mrs. Trotteville, and I thought you might like to ask him in for a few minutes. He would like to see your things, I'm sure. He's French, and doesn't seem to understand much English. But still, as Pip was top of his form in French last term, I expect he can talk to him all right.'

The boy hung back. Pip went forward and held out his hand. The boy took it and gave it a limp shake.

'Comment allez-vous ? ' he said.

' That means, " How do you do," Bets,' explained Larry.

' Très bien, merci,' said Pip, feeling that he must say something to justify his mother's pride in his French. But it was one thing to write French sentences in school, when you could look up every single word, and quite another to say something ordinary. For the life of him Pip couldn't think of a single thing to say in French.

Bets was sorry for the boy. She went forward and took his hand. ' Don't be shy,' she said. ' Why didn't Fatty come with you ? '

' Je ne comprends pas,' said the boy, in a rather silly, high voice.

' That means he doesn't understand,' said Pip to Bets. ' Let *me* try now ! ' He cleared his throat, thought hard, and addressed the boy.

' Où est Fatty—er, Frederick, I mean.'

' Je ne comprends pas,' said the boy again, and twisted his cap round and round furiously.

' Golly ! he doesn't even understand his *own* language,' said Pip, in disgust. ' I wonder what his name is. I'll ask him. I know the French sentence for " What is your name ? " '

He turned to the boy again. ' Comment appellez-vous ? ' he said.

' Ah ! ' said the boy, evidently understanding this. He smiled, and the children saw his enormous, jutting-out teeth, which gave him a very queer look. ' My name it ees—Napoleon Bonaparte.'

There was a silence after this extraordinary statement. The children didn't know what to think. Was the boy called after Napoleon Bonaparte, the famous Frenchman—or was he pulling their legs ?

The boy walked across the room, limping badly. Bets wondered what he had done to his leg.

'Is your leg bad?' she asked sympathetically. To her horror the boy fished out a very dirty handkerchief and burst into floods of tears. He muttered strings and strings of French-sounding words into his handkerchief, whilst the others stared at him in discomfort, not in the least knowing what to do.

Mrs. Hilton put her head into the room again to see how the children were getting on with their new friend. She was simply horrified to see him apparently in floods of tears.

'What's the matter?' she said. 'What have you been doing to the boy?'

'Nothing,' said the children indignantly. 'I only just asked him about his bad leg,' added Bets.

The boy gave a loud howl, limped across the room to the door, pushed by the distressed Mrs. Hilton, and disappeared down the stairs. 'Ah, ma jambe, ma jambe!' he wailed as he went.

'What's jambe?' asked Bets, bewildered.

'Leg. He's yelling out, "Oh, my leg, my leg!"' said Pip. 'He's mad, I think.'

'I must ring up Mrs. Trotteville and ask her about the boy,' said Mrs. Hilton. 'Poor child—he doesn't seem at all well. I wish I hadn't brought him up to you now. He did seem very tongue-tied and shy, I must say.'

The front door crashed shut. The children crowded to the window and watched the extraordinary French boy go limping down the drive. He still had his handkerchief in his hand, which every now and again he dabbed at his eyes.

'Well, if that's one of Fatty's friends I'm glad he didn't ask us to play with him,' said Larry in disgust.

'I'll just leave the boy time to get back to Mrs. Trotteville's,' said Mrs. Hilton, 'and then I really must telephone her to ask if he's arrived all right and to apologize for your upsetting him so.'

The children stared at her indignantly.

' *Upsetting* him ! ' said Pip. ' We didn't do anything of the sort. He's potty.'

' Don't use that silly word about people,' said Mrs. Hilton.

' Well, dippy then,' said Pip, and got a glare from his mother. She was very particular about the way Pip and Bets spoke and acted.

' I'm sorry to think that you couldn't put a little foreign boy like that at his ease,' she said, and spent a few more minutes saying the same kind of thing. Then she went to the telephone to ring up Mrs. Trotteville.

But she apparently got on to Fatty, who politely informed Mrs. Hilton that his mother was out and could he take any message for her ?

' Well, no, not exactly,' said Mrs. Hilton. ' It's only that I'm rather worried about a friend of yours, Frederick, who called here with a note just now. I took him up to be with the others for a few minutes, and when I went in later something had happened to make him very upset. He fled from the house, weeping bitterly. I just wondered if he had come back all right.'

' Yes, he's back,' said Fatty cheerfully. ' He came and told me how nice the others had been to him, and what fun he had had. He said could he come to tea with them this afternoon, he would so enjoy it.'

Mrs. Hilton was extremely surprised to hear all this. She didn't say anything for a moment, then she turned to the listening children.

' Er—the boy seems to have got back all right, and to have recovered,' she said. ' He wants to come to tea with you this afternoon.'

There was an astonished and horrified silence.
Nobody wanted the boy.

'Mother, we can't have him!' said Pip, in an
agonized whisper. 'He's awful; he really is. Do
say we're all going up to Larry's to tea. Larry, can
we come? We simply can't have that awful boy
here again.'

Larry nodded. Mercifully Mrs. Hilton seemed
to agree with them, and she turned to the telephone
again.

'Oh, Frederick, are you there? Will you tell
your friend that Pip and Bets are going out to tea
with Larry and Daisy this afternoon, so they won't be
able to have your little French friend. I'm so sorry.'

'Good for you, Mother!' said Pip, when she
put the telephone down. 'Golly, wouldn't it have
been simply awful to have that boy stuck here for
hours. I bet old Fatty wanted us to have him to tea
just to get rid of him. I bet the boy didn't really
ask to come. He was scared stiff of us all.'

'Well, you'd better come up to us this afternoon,' said Daisy, 'seeing that we've told Fatty
that. Come up as soon after dinner as you can—
about half-past two, if you like.'

'Right,' said Pip. 'We'll be along. Golly, how
can Fatty put up with friends like that?'

5   CLEVER FATTY

ABOUT half-past two that afternoon Pip and Bets
set off to go to Larry's. They had to go through the
village, and to their horror they saw the French boy
limping along the street.

'Look! there's that awful boy again,' said Pip. 'We'll just grin at him and go on. Don't let's stop, for goodness' sake, Bets. He might start jabbering at us again, or howling into his hanky.'

The boy went in at a gate. It was Mr. Goon— the policeman's—gate. He had a note in his hand.

'Look! I bet Fatty has got his Frenchy friend to deliver that invisible letter!' said Pip. 'Let's just wait and see what happens. He's knocked at the door, so old Clear-Orf may open it.'

The two waited near the gate, half-hidden by a bush. They saw the door open, and Mr. Goon's red face appeared.

'I have zumsing for you,' said the boy in a foreign accent. 'Mistaire Goon, is it not?'

'Yes,' said Mr. Goon, looking in surprise at the boy. He never remembered having seen him before. The boy presented him with a letter, bowed deeply and courteously, and waited.

'What you waiting for?' said Mr. Goon.

'I not understand,' said the boy politely.

Mr. Goon appeared to think the boy was deaf. So he raised his voice and shouted, 'I said—what you waiting for?'

'I wait for a—what you say?—answer. Ah, yes, I wait for the answer,' said the boy.

'H'm!' said Mr. Goon, and slit the envelope open. He unfolded the blank sheet and stared at it. His face went purple.

'See here!' said Mr. Goon, and he thrust the blank letter in the boy's face. 'Some one's been playing a joke on me—silly sort of joke, too—wasting the time of the Law like this. Who gave you the letter?'

'I not understand,' said the boy, and smiled politely at the policeman, showing all his jutting-out

365

teeth. ' It is a mystery, is it not ? A letter with nothing in it. Ah, truly a great mystery ! '

The word ' mystery ' seemed to strike Mr. Goon. Since the children had solved two strange mysteries before he did, he had been rather sensitive about mysteries, and terribly afraid that the children might happen on a third one before he did. He gazed at the letter.

' Maybe it's a secret letter,' he said. ' Maybe it's got a secret message. Who gave this to you, boy ? '

' I not understand,' said the boy irritatingly.

' Well—I'll test the paper for secret ink,' said Mr. Goon most surprisingly.

Bets gave a gasp. ' Oh, Pip ! ' she said in a whisper. ' It's got such a rude message ! '

The boy seemed to think it was time to go. He raised his cap, bowed deeply once more, and limped down the path, almost bumping into Bet and Pip.

' Bon jour,' he said courteously. Bets knew that meant good-day. She hardly dared to answer, because she was so afraid she might make him burst into tears again. Pip nodded curtly to the boy, took Bets by the arm, and moved smartly up the street.

To their annoyance the boy followed. ' You will take me to tea with your friends ? ' he said, to their great horror.

' Certainly not,' said Pip, getting annoyed. ' You can't ask yourself out to places like that.'

' Ah, thank you a million times. You are so kind,' said the boy, and walked with them.

' I said, *no*, we can't take you,' said Pip. ' Go home.'

' I come, I come,' said the irritating boy, and linked his arm in Pip's. ' You are so, so kind ! '

' Goodness, what are we to do with him ? ' said Bets. ' I bet Fatty told him to come and meet us and ask to go with us. Fatty would be sure to want to get rid of him. He's awful.' She turned to the boy.

' Go home,' she said. ' Oh dear, I feel as if I'm talking to Buster when I say that ! Do go home ! '

To her horror the boy pulled out his hanky and began to sob into it—but they were queer sobs. Pip suddenly snatched away the boy's hanky and stared at him. There wasn't a single tear in his eyes—and he was laughing, not crying !

' Oh ! ' said this amazing boy, ' oh, you'll be the death of me ! I can't keep it up any more ! Oh, Bets, oh, Pip, I shall crack my sides with laughing ! '

It was Fatty's voice ! *Fatty's* voice ! Bets and Pip stared in the utmost amazement. How could this boy talk with Fatty's voice ?

The boy suddenly put his hand to his mouth and whipped out the curiously jutting teeth ! With a quick look round to make sure no one was looking, he lifted his curly hair—and underneath the wig was Fatty's own smooth hair !

' Fatty ! Oh, Fatty ! It's you ! ' cried Bets, too astonished even to hug him.

' Golly, Fatty ! You're a marvel,' said Pip, in awe. ' You absolutely took us in. How did you get such a pale face ? And those teeth—they're marvellous ! Your voice too—you talked just like a silly, shy French boy—and to think I tried to talk French to you too ! '

' I know ! The hardest thing for me was trying not to laugh,' said Fatty. ' I did burst out just before your mother came into the room this morning, and I had to pretend I was howling. I say—didn't I take you all in ! '

'How did you dare to go and face old Clear-Orf like that?' said Pip. 'However did you dare?'

'Well, I thought if I could deceive you as easily as all that, Clear-Orf would never, never guess,' said Fatty, walking on with them. 'Come on— let's go to Larry's, and you can say I joined you on the way up. We'll get another laugh. And then we'll have to talk about old Clear-Orf and that letter. I hope to goodness he doesn't know how to test for invisible writing. That wasn't a very polite letter.'

They went in at Larry's gate, walked in at the side door and up to Larry's room. Larry and Daisy were there. They stared in horror when they saw the French boy again.

'He wants to come too,' said Pip, hoping he wouldn't giggle. 'He met us in the road.'

'They were so, so, *so* kind,' put in Fatty, and he bowed deeply again, this time to Daisy.

Bets exploded into a laugh. Pip gave her a nudge.

'I can't help it, I can't help it,' giggled Bets. 'Don't glare at me, Pip, I just can't help it.'

'What can't she help?' said Larry, in astonishment. 'Honestly, she's potty too.'

Fatty spoke suddenly in his own voice. 'I hope you don't mind me coming to tea, Larry and Daisy.'

Larry and Daisy jumped violently. It was so unexpected to hear Fatty's voice coming from some one they thought was a queer French boy. Daisy gave a squeal.

'You wretch! It was you all the time! Fatty, you're simply marvellous! Is that one of your disguises?'

'Yes,' said Fatty, and he took off his curly wig and showed it to them. They all tried it on in turns It was amazing the way it altered them.

'The teeth are fine too,' said Larry. 'Let's rinse them and I'll put them on. I bet you won't know me !'

They didn't ! It made Larry look completely different to wear the odd, jutting-out teeth. They were not solid teeth, but were made of white celluloid, with pink celluloid above to make them look as if they grew from the gum.

'And your limp—and your voice ! They were both awfully good,' said Pip admiringly. 'Fatty, you took Mother in completely, too—it wasn't only your disguise—it was your acting as well.'

'Oh, well—I was always good at acting,' said Fatty, in a modest kind of voice. 'I always get the chief part in the school plays, you know. Before I decided to be a detective I thought I'd be an actor.'

For once the four children did not stop Fatty's boasting. They all gazed at him with such rapt, admiring attention that Fatty began to feel quite uncomfortable.

'I think you're wonderful,' said Bets. 'I couldn't possibly act like that. I should be scared. Fatty, how *dared* you go and face old Clear-Orf—and give him that letter too !'

'I think that was a bit of a mistake now,' said Fatty, considering. 'If he does run a warm iron over the blank sheet, he'll read the letter—and it's a bit rude, really.'

'Awfully rude,' said Daisy. 'I only hope he won't go and show it to our parents. That really would be sickening.'

Pip felt alarmed. His mother and father were strict, and would not allow rudeness or bad behaviour of any sort if they could help it.

'Golly !' said Pip, 'this is awful. I wish we could get the letter back.'

It made Larry look completely different

Fatty, looking like himself now that he had taken off the wig and the teeth, looked at Pip for a moment. ' That's a good idea of yours, Pip,' he said. ' We *will* get it back. Otherwise he'll certainly show it round to all our parents and we'll get into a row.'

' I don't see how in the world we can possibly get it back,' said Larry.

' What about one of us putting on a disguise, and——' began Fatty. But they all interrupted him.

' No ! *I'm* not going to face old Clear-Orf now ! '

' I wouldn't *dare* ! '

' Golly—he'd arrest us ! '

' He'd see through any disguise *I* wore ! '

' All right, all right,' said Fatty. ' *I'll* go and face old Clear-Orf—in my French-boy disguise again—and I bet I'll get that letter back too.'

' Fatty—you're marvellous ! ' said every one together, and Fatty tried in vain to look properly modest.

6   FATTY AND MR. GOON

' HOW can you possibly get our letter back, though ? ' asked Larry. ' I mean—old Clear-Orf isn't likely to hand it meekly to you, is he ? '

' Fortune favours the bold,' said Fatty. ' I propose to be bold. First of all, I want to write another letter in invisible writing. Hand me an orange, Larry.'

Larry gave him an orange and he squeezed juice from it into a cup. Then he took out his pen, with its clean nib, got a sheet of white notepaper just like the one he had written on before, and began to write :

'DEAR CLEAR-ORF,—1 suppose you think you will solve the next mystery first. Well, as your brains are first class, you probably will. Good luck to you ! From your five admirers,
'THE FIVE FIND-OUTERS (AND DOG).'

Fatty read it out loud as he wrote. The others laughed. 'There !' said Fatty, 'if I can possibly exchange this letter for the other one, it won't matter a bit if he goes parading round showing it to our parents !'

He stuck his teeth back under his upper lip, and at once his face altered out of all knowledge. Then he carefully fitted on the curly wig. It was a beauty.

'What else did you buy ?' asked Larry.

'Not much, after all,' said Fatty. 'The things were much more expensive than I thought they'd be. This wig took nearly all my money ! I got these teeth, and two or three pairs of different eyebrows, some make-up paint that gives you a pale skin, or a red one, or whatever you like— and that foreign - looking cap. I got a cheaper wig too, which I'll show you — mousy hair, and straight.'

He put on the foreign-looking cap, and stuck it out at an absurd angle. Nobody would have thought he was Fatty. He began to limp across the room.

'Adieu !' he said. 'Adieu, mes enfants !'

'He means " Good-bye, my children," ' Pip explained to Bets, who watched with admiring eyes whilst Fatty limped along the passage to the head of the stairs.

' Good-bye, Napoleon ! ' called Bets, and every one giggled.

' I hope old Clear-Orf won't get him,' said Larry. ' He's frightfully brave and bold, and awfully clever at this sort of thing—but Clear-Orf doesn't like jokes played on him.'

' I wonder if Clear-Orf has been able to read the invisible writing yet,' said Bets. ' I bet he was angry if he has ! '

Clear-Orf *was* angry. In fact, he was almost bursting with fury. He had heated an iron, knowing that heat was one of the things that made most invisible writing show up plainly—and he had carefully ironed the sheet of notepaper.

He could hardly believe his eyes when he read the faint brown letters ! He swallowed hard, and his froggy eyes almost fell out of his head.

' All right. We'll see what your parents say to *this* ! ' said Mr. Goon, speaking as if the children were there in front of him. ' Yes, and the Inspector too ! This'll open his eyes, this will. Rude, cheeky toads. No respect for the Law ! Ho, now I've got you ! You didn't think as I'd be smart enough to read your silly invisible writing, did you ? '

Mr. Goon had several things to do that day, and it was not until the afternoon that he decided to go and display the letter to the children's parents.

' Don't wonder they dursent come and deliver the note themselves ! ' he thought, remembering the queer boy who had delivered it. ' Got some friend of theirs, I suppose. Staying with one of them, I'll be bound.'

He decided to go to the Hiltons first. He knew how strict Mr. and Mrs. Hilton were with Pip and Bets.

' Open their eyes nicely, this will,' he thought,

trudging off. 'Hallo!—there's that little Frenchy fellow. I'll just find out where he's staying.'

'Hi!' yelled Mr. Goon to Fatty, who was sauntering along on the other side of the street, hoping that the policeman would see him. 'You come here a minute.'

'You call me?' said Fatty politely, in the high, foreign kind of voice he had used before.

'I got a few questions to ask you,' said Clear-Orf. 'Who gave you that there rude note to deliver to me this morning?'

'*Rude?* Ah, non, non, non—surely it was not *rude!*' said Fatty in a shocked tone, wagging his hands just as his French master did at school. 'That I cannot believe, Mr. Poleeeceman.'

'Well, you look here at this,' said Mr. Goon. 'Maybe you can tell me whose writing this is, see?'

He took the envelope from his pocket, and pulled out the sheet of paper. 'There you are—you take a squint at that and tell me if you know who wrote that rude letter.'

Fatty took it—and at that moment the wind most conveniently puffed down the street. Fatty let go the paper and it fluttered away. Fatty sprinted after it at once, and, when he bent down to pick it up, it was easy to slip it into his pocket and turn to Clear-Orf with the other letter in his hand.

'Drat it, it nearly went!' said Mr. Goon, and he almost snatched it from Fatty's hand. 'Better not flap it about in the wind. I'll put it back into the envelope.'

He did, and Fatty grinned to himself. It had been so easy—much, much easier than he had expected. What a kind puff of wind that had been!

'Where are you walking to, Mr. Poleeeceman?' asked Fatty politely.

' I'm going down to Mr. and Mrs. Hilton,' said Mr. Goon righteously.

' Then we part,' said Fatty. ' Adieu, dear Mr. Poleeeceman.'

He went off round a corner, and Mr. Goon stared after him. He felt puzzled, but he didn't know why. ' That French boy isn't half queer,' he thought. He would have thought him queerer still if he had seen what Fatty did round the corner !

Fatty pulled off his wig, took out his teeth, removed his queer-looking cap, and took off the rather gaudy scarf he wore. He hid them all in a bush.

Then, looking once more like Frederick Algernon Trotteville, he hastened to the house where Pip and Bets lived, and where Mr. Goon had already gone. He went in and gave his usual call for Pip, although he knew quite well he wasn't there, but was at Larry's.

' Oh, there you are, Frederick,' said Mrs. Hilton, looking out of the door of the sitting-room. ' Come here a minute, will you ? Pip is out, and so is Bets. Mr. Goon is here with a very extraordinary story. Apparently he thinks that you and the others have been guilty of most unnecessary rudeness.'

' How extraordinary ! ' said Fatty, and went into the sitting-room. He saw Mr. Hilton there too, and Mr. Goon sitting on a chair, his knees turned out widely, his great hands flat on them.

' Ho ! ' he said, when Fatty went in. ' Here's one of them what wrote that invisible letter. Now, ma'am, I'll just show it to you, and you'll be able to read it. Talks about my brains creaking for want of oil ! '

Mr. Goon took out the sheet of paper from the envelope and laid it on the table. It was blank, because the writing had not been warmed up. Mr.

Goon looked at it, and was annoyed. The lettering had been there last time he had looked at it.

'It wants a hot iron again,' he said, much to Mrs. Hilton's surprise. 'Could I trouble you to procure me a hot iron, ma'am?'

One was warmed and then Mr. Goon ran it over the sheet. 'There you are!' he said in triumph, as the faint brown lettering became visible, 'you just read that, ma'am and sir—what do you think of that for a letter sent to a repre—er—representative of the Law!'

Mrs. Hilton read it out loud:

'"DEAR CLEAR-ORF,—I suppose you think you will solve the next mystery first. Well, as your brains are first class, you probably will. Good luck to you! From your five admirers,

'"THE FIVE FIND-OUTERS (AND DOG)."'

There was a silence. Mr. Goon's eyes bulged. This was not what he had read before! He snatched the letter.

'Well, Mr. Goon,' said Mr. Hilton, entering into the matter suddenly, 'I can't see what you have to complain about in that. Quite a nice, complimentary letter, I think. Nothing about your brains er—er —creaking and wanting oiling. I don't understand what you are complaining of.'

Mr. Goon read the letter again hurriedly. He couldn't believe what he saw! 'This here ain't the letter,' he said. 'There's some dirty work going on. Did you write this letter, Master Frederick?'

'I did,' said Fatty, 'and I can't think why you should object to us expressing our admiration for you—or perhaps you think you *have*n't got first-class brains?'

' That will do, Frederick,' said Mrs. Hilton.

Fatty looked hurt.

' What's become of the letter I first had ? ' said Mr. Goon, feeling more and more puzzled. ' Yes, and what I want to know is—are you children messing about with any more mysteries ? Because if you are, you'd better tell me, see ? If you go snooping around trying to find out things, you may get into Serious Trouble.'

Fatty couldn't resist the temptation to let Clear-Orf think he and the other children really were trying to solve another mystery. So he looked very solemn indeed.

' I can't give any secrets away, Mr. Goon, can I ? It wouldn't be fair.'

Mr. Goon at once thought there must *be* a secret, a mystery he didn't know about. He got so red in the face that Fatty thought it was about time he was going.

' Well, I must be off,' he said to Mrs. Hilton, in his politest voice. ' Good-bye ! '

And before Mr. Goon could think of any good reason for stopping him, he went ! He exploded into loud laughs as soon as he was out of earshot. Then he decided he had better go and get his disguise from the bush. He would put it on again to save carrying it, and would pop back to his house to fetch old Buster.

So, in a few minutes Fatty, once more in disguise, was walking home looking the same curly-haired, queer, rabbit-toothed boy that Mr. Goon had already seen twice that day.

And Mr. Goon spotted him just as he walked in at his gate ! ' Ho ! ' said Mr. Goon, pleased, ' so that's where that little varmint is staying—with that Frederick Trotteville ! I'll be bound he had some-

thing to do with altering that there invisible letter—
though how it was done beats me ! I'll just go and
make a few inquiries there, and frighten the life out
of that Frenchy fellow.'

So, to Mrs. Trotteville's enormous surprise,
Mr. Goon was announced and came ponderously
into her drawing-room.

'Good afternoon, ma'am,' said Mr. Goon. ' I
just came to ask a few questions of that foreign boy
you've got here.'

Mrs. Trotteville looked as if she thought Mr.
Goon had gone mad. 'What boy ? ' she said.
' We've got no foreign boy here at all. There's
only my son, Frederick.'

Mr. Goon looked at her disbelievingly. 'Well,
I see him come in to your front gate just half a
minute ago ! ' he said.

' *Really ?* ' said Mrs. Trotteville, in astonishment.
' I'll see if Frederick is in and ask him.' She called
Fatty. ' Frederick ! Are you in ? Oh, you are !
Well, come here a minute, will you ? '

' Hallo, Mr. Goon ! ' said Fatty, coming into the
room. ' You seem to be following me about this
afternoon, don't you.'

' None of your sauce, now,' said Mr. Goon,
beginning to feel he couldn't keep his temper much
longer. ' Where's that foreign-looking chap that I
see coming in here a minute ago ? '

Fatty wrinkled his forehead and looked in a
puzzled manner at Mr. Goon. ' Foreign-looking
chap ? I don't know who you mean. Mother, have
we got any foreign-looking chaps here ? '

' Of course not. Don't be silly, Frederick,' said
his mother. ' I wondered if a friend of yours had
come to call.'

' There's nobody here but me,' said Fatty truthfully. 'No other boy, I mean. Mr. Goon, do you think you need glasses ? There was that letter you thought was different—and now you keep seeing foreign-looking boys.'

Mr. Goon got up. He felt he would explode if he stayed there one minute longer talking to Fatty. He went, vowing to himself that the very next time he saw that there Frenchy-looking fellow he'd drag him off to the police station, that he would !

7   AN ESCAPE—AND A SURPRISE

THE next time the Five Find-Outers met they roared with laughter at Fatty's story. He acted it well, and the children could imagine exactly how poor Mr. Goon had looked.

'And now he really does think we're on to some mystery he doesn't know about,' said Fatty. 'Poor old Clear-Orf—we've got him really puzzled, haven't we ! Mother tells me he has been making inquiries all over the place to find out where the " Frenchy fellow " is staying, but nobody can tell him anything, of course.'

'I do, do wish there *was* a mystery to solve now,' sighed Bets, tickling Buster. 'We've got all sorts of good detective tricks—invisible writing—how to get out of a locked room—disguises—but there's nothing to solve.'

'We'll just have to go on playing a few tricks on Clear-Orf,' said Fatty. 'That will keep our wits sharp, anyway. Pip, would *you* like to wear a disguise to-day, and go and do a bit of parading where Clear-Orf is ? '

'Yes,' said Pip, who had now tried on all the eyebrows, teeth, and wigs and painted his face a curious collection of colours. 'I'd love to. Let me wear the other wig—the straight-haired one, Fatty —and the teeth—and those big black eyebrows. They're lovely. And I might give myself a red face like Clear-Orf's too.'

This sounded exciting. Every one helped Pip to put on his disguise.

'I don't see why you haven't bought any moustaches too,' said Pip, thinking that he would look grand in a black moustache.

'Well, we haven't got voices to match moustaches,' said Fatty. 'You want a man's voice for that. I did think of bringing back a moustache or two, but it wouldn't be a proper disguise for us. We can only disguise ourselves as some kind of children. There—you look positively frightful!'

Pip did. He had a fiery red face, black, fierce eyebrows, the awful jutting-out teeth, and the straight-haired wig. He borrowed a red scarf from Daisy, put on his mackintosh inside out, and then felt himself sufficiently disguised.

'Goon always goes down the village and round the corner at half-past eleven,' said Larry. 'There won't be any one much about to-day, it's such an awful day, and there's a fog coming on. Wait round the corner for him, and then ask him the time or something.'

'Please, sir, what's the time?' said Pip, in an astonishingly deep, hoarse voice. Every one laughed.

'That's fine,' said Larry. 'Well, off you go, and come back quickly and tell us what happened.'

Pip set off. Down in the village it was foggy. He could hardly see more than a yard in front of him. He waited about at the corner, listening for Clear-Orf's heavy feet. Some one came unexpectedly round the corner, walking quietly and lightly.

Pip jumped—but the other person jumped much more ! The sight of Pip's fiery face, fierce eyebrows, and awful teeth made old Miss Frost scream.

' Oh ! Help ! Who is it ? ' she squealed, and turning back, she raced down the village street. She bumped into old Clear-Orf.

' There's a horrible person round the corner,' she panted. ' Awful red face and great eyebrows— and the wickedest teeth I ever saw—sort of hanging out of his mouth ! '

The mention of sticking-out teeth reminded Mr. Goon of the French boy, and he wondered if it was he who was hanging about round corners. So, trying to walk as lightly as he could, he tiptoed to the corner and went round it very suddenly.

Pip was there ! Mr. Goon was on him almost before he could move. The policeman stared in amazement at the boy's fiery face, the absurd eyebrows, and the familiar jutting-out teeth.

' 'Ere, what's all this ? ' he began, and shot out a powerful arm to get hold of Pip. Pip felt his grip on his mackintosh, and had to wriggle right out of it before he could escape. Mr. Goon was left standing with a mackintosh in his hands—but he didn't stand for long. He went after Pip at top speed.

Pip was frightened. He hadn't really thought Mr. Goon would catch hold of him so quickly— and now he had got his mackintosh. Blow ! Well, he mustn't be caught, or there would be very awkward questions to answer. For a minute he was sorry he had gone out in such an extraordinary

381

disguise. Then, as he gained a little on the panting policeman, he began to enjoy the adventure.

They tore up the road. They raced up the hill and over it. Pip made for open country, thinking that he might be able to get behind a hedge and let Mr. Goon go lumbering by in the mist.

He came to a gateway, and remembered that it led up the drive to an old empty house. No one had lived there for ages and ages. It belonged to somebody who seemed to have forgotten all about it !

He tore into the drive, hoping that Mr. Goon would go on without seeing him. But the policeman was not to be put off so easily. He tore up the drive too.

Pip fled round the old house, and came into a tangled, untidy garden, with many trees standing about. He spotted one that seemed easy to climb, and in a trice had shinned up it, just before Mr. Goon came round the corner, puffing like a goods train.

Pip sat high up in the tree, as silent as could be. There were no leaves on it and if Mr. Goon looked up he was lost ! He watched the policeman go all over the garden, and took the chance of climbing up still farther, so that more branches hid him from Mr. Goon. He was almost at the top of the tree now, level with the highest storey of the house. He watched Mr. Goon, hardly daring to breathe.

' Jolly good thing this is an empty house,' thought Pip, ' else the people would all be coming out to see what the matter is—and I'd be spotted.'

He crouched against the trunk of the tree, level with a window. He looked at it, and saw to his surprise that it was barred.

' Must have been a nursery window at one time, I suppose,' he thought. ' Jolly strong bars, though.'

Then he glanced in at the window—and he almost fell out of the tree with shock !

The room inside was not empty. It was fully furnished !

Pip couldn't understand it. If the house was empty, how could a room on the top storey be furnished ? People didn't move away and forget all about one room !

' Golly !—I wonder if this *is* the old empty house after all,' thought Pip. ' Perhaps in the fog I've run in at a different gate. Maybe the house is lived in, and all the rooms are furnished. I wish old Clear-Orf would go, then I could have a look round.'

Clear-Orf was hunting everywhere. The garden was well hedged in, and no one could squeeze out of the sides. Then where had that queer fellow gone ? It was a real puzzle to the policeman. It never once occurred to him to look up into any of the trees.

At last he gave it up. His prey had escaped him —but next time — ah, next time he saw any one with those awful teeth, he'd get them ! There was something funny about two people having the same sticking-out teeth.

' I never did see teeth that stuck out so,' thought the defeated Mr. Goon, as he made his way round the side of the house and walked to the front gate. ' That Frenchy fellow had them, and so had this one I'm after now. Wish I could have caught him. I'd have asked him a few straight questions, I would ! '

Pip was very thankful to see him go. He waited till the policeman had disappeared round the house, and then he cautiously slid along a branch to the window, in order to get a better look inside.

There was no doubt about it at all. The room had plenty of furniture in it—a couch that was big

383

enough for a bed, an arm-chair, two smaller chairs, a table, a book-case with books in, a carpet on the floor. It was all most extraordinary.

'There's an electric fire there too,' said Pip to himself. 'But there's no one there—and judging by the dust everywhere, there hasn't been any one for some time. I wonder who the house belongs to.'

He looked at the bars on the window. No one could possibly get in or out of the window, that was certain. The bars were as close together as most nursery-window bars are—not even a child could slip between them.

Pip climbed cautiously down the tree, keeping a sharp look-out in case Mr. Goon was lurking somewhere. But that puzzled man had gone back to the village, comforting himself with the thought that though he had lost the boy with the teeth and eyebrows, he had at least got his mackintosh! Wait till he saw if there was a name inside!

Pip felt cold without his mackintosh. He thought ruefully of how he could explain its loss to his mother. Perhaps she wouldn't notice it was gone. On the other hand, mothers invariably noticed anything like that almost immediately.

The fog was now getting very thick. Pip would have liked to stay and snoop round a bit, but he was afraid of getting lost if the fog grew much thicker. So he contented himself with making quite sure that the house was indeed the empty one he knew.

It was. There was no doubt about it—and the rooms on the ground-floor were perfectly empty. On the gate was the name Pip had seen before— Milton House.

'It's a mystery!' said Pip, as he plodded back in the fog. 'A real mystery.' Then he stopped suddenly and hugged himself. 'This might be our *third* mystery ! We shall have to solve it somehow. There's something *very* queer going on in that old empty house ! '

8   A FEW PLANS

PIP made his way back to Fatty's house, where the others were waiting for him to report on anything that had happened. Fatty had what he called a ' den '—a small crowded room, full of books, games, sports things, and a cosy basket for Buster. The fog clung round Pip and made him feel damp and cold.

He was shivering when at last he went in at the side-door of Fatty's house. He listened to see if any one was about, because he was not anxious to bump into the maid or Mrs. Trotteville in his present disguise.

He heard nothing, and made his way up the stairs. The others were playing a card-game on the floor. They looked up when Pip came in.

' Oh—here's Pip ! ' said Bets, pleased, and Buster went to greet him as if he had not seen him for weeks. ' Did you do anything exciting, Pip ? '

' I should jolly well think I *did* ! ' said Pip, his eyes shining. He got as close to the fire as he could. ' And what's more, Find-Outers—I believe I've got our third mystery for you ! '

They all stared at him in delight and surprise. Bets jumped up. ' Tell us, quick ! What do you mean ? What is the mystery ? '

' I'll tell you it all from the beginning,' said Pip. ' Golly, I'm cold ! '

'Where's your coat?' said Daisy, seeing how cold Pip was.

'Old Clear-Orf has got it!' said Pip. 'Sickening, isn't it?'

'*Clear*-Orf! But how did he get it?' said Fatty. 'Was your name in it?'

'Do you remember if it was, Bets?' asked Pip, turning to his little sister.

'No, it wasn't,' said Bets. 'So Clear-Orf won't know whose it was—unless he goes round asking our parents if one of us has lost a mack!'

'Don't worry,' said Fatty. 'My old mack is almost exactly like Pip's. I've got a new one. Pip can take mine, then if Clear-Orf goes round asking our parents if we've lost one, Pip can produce mine.'

'Thanks, Fatty,' said Pip, relieved. 'You always come to the rescue. Well—let me tell my story.'

He began, and the children giggled to hear how poor old Miss Frost got such a fright to see the fierce eyebrows, red face, and awful teeth just round the corner—and roared when Pip described what a dance he had led Mr. Goon in the fog.

'Fancy him not looking up into the trees,' said Fatty. 'He'll never make a detective! But you haven't come to the mystery yet, Pip—what is it?'

'Well,' said Pip importantly, 'as you all know, Milton House is empty—has been empty for ages, hasn't it?'

The others nodded. They knew the house quite well.

'All right,' said Pip, 'well, listen to this. *One of the rooms at the very top of the house is fully furnished!*'

Every one stared in amazement.

'Fully furnished!' said Fatty. 'How very extraordinary! Does some one live there after all, then—and if so, why does he live at the *top* of the house ? Pip, this is certainly very queer.'

' It is, isn't it,' said Pip, pleased at the interest he had caused. ' Don't you think it's going to be our third mystery ? I'm sure there's something queer about it.'

' Well, it certainly sounds jolly strange,' said Fatty. ' Yes, it's a mystery all right.'

'Hurrah ! ' said Bets. ' We've got one for these hols, after all ! How shall we solve it ? '

' Well—it's not our usual sort of mystery,' said Fatty thoughtfully. ' I mean—in the ones before we have had Clues and Suspects to work on—this time all we've got is a fully furnished room at the top of an empty house. We don't even know if there's anything wrong about it. But it's certainly queer and unusual enough for us to try and find out what's behind it.'

' Oooh, how lovely ! ' said Bets joyfully. ' I did so want a mystery these hols. Especially as we've got so many good detective tricks.'

' Well, Pip, you certainly had a good afternoon,' said Larry. ' Do take off that awful disguise now. I can't bear to look at you. It's the teeth that make you look so revolting.'

' I know,' said Pip, taking them out and going to a basin to rinse them and dry them. ' They're marvellous. Old Clear-Orf nearly had a fit when he saw them flashing at him again, after seeing them in the French boy's mouth ! '

The others laughed at the thought of Mr. Goon's surprise. Fatty suddenly looked thoughtful.

' I only hope old Clear-Orf won't go snooping round after us,' he said. ' I know it was fun to make him think we were in the middle of a new mystery he knew nothing about—but now that we really *have* stumbled on one, it will be sickening if he follows us around. It will cramp our style terribly.'

'Blow!' said Larry. 'We shan't be able to keep this mystery to ourselves if Clear-Orf sniffs it out. I must say it sounds a first-class one—I find myself asking all kinds of questions! *Who* uses the room? Why in an empty house? Does the owner know about it? When does the one who uses it come and go?'

'Yes—there are all sort of questions to answer,' said Fatty. 'It's going to be interesting—but difficult! I vote we try and get into the room.'

'Oh *no*!' said every one at once.

'We daren't do that,' said Larry. 'We can't break into houses—even empty ones. You know we can't.'

'We don't need to break in,' said Fatty, in a dignified manner. 'There's no reason why we shouldn't go to the house-agent's and ask for the key to look over the house, is there?'

No one had thought of that. Daisy stared doubtfully at Fatty. 'They wouldn't give the key to children, silly,' she said.

'They might give it to *me*,' said Fatty, who thought he could do anything. 'Anyway I can but try. Did you happen to notice the name on the House for Sale board, Pip—I mean the name of the house-agent?'

'No. I don't remember seeing a board,' said Pip. 'But it was so foggy. We could go and find out sometime.'

'Let's go now,' said Bets eagerly. But the others shook their heads.

'Too foggy, Bets,' said Larry. 'You can't see a thing now. It's a good thing we all know our way home so well or we'd get lost!'

The fog was indeed very thick. It wasn't any good doing anything that day. The Find-Outers felt a little impatient. They wanted to get on with this new mystery !

' We shall have to be jolly careful we don't let Clear-Orf know what we're doing,' said Larry. ' We'd better try and put him on the wrong track. if we think he is snooping after us.'

' Oh yes ! ' said Bets. ' Let's do that. That would be fun. We could make up a mystery for him, couldn't we ?—a big robbery or something.'

' That's not a bad idea,' said Larry. ' If we could get Clear-Orf on to the track of a false mystery, he wouldn't spend any time or attention on our real one. So, if we do find he's snooping around, following us, or making inquiries, we'll present him with a first-class mystery—that we'll make up for him ourselves ! '

This seemed a fine idea. It didn't occur to any of the children to take Mr. Goon into their confidence and let him work with them. He disliked them so much, and was such a blunderer, that if any one was to be told, they preferred to tell their friend, Inspector Jenks—the ' very high-up policeman ' as Bets called him. He would listen to them with attention and interest, and would certainly not take any credit that was due to them. Clear-Orf, they knew, would pooh-pooh anything they did, and pretend that he had done all the brainwork.

But he was a suspicious fellow, and if he thought they really were at work on some mystery again, he would certainly try to interfere. The children felt terribly excited when they thought of this new mystery. They had so much enjoyed their first two mysteries — now here was another — and a very peculiar one too.

'Let's see,' said Fatty, considering. 'I think the first thing to do is to find out who the house-agent is, as I've said, and try and get the keys. Then we could explore that room and find out if possible what it's for and why it's fully furnished.'

'Right,' said Larry. 'You can tackle the house-agent to-morrow, then. You're good at that sort of thing. But if you manage to get the keys out of him, I'll be surprised!'

'You wait and see,' said Fatty, who now had such a high opinion of himself that he thought nothing was impossible. He could already see himself at the head of all the British police, the most famous solver of mysteries the world had ever known.

Nobody seemed to want to play a game. The thought of the new mystery made them feel unsettled and excited.

'Do you think it will be a dangerous mystery?' asked Bets rather anxiously. 'The other two we did weren't dangerous. I don't think I'd like a dangerous mystery.'

'Well, if it *is* dangerous, we three boys will tackle it,' said Fatty rather pompously. 'And you two girls must keep out of it.'

'I certainly shan't!' said Daisy indignantly. 'Bets can do as she likes—but I'm sharing this mystery from the beginning to the end, Fatty. I'm as good as you boys any day.'

'All right, all right,' said Fatty. 'Keep your hair on. Good!—there's the bell for tea. I'm frightfully hungry.'

'You always are,' said Daisy, still feeling cross.

But at the sight of the fine tea Mrs. Trotteville had provided, not one of them had any feelings but pleasure. A good tea—and a first-class mystery waiting to be solved. What could be nicer?

9 OLD CLEAR-ORF IS A NUISANCE

IT was decided that all the Find-Outers should meet next day and walk to Milton House, to see the house-agent's board.

'We could also do a bit of snooping round,' said Daisy. 'I want to climb that tree, for one thing!'

'Well, we mustn't let Clear-Orf see us doing it,' said Pip. 'That *would* give the game away.'

'As soon as we've got the name of the house-agent we'll let Fatty go and do his stuff,' said Larry. 'We could wait at the house till he comes back. Then we could use the keys he brings, and go in.'

This seemed a good plan. They all hoped that the fog would clear away the next day, otherwise their parents might not let them go walking away from the roads they knew well. Milton House lay over the hill, rather off the usual track. Beyond it lay the open country, and big empty fields stretched away for miles.

The day was fine and sunny. Every one rejoiced. Now they could certainly go to Milton House. They set off soon after breakfast, joining up at different corners. Buster went with them, of course, and walked along more solemnly than usual, just as if he knew a mystery was somewhere near.

They walked over the hill, and made their way down the rather secluded lane to Milton House. It was the last house, and stood well back in its own overgrown grounds. It was plain that no gardener had worked there for years. It looked a lonely and desolate place. The house itself was large, high, and rambling, and had two or three absurd little towers.

'Well, there it is—our Mystery House,' said Pip, as they stood and looked at it from the drive. 'Now wouldn't you say that house was completely empty and unlived in ? And yet there's a furnished room at the top of it, where some one must come and live at times ! '

The children felt a little shiver go down their backs. It was exciting. Probably no one but themselves and the one who furnished the room knew about that secret.

'Well—let's take down the house-agent's name and address,' said Fatty. 'Any one seen the board ? '

Nobody had. And what was more, there didn't appear to be one to see. Other empty houses they had passed on their way all had at least one, if not two boards up, with the notice ' For Sale. Apply to —— ' on them. But Milton House didn't seem to have a board at all.

'But surely it's for sale ? ' said Larry, puzzled, when they had made quite certain that there was no For Sale board. ' Surely all empty houses are for sale or to be let ? The owner wouldn't want them to stand empty, gradually falling into ruin.'

'Well—it's funny,' said Fatty. 'I can't understand it either.'

'It's not much use you going to any house-agent now and asking for the keys,' said Daisy. ' If no one is selling it, there won't be any keys to get.'

'Blow ! ' said Fatty, upset to find his plans coming to a full stop. He thought for a minute. 'Well, I'll tell you what I *could* do—I could go to the biggest house-agent's in the village, and ask about houses for sale—and mention Milton House. I could see if he says anything interesting.'

'Yes—you could do that,' said Daisy. 'You'd better be the one to do it, anyway. You've got cheek enough for anything, and you can be more grown-up than any of us. You could pretend you were asking for your mother or your aunt.'

'Yes,' said Fatty. 'I think I can manage it all right, without arousing the house-agent's suspicions. But before I go, let's snoop round a bit. And I want to climb that tree too, and look into that room.'

'Had we better post a guard to look out in case any one comes?' said Pip. 'We don't want to be caught on somebody else's property. Bets, you keep guard.'

'No!' said Bets, indignant at being left out of the exploring. 'You keep guard yourself, Pip.'

'Buster can keep guard,' said Fatty. 'Here, Buster, stand at the gate and bark if any one comes!'

Buster stood by the gate, near Fatty, looking up into his master's face as if he understood every word.

'There!' said Fatty, pleased. 'He'll stay on guard all the morning if we want him to.'

But as soon as they went down the drive again, Buster scampered after them! He didn't want to stand at the front gate if they were all going to leave him!

'He's not so clever as we thought,' said Pip. 'You'll never get him to stay there, Fatty.'

'Yes, I shall,' said Fatty, and took Buster firmly back to the gate. He took off his overcoat and removed his pullover. He put it down just inside the gate, at the edge of the drive.

'Guard it, Buster, guard it!' said Fatty commandingly. 'Sit on it—that's right. It's my best pullover. Guard it for me, old fellow!'

Buster knew perfectly well how to guard things, and once he sat on them, would stay with them till

Fatty came back and called him off. Now he made no attempt to leave the pullover and follow the others ; he sat there as good as gold, looking mournfully after them.

'Poor Buster ! He does want to come. I bet he knows you've played a trick on him, Fatty,' said Pip. 'His ears are down and his tail hasn't got a wag left in it.'

'Well, anyway he'll give us warning if any one comes,' said Fatty. 'Not that I'm expecting any one. But you never know. Detectives have to be prepared for anything.'

'It's nice to be Find-Outers again,' said Bets happily. 'Oh, Pip !—is this the tree you climbed ?'

It was. It was such an easy one to climb that even Bets, with Fatty's help, could climb from branch to branch, and reach the place from which she could peer into the secret room.

It was just as Pip had seen it the day before —fully furnished, comfortable looking, and very dusty. The children all took their turn at staring in. It had been exciting to hear of it, but it was even more thrilling really to see it. Whatever was the room used for ?

'Well, I'm going off to the house-agent's,' said Fatty, shinning down the tree. 'You take charge now, Larry, and snoop round the house. Look out for footprints, bits of torn paper, cigarette-ends— anything that might be clues.'

'Oooh !' said Bets joyfully. 'I do love looking for clues.'

'You called them glues last year,' said Pip. 'Do you remember ?'

Bets didn't want to remember things like that, so she didn't answer. They all climbed down the tree and began to look round the house.

'Everywhere is empty,' said Larry. 'I wish we could find a window left open or something. Then we could get inside.'

But not a window was left open, not even a crack. Not only that, but it seemed as if every window had a double fastening.

'Whoever lived here before must have been afraid of burglars,' said Daisy. 'Short of smashing a window or breaking down a door, I don't see how any one could possibly get into this house.'

They looked for footprints, but found none. Neither was there a cigarette-end, or even a scrap of paper to be seen.

'Not a single clue!' said Bets sorrowfully.

'Look at all *our* footprints!' said Daisy, pointing to where they showed in the muddy ground. 'Plenty of clues left by *our* feet to show we've been here! I think we ought to have been more careful.'

'Well, we can't do anything about it now,' said Pip. 'Listen—is that Buster barking?'

It was. He was barking madly, and the four children listened uneasily. Fatty had gone to the village. He wasn't there, with his quick cleverness to take charge. Pip, Daisy, and Bets looked at Larry.

'What shall we do?' said Bets. 'I can hear some one coming down the drive!'

'Hide!' said Larry. 'Quick, scatter behind bushes!'

They scattered, and Bets with a beating heart hid behind rather a small bush, hoping she would not be seen.

To her horror it was the familiar dark-blue uniform worn by the village policeman that she saw coming round the corner of the house! He was wheeling his bicycle.

'Quick! Scatter behind the bushes!'

It was a real piece of bad luck that he had passed that way this morning, for he rarely cycled down the lane that led to Milton House. But he had to go to an outlying farm to speak to a farmer about straying cows, and, as the usual field-path was under water, Mr. Goon had taken a longer way round, which took him by Milton House.

He was thinking of a nice hot dinner when he cycled slowly by. He hadn't even seen Buster sitting patiently on Fatty's pullover; but Buster not only saw him and heard him, but smelt him too —and it was not a smell that Buster liked.

Mr. Goon was his enemy. In fact, Mr. Goon was the natural enemy of all little dogs, though big ones he tried to make friends with. Buster couldn't help barking defiantly when he saw Mr. Goon sailing ponderously by on his bicycle. He made the policeman jump. Mr. Goon looked to see where the barking came from, and to his enormous surprise saw Buster, sitting down on a heap of wool, barking furiously.

'Ho!' said Mr. Goon, getting off his bike at once. 'You the dog belonging to that fat boy? If you're here, *he's* here—and up to some mischief, I don't doubt!'

He walked in at the gate. Buster barked more loudly than ever, but he didn't get up off Fatty's pullover. No, he had been trusted to guard that, and he would guard it with his life, if need be!

Mr. Goon was pleased to find that Buster didn't hover round his ankles as he usually did, but he was very curious to know what Buster was sitting on. He bent down and gave the pullover a jerk.

Buster was so furious that he almost snapped one of Mr. Goon's fingers off. The policeman hurriedly took his hand away.

'Spiteful creature! Vicious dog! You ought to be destroyed, you ought,' said Mr. Goon severely. 'What you want is a good thrashing, and wouldn't I like to give it you?'

Buster said some rude things to Mr. Goon in a perfect torrent of barks. The policeman walked by him, keeping his bicycle between himself and Buster, and went up the drive. He felt certain he would soon see Fatty.

He came round the side of the house into the big garden at the back. He saw no one. But he did see all the many footprints in the mud. He leaned his bike against the house and began to examine them with interest.

Then he suddenly caught sight of the top of Bets' red beret behind her bush. He straightened himself up and shouted:

'Hie, you! *I* can see you! You come on out from behind that bush!'

Poor Bets came out, trembling. Mr. Goon looked her up and down.

'Ah! One of them Hilton kids again. Can't keep out of mischief, can you? Where are the others? Where's that fat boy—and have you got that Frenchy fellow with you? I want to talk to him, I do!'

As soon as poor trembling Bets showed herself, the others came out too. They couldn't let little Bets bear the brunt of Clear-Orf's scolding. The policeman was surprised to see so many children coming out from behind bushes.

'Now what you doing? Playing hide-and-seek on somebody's private property?' he said. 'I suppose you think because you're friendly with Inspector Jenks you can do anything you like. But let me tell you, you can't. I'm in charge of this here village, see ? And any nonsense I shall report straight to your parents ! '

' Oh, Mr. Goon, is it wrong to play hide-and-seek in the grounds of an empty house ? ' said Larry, in an innocent voice. ' We're so sorry. Nobody ever told us that before.'

Mr. Goon did one of his snorts. ' You're up to some mischief, I'll be bound,' he said. ' What are you here for ? You'd better tell me, see ? If there's anything going on, I've got to know about it sooner or later.'

Larry knew that Clear-Orf suspected them of being there because of some new mystery, and he was annoyed to think the policeman had stumbled upon the very place where the mystery was. He decided the best thing to do was to go at once, and make Mr. Goon think they had only been playing hide-and-seek, as he had so obligingly suggested to them.

' Come on,' he said to the others. ' Let's go and play hide-and-seek somewhere else.'

' Yes—you clear orf ! ' said Mr. Goon majestically, feeling that he really had got the better of those interfering kids this time. ' You just clear orf, see ? '

10   FATTY MAKES INQUIRIES

THE children went down the drive, watched Mr. Goon mount his bicycle and ride off, and then went down the lane to meet Fatty. Buster refused to come with them. Fatty had not released him from his trust, and he couldn't leave the pullover !

'I wonder how Fatty's got on,' said Pip. 'I bet he won't have got any keys!'

Fatty had gone back to the village, and had gone into the office of the bigger of the two house-agents. An elderly man sat at a desk. He looked up impatiently when Fatty came in.

'What do you want?' he said.

'Have you any secluded properties standing well back from the road?' asked Fatty in a smooth, dignified voice. 'My aunt would like to hear of some. She wants a large house and garden, if possible on the outskirts of the village.'

'Well, you tell your aunt to ring me up or write to me,' said the elderly man, looking suspiciously over the tops of his large glasses. 'Or give me her address and I'll write to her.'

This didn't suit Fatty at all. What would be the good of that!

'Well, she rather wanted me to take her some particulars to-day,' said Fatty. 'Er—a house something like that one called Milton House might do for her.'

'What price house does she want?' asked the house-agent, still looking suspiciously at Fatty. He didn't like boys.

Fatty didn't know what to say. He had a good deal of general knowledge, but the price of houses didn't come into it. He hesitated.

'Well—about five hundred pounds,' he said boldly, thinking that that was such a lot of money surely it would buy a house like Milton House.

The house-agent gave a short bark of a laugh. 'Go away!' he said. 'Trying to have me on, aren't you? Five hundred pounds indeed! Why, that would hardly buy a cottage these days. You go and tell your aunt she'd better spend her money on a dolls' house ! And by the way, just give me your aunt's address, will you ? '

Fatty was equal to this, and at once gave a perfectly marvellous address, which the house-agent wrote down rather doubtfully.

' Er—perhaps you'd better give me her telephone number too,' said the man, hoping to catch Fatty out.

' Certainly,' said Fatty. ' Whiskers oooo.'

Before the astonished agent could make any comment about this curious telephone number, Fatty had bade him a polite good-day and gone.

' Phew ! ' said Fatty to himself, as he sprinted down the road at top speed. ' What a nasty suspicious fellow ! Well—I didn't get much information out of *him* about Milton House. I'd better try the other agent—and this time my dear aunt will have to spend five thousand pounds on a house.'

He marched into the other house-agent's, and saw to his relief a boy sitting at a table. The boy did not look much older than himself, and was rather pale and pimply. In the ordinary way Fatty would have greeted him by saying, ' Hallo, Pimples ! ' but this time he thought he had better not.

' Good morning,' said Fatty, putting on his deepest, most important voice.

' 'Morning,' said Pimples. ' What do you want ? '

' Well—it's not so much what *I* want as what my Aunt Alicia needs,' said Fatty. ' She is desirous of—er—purchasing a property, a secluded property, at about—er—five thousand pounds.'

' Pom-pom-pom, aren't we high and mighty ! ' said Pimples. ' Who's your aunt ? '

' She's my uncle's wife,' said Fatty, and grinned. He took out a bag of big bull's-eye humbugs and offered Pimples one. Pimples grinned back and took one.

'We aren't used to people popping in and wanting to spend five thousand pounds on any property hereabouts,' said Pimples, grinning again. 'But we've got plenty of empty houses if your aunt would like to choose one. There's Elmhurst and Sunlands, and Cherry Tree and Burnham House, and——'

'Got any down Chestnut Lane?' asked Fatty, sucking his humbug. Chestnut Lane was the road in which Milton House was.

'Yes. House called Fairways,' said the boy, consulting a big book and putting his peppermint into his other cheek.

'What about Milton House?' said Fatty. 'That's empty too.'

'It's not for sale,' said the boy.

'Whyever not?' asked Fatty, surprised.

'Because somebody's bought it, fathead,' said Pimples. 'It was on the market for four years, and somebody bought it about a year ago.'

'Oh!' said Fatty, puzzled. 'Well, why haven't they moved in?'

'How should I know?' said Pimples, crunching up his peppermint. 'I say, where do you get these humbugs? They're jolly good.'

'I got them in London the other day,' said Fatty. 'Have another? Do you know when the new people are moving in?'

'No idea,' said Pimples. 'Once a house is sold, my boss, Mr. Richards, doesn't take any more interest in it. Don't tell me your Aunt Alicia has fallen in love with that desolate old place!'

'Well—it might be just what's she looking for,' said Fatty. 'I wonder now—perhaps the people who bought it don't like it after all—and might sell it to my aunt. Do you know their name and address ? '

' Gosh !—you do seem keen on your aunt having that house,' said Pimples. ' Wait a minute. I may be able to put my hand on the name. It's in this book, I believe.'

Fatty waited whilst Pimples ran a dirty thumb down lists of names. He was very anxious to know the name and address of the person who had bought the house. He felt he must get hold of something, or the other Find-Outers wouldn't think him very clever.

' Yes, here we are,' said Pimples at last. ' Name of Crump. Miss Crump, Hillways, Little Minton— that's quite near here, you know. Well, Miss Crump bought it, but why she didn't live in it, goodness knows ! She paid three thousand pounds for it.'

' Oh ! ' said Fatty. ' Well—thanks awfully. I'll get my aunt to go and see Miss Crump. Perhaps, if she doesn't want Milton House herself, she'll be willing to sell it to my aunt.'

' So long ! ' said the boy, as Fatty got up to go. ' Give my love to Aunt Alicia and tell her I wouldn't mind a bit of her five thousand pounds.'

Fatty went. He was puzzled. Miss Crump didn't sound at all mysterious. He could almost imagine what she looked like—a prim little old lady with a bun of hair at the back, high collars to her dresses, and skirts that swept the ground. She would probably have a cat or two.

Fatty took the road back to Milton House. Before he got there he met the other Find-Outers, looking rather woebegone.

' Oh—there's Fatty ! ' cried Bets. ' Fatty, how did you get on ? Oh, Fatty, Clear-Orf found us and turned us out ! '

'Golly!—did he really?' said Fatty, looking concerned. 'That's bad luck. We particularly didn't want him snooping round about our mystery. If he really thinks we're on to something, he'll keep a watch on that house—and on us too now—and spoil things for us properly. Who was silly enough to get spotted by Clear-Orf?'

'Well—it was Buster who gave the game away,' said Larry. 'It wasn't really such a very clever idea of yours to put him on guard by the gate, Fatty, because as soon as Clear-Orf came by, Buster nearly barked his head off. And of course Clear-Orf looked at him, knew he was your dog, and came in to see what you were doing. He found *us*, not you!'

'Blow!' said Fatty. 'I never thought of Buster making Clear-Orf suspicious if he came by. I only thought of him warning *you*. Where is he?'

'Still sitting on your pullover, and he'll be guarding it till to-morrow morning if you don't go and get him,' said Larry. 'He's only got one thought in his doggy head now—to guard that pullover of yours.'

'I'll go and get him,' said Fatty. 'You walk on slowly and I'll catch you up.'

He ran on down the lane to Milton House. Buster burst into a hurricane of delighted barks as soon as he saw him. 'Good dog,' said Fatty, patting him. 'Off guard now, old fellow—*off* guard. Let me get my pullover.'

Buster allowed Fatty to get his pullover and put it on. Fatty, who had not been thoroughly round the house as the others had, thought he would just take a quick look round. Maybe he might see something they had missed. So he trotted round the house and began to look carefully in at every window.

He jumped terribly when a stern voice came

across the garden. ' Now then ! What you a-doing
of ? Didn't I send you all off a few minutes ago ? '

' Clear-Orf—back again,' thought Fatty, annoyed
with himself for being found there. ' Blow ! '

Clear-Orf wheeled his bicycle over to him.
' Now you tell me what you're doing here,' he
demanded.

Fatty looked all round as if hunting for something.
' I left the others here,' he said. ' But now they're
gone.'

' And you was peeking in at all the windows to
see if they'd slipped through a crack ! ' said Clear-
Orf smartly.

' How clever you are, Mr. Goon,' said Fatty.
' You always think of such bright things. Do you
know where the others are ? '

' Maybe I've arrested them all for playing on
private property,' said Mr. Goon darkly. ' You tell
me what you're all so interested in here, and I'll tell
you where the others are.'

' Oh, Mr. Goon—will you really ? ' said Fatty,
edging away. ' Will you let them out of prison if I
tell you ? Have you told their parents yet that you've
arrested them ? What did they say ? '

' You stop cheeking of me,' said Clear-Orf.
' And you tell me what's making you hang about
here ? This house is empty, and children aren't
allowed here.'

Fatty went on edging away, and Mr. Goon went
on edging after him, growing purple in the face.
Of all the Five Find-Outers he detested Fatty most.
Fortunately for Fatty he had Buster with him, and
Buster, feeling that matters had gone quite far
enough, began to growl.

He then went to sniff at Mr. Goon's ankles and
the policeman kicked him away.

'Look here, Mr. Goon, if you kick Buster, he'll bite you, and I don't blame him,' said Fatty, angry to hear the yelp that Buster made. 'I shan't call him off either, if he goes for you. You'll deserve it.'

Mr. Goon kicked at Buster again, and the dog flew at him, growling furiously. Mr. Goon, seeing two rows of sharp white teeth, got on his bicycle and rode off down the drive at top speed, Buster scurrying after him, barking all the way.

'You haven't heard the last of this!' yelled Clear-Orf, as he swung out of the gate. 'I'll get to the bottom of this, see if I don't!'

'Good-bye, and send me a post card when you get to the bottom!' yelled Fatty. 'Buster, come here!'

11   SURPRISING NEWS FROM MISS CRUMP

THE others were disappointed but not surprised to hear that Fatty had not been able to get the keys of Milton House.

'It seems funny for Miss Crump to buy a house and not move into it,' said Larry. 'Why should she just furnish one room at the top, and not tell any one about it? It's a funny secret to have.'

'We can't very well go and ask her why she's got that room at the top of the house like that,' said Daisy. 'She'd be wild to think we had climbed the tree and looked in.'

'Of course we can't,' said Fatty. 'But we could quite well go over and see her—think up some excuse, you know—and try to get her talking.'

'What excuse can we give for going to see her in the dead of winter ? ' said Daisy.

'Oh !—we shall be able to think of something,' said Fatty. 'Good detectives can always find some way of getting into talk with people.'

'What's the address ? ' asked Pip.

Fatty told him.

'Well—we could easily go over there on our bikes,' said Larry. 'I vote we do. I'm longing to get on with this mystery if we can.'

'Yes, but *what* excuse can we give for going to see Miss Crump ? ' asked Daisy, who didn't like the idea of butting in on an old lady without some very well-thought-out excuse.

'Oh, Daisy, don't fuss so ! ' said Fatty, who hadn't yet thought of any excuse. 'Leave it to me. We'll go over there, look around a bit, and then see what's the best way to get into talk with Miss Crumpet.'

'Miss Crump, you mean,' said Bets with a giggle. 'Don't go calling her Crumpet.'

'We can't *all* go and see her,' said Daisy. 'She'd be suspicious if five children descended on her to talk about Milton House.'

'Well, *I've* gone to see two house-agents, and *Pip* discovered the mystery, so it's your turn, or Larry's or Bets' turn to do something,' said Fatty generously. He would have liked to do everything himself, really, but a good leader gives every one else a chance, and Fatty was a good leader.

'Oh ! ' said Daisy, not quite liking the idea. 'All right. But I think you could do it better than any one, Fatty.'

'Well, I could,' said Fatty, not very modestly. 'But then I've been training myself for this kind of work all last term. Anyway, it will be quite easy.'

They decided to bike over and see Miss Crump that afternoon. Buster could ride in Fatty's bicycle basket as it wasn't very far.

'And for goodness' sake, Buster, don't try baling out from my basket,' said Fatty. 'You did that last time I took you—saw a rabbit or something, and jumped out of my basket and nearly caused an accident.'

'Woof!' said Buster, looking upset. He always knew when Fatty was telling him not to do something or other.

'Good dog,' said every one at once, and patted Buster. They couldn't bear it when he looked sad.

They set off on their bicycles immediately after dinner, meeting at the corner at the top of Pip's lane. Off they went, ringing their bells at everything they saw, with Buster sitting up straight in Fatty's basket, his tongue hanging out in excitement.

They got to Little Minton in just under twenty minutes, and began to look for Hillways. An errand-boy directed them.

It was a nice house, old and beautiful, with leaded windows and tall chimneys. The garden was beautifully kept.

'Well, I don't wonder Miss Crumpet preferred to live here rather than in that desolate, ugly old house,' said Fatty, getting off his bicycle. 'Now —what's our plan?'

Nobody had a plan. It suddenly seemed unexpectedly difficult to find a way to go and talk to Miss Crump about Milton House.

Fatty lifted Buster down from the bicycle basket. Buster was glad to stretch his legs. He ran into the gate of the garden.

Then things happened. A large dog suddenly

rushed up the path, barking, and flew at Buster. Buster, astonished, growled and swung round. The big dog growled too and all the hairs at the back of his neck rose up.

'They're going to fight !' shrieked Bets. 'Oh, get Buster, Fatty !'

But before Fatty could get hold of Buster, the big dog pounced on him, and a fight began. Bets howled. The dogs barked angrily and growled furiously. All the children yelled at Buster.

'Come here, Buster—come here, sir ! BUSTER, come here !'

But Buster was not going to turn tail and run away in the middle of a fight. He enjoyed a fight, and he hardly ever got one. He didn't mind about the other dog being bigger than he was—he could bite as hard as he did !

The front door opened and some one came out. It was a pleasant, plump, middle-aged lady, looking very worried. She ran up the path.

'Oh dear !—is Thomas attacking your dog ?' she said. 'Thomas, stop it !'

But neither Thomas nor Buster took the slightest notice. This was their own enjoyable, private fight, and they were going on with it.

Bets cried bitterly. She was very upset at the noise and scuffling, and terribly afraid that Buster might be killed. The plump lady was distressed to hear Bets' sobs.

'Half a minute, dear—I know how to stop them !' she said to Bets. 'Don't cry any more !'

She rushed indoors and came out again with a large pail of water. She threw it over both the snarling dogs.

They had such a shock as the icy water drenched them that they both leapt back from one another in

Buster enjoyed a fight

horror. Miss Crump at once caught hold of Thomas, and Fatty made a grab for Buster.

'You bad dog, Thomas!' scolded the plump lady. 'You shall be locked in your kennel yard all day.'

She turned to the children. 'Just wait whilst I put him into his kennel,' she said, 'then I'll be back.'

She went off round the house, leading a cross and disappointed Thomas.

'Is that Miss Crump?' whispered Larry.

Fatty nodded. 'I expect so. I say—look at poor old Buster. He's been bitten on this leg. He's bleeding.'

Bets sobbed with shock and misery. She couldn't bear to see Buster bleeding. Buster was the only one who didn't seem to mind about his bite. He licked his leg, then wagged his tail hard as if to say, 'Jolly good fight, that. Pity it ended so soon.'

'It wasn't your fault, Buster,' said Daisy. 'That horrid big dog flew at you.'

Miss Crump came back, looking very sorry about the whole affair. Bets was still crying. She put her arm round the little girl and hugged her.

'Stop crying, dear,' she said. 'That bad dog Thomas hasn't hurt your little dog very much. Thomas is such a fighter. He's my brother's dog, and if any other dog or cat so much as sets a foot in this garden, he flies into a temper and pounces on them.'

'Poor B-b-b-buster's b-b-b-bleeding,' wailed Bets, who never liked the sight of blood.

'Well, we'll take him indoors and bathe his leg and put a bandage on. How would you like that?' said Miss Crump.

'Yes. I'd like that,' said Bets, drying her eyes.

She thought Buster would look lovely with a bandaged leg. She would love him a lot.

'Well, come along, then,' said Miss Crump. 'Leave your bicycles by the gate. That's right. My name is Miss Crump, and I live here with my brother.'

'Oh!' said Daisy, and thought she had better tell Miss Crump their names too. So she introduced every one politely. Soon they were in a comfortable, cosy sitting-room, and Miss Crump was bathing Buster's leg and bandaging it beautifully. Buster liked all the attention immensely.

'I believe Cook has just made some buns,' said Miss Crump, beaming round at the children when she had finished the bandaging. 'Could you manage one or two, do you think?'

Every one was sure that plenty of buns could be 'managed'. They thought Miss Crump was very nice. When she went to get the buns, Fatty nudged Daisy.

'You'd better start off asking questions,' he said. 'It's a wonderful chance, this.'

Daisy wondered how to begin asking questions about Milton House, but it was all unexpectedly easy.

When Miss Crump came back with the buns, she handed them round and said, 'Where have you bicycled from? Very far?'

'Oh no,' said Daisy. 'Only from Peterswood. We live there.'

'Do you really?' said Miss Crump, offering a bun to the surprised and grateful Buster. 'Well, you know, I nearly went to live there a year ago. I don't expect you know a place called Milton House, do you?'

'Oh yes, we do,' answered every one in a chorus.

412

Miss Crump looked surprised to think that Milton House should apparently be so well known.

'I bought Milton House,' said Miss Crump, taking a bun herself. 'My brother wanted to live in this county, and he seemed to think Milton House would do for us.'

'Oh!' said Daisy, after a nudge from Fatty. 'Well—er—why didn't you go and live there, then? I mean—you seem to live here.'

This wasn't very clever, but Miss Crump went on cheerfully, 'Well, after I'd bought it, a funny thing happened.'

The children pricked up their ears at once. Buster, sensing the general feeling of interest, pricked his up too. 'What funny thing happened?' asked Bets eagerly.

'A man came to see me, and begged and begged me to let him buy the house from me,' said Miss Crump,' and all because it used to belong to his dear old mother, and he had been brought up in it, and wanted to go there with his wife and children and live there himself! As he offered me very much more than I had paid for it, which was, let me see, now——'

'Three thousand pounds,' said Pip obligingly, remembering what Fatty had told him.

He got a sharp and angry nudge from both Fatty and Larry immediately. Miss Crump stared at Pip in great astonishment.

'Now how in the world did you know that?' she said. 'What an extraordinary thing! That *was* the price I paid. But how did you know?'

Pip was scarlet. He couldn't think what to say. Fatty as usual came to the rescue.

'He's an *awfully* good guesser!' he said earnestly. 'Simply awfully good. It's a sort of gift, I suppose. It's wonderful what a good guesser Pip is, isn't it?'

he said, turning to the others and glaring at them to make them say yes.

They said it at once. 'Oh *yes*—a very good guesser,' they all said in chorus.

Fortunately Miss Crump seemed satisfied with this simple explanation. 'Well, I don't know why I'm rambling on like this to you,' she said. 'It must be very dull—but it was you mentioning that you came from Peterswood, you know, that reminded me of Milton House. Of course, I'm glad now that we didn't go there, because almost at once I found this place, which is *much* nicer.'

'Oh, much!' said Fatty. 'It's delightful. Fancy that man wanting to live in Milton House just because he had been brought up there himself, Miss Crump! What did you say his name was?'

'Well—I didn't say, did I?' said Miss Crump, surprised. 'But possibly you know him. I expect he lives there now, and maybe you know the children.'

Nobody said that Milton House was empty. Nobody said that there were certainly no children there. They did not want to give anything away. The mystery seemed to be getting deeper and deeper!

'Is his name Popps?' said Fatty, saying the first name that came into his head in order to make Miss Crump think of the right name.

'No, no—nothing like that,' said Miss Crump. 'Wait a minute—I believe I've got a letter from him somewhere. I usually keep all business letters for two years, you know, then destroy them. Ah, here it is! Oh dear! where are my glasses?'

It was clear that Miss Crump couldn't read anything without her glasses. She stood by her desk, holding a letter in her hand, looking helplessly round for her glasses.

Then Pip showed himself to be really very clever.

He saw the glasses on the table near by him in their case. He pushed them quickly down the side of the chair he was sitting on, and then got up. He went to Miss Crump's side.

'Let me help you,' he said. 'I can read the name for you.'

'But where *are* my glasses?' said Miss Crump. 'I really must find them.'

She couldn't find them, of course, and in the end she let Pip read the name for her. He read it out loud, 'John Henry Smith.' But, whilst he was reading out this very ordinary name, his eyes were also taking in the address at the top! Yes, Pip was being very smart just then—he was annoyed with himself for having blurted out, 'Three thousand pounds,' and he wanted to make up for it.

'Yes, that's right,' said Miss Crump. 'It was such an ordinary name I'd forgotten it. Well, do you know the Smith children?'

'Er—no, we don't,' said Daisy. 'We don't seem to have met them. Well, thank you very much indeed, Miss Crump, for being so kind to us and Buster. I think we'd better go now, or we shan't get home before dark.'

They all said good-bye, and Miss Crump told them to come again. Then off they went on their bicycles, but at the very first corner, they got off to talk!

12   LARRY TAKES A TURN

'GOLLY! We've found out something now!' said Fatty. 'Pip, did you notice John Henry Smith's address?'

'Of course,' said Pip importantly. 'Didn't you guess that's why I offered to help to read the name ? '

'I saw you push Miss Crump's spectacle-case down the side of your chair,' said Daisy.

'Yes. But I put them on the table again before I went,' said Pip. 'I got the address all right. It was 6, The Causeway, Limmering. And the telephone number was Limmering 021.'

'Jolly good, Pip,' said Fatty admiringly. 'You made an awful blunder about the three thousand pounds, but you were certainly very smart afterwards. I couldn't have done better myself.'

'You couldn't have done so well ! ' said Bets, very proud of Pip. 'I say—it's all very queer, isn't it ? If Mr. Smith so badly wanted the house because his mother lived there, and because he was brought up there, why did he only furnish one room ? '

'That room has a barred window,' said Fatty, thinking hard. 'Maybe that was the nursery window in the days when he was there as a child— and perhaps that's why he has taken that one room and furnished it—he may be a frightfully sentimental person. Though I admit it doesn't sound a very good explanation. Still, detectives have to think out every *possible* explanation.'

Nobody thought it was a good explanation.

'We'll find out if a Mrs. Smith lived there in years gone by,' said Larry thoughtfully. 'And if one of her children was called John. And if that room was the nursery.'

'Yes. We can do that,' said Fatty. 'And we might find out if John Henry is still at Limmering.'

'Limmering is *miles* away ! ' said Larry. 'We would never be allowed to go there.'

'Well, we've got the telephone number. We can telephone, silly,' said Fatty.

They got on their bikes and cycled away fast, for it was now getting dark.

'Whose turn is it to make inquiries now?' said Daisy. 'I've done my share. I should think it's Larry's or Bets'.'

'How can we find out who lived at Milton House before?' said Larry. 'Nobody will know!'

'Use your brains, fathead,' said Fatty. 'There are lots of ways of finding out. I could tell you plenty. But you can jolly well think up some for yourself. A good detective would never be stumped by a simple thing like that. Pooh!—I could find out in ten minutes.'

'You're always so clever!' said Larry crossly.

'I can't help that,' said Fatty. 'Even as a baby I used to——'

'Oh, shut up!' said Pip and Larry, who never would allow Fatty to tell them of his wonderful babyhood.

Fatty looked offended. 'Well,' he said, when they parted at Pip's corner,' 'see you all to-morrow. You get the information we want, Larry, and report it.'

This sounded very official and important. Bets sighed happily. 'It *is* nice to be solving such a dark mystery, isn't it?' she said.

'Well—we haven't got very far with it yet!' said Fatty, smiling at her. 'And if old Buster hadn't got into that fight, I doubt if we would have got so much out of Miss Crump.'

'Poor darling Buster,' said Bets, looking at the little Scottie as he sat patiently in Fatty's bicycle basket. 'Does your leg hurt?'

It didn't, but Buster was not going to refuse any sympathy offered to him. He held out his bandaged leg and put on a miserable expression.

417

' He's a humbug,' said Fatty, patting him.
' Aren't you, Buster ? You enjoyed that fight,
didn't you—and all the fuss afterwards ? And
I bet you got in two or three jolly good bites
yourself. Now you'll expect to be spoilt the
next few days all because of a bandage round
your leg ! '

' Well, *I* shall spoil him,' said Bets, and she
kissed the top of his head. ' I was terrified when I
saw that big dog fighting him.'

' Poor little Bets,' said Fatty. ' Well, what with
Buster's snarling and your howling, we managed to
get right into Miss Crump's house and get all the
information we needed, and a lot more than we
expected ! '

They all said good-bye and cycled off to their
homes, getting in just at tea-time, as dusk was
falling. It was a cold December evening, and
thoughts of a cheerful fire and a good tea were very
welcome to all the Find-Outers !

Larry and Daisy discussed how to find out about
John Henry Smith and his mother. They soon
thought of quite a lot of ways.

' We could go to the next house and ask if Mrs.
Smith lived there,' said Daisy. ' Then they would
say no, she lived at Milton House years ago, or
something like that.'

' Or we could go and ask the village grocer,'
said Larry. ' He serves every one, and he would
remember Mrs. Smith, I should think. We could
ask the old man—he's been here all his life.'

' We could even ask Mother,' said Daisy.

' Better not,' said Larry. ' She would wonder
whyever we suddenly wanted to know a thing like
that.'

' We could ask at the post office too,' said Daisy.

' They know every one, because the postman delivers letters.'

' Oh—we could ask the *post*man ! ' said Larry, pleased. ' Of course. He's been postman here for years and years. He would be sure to know who used to live at Milton House.'

' Yes. That's a good idea,' said Daisy. ' We can easily ask him. How shall we do it ? We can't ask him straight out. I mean, it would seem a bit funny to say, " Did a John Henry Smith live with his mother at Milton House years ago ? " Wouldn't it ? '

' Yes,' said Larry. ' I'll think out something to-night, and I'll hang about to-morrow morning about eleven, when he delivers the second lot of letters.'

So, just before eleven the next morning, Larry and Daisy were swinging on their front gate, watching for old Sims the postman.

He came along as usual, disappearing into first one house and then another. Larry called to him as he came near :

' Hallo, Sims ! Any letters for me ? '

' No, Master Larry. Why, is it your birthday or something ? ' said Sims.

' Oh no ! ' said Larry. ' Gracious ! What a crowd of letters you have to deliver, Sims ! Have you got to deliver all those by the second post ? Do you have a completely empty bag by the time you get back to the post office ? '

' Yes,' said Sims, ' unless some one has addressed a letter wrong-like. Then, if I can't find out where the person lives, I have to take it back. But I knows where most people lives ! '

' I bet you can't remember the names of all the people who have lived in Peterswood since you were postman ! ' said Larry cleverly.

'Oh, can't I, now!' said Sims, stopping to lean on the gate. 'Well, that's one thing I *can* do! My old woman, she says I ain't forgotten a single name. I can tell you who lived in *your* house afore you came. Yes, it was a Mrs. Hampden, it was, and mighty feard I was of coming every morning because of her two fierce dogs. And afore she had the house it was a Captain Lacy. Nice old gentleman he was. And afore that——'

Larry didn't want to hear any more about his own house. He interrupted old Sims.

'Sims, you *have* got a wonderful memory. You really have. Now—I'll try and catch you out. Who lived at Milton House years ago?'

'Milton House? Ah, that's an easy one, that is!' said Sims, brightening up. 'Why, the three Misses Duncan lived there, so they did, and well I remember them too.'

'Duncan?' said Larry, astonished. 'Are you sure? I thought somebody named Smith lived there.'

'No. There was never any one by name of Smith there,' said Sims, wrinkling his forehead. 'I remember that house being built. It was built by Colonel Duncan for himself and his three daughters. What be their names now? Ah yes! —there was Miss Lucy and Miss Hannah and Miss Sarah. Real nice ladies they was, and they never married neither.'

'Did they live there long?' said Larry.

'Oh yes—they lived there till about six years ago,' said Sims. 'The old gentleman died, and then two of the ladies died, and the last one she went and lived with her friend, she was that lonely.'

Larry remembered the barred window. 'Was there ever a nursery at Milton House?' he said. 'Were there young children?'

' Oh no. The young ladies were in their twenties
when they came,' said Sims. ' There weren't never
no children there. Never have been children there.'

' Who came after the Duncans ? ' asked Daisy,
wondering if the Smiths could have come then.

' Oh, it was taken by a Miss Kennedy who ran
it as a kind of boarding-house,' said Sims. ' But
that were a failure. Only lasted two years. Since
then it's been empty. I did hear as some one had
bought it—but they've not moved in. I never take
no letters there.'

' And nobody of the name of Smith ever lived
there ? ' said Daisy, puzzled.

' You seem set on the Smiths, whoever they be ! '
said old Sims, straightening himself up to go.
' Maybe you're thinking of old General Smith, him
as lived in Clinton House ! '

' I dare say we are,' said Larry. ' Well, Sims, I
think your memory is wonderful. You tell your
wife we tried to catch you out and couldn't ! '

Sims grinned and went trudging on up the hill.
Larry and Daisy looked at one another.

' Well—what do you think of *that* ! ' said Larry.
' Mr. John Henry Smith told a pack of the most
awful lies to get that house ! Whoever is he, and
what's his little game ? '

13   WHO IS JOHN HENRY SMITH?

WHEN Larry went down to Pip's to meet the others,
his news caused a good deal of surprise.

' You did jolly well to think of asking old
Sims,' said Fatty warmly. ' A very good idea—

worthy even of that great detective, Sherlock Holmes.'

This was indeed high praise from Fatty, but honesty made Larry admit that it was Daisy who had given him the idea.

'Still, it was well carried out,' said Fatty. 'But, I say—things are curiouser and curiouser, as Alice in Wonderland would say. I did think, when I heard the name, that John Henry Smith sounded a little bit *too* ordinary—the sort of name people take when they don't want to be found out in anything.'

'Fancy! All that tale about his mother living there was made up,' said Bets. 'I wonder why he wanted that particular house so badly. Does *he* use that secret room, do you think?'

'Don't know,' said Fatty. 'We've certainly got hold of a queer mystery. We shall have to find out who John Henry Smith is.'

The others stared at him, and little shivers went down Bets' back. To her John Henry Smith seemed to be a queer and rather frightening person. She didn't think she particularly wanted to meet him.

'We—we can't go to Limmering,' she said, in a small voice.

'No. I told you before—we can telephone,' said Fatty. 'What was the number now, Pip? Limmering 021?'

'Yes,' said Pip. '*You* telephone, Fatty. This is rather important. If any one is going to speak to John Henry Smith himself, it had better be you.'

'All right,' said Fatty, looking important. 'I'll go down to the call-box and phone from there. If your mother hears me phoning from your house here, Pip, she may want to know what it's all about.'

'Yes, she would,' said Pip. 'You go on down

to the call-box. Buster can stay here because of his bad leg.'

' Woof ! ' said Buster pathetically. He was very funny that day, because whenever he wanted a little fussing, he got up and limped badly, which made all the children very sorry for him. Actually his healthy little leg was healing fast, and did not even need a bandage on it. But Buster was going to make the most of it whilst it lasted !

All the same, he went with Fatty. He wasn't going to be left behind, if his master was going anywhere. So, limping badly, he followed Fatty down to the call-box.

Fatty felt rather excited. John Henry Smith was the key to the mystery—and he was just about to talk to him !

He put the receiver to his ear and asked for the number he wanted.

A voice told him what money to put into the slot. He pressed it in, and then listened for an answer, his heart beating rather fast.

Then he heard a voice at the other end : ' Hallo ! '

' Oh—hallo ! ' said Fatty. ' Does a Mr. John Henry Smith live there, please ? '

There was a silence. Then the voice said cautiously, ' What number do you want ? '

Fatty repeated the number.

' Who told you that you could get Mr. Smith at this number ? ' said the voice. ' Who are you ? '

Fatty made up a name out of his head. ' This is Donald Duckleby,' he said.

There was another astonished silence. ' *What* name did you say ? ' said the voice at last.

' Could you tell me if Mr. Smith still lives at Limmering, or if he has moved to Peterswood ? ' said Fatty, deciding on boldness. He knew quite well that John Henry Smith had *not* moved to Peterswood, but there would be no harm in giving him a shock.

There was another silence. This time it was so long that Fatty spoke again, ' Hallo ! Hallo ! '

But there was no reply. The person at the other end replaced his receiver. Fatty put his down too and thought hard.

He hadn't learnt much ! He didn't even know if the man he had spoken to was John Henry Smith or not ! It was most unsatisfactory, really. Fatty didn't quite know what he had hoped to get from his telephone call, but he had certainly hoped for something a little more definite.

He went out of the call-box—and stepped right in front of old Clear-Orf, who had been watching him through the glass. No wonder Buster had been growling !

Mr. Goon felt very suspicious. Who was this boy telephoning to ? Hadn't he got a telephone in his own house ? Yes, he had. But probably he didn't want his mother to hear what he was saying, so he had gone out to the public call-box. Therefore Fatty must have been phoning about the mystery that Clear-Orf was certain the children were meddling in !

' Who you been phoning to ? ' he said.

' I don't really think it's any of your business, is it ? ' said Fatty, in the polite voice that always infuriated Mr. Goon.

' You been to Milton House any more ? ' said Mr. Goon, who had a definite feeling that that house had something more to do with the mystery than he knew.

' Milton House ? Where's that ? ' said Fatty innocently.

Mr. Goon swelled, and his face began to turn the purple colour that fascinated the children.

'None of your sauce,' he began. 'You know where Milton House is as well as I do—better, perhaps!'

'Oh!—you mean that old place we played hide-and-seek in the other day,' said Fatty, as if he had only just remembered. 'Why don't you come and have a game with us some time, Mr. Goon?'

Buster began to growl again. Mr. Goon edged away from him. That was the worst of talking to Fatty. He always had Buster with him, and Buster could always bring any conversation to a remarkably quick end.

Buster ran at Mr. Goon's ankles, and the policeman kicked out. 'Now don't you hurt his *other* leg!' cried Fatty, and Mr. Goon immediately thought that it was his kicks two or three days before that had caused Buster's leg to be bandaged.

'Well, you call him orf,' he said. 'And clear-orf yourself. Hanging about in telephone boxes! Always messing about somewhere, and hanging around!'

He went off, and Fatty grinned. Poor old Clear-Orf! Fatty's quick tongue could always get the better of him. Fatty strolled back to Pip's house.

The others were interested to hear about his telephone call, and amused to hear about Clear-Orf going all suspicious about it.

'But I say, Fatty—I'm not sure you ought to have said anything about Peterswood,' said Larry, after thinking a little. 'You may have put him on his guard, you know. I mean—if Mr. Smith is up to some sort of underhand game at Milton House, he'll get a shock to find out that somebody apparently knows about him in Peterswood—where his house is!'

'Blow!—yes, I think you're right,' said Fatty, thinking of the quiet, quick way in which the person he had spoken to had replaced his receiver when he had mentioned Peterswood. Milton House was on the outskirts of Peterswood. Yes—he might have put Mr. John Henry Smith on his guard.

'Well—if I've put him on his guard—he'll probably come racing down to Peterswood to see if his precious secret room is all right,' said Fatty. 'So we may have set things happening. We'll keep a very, very strict eye on Milton House from now on. If Mr. Smith does come down, we'll be able to see him and find out what he's like.'

'We can't watch at night,' said Larry doubtfully.

'*I* can,' said Fatty. 'My mother would never know if I'm in bed or not.'

'But, Fatty—you'd never dare to go down to Milton House in the dark of night!' said Bets, horrified. 'It'll be so cold—and pitch dark—and simply awful.'

'It won't be dark,' said Fatty. 'The moon is nearly full. And I shan't be cold. I spotted a sort of tumble-down summer-house there in the garden, and I can take a couple of thick rugs and make myself comfortable.'

The others stared at him in awe. Not one of them would have liked to go down to Milton House alone at night.

'I'm perfectly fearless,' said Fatty, basking in their admiration. 'Why, when I was two years old, I went——'

'Shut up!' said Larry and Pip. 'You spoil everything when you start boasting.'

'Will you take Buster with you?' asked Bets.

'Don't know,' said Fatty. 'He'd be company. On the other hand, he might bark if any one came.

426

'Do you know it's snowing?' said Daisy suddenly.

So it was. The big white flakes came down silently. The children stared at them out of the window.

'This will mean I ll have to be awfully careful not to give myself away by footprints,' said Fatty. 'I shall have to try and creep in through the garden hedge. Anyway, *I* shall be able to see if any one has been to the house, because their footprints will show too!'

'Shall we pop down to Milton House now?' said Pip. 'Just to see if anything is different?'

'No. We'll go to-morrow,' said Fatty. 'Our Mr. John Henry Smith isn't likely to rush over to-day—but most likely he will to-morrow—and we may see some sign of him then. Let's play a game now.'

So they played Happy Families, and roared at Bets when she forgot the game for a moment and asked Daisy if she had got 'Mr. John Henry Smith' instead of Mr. Bones the Butcher.

'I feel as if our mystery is warming up a bit,' said Fatty, when he said good-night to the others. 'I shouldn't be surprised if things begin to happen soon!'

14   DOWN TO MILTON HOUSE AGAIN

NEXT morning the Five Find-Outers and Buster set off to Milton House. The snow was very thick, and they left the marks of their footprints behind them.

Pips and Bets had to pass Mr. Goon's house to meet the others, and the policeman saw them. He wondered if they were doing something he ought to know about. He felt so certain that the children were on the track of some mystery, and old Clear-Orf couldn't bear the idea of their getting in first again.

He decided to follow them. He couldn't very well ride his bicycle in the thick snow, so he set out on foot, keeping them in sight, but trying not to be seen himself.

However, as soon as Pip and Bets joined up with the others, Buster knew they were being followed. He stopped and growled, looking back along the road. The children turned too, and caught sight of the familiar dark-blue uniform slipping into a gateway.

' It's Clear-Orf following us,' said Fatty, in disgust. ' What a nuisance he is ! We can't possibly go to Milton House with him hard on our heels all the time. What shall we do ? '

' We're not very far from my house,' said Larry. ' Shall I slip in and write a note of some sort that will make him think we *are* solving a mystery—but not the one we really are in the middle of ? A make-up one ? '

Every one giggled.

' Yes,' said Fatty, ' and we'll drop it behind us for him to pick up ! I bet he'll pounce on it and read it—and then he'll be properly on the wrong track ! Maybe he will give up bothering us then.'

So Larry popped in at his gate and wrote a hurried note in pencil :

' DEAR FATTY,—Just to tell you that I am on the track of the robber who stole those jewels. Meet me on Felling Hill, and I will show you where he hid the things before he took them away again.—Yours, LARRY.'

Larry grinned as he stuck up the envelope. He ran out to the others, and they set off down the road again, hoping that Mr. Goon was still watching them.

Fatty laughed when Larry told him what he had written. ' Good ! ' he said, ' now old Clear-Orf will think we are tracking a jewel-thief, and he'll hare off to Felling Hill and do a bit of exploring there. Keep him quiet for a bit ! '

' There he is — behind that tree,' said Bets. ' Don't look behind, anybody. You two boys begin to push one another about, and then drop the note as you do it. Clear-Orf will think you really did drop it by accident then.'

' Good idea, Bets,' said Fatty, approving. ' You're getting to be quite a good detective.'

The children set off again, and when they thought they were nicely in view of Clear-Orf they began to jostle one another, as if in play.

Larry and Fatty tried to push each other off the kerb, and in the middle of the tussle Larry dropped the note. Then the five children, with Buster, went on their way again. Buster nearly spoilt things by running back to the note and sniffing at it.

' Buster ! Idiot ! Come here and leave that alone,' said Fatty, in a low voice. ' Don't you dare to pick it up and bring it ! '

Buster, though surprised, had the sense to leave the note where it was. Limping badly, he went after the others, feeling rather hurt that Fatty should have scolded him.

' Can we manage to see if old Clear-Orf picks it up ? ' said Larry excitedly. ' I do so hope he does.'

' I'll go into the sweet-shop and watch, whilst you others go on,' said Fatty.

So Fatty watched from the sweet-shop, whilst

he was buying chocolate, and to his great delight he saw Mr. Goon pick up the note !

' I bet he'll read it ! ' thought Fatty, pleased. ' He's so jolly snoopy.'

Mr. Goon put the note in his pocket. He certainly meant to read it ! He pondered whether to go on following the children or to slip home and read the note. It might tell him something he wanted to know !

He went home. He opened the note and gave a snort. ' Ho ! Didn't I know they were up to something ? On the track of some thief now. I suppose it's the Sparling Robbery they've heard about. Well, who would have thought the thief would have come in this direction ? Felling Hill, they say. Well, I'll be along there sometime or other, and if I don't sniff something out, my name's not Theophilus Goon ! '

Mr. Goon felt very pleased. ' Those children think they're clever—but they go and drop a note like this and give their game away,' thought the policeman. ' Now I know what they're after. I knew they were interfering in something again. Can't keep them children out of meddling ! '

He sat and thought for a moment. ' Now wait a bit—this boy Larry says the thief put the things on Felling Hill and took them away again. Where did he take them to ? Why are those kids so interested in Milton House ? Ah—now I've got it—the thief has hidden the jewels somewhere in that empty house ! '

This wasn't at all what Larry had wanted Mr. Goon to think. But Mr. Goon felt very pleased with himself. He thought he could see everything clearly now. Somehow those kids had got on the Sparling Robbery mystery, and somehow they had got on

430

the track of the thief, and had found out where he had first hidden his booty. Now they were on the track of the booty again—and maybe Milton House was the key to the mystery !

' Ah !—I'll keep a good watch on that there house now,' he thought. ' If there's any jewels hidden there, *I'll* be the one to find them and not that fat boy. Got brains, he has—but mine are better than his. Ho ! I'll pay him out for saying mine want oiling ! '

Meanwhile, not knowing that Mr. Goon was thinking all these tiresome things, the children were on their way to Milton House, keeping a sharp look-out in case Mr. Goon was still following them.

' I don't think he is,' said Fatty. ' He's probably on his way to Felling Hill by now ! '

They came to Milton House—and almost at once Fatty gave a low exclamation.

' Look there ! What do you think of that ? Footprints to the front door ! '

The children stared at them. They saw a line of prints, very big prints too, leading down the drive, right to the front door. And they saw another line, criss-crossing the others, leading back !

' Some one's been here,' said Fatty, excited.

' Yes—I bet you *did* put John Henry Smith on his guard, and he came down here in the night ! ' said Larry.

' How did he come ? ' said Pip.

' By car, I bet ! ' said Daisy. ' I saw some car-prints outside, but I didn't take much notice of them. Come and see.'

They all went to see—and sure enough, a car had been down Chestnut Lane the night before, and had stopped outside Milton House ! And it had turned round there too and gone back up the lane

They saw a line of prints to the front door

again, for there were the same wheel-prints on opposite sides of the road.

'Now we're getting somewhere!' said Pip. 'We know that whoever you phoned to knew about Milton House, and was worried to know some one had mentioned it, and came down to inspect. Who was it? John Henry Smith? And who *is* Mr. Smith, anyhow? I wish I knew.'

'Let's shin up the tree and see if anything is different in the room,' said Larry.

So they all climbed the tree and one by one looked in at the window. And they saw several things that interested them!

'Some one's put a kettle on top of the electric stove,' said Daisy.

'And some one's put tins of food on that shelf opposite,' said Pip.

'And there are some books on the window-sill that weren't there before—books in a foreign language I don't know,' said Larry.

'And the room's been dusted,' said Bets. 'It looks quite clean. And there are two thick rugs on the sofa. What does it all mean?'

'It means that the room has been got ready for a visitor!' said Fatty. 'Yes—it can only mean that. Who's the visitor? Not Mr. John Henry Smith, *I* bet! Some one who uses the room at intervals when he wants to be well hidden. It's jolly queer.'

'I wish we could get in and explore the whole house,' said Pip. 'But there's no way in at all.'

'Wait a minute,' said Fatty, thinking hard. 'There *may* be a way. I've just thought. That is, if there's an outside coal-hole.'

'What do you mean?' said the others, puzzled.

'Come and see,' said Fatty.

So down the tree they went, and, led by Fatty,

went round to the kitchen entrance. It began to snow again as they walked round, and Fatty was pleased.

'The snow will hide our footmarks,' he said. 'I was a bit worried about those. Ah, look—this is what I hoped to see!'

He pointed down to the ground to a spot that he had rubbed clear of snow with his boot. The others saw a round iron lid, whose crevices were black with old coal-dust.

'An outside coal-hole,' said Fatty. 'Now you all know that a coal-hole leads into a coal-cellar—and that steps lead up to the kitchen from the coal-cellar—and so any one slipping down this coal-hole can get into the house!'

'Jolly good, Fatty!' said every one admiringly.

'But do you think we'd better go down in these clothes?' added Pip. 'We'd get filthy, and I know my mother would ask all sorts of awkward questions.'

'Yes—we can't go down now,' said Fatty. 'I shall go down myself to-night!'

The others looked at him in awe. To go down to Milton House, the mystery place, at night, and get down the coal-hole! It seemed a most heroic feat to every one.

'I shall put on a disguise,' said Fatty. 'Just in case.'

'In case of what?' said Bets.

'Oh, just in case,' said Fatty. 'I don't want to be recognized, do I?'

'Oh!—you mean Mr. Goon might see you,' said Bets.

Fatty didn't mean that at all. He just wanted to disguise himself because he liked it. What was the good of buying disguises if you didn't use them?

He felt pleased and important. The mystery, as

he had said the day before, was decidedly warming up ! Soon, no doubt, the Find-Outers would have solved it, and could tell Inspector Jenks all about it.

' We won't tell the Inspector a word about all this till we've got to the bottom of the mystery and can tell him everything, down to the last detail,' said Fatty. ' Then, if we find there's any arresting or anything to be done, he can do it.'

' Oooh !—do you think there will be people to be arrested and sent to prison ? ' said Bets, with large eyes.

' You never know,' said Fatty grandly. ' Well— we'd better go now, and I'll lay my plans for to-night.'

15   THE SECRET ROOM

IT was most enjoyable talking over Fatty's plans for the night. All the Find-Outers and Buster gathered round the fire in Pip's playroom, and talked.

' My mother and father will be away for two days,' said Fatty. ' That's lucky. They won't know if I'm there to-night or not. I shall go down to the summer-house in the grounds of Milton House and make myself comfortable there with a couple of rugs. If I don't hear anything by midnight, I shall get in at the coal-hole.'

' Fatty—suppose you're caught ? ' said Pip.

' Yes—I'd thought of it,' said Fatty, considering. ' If I'm caught, one of you had better know. I'll tell you what—if I'm caught, I shall throw a note out of the window of whatever room I am locked up in—I imagine if I'm caught I shall be locked in somewhere—and one of you must scout round the grounds to-morrow morning and look out for the note. See ? It will be in invisible writing, of course.'

This sounded terribly exciting. Bets looked solemn. ' Don't be caught, Fatty. I don't want you to be caught.'

' Don't worry. I'm pretty smart,' said Fatty. ' People would have to be pretty clever to catch *me* ! '

' Well—that's settled, then,' said Larry. ' You are going down to Milton House to-night in disguise, and you're going to wait till midnight to see if any one comes. If nobody comes, you're going to get down the coal-hole and explore the secret room, to see if you can get any information about the mysterious John Henry Smith. By the way—I do wonder why that window was barred if there were no children in that house.'

' Don't know,' said Fatty. ' But I expect I shall find out.'

' If you don't get caught, you'll come back home, go to bed, and meet us in the morning with whatever news you've got,' said Larry. ' But if you don't turn up, one of us will snoop round the grounds and wait for a letter written in invisible ink. Don't forget to take an orange with you, Fatty, in case you have to write that note.'

' Of course I shan't forget,' said Fatty. ' But as I shan't be caught, you needn't worry—there won't be any letter floating out of a window ! '

' Anyway, Fatty, you know how to get out of a locked room if you have to,' said Bets.

' Of course ! ' said Fatty. ' I shall be all right, you may be sure.'

As Fatty's parents were away, the Find-Outers decided to go down to his house after tea and watch him disguise himself. They all felt excited, though

Bets had now got the idea that this mystery was a dangerous one, and she was rather worried.

'Don't be silly,' said Fatty. 'What danger can there be in it? I shall be all right, I tell you. This is an adventure, and people like me never say no to an adventure.'

'You *are* brave, Fatty,' said Bets.

'This is nothing!' said Fatty. 'I could tell you of a time when I really *was* brave. But I expect I should bore you?' He looked round inquiringly.

'Yes, you *would* bore us,' said Pip. 'Are you going to wear those terrible teeth again, Fatty?'

'You bet!' said Fatty, and slipped them into his mouth. At once his whole appearance changed as he grinned round, the frightful sticking-out teeth making him look completely unlike himself.

Fatty looked fine when the Find-Outers at last left him, taking Buster with them. Fatty had decided that it wouldn't do to leave the little dog behind in the house as he might bark all night long. So he was to spend the night with Larry and Daisy. Bets wanted him, but Pip said that their mother would be sure to ask all kinds of why and wherefore questions if Buster suddenly appeared for the night, and that might lead to something awkward.

So Larry took him home, and Buster, rather surprised, trotted along with him and Daisy, limping every now and again whenever he remembered. He quite thought that Fatty would be along to fetch him from Larry's sooner or later.

Fatty sat up fairly late reading. He was in his French-boy disguise, and looked fine. If the maid had popped her head into his room she would have got a shock. But nobody saw him at all.

At about ten o'clock Fatty slipped out of the house. The moon was almost full, and shone brightly down on the white snow. Fatty's footsteps made no sound at all.

He went down the road, took the way over the hill, and at last walked down Chestnut Lane, keeping well to the hedge, in the black shadows there. He saw nobody. Mr. Goon was not about that night, being busy nursing a very bad cold which had suddenly and most annoyingly seized him. Otherwise he had fully meant to hang about Milton House to see if he could find out anything that night.

Now he was in bed, sneezing hard and dozing himself with hot lemon and honey, determined to get rid of the cold by the next day, in case those tiresome children got ahead of him in this new mystery.

So there was no one to watch Fatty. He slipped in at the drive gate, kept to the shadows, and made his way round the house, hoping that no one would notice his footprints the next day. He came to the little tumble-down summer-house and went in. He had two thick rugs with him, and put them down on the seat.

He had a look up at the secret room, with its strange bars. Was there any one there yet? Would any one come that night?

It was cold. Fatty went back to the summer-house and cuddled himself up in the rugs. He soon felt warm again. He grew rather sleepy, and kept blinking to keep himself awake. He heard the church clock in the village strike eleven. Then he must have fallen asleep, for the next thing he knew was the clock striking again! This time it struck twelve.

'Golly!' said Fatty, 'midnight! I must have fallen asleep. Well—as nothing has happened, and no one has come, or is likely to come as late as this, I'll just pop down the coal-hole!'

Fatty had put on his oldest clothes. His mother was not as particular as Pip's, but even she would remark on clothes marked with coal-dust. Fatty looked a proper little ruffian as he threw off the rugs and stood listening in the moonlight. He had on the curly wig, he had made his face very pale, he had stuck on dark eyebrows, and, of course, he had the awful teeth. He was certainly enough to startle any one if there had been some one to see him.

He made his way round the hedges of the garden to the kitchen entrance, keeping well in the shadows. He came to the coal-hole. Snow had covered it again, but Fatty knew just about where it was. He cleared the snow away from it, and bent down to pull up the round iron lid.

It needed a jolly good tug, but at last up it came, unexpectedly suddenly, so that Fatty sat down with a bump, and the lid clanged down, making quite a noise.

Fatty held his breath, but nothing happened. He got up cautiously, pushed the lid to one side, and then shone his torch down the dark opening to see how far below the floor was.

Fortunately for him there was a heap of coal just below the hole. He could let himself down on it fairly easily. So down he went, and landed on the coal, which at once gave beneath him, so that he went slithering down the side of the heap.

He picked himself up and switched on his torch. He saw a flight of stone steps leading upwards to a shut door—the kitchen or scullery door, he guessed. He went up slowly, and turned the handle of the door.

It opened into a large scullery, into which the moon shone brightly. It was completely empty. He went into the next room, which was a kitchen.

That, too, was empty, but in the dust of the floor Fatty saw the same large footprints that he had seen in the snowy drive the day before.

'Perhaps I can see into the secret room!' thought the boy, his heart beating fast. It was a queer feeling to be all alone in a deserted house, knowing that people came there secretly for some mysterious reason!

Fatty felt certain there was nobody at all in the house, but all the same he jumped at any moving shadow, and almost leapt out of his skin when a floor-board creaked loudly under his foot.

He looked into room after room. All were completely empty. He explored all the ground floor, the first floor, and the second floor. The secret room was on the third floor, at the top of the house. Fatty went up the stairs to the last floor, trying to walk as quietly as possible even though he felt so certain that there was nobody else in the house but himself.

He came to the top floor. He looked into the first room he came to. It was empty. He looked into the next one ; that was empty too. But the third one was the secret room !

Fatty pushed open the door quietly and slowly. He peeped in. It lay silent and still in the brilliant moonlight—a very comfortable room, large, high-ceilinged like all the rooms, and very well furnished.

Fatty walked round the room. It had evidently been roughly cleaned and thoroughly dusted not long before. A little pile of tins of meat and fruit stood on a shelf. The kettle on the stove had water in it. A tin of tea was on the table. Books stood on the window-sill, and Fatty turned over the pages of some. They were in a foreign language and he couldn't understand a word.

The sofa had been prepared as a kind of bed, for the cushions were piled at one end, and cosy rugs had been folded there. It was all very strange.

'I suppose I'd better get back to the summer-house,' thought Fatty. 'I wish I could find some letters or documents of some sort that would tell me a bit about this queer room. But there don't seem to be any.'

He sat down on the sofa and yawned. Then his eye caught sight of a small cupboard in the wall. He wondered what was in it. He got up—but the cupboard was locked. Fatty put his hand into his pocket and brought out a perfectly extraordinary collection of keys. He had secretly been making a hoard of these, as he had learnt that most detectives can lock or unlock doors or cupboards. They had queer keys called skeleton keys which could apparently unlock with ease almost anything that needed a key.

But a skeleton key had proved impossible to buy, and, indeed, had led to many awkward questions being put by the shopkeepers whom he had asked for one. So Fatty had been forced to collect any old key he could find, and he now had a very varied collection which weighed down the pocket of his coat considerably. He took them all out.

Most patiently and methodically Fatty tried first one key and then another in the lock of the little cupboard, and to his delight, and also his surprise, one key did manage to unlock the door!

Inside was a small book, a kind of notebook, and entered in it were numbers and names, nothing else at all. It seemed very dull to Fatty.

'Perhaps Inspector Jenks may like to have a look at it,' he thought, and he pocketed the little book and locked the cupboard door again. 'We shall soon be reporting this mystery to him, and he may like to have all the bits of evidence we can find.'

He sat down on the sofa again. He no longer felt excited, but very sleepy. He looked at his watch. It was a quarter past one ! Gracious ! he had been a long time in Milton House.

' I'll just have a bit of a rest on this comfy sofa,' said Fatty, and curled himself up. In half a minute he was sound asleep. What a mistake that was !

16   A BAD TIME FOR FATTY

FATTY slept soundly. His adventure had tired him. The couch was extremely comfortable, and although there was no warmth in the room, the rugs were thick and cosy. Fatty lay there dreaming of the time when he would be an even more important detective than the famous Sherlock Holmes.

He did not hear the sound of a car about half-past four in the early morning. The wheels slid silently over the snow, and came to a stop outside Milton House.

Fatty did not hear people walking up the drive. Nor did he hear a latch-key being put into the lock of the front door. He heard no voices, no footsteps, but the old empty house suddenly echoed to them.

Fatty slept on peacefully. He was warm and comfortable. He did not even wake up when some one opened the door of the secret room and came in.

Nobody saw him at first. A man crossed to the window and carefully drew the thick curtains across before switching on the light. Not a crack of light could be seen from outside once the window curtains were drawn.

Another man came into the room—and he gave a cry of surprise. ' Look here ! '

He pointed to the couch, where Fatty still slept as peacefully as Goldilocks had slept in the Little Bear's bed long ago !

The two men stared in the utmost astonishment at Fatty. His curly wig of black hair, his big black eyebrows, and the awful teeth made him a peculiar sight.

' Who is he ? And what's he doing here ? ' said one of the men, amazed and angry. He shook Fatty roughly by the shoulder.

The boy woke up and opened his eyes under the shaggy eyebrows. In a trice he knew where he was, and realized that he had fallen asleep in the secret room—and now he was caught ! A little shiver of fear went down his back. The men did not look either friendly or pleased.

' What are you doing here ? ' said the bigger fellow of the two, a ruddy-faced man with eyes that stuck out like Mr. Goon's, and a short black beard. The other man was short, and had a round white face with black button-eyes and the thinnest lips Fatty had ever seen.

The boy sat up and stared at the two men. He really didn't know what to say.

' Haven't you a tongue in your head ? ' demanded the red-faced man. ' What are you doing on our premises ? '

Fatty decided to pretend he was French again.

' Je ne comprends pas,' he said, meaning that he didn't understand.

But unfortunately one of the men spoke French

and he rattled off a long and most alarming sentence in French, which Fatty couldn't understand at all.

Fatty then decided he wouldn't be French; he would speak the nonsense language that he and the others sometimes spoke together when they wanted to mystify any one.

'Tibbletooky - fickle - farmery - toppy - swick,' he said quite solemnly.

The men looked puzzled. 'What language is that?' said the red-faced man to his companion. He shook his head.

'Speak French,' he commanded Fatty.

'Spikky - tarly - yondle - fitty - toomar,' answered Fatty at once.

'Never heard a language like that before,' said the red-faced man. 'The boy looks foreign enough. Wonder where he comes from. We'll have to find out how he got here.' He turned to Fatty again, and addressed him first in English, then in French, then in German, and then in a fourth language Fatty had never heard.

'Spikky-tarly-yondle,' said Fatty, and waggled his hands about just like his French master at school.

The pale-faced man spoke to his companion. 'I believe he's foxing,' he said in a low voice that Fatty could not hear. 'He's just pretending. I'll soon make him talk his own language. Watch me!'

He suddenly bent over Fatty, took hold of his left arm, dragged it behind him and twisted it. Fatty let out an agonized yell. 'Let go, you beast! You're hurting me!'

'Aha!' said the pale-faced man. 'So you *can* talk English, can you? Very interesting. Now— what about talking a little more, and telling us who you are and how you came here.'

Fatty nursed his twisted arm, feeling rather

alarmed. He was very angry with himself for falling
asleep and getting so easily caught. He looked
sulkily at the man and said nothing.

'Ah !—he wants a little more coaxing,' said the
pale-faced man, smiling with his thin lips and showing long yellow teeth. 'Shall we twist your other
arm, boy ?'

He took hold of Fatty's right arm. Fatty decided
to talk. He wouldn't give away more than he could
help.

'Don't you touch me,' he said. 'I'm a poor
homeless fellow, and I'm doing no harm sleeping
here.'

'How did you get in ?' said the red-faced man.

'Through the coal-hole,' said Fatty.

'Ah !' said the man, and the thin-lipped one
pursed up his mouth so that his lips completely
vanished.

He looked very hard and cruel, Fatty thought.

'Does any one else know you're here ?' said the
red-faced man.

'How do I know ?' said Fatty. 'If any one had
seen me getting down the coal-hole they'd know I
was here. But if they didn't see me, how would they
know ?'

'He is evading the question,' said the thin-
lipped man. 'We can only make him talk properly
by giving him much pain. We will do so. A little
beating first, I think.'

Fatty felt afraid. He was quite sure that this
man would go to any lengths to get what he wanted
to know. He stared sulkily at him.

Quite suddenly, without any warning, the thin-
lipped man dealt Fatty a terrific blow on his right
ear. Then, before the boy could recover, he dealt
him another blow, this time on his left ear. Fatty

gasped. Bright stars danced in front of his eyes, and he blinked.

When the stars went, and the boy could see again, he gazed in fear at the thin-lipped man, who was now smiling a horrible smile.

'I think you will talk now?' he said to Fatty. 'I can do other things if you prefer.'

Fatty was very frightened now. He felt that he would rather give away the whole mystery than have any more blows. After all, he wouldn't be harming the other Find-Outers, and he knew they would be only too glad for him to save himself from harm or injury. This was just very, very bad luck.

'All right. I'll talk,' said Fatty, with a gulp. 'There's not much to tell you, though.'

'How did you find out about this room?' demanded the red-faced man.

'By accident,' said Fatty. 'A friend of mine climbed that tree outside, and looked in and saw this room.'

'How many know about it?' rapped out the thin-lipped man.

'Only me and the other Find-Outers,' said Fatty.

'The other what?' said the man, puzzled.

Fatty explained. The men listened.

'Oh!—so there are five children in this,' said the red-faced man. 'Any grown-up know about this affair?'

'No,' said Fatty. 'We—we are rather keen on solving mysteries if we can—and we don't like telling grown-ups in case they interfere. There's only me and the other four in this. Now that I've let you know, you might let me go.'

'What!—let you go and have you spread the news around?' said the thin-lipped man scornfully.

'It's bad enough to have you interfering and messing up our plans without running the risk of letting you go.'

'Well, if you don't, the others will come snooping round to see what's happened to me,' said Fatty triumphantly. 'I've already arranged for them to come and find out what's happened if I'm not at home this morning.'

'I see,' said the thin-lipped man. He spoke quickly to the other man in a language Fatty could not follow. The red-faced man nodded. The thin-lipped man turned to Fatty.

'You will write a note to the others to say that you have discovered something wonderful here, and are guarding it, and will they all come to the garden as soon as possible,' he said.

'Oh !—and I suppose you think that you can catch them too when they come, and lock them up till you've finished whatever secret business you are on !' said Fatty.

'Exactly,' said the man. 'We think it would be better to hold you all prisoner here till we have finished our affairs. Then you can tell what you like.'

'Well, if you think I shall write a letter that will bring my friends into your hands, you're jolly well mistaken !' said Fatty hotly. 'I'm not such a coward as that !'

'Are you not ?' said the thin-lipped man, and he looked at Fatty so strangely that the boy trembled. What would this horrible man do to him if he refused to write the note ? Fatty didn't dare to think.

He tried to stare back bravely at the man, but it was difficult. Fatty wished desperately he had not gone into this midnight adventure so light-heartedly. He longed for old Buster. But perhaps it was as well that Buster was not there. These men might kick him and misuse him cruelly.

' We shall lock you up,' said the thin-lipped man. ' We have to go in a little while, but we shall come back soon. You will write this note whilst we are gone. If it is not done by the time we come back, there will be trouble for you, bad trouble—trouble you will not forget all the rest of your life.'

Fatty's spirits went up a little when he heard he was to be locked up. He might be able to escape if so ! He had a folded newspaper in his pocket. He was sure he could use his trick of getting out of a locked room all right. Then his spirits sank again.

' We will lock you into this so-comfortable room,' said the red-faced man. ' And we will give you paper and pen and ink. You will write a nice, excited note that will bring all your friends here quickly. You can throw it out of the window.'

Fatty knew he could never escape from the secret room. A thick carpet ran right to the door. There was no space beneath the edge of the door to slip a key. None at all. He would be a real prisoner. He could not even escape down the tree because the window was so heavily barred.

The thin-lipped man placed a sheet of note-paper on a table, and laid beside it a pen and a little ink-stand.

' There you are,' he said. ' You will write this note in your own way and sign it. What is your name ? '

' Frederick Trotteville,' said Fatty gloomily.

' You are called Freddie, then, are you not ? ' said the thin-lipped man. ' You will sign your letter " Freddie," and when your friends come into the garden, I will fling your note from the window —but you will not speak to them.'

The red-faced man looked at his watch. ' We must go,' he said. ' It is time. Everything is ready here. We will get the rest of these interfering kids and lock them up till we have finished. It won't hurt them to starve for a day or two in an empty room ! '

They went out of the room. Fatty heard the key turn in the lock. He was a prisoner. He stared gloomily at the shut door. It was his own fault that he was in this fix. But he wasn't going to get the others into it too—no, not even if those men beat him black and blue !

17   THE SECRET MESSAGE

FATTY heard the footsteps of the men clattering down the uncarpeted stairs. He heard the front door close quietly. He heard the sound of a car starting up. The men had gone.

He tried the door. It was locked all right. He went to the window. It was pitch-dark outside. He opened the window and felt the bars. They were too close together for him to slip out between them. He was indeed a prisoner.

He went and sat down again, shivering. Fright and the winter's chill made him shake all over. He saw the electric fire and decided to put it on. He might as well be warm, anyway !

He sat down once more and gazed gloomily at the sheet of notepaper. What a bad detective he was, to allow himself to be caught like this ! It was terribly careless. The others would never admire him again.

'Well, I shan't write that letter, anyway,' thought the boy, but he trembled to think what his punishment might be if he didn't.

Then an idea came to him. It was really brilliant. He sat and thought about it for a while. Yes—it would work if only the others were bright enough to catch on to the idea too !

'I'll write an invisible letter on this sheet of paper, and I'll write a letter in ink on it as well !' thought Fatty. ' I bet Pip and the others will think of testing it for secret writing. Golly—what an idea this is ! To write two letters on one sheet, one seen and the other unseen ! I bet the men will never think of *that* ! '

He looked at the sheet of paper. It was faintly ruled with lines. He could write his secret letter *between* the lines and the other letter *on* the lines ! When the others tested it for secret writing, they would then be able to read his real letter easily.

Fatty's hands shook with excitement. He might be able to do something startling now ! He must think carefully what to write. The men who used this room were evil, and they used it as a meeting-place for evil reasons. They must be stopped. They were evidently in the middle of some big affair at the moment, and it was up to Fatty to stop them.

He took a rather squashy orange from his pocket. He looked round for a glass. There was one on the shelf. He squeezed his orange into it, then picked up the pen the men had left. The nib was clean and new.

Should he write the visible letter first, or the secret one ? Fatty decided on the visible one, because it would be easier then to write the invisible one, as he could see where he had written the first letter.

He began :

' DEAR FIND-OUTERS,—I have made a wonderful discovery, most awfully exciting. I can't leave here, because I am guarding something—but I want to show you what it is. All of you come as soon as you can, and I will let you in when you knock.—Yours,
' FREDDIE.'

That seemed all right—just what the man had commanded him to write. But the others would smell a rat as soon as they saw the name ' Freddie ' at the bottom. He always signed himself Fatty in notes like this.

Then he set to work to write the letter in secret ink—or rather in orange juice.

' DEAR FIND-OUTERS '—he wrote—' Don't take any notice of the visible letter. I'm a prisoner here. There's some very dirty work going on ; I don't quite know what. Get hold of Inspector Jenks AT ONCE and tell him everything. He'll know what to do. Don't you come near the place, any of you.—Yours ever, FATTY.'

That just took him to the bottom of the sheet. Not a trace of the secret writing was visible ; only the few sentences of the inked writing were to be seen. Fatty felt pleased. Now, if only the others guessed there was a secret message and read it, things might be all right.

' Inspector Jenks will see to things,' thought Fatty, and it was comforting to think of the clever, powerful Inspector of Police, their very good friend, knowing about this curious affair. Fatty thought of him—his broad cheerful face, his courtesy, his tallness, his shrewdness.

It was now about six o'clock. Fatty yawned. He had had a poor night. He was hungry and tired, but warmer now. He curled himself up on the sofa again and slept.

He was awakened by the men coming into the room again. He sat up, blinking. Daylight now came in through the window.

The thin-lipped man saw the paper on the table and picked it up. He read the letter in silence and then handed it to the other man.

'This is all right,' he said. 'We'll bag all the silly little idiots, and give them a sharp lesson. Will they all come down to see where you are, boy?'

'I don't know,' said Fatty. 'No, probably not. Maybe just one or two of them.'

'Then they're sure to take the letter to show the others, and bring them back here,' said the thin-lipped man. 'We'll keep a look-out for them. We'll hide in the garden and catch the lot. Jarvis is downstairs now too. He can help.'

They opened some tins and had breakfast. They gave the hungry Fatty a small helping of ham sandwich, and he gobbled it up. They suddenly noticed his glass of yellow juice and one of them picked it up.

'What's this?' he said, smelling it suspiciously. 'Where did it come from?'

'It's orange juice,' said Fatty, and he drank it up. 'I had an orange with me and I squeezed it. I can't help being thirsty, can I?'

He set down the glass. The men evidently thought no more of it but began to talk together in low voices, again using the language that Fatty did not understand. He was very bored. He wondered if one of the others would come soon. As soon as some one found he hadn't got home, surely they

would come and look for him! What were the
Find-Outers doing?'

They were all wondering how Fatty had got on
that night. Bets was worried. She didn't know
why, but she really did feel anxious.

'I hope Fatty is all right,' she kept saying to
Pip. 'I do hope he is.'

'That's about the twenty-third time you've said
that!' said Pip crossly. 'Of course he's all right.
Probably eating an enormous breakfast this very
minute.'

Larry and Daisy called in at Pip's soon after
breakfast, looking cross.

'We've got to catch the bus and take some things
to one of our aunts,' said Daisy. 'Isn't it a bore—
just when we wanted to hear if Fatty had found out
anything. You and Bets will have to see if he's home,
Pip.'

'He may come wandering down, if he's at home,'
said Pip. 'Oh, you've got Buster with you! Well,
I'll take him back to Fatty's for you, shall I?'

Pip's mother wouldn't let him go out till about
twelve o'clock, as she had made up her mind that he
and Bets were to tidy out their cupboards. This was
a job Pip hated. It took ages. Grumbling loudly,
he began to throw everything out on to the floor.

'Oh, Pip, let's hurry up and finish this job,'
begged Bets. 'I can't wait to find out if Fatty's
home all right.'

Buster fussed round, sniffing at everything that
came out of the cupboards. He was upset and
worried. His beloved master hadn't fetched him
from Larry's the night before, and here was the
morning and nobody had taken him back to Fatty
yet. Not only that, but they apparently wouldn't
let him go by himself! He was so miserable that

he limped even more badly than usual, though his leg was now quite healed.

At last the cupboards were finished and Pip and Bets were told they might go out in the snow. They put on hats and coats, whistled to Buster, and set off to Fatty's.

They slipped in at his garden door and whistled the tune they always used as a signal to one another. There was no reply.

A maid popped her head out into the passage. ' Oh ! ' she said, ' I thought it was Master Frederick. He didn't sleep here last night, the naughty boy. I suppose he stayed the night with you or Master Larry—but he ought to have told me. When is he coming back ? '

This was a real shock to Pip and Bets. So Fatty *hadn't* come back from Milton House ? What had happened ?

' Oh !—he'll be back to-day I expect,' Pip said to the anxious maid. He dragged Bets out into the garden. She was crying.

' Don't be so silly,' said Pip. ' What's the good of crying before you know what's happened to Fatty ? '

' I knew something had happened to him. I knew he was in danger, I did, I did,' wept poor Bets. ' I want to go down to Milton House and see what's happened.'

' Well, you won't,' said Pip. ' There may be danger. You look after Buster for me. I'll go down myself.'

' I'll come too,' said Bets bravely, wiping her eyes.

' No, you won't,' said Pip firmly. ' I'm not going to have you running into danger. You don't like danger, anyway. So you be a good girl and take Buster home with you. I'll be back as soon as I can —and maybe I'll bring Fatty with me, so cheer up.'

Still crying, poor Bets went off with the puzzled Buster, who simply could *not* understand what had happened to Fatty. He seemed to have disappeared into thin air !

Pip was much more worried than he had let Bets see. He couldn't help thinking that something serious must have happened. But what could it be ? Fatty would surely never allow himself to be caught. He was far too clever.

Pip went over the hill and down Chestnut Lane. He came to the gate of Milton House. He gazed in cautiously. He could see more footprints, and there were new car-wheel prints.

He went round the hedge, slipped in at a gap, and found himself by the summer-house. Inside were the rugs Fatty had taken to keep himself warm. But there was no Fatty there.

He stepped cautiously into the garden, and one of the men, who was watching, saw him from a window. He had with him the sheet of notepaper on which Fatty had written the two letters.

The man bent down, so that he could not be seen, opened the window a crack at the bottom, gave a loud whistle to attract Pip's attention, and then let the paper float out of the window.

Pip heard the whistle and looked up. To his enormous surprise he saw a sheet of paper floating out of one of the second-storey windows. Perhaps it was a message from Fatty.

The boy ran to where the paper dropped and picked it up. He recognized Fatty's neat hand-writing at once. He read the note through, and his heart began to beat fast.

' Fatty's on to something,' he thought. ' He's found some stolen jewels or something and he's guarding them. He wants us all to be in it ! I'll run back to the others, and bring them back with me. What an adventure! Good old Fatty!'

He scampered off, his face bright. The man watched him go and was satisfied. That young idiot would soon bring the other children down with him, and then they could all be locked up safely before they gave the game away!

Fatty saw Pip too and began to have a few horrid doubts. Were the Find-Outers smart enough to guess there was a secret letter in between the lines of inked writing? Suppose they didn't? He would have led them all into a trap!

18   A SMELL OF ORANGES

PIP ran all the way home. He was tremendously excited. What had Fatty discovered? It must be something very wonderful for him to be guarding it like that!

Bets was waiting for Fatty very anxiously. She was at the window of the playroom, and Buster was sitting on the window-sill beside her, his black nose pressed against the pane.

Pip grinned widely and waved the letter at Bets. She guessed at once that he had good news, and her heart felt lighter. She tore downstairs to meet him, Buster at her heels.

'Is Fatty all right? What has happened? Is that a letter from him?' she asked.

Pip pushed her upstairs again. 'Don't yell questions at me like that!' he said crossly. 'You'll have all the household knowing about our mystery soon!'

Just then the luncheon gong sounded, and Pip's
mother put her head in at the door. 'Come along,'
she said. 'Don't keep me waiting, Pip, because I
have to go out immediately after lunch.'

So there was no time to show poor Bets the letter,
and she was so terribly curious about it that she
fidgeted all through the meal, much to her mother's
annoyance.

As soon as lunch was over, Pip and Bets flew
upstairs, and Pip spread the note out on the table.

'Look there!' he said. 'Fatty's found something marvellous—and he's guarding it. He wants
us all to go down and join him. So we'd better go
up to Larry's and get him and Daisy as soon as we
can.'

Bets read the note. Her eyes sparkled with
excitement. This sounded too thrilling for words.

'Fatty must have solved the mystery,' she said.
'Isn't he awfully clever?'

'Let's put on our things and go and fetch Larry
and Daisy now,' said Pip. 'Fatty will be expecting
us as soon as possible. We'll march up to the front
door and knock loudly.'

They put on their things and ran all the way to
Larry's house. They went in at the garden door
and whistled for Larry, using the signal they always
kept for themselves.

'Here we are, up here,' said Daisy, popping her
head out of a room upstairs. 'Any news?'

'Yes, heaps,' said Pip, leaping up the stairs two
at a time. 'We went to call on Fatty this morning,
and the maid said he hadn't been home all night!'

'Goodness!' said Daisy.

'So I went down to Milton House, without Bets
or Buster,' said Pip. 'And suddenly this letter
floated out of a window! It's from old Fatty.'

He showed it to Larry and Daisy. They read it in great excitement.

'I say! He's certainly found out something!' said Larry. 'He must have got in at the coal-hole and gone up to that secret room. I vote we all go down to Milton House now, this very minute.'

'Bets was awfully silly all last night and this morning,' said Pip. 'She kept on worrying and worrying because she felt sure Fatty was in trouble! She cried like anything when we found he wasn't at home. She's an awful baby.'

'I'm not,' said Bets, going red. 'I did feel awfully worried, but I couldn't help it. Something sort of told me that Fatty was in danger—and, as a matter of fact, I still don't feel quite right about him. I mean—I've still got that uncomfortable sort of feeling.'

'Have you?' said Daisy. 'How funny! But nothing can be wrong with Fatty now! You've read his note.'

'I know,' said Bets, and she read it again. 'I wonder why he signed himself " Freddie," ' she said suddenly. 'He nearly always puts " Fatty " now. I suppose he just didn't think.'

The little girl looked thoughtfully at the letter. Then she sniffed a little, turning this way and that.

'What's the matter? You look like Buster when he smells a nice smell and doesn't quite know where it comes from!' said Larry.

'Well—I did get a whiff of a smell that reminded me of something,' said Bets. 'What was it now? Yes—I know—oranges! But there aren't any in the room.'

'Imagination,' said Pip. 'You're always imagining things.' He took the letter and began to fold it up, but as he did so, he too began to sniff.

458

' How funny ! I can smell oranges too now ! '
he said.

Bets suddenly snatched the letter from him, her
eyes bright. She held it to her nose.

' *This* is what smells of oranges ! ' she said
excitedly. ' Smell it, all of you.'

They smelt it. Yes, it smelt of oranges—and
that could only mean one thing. Fatty had written
another letter on the same sheet—in orange juice, for
secret ink !

Bets sat down suddenly because her knees began
shaking.

' I've got that feeling again,' she said earnestly.
' You know—that something is wrong with Fatty.
Let's test the letter quickly for secret writing.'

Daisy flew down to get a warm iron. It seemed
ages to wait whilst it got hot enough. Then Pip
deftly ran the warm iron over the letter.

At once the secret message came up, faintly
brown. The children read it with beating hearts :

' DEAR FIND-OUTERS,—Don't take any notice of
the visible letter. I'm a prisoner here. There's
some very dirty work going on ; I don't quite know
what. Get hold of Inspector Jenks AT ONCE and
tell him everything. He'll know what to do. Don't
you come near the place, any of you.—Yours ever,
' FATTY.'

There was a silence. The Find-Outers looked
solemnly at one another. Suddenly their mystery
seemed to be very deep and dark and dangerous.
Fatty was a prisoner ! Why had he written that
other letter in ink ?

' The men who caught him must have made him
write it ! ' said Larry, thinking hard. ' They wanted

us all to be caught—because we know about the secret room. But clever old Fatty managed to write a secret letter on the same paper.'

'We nearly didn't find out about the secret one,' said Daisy. 'My goodness!—we were *just* going down to Milton House—to knock at the door—and it would have opened, and we'd have gone in—and *we* would have been prisoners too.'

'I think we were all very feeble not to think of testing for a secret message,' said Pip. 'We ought to have done that as a matter of course.'

'Bets and her sniffing saved us,' said Larry. 'If she hadn't smelt orange juice, we would all have been in the soup! Good old Bets! She's really a fine Find-Outer. *She* found out about the secret message.'

Bets glowed with pleasure at this praise. 'My uncomfortable feeling about Fatty was right, wasn't it?' she said. 'Oh dear!—I hope he isn't too unhappy. Pip, shall we telephone the Inspector at once? I feel as if I want to tell him everything as soon as possible.'

'I'll telephone now,' said Larry. He went down the stairs with the others, and took up the telephone receiver. He asked for Inspector Jenks' number. He lived in the next big town.

But alas, the Inspector was out and would not be back for an hour. What was to be done?

'It's no good going down to Milton House,' said Larry. 'Not a bit. If those men have caught Fatty, they would somehow catch us, and then we couldn't be any help to him at all. We'll have to wait patiently.'

'It—it would be silly to tell Clear-Orf, wouldn't it?' said Bets. She disliked Mr. Goon extremely, but she felt that it was very urgent to get help to Fatty.

' What ! Make old Clear-Orf a present of our mystery ! ' said Pip, in disgust. ' You're mad, Bets. Anyway, he's in bed with a cold. Our charwoman, who goes to turn out for him, told me that this morning. He won't go snooping down to Milton House for a bit.'

But Pip was wrong. It was true that Mr. Goon had kept in bed for one day, but the next morning he was up and about, still sniffing and sneezing, but quite determined to go down to Milton House as soon as he could.

In fact, even as Pip was telling Bets that Mr. Goon would not be going down to Milton House for a bit, he was on his way there ! He had to walk, because the snow was still lying thickly. He set off over the hill, and came to Chestnut Lane.

He noticed the car-wheels going down the lane, and wondered if they went as far as Milton House. He felt pleased when he saw that they stopped outside.

' Ho ! Somebody coming to this old empty house in a fine big car ! ' said Mr. Goon to himself. ' A bit funny, that. Yes—there's somethink going on here—and those kids have got wind of it. Well, if they think they're going to have another mystery all to themselves, they're mistaken ! '

Mr. Goon became all business-like. He hitched up his belt. He put his helmet more firmly on his round head. He walked very cautiously indeed to the gate of Milton House, trying to keep out of sight of the windows.

He saw the many footprints leading to and from the front door. He scratched his head, thinking hard. It looked as if people might be there. Were they the rightful owners of the place ? What were they doing ? And why did the children keep messing about there? Could it be that the thieves of the Sparling Jewels were there, hiding their booty?

Mr. Goon longed to get into that empty house. He longed to explore it. He wanted, however, to explore it without being seen. He felt sure the children had done so.

It was beginning to get dark, for it was a very gloomy, lowering winter's afternoon, with more snow to come. Mr. Goon went cautiously round the house, and, to his enormous surprise, suddenly saw a black hole in the ground near the kitchen.

Almost at once he saw it was a coal-hole with the iron lid off. He stared at it in surprise. Had somebody got down there? Yes—one of those tiresome children, probably—and maybe they were even now exploring that house to find if any stolen goods were hidden there.

Mr. Goon's face went slightly purple. He couldn't bear to think that those children might get more praise from Inspector Jenks for finding stolen goods hidden in his, Goon's, district. He determined to get into the house himself, find any of the children there, and scare the life out of them. My word, wouldn't he shout at them!

Very quietly and cautiously Mr. Goon lowered himself down into the coal-hole. He almost stuck, for he was plump. But he managed to wriggle through and landed on the coal.

'Now!' thought Mr. Goon triumphantly, as soon as he had got his breath, 'now to go up and explore the house and catch those interfering little nuisances! Won't I scare them! Won't I shake the life out of them! Ha, I'll learn them to go snooping round, doing the things that policemen ought to do! I'll learn 'em!'

19   ESCAPE—
AND A SHOCK FOR MR. GOON

MEANTIME, what had happened to Fatty ?

The men had taken the letter from him and had gone out of the room, locking it again. Fatty guessed they were going to wait for one of the Find-Outers to come. He, too, went to the window and watched.

Nobody came that morning, as we know, until just before dinner-time. Then Pip arrived, and Fatty saw him pick up the letter, which had apparently been flung out of one of the lower windows.

Fatty watched Pip, but did not dare to whistle to him. The only hope for Pip would be for him to get away back to the others, and for them to read the secret note—if only, *only* they guessed there *was* a secret message for them !

In a little while the two men came back. ' Well,' said the thin-lipped man, ' I expect we shall soon have your friends down here — and you will be pleased to have company ! You can have your dinner in a room not quite so comfortable as this, my boy —and as soon as your friends come, we will throw them all into the room with you ! '

Fatty was made to go out of the comfortable secret room, and taken to a room on the floor below. It was quite empty, and very cold.

' Here are some sandwiches for you,' said the red-faced man, and he handed some to Fatty. ' And here is a glass of water. We shall lock you in and bring your friends here as soon as we catch them. And here, I am afraid, you will have to stay for a day

463

or two, till our important business is finished. Then maybe we will telephone to the police or your parents and tell them where to find their poor missing children ! After this experience maybe you will not interfere again in what doesn't concern you ! '

He gave Fatty another box on the ear, and then the two men went out. Fatty heard the key turning in the lock.

' Well,' he thought, ' it's jolly cold and uncomfortable in here—but on the other hand I believe I might be able to get out of *this* locked room ! There's no carpet on the floor here, and a jolly good space under the door. I'll wait till everything is quite quiet and then I'll try my little trick.'

He went to the window. There was certainly no way out there, for it was a sheer drop to the ground. No tree grew conveniently near by !

Fatty squatted down in a dusty corner and ate his sandwiches hungrily. He considered that the men had been very mean to him over food. They had plenty up there in that secret room, but all they had given him that day were two or three measly ham sandwiches ! Fatty, who was used to tucking in well at least four times a day, felt very annoyed.

He finished his meal, drank the water, and then went to the door. He listened hard. He could hear no sound at all.

He wondered if it would be a good idea to try and escape then and there. Perhaps the men were having a nap upstairs in the secret room. He knew there were three of them, though he had not seen the one called Jarvis, who was probably some kind of servant. Maybe Jarvis had been left to watch for the children.

Just as he was thinking he would push his newspaper under the door, ready to receive the key when it dropped the other side, he heard footsteps. He drew back, and sat down in a corner of the room. But no one came in. Fatty looked at his watch. The afternoon was getting on now. Perhaps it would be best to wait till it began to get dark. Nobody would spot a newspaper sticking out from under the door in the darkness, but any one passing by now would certainly be suspicious.

So the boy set himself to wait in patience. He felt dirty and cold, hungry and tired. He thought this adventure was not at all pleasant at the moment — but then adventures often had unpleasant moments, and certainly he had brought this unpleasantness on himself !

Just as it began to get dark, Fatty looked out of the window. He felt certain he could see somebody skulking in the hedge. Who was it ? He did hope it wasn't one of the Find-Outers ! He couldn't make out Clear-Orf's uniform, or he would have recognized the policeman, who had just arrived.

Fatty decided that he had better escape immediately in case the skulking figure he had seen *was* one of the Find-Outers ! Then he could warn whoever it was—Pip or Larry, maybe—and they could escape together and tell Inspector Jenks everything.

He listened at the door. There was nothing to be heard. He unfolded his newspaper and pushed it carefully under the door until only a corner was left inside the room. Then he began to try and push the key out of the lock. It fell quite suddenly, making a little thud on the newspaper.

Fatty's heart beat fast. Escape was very near now ! He began to pull the newspaper sheet back into the room again. This was the anxious part—

would the key slip under the door on the paper or not?

It did! Fatty saw it coming and picked it up thankfully. He slipped it into the lock on his side of the door.

He turned the key, and the lock slid back. He opened the door quietly and looked out on to the landing. No one was there. He locked the door again and left the key in the lock. Then, if any of the men came by, they would see the key there and imagine he was still in the locked room.

He wondered how to get out of the house. He was afraid of going out of the front door, because he would not dare to slam it—and if he left it open, some one might notice.

He thought he had better go down into the coal-cellar again and slip out of the hole. It was so dark that no one would see him.

So Fatty cautiously made his way downstairs and crept through the kitchen to the door that led down into the coal-cellar. He felt for the key. He thought it would be a very good idea to lock the door after him once he was in the cellar, then no one could come down after him if he found it impossible to get up through the hole into the garden.

He took out the key. He went through the cellar door and stood on the topmost step. He shut the door behind him, slid the key into the lock, and turned it. Then he took a deep breath. He was safe for the time being!

He stepped down into the cellar, and then he stopped in horror. Some one—some one was coming down the coal-hole! He could hear them grunting and groaning. Who was it? Certainly not any of the Find-Outers!

Fatty's heart began to beat painfully again. He heard the newcomer jump down on the coal. Fatty felt sure it was one of his captors, though why he should enter the house that way Fatty couldn't imagine.

He made up his mind quickly. As the newcomer was slithering down the coal, Fatty jumped on him, made him overbalance and fall headlong into the farthest corner of the cellar.

Then, before he could pick himself up, Fatty struggled up the coal to the coal-hole. He felt it with his hands, gave himself a terrific heave up, and managed to balance himself in the middle of the opening. Gasping hard, he scrambled out, whilst from down below came the sound of mutterings and groanings.

Fatty had no idea at all that it was Clear-Orf down in the cellar. Once out of the hole, he felt about for the iron lid. Just as he was about to put it over the hole, Mr. Goon staggered to his feet, took his torch from his belt, and switched the light on so that the beam shone at the hole.

To Mr. Goon's enormous astonishment he saw the face of ' that Frenchy fellow ' looking down at him ! Yes, there was no doubt about it—there was the black curly hair, the pale face, the sticking-out teeth.

' Gr-r-r-r-r ! ' said Mr. Goon, so angry that he couldn't speak properly. Fatty, blinded by the glare of the torch, blinked and hastily put the heavy lid back on the entrance to the coal-hole.

Then, afraid that his prisoner might do as he had done and climb out, Fatty dragged a barrel over to the hole and stood it on top of the lid. It was about a quarter full of icy water, and it was quite certain that whoever was now down in the

467

He gave himself a terrific heave up

cellar could not get out either through the door or through the hole.

Fatty breathed more easily. The prisoner in the cellar began to shout and yell. But hardly a sound came up. Fatty did not think any one would hear the captive.

He crept silently round the hedges of the garden, on the look-out for any one else. But he saw nobody.

Then he heard a curious noise. What could it be ? It was like a low and distant humming or throbbing.

' Sounds like an aeroplane,' said Fatty, puzzled. He looked up. To his surprise he saw what looked like a beam of light shining from the roof of Milton House.

' There's a light of some sort being shown up there,' thought Fatty. ' Could that be an aeroplane making that noise—and could that be a light to guide it to the fields near by ? They are big enough for an aeroplane to land on them, that's certain.'

The boy waited for a while. The noise came nearer. It seemed to circle round. Then, after a while, it stopped. Fatty felt certain it was an aeroplane that had landed in the fields behind Milton House. The beam on the roof-top of Milton House went out.

Fatty went into the summer-house, cuddled himself in the rugs there, and waited. Presently, in at a gate that led into the back part of the garden, came the sound of footsteps and the light of a lantern. Evidently the aeroplane passengers were to meet some one at Milton House !

Fatty suddenly felt terribly afraid. He didn't understand at all what was going on. He only knew it was a mystery, and a dangerous mystery, and he had better get out of it as soon as ever he could.

Had the others read his secret message? Had they telephoned to Inspector Jenks? Were they doing something to help him? No one, as far as he knew, had come in search of him since Pip had taken the note. Fatty thought he had better go back to Pip's or Larry's and really find out if anything had been done. If something wasn't done soon, the men would finish up their business, whatever it was, and clear off for good.

They would never come back to Milton House again, that was certain. They had been using it secretly for some time, but now that their meeting-place, or hiding-place, had been discovered, it would be of no use to them.

'So, unless I can get help straightaway, these men may escape for good!' thought Fatty. 'Anyway, at any moment they may find I've escaped from that room, and be alarmed. They have only got to hop into that aeroplane and be off to another country if they wish!'

He slipped through the hedge into Chestnut Lane. He crept quietly up the lane, still keeping in the darkness of the hedge.

And quite suddenly he bumped hard into some one who was creeping *down* the lane, also keeping well in the shelter of the hedge! That some one clutched hard at Fatty, and held him tightly in a grip there was no getting away from.

A light was flashed into his eyes and a grim voice said, 'And who are you, and what are *you* doing here?'

It was a voice Fatty knew well. He listened in delighted surprise.

'Inspector Jenks! Golly, I *am* glad to hear you!'

THE torch flashed into Fatty's face again.

'You know me?' said Inspector Jenks' voice. 'Who are you?'

The Inspector did not recognize Fatty in his curious disguise. Also Fatty was now extremely black and dirty, and looked more like a negro than himself.

'I'm Frederick Trotteville,' said Fatty. 'I'm —er—disguised, Inspector, that's all.'

'Quiet, now,' said the Inspector, and pulled Fatty into a field beyond the hedge. 'Talk in a whisper. What are you doing here? The others telephoned to me and told me enough to puzzle me. I can't say I thought very much of their story, but I came over to see what was up.'

'Good!' said Fatty. 'The others guessed then that I had written a secret message, and they read it.'

'Yes,' said Inspector Jenks. 'Well, as I said, I came over as soon as I could by car, and after I had heard what the others had to say, I went to see Mr. Goon. I wanted to see if *he* knew anything about this, because it was quite likely he did, and hadn't told you.'

'Oh!' said Fatty. 'We didn't want Clear-Orf to know about it.'

'Well, he doesn't,' said Inspector Jenks. 'He wasn't there, and no one knows where he is. Do you?'

'No,' said Fatty, not dreaming that Mr. Goon

471

was well and truly locked into the coal-cellar of Milton House.

'Then I thought I'd come along down to Milton House myself,' said the Inspector, 'and I bumped into you. What *has* been happening, Frederick ? Is it really something serious, or just a little local robbery or something ? '

'I don't know what it is, sir,' said Fatty. 'I really don't. I can't make it out. I'll tell you what I know.'

So the boy related everything : he told of the secret room he had been locked in—the two men he had seen—the one he hadn't seen, called Jarvis— the coming of the aeroplane, bringing more men to meet in the secret room—and how he had locked somebody into the cellar.

'So you'll catch *one* of the men, anyway, sir,' he said, 'even if the others escape. Oh !—I nearly forgot—I—er—I managed to get hold of this book for you to see. I thought it might tell you something. I don't understand a word of it.'

By the light of his torch Inspector Jenks examined the queer little notebook that Fatty had taken from the cupboard in the secret room. He whistled.

'Yes—I understand this all right ! ' he said, and Fatty heard the real excitement in his low voice. 'This is a code-book containing the names, both true and false, of members of a well-known gang and their various addresses ! Pretty good work on your part, Frederick. Now, look here, you scoot up to the nearest telephone, ring the number I tell you, and say I want all the Squad down here immediately. There's not a moment to spare. *Immediately !* Understand ? '

Fatty understood. He felt thrilled. The other

mysteries he and the Find-Outers had solved had been exciting, but really, this one was the most exciting of the lot. He shot off up the lane, leaving the Inspector to do a little more watching.

He got the number immediately. It was evidently a private police number. He gave his message. A sharp, commanding voice answered him :

'Right ! Over in about ten minutes' time.'

Fatty rang off. His heart beat fast. What should he do now ? Surely he must go down and see what was going to happen ? It promised to be extremely exciting.

On the other hand, would it be fair to leave the other Find-Outers out of this ? They would so love to be in it too. Surely there wouldn't be any danger if they all kept in the lane ?

Fatty sped off to Pip's. By good luck all the other Find-Outers were there, very worried, but very glad to think that Inspector Jenks had come and taken charge of things.

Buster suddenly began to bark his head off, and Bets knew that Fatty was coming up the stairs. She ran to the door, flung her arms round him, and dragged him into the room.

'Fatty ! Are you safe ? How did you get out ? Oh, Fatty, we were so worried about you ! '

'Get me some biscuits or something,' said Fatty. 'I'm starving. You needn't have worried about me. I was perfectly all right.'

'You look simply *aw*ful ! ' said Pip. 'Black and dirty and really disgusting ! '

'Don't care,' said Fatty, and gobbled down some biscuits. 'Had the time of my life. I'll tell you all about it as we go.'

'*Go?*' said Daisy. 'Go where ? '

'Down to Milton House to see the fun,' said

Fatty. ' I've just telephoned for a squad of armed policemen to come over—Inspector Jenks' orders ! '

There were squeals and gasps. The other Find-Outers stared at Fatty with amazed eyes. Buster tried in vain to get on his knee. He was overjoyed at having Fatty again.

' Is it—is it dangerous ? ' asked Bets.

' Very—but not for us ! ' said Fatty. ' Now do you want to come or not ? I'll tell you everything on the way. We must go at once or we shall miss the fun.'

They went, of course. They flung on hats and coats and trooped out into Pip's drive, excited. They set out over the hill, and just as they got to the other side a powerful police car swept by them !

' That's it—that's the armed Squad ! ' said Fatty. ' Did you see them ? My, they've been quick ! '

The big police car roared down Chestnut Lane, and the children hurried as fast as they could after it. Their hearts thumped, and Bets clung tightly to Fatty's sturdy arm. Buster, his tongue hanging out, his tail wagging all the time, hurried along too, quite forgetting to limp in his excitement.

They arrived at the gateway of Milton House. The police car was outside in the lane. Black shadows here and there showed where members of the Squad were. Orders were being given by the Inspector in a low voice.

' He's putting men in a ring round the house,' whispered Fatty to the others, almost choking with excitement. ' See—there goes one that way—and there's another going the other way round the house. I wonder how they will get in.'

Inspector Jenks had a very simple way of getting in. He had read Fatty's letter to the Find-Outers, and had noticed that he had told them to knock at the door.

So, if he or his men walked up the steps to the door and hammered with the knocker, the men inside would quite probably think it was the children coming along in obedience to Fatty's letter.

When all his men were in position around the house, the Inspector went to the front door and lifted the knocker. All the children jumped when they heard the loud rat-a-tat-tat.

The door opened wide. Evidently the one who opened it—probably Jarvis—expected four children to walk quietly in.

Instead of that a burly figure crowded on top of him, the round barrel of a revolver was pressed into his chest, and a low voice said, ' Not a word ! '

Immediately on the Inspector's heels came three more men. The door was quietly shut. Then one of the men put handcuffs on the frightened Jarvis.

The Inspector went silently up the stairs followed by two of his men. They all wore rubber-soled shoes and made no sound at all. Right up to the top of the house they went, to a room where light came from the keyhole. It was the secret room.

The Inspector swung it open suddenly, his revolver in his hand. He said nothing at all. There were five men in the room, and they all leapt to their feet at once. One glance at the Inspector's stern face, and they put up their hands.

Then the Inspector spoke, in quite an amiable voice, looking round the room.

' Ah !—got yourself a cosy little nest here, haven't you ? Pleased to see you again, Finnigan—or is your name John Henry Smith now ? And you're here too, I see, Lammerton—well, well, well, this is an unexpected pleasure, if I may say so ! '

The two men spoken to scowled. One was the thin-lipped man, and the other was the red-faced man. The Inspector looked at the others.

One of them spoke eagerly. ' I'm not in this, Inspector ! I didn't know till to-night, when I was brought over here by plane, that there was any dirty work afoot.'

' Really ? ' said the Inspector disbelievingly. ' You hadn't got anything unusual in the way of antiques to sell, I suppose ? Oh no—you don't know anything about the theft of the priceless Chinese vases owned by the Belgian Count, I suppose ? You are quite innocent ! '

' And you ! ' he said, turning to another man, ' you hadn't anything to do with getting the valuable picture from the Paris gallery, had you ? You don't know anything about that, I'm sure ! Well, well— I can only say it is unfortunate that such clever and notorious rogues as you should be found here, in a secret place, with equally well-known buyers of antiques, rogues too, known to be hand in glove with the same kind of fellows on the other side of the Atlantic ! '

' The game's up,' said the fifth man, in a sulky voice. ' I always said this was a dangerous place to meet in.'

' It's been all right up till now, hasn't it ? ' said the Inspector. ' A very nice quiet spot ! A good place to meet and to plot—a good place even to store valuable goods until the hue and cry has died down, and you can take them over to America to sell. Barred windows to protect your goods and all ! A good many police all over the world have been on the look-out for your clever gang for years. I am happy to think it will be broken up for a long time to come ! '

The other men who had come up with Inspector Jenks moved into the room and deftly put handcuffs on each of the five sullen men.

'Any more of you?' inquired the Inspector. 'We've got a fellow downstairs.'

'Find out for yourself,' said Lammerton viciously.

'We will,' said the Inspector. 'There are men all round the house, as you will probably guess. A very proper precaution, as I am sure you will agree?'

The men scowled and said nothing. The Inspector gave a sharp order, and every one went out of the room. For a minute or two Inspector Jenks examined the secret room, his eyes sharp and shrewd. Then he went downstairs too.

The five men and Jarvis were lined up in the hall. One of the policemen had put a lantern on a ledge and the scene was lighted up. The five children at the gate, feeling certain that things were safe now, crept up to the door and looked in.

'Golly!' said Larry, in awe. 'Look at them all —what scoundrels they look! What are they, Fatty, do you think? Thieves? Spies? Or what?'

'They might be anything,' said Fatty, squinting in. 'They look bad enough!'

Suddenly Fatty slipped and fell, making a slithering noise. At once the front door was flung open and a policeman looked out.

'Who's there?'

'It's only us,' said Fatty, grinning up into the beam thrown by the torch. 'Hallo, Inspector—we just came to see the fun.'

'Then you've no right to,' said the Inspector. 'There might have been shooting. Frederick, which of these men did you see most of?'

Fatty pointed to the thin-lipped man and the

red-faced one. ' Have you got them all ? ' he said.
' What about the one I locked into the coal-cellar ? '

The prisoners looked astonished. The thin-
lipped man spoke sharply to Fatty.

' How did you get out of that locked room ? '

' I don't give my secrets away,' said Fatty.
' Inspector, the one in the cellar makes seven. Shall
we get him ? '

' There's nobody else,' said the thin-lipped man.
' Only six of us.'

Another black figure loomed up in the darkness
outside and a policeman came into the light.

' Sir,' he said to the Inspector, ' there's some one
underground somewhere. I was standing on guard
at the back there, and I kept hearing muffled shouts,
but couldn't make out where they came from.'

' That's the fellow I locked in the coal-cellar ! '
said Fatty. ' Let's go and get him ! '

21   THE END OF THE MYSTERY

' COME along, then,' said the Inspector, getting
out his gun again. ' You others keep back. Only
Frederick is to come, to show me the way. You
keep back when I open the cellar door, Frederick.'

Fatty proudly led the way to the cellar door,
and produced the key from his pocket. From
below came a violent voice, shouting and yelling,
and now and again the sound of falling coal as poor
Clear-Orf tried to find a way out.

The voice sounded vaguely familiar to Fatty as
he gave the key to the Inspector to open the door.
The Inspector put it in the lock and turned it.

'Come on out!' he roared. 'Up the steps, man, and put your hands up!'

Some one came tumbling up the steps. It was poor Mr. Goon, without his helmet, which was lost somewhere in the coal, and as black as night. He stumbled out of the door, blinking in the bright torch-light shone on him by the Inspector. He was so dirty and black that neither Fatty nor the Inspector recognized him.

Mr. Goon was angry, afraid, and puzzled. He walked through the kitchen, with the Inspector prodding him from behind, and gaped to see the crowd of men in the hall. He also gaped to see the children there, opening and shutting his mouth like a goldfish.

Buster was the only one who recognized poor Mr. Goon. With a torrent of loud barks he flung himself joyfully at the ankles of his enemy.

'You clear-orf!' said Goon angrily, and kicked out at the dog. 'What's all this-ere?'

'It's *Clear*-Orf!' cried all the Five Find-Outers in the greatest surprise.

'Goon!' said the Inspector, also in the utmost astonishment. 'How did you—how is it—what has . . .' But the Inspector didn't finish. Instead he burst out into such hearty laughter that the other members of the Squad grinned too.

'Well, Goon, this is an extraordinary meeting,' said the Inspector, eyeing the dirty, angry policeman with amusement. 'I called at your place to find out if you knew anything about the goings-on here— but you were not there.'

'I were locked up in that filthy coal-cellar!' said Goon, and he glared at Fatty. 'And that's the one who locked me in! He wants watching, he does. He's a Frenchy fellow, up to no good—in

479

with the thieves, I don't doubt—or whatever these fellows are you've caught. Wait till I get my hands on him!'

'Don't you know me, Mr. Goon?' said Fatty, in his ordinary voice, and Mr. Goon jumped. He stared at the black curly wig, the big eyebrows, the sticking-out teeth—the face of that 'Frenchy fellow,' not a doubt of it, but the voice was Fatty's.

'I don't think I want you to molest this helper of mine,' said the Inspector smoothly. 'I'm surprised that a smart policeman like you, Goon, didn't see through Master Frederick's disguise!'

Fatty snatched off wig and eyebrows and with a little more difficulty removed the teeth. Mr. Goon stared and swallowed violently several times. He became deep purple. The six prisoners watched Fatty in amazement. The other Find-Outers giggled. Good old Fatty!

'We will leave any more explanations till later!' said the Inspector. 'Now—lead the way, you men. There's room in the police car for the prisoners and three guards. You others can get over to the aeroplane and stand guard there till relieved.'

The company dispersed. Mr. Goon, looking queer without his helmet, stood looking sulkily on.

'Better get home, Goon,' said the Inspector. 'You look bad.'

'I *feel* bad,' said Mr. Goon, in a most aggrieved tone. 'Didn't I know those kids were interfering again? And then, just as I was finding out things, didn't that boy go and lock me up so that he could get all the credit?'

'I didn't know it was you, Mr. Goon,' said Fatty truthfully.

'Wouldn't have mattered if you *had* known. You'd have done it just the same!' said Mr. Goon.

'Proper lot of nuisances you are, see? Messing about. Interfering with the Law.'

'No, no, Goon—*helping* the Law!' corrected the Inspector. 'We've done a good night's work here—caught nearly the whole gang of international thieves and their agents. You've heard of the notorious Finnigan, I have no doubt, Goon—and the equally infamous Lammerton? They are the men who specialize in procuring valuable pictures, jewels, china, and so on—and ship them to other countries to sell them!'

'Coo, yes, sir,' said Goon, his eyes nearly dropping out of his head. 'Don't mean to say we got *them*, sir! Coo—to think they've been meeting here under my very nose, like!'

'Yes—your nose must do a little better in future, Goon,' said the Inspector.

'A-TISH-oo!' sneezed Goon. 'Well, sir — a-TISH-oo!'

'Go home, Goon, and get to bed,' said the Inspector. 'You've got a bad cold.'

'Yes, I have,' said Goon, wiping his nose with a tremendous pocket-handkerchief. 'Oughtn't to be up at all by rights, but I felt it was me duty, sir, when I knew there was queer goings-on here, like. Thought I'd better risk getting pewmonia than neglect me duty, sir.'

'Very noble of you, Goon,' said the Inspector gravely. 'Now get back home. I'll have a talk with you to-morrow.'

Goon disappeared into the night, sniffling and sneezing. He gave Fatty one last spiteful look, but Fatty didn't mind. Buster gave Mr. Goon a few parting barks.

'And now,' said the Inspector, 'do you think, Pip, that your good mother would let me share your

supper ? I have a feeling that she may like to hear
a little of all this—I hope you agree with me ? '

' Oh *yes* ! ' said Pip joyfully. He had been
wondering how to explain everything to his mother
and father. He knew his mother liked and admired
the Inspector. Now things could all be straightened
out, and there would be no scoldings for anything.

It ended in being a big supper-party, and a most
enjoyable one. When Pip's mother heard that
something extraordinary had happened, and that
the Inspector felt very pleased with the Five Find-
Outers once again, she telephoned to Fatty's parents,
who were now back, and to Larry's, asking them to
come down and join them in supper that night.

The children all stayed up too, and the conversation was most interesting. The grown-ups listened
in amazement to the tale of the third mystery, and
though Pip's mother secretly thought she really
didn't like Pip and Bets being mixed up in such
queer doings, she didn't say so.

Fatty, of course, was the hero of the evening.
His description of secret writing, getting out of
locked rooms and wearing disguises was listened to
with the utmost astonishment.

' Well, really, Fredeirck ! ' said his mother.
' I had no idea you were doing all these things.
I didn't even know you knew about them ! '

' Well, Mother—you see I've been studying
detective methods lately,' said Fatty. ' I can't help
thinking I have a gift that way, really. I hope you
won't insist on my going in for soldiering, because
I'm sure I should be wasted in the army. I'm a
born detective. I could tell you things you could
hardly believe. Why once——'

' Shut up ! ' said Pip, unable to bear Fatty's
vanity any longer. ' You're jolly clever at times, I

agree ; but, after all, it was me climbing that tree that first set us on the track of the Mystery of the Secret Room. You know it was.'

' You all deserve praise,' said the Inspector, beaming round. ' Yes, even little Bets here, who was clever enough to smell the orange juice in that note of Frederick's—and stopped the whole of the Find-Outers from walking into a trap ! '

Bets went red. It was tiresome being the youngest Find-Outer, but it was lovely to be praised by the Inspector.

It was a happy and exciting evening. Nobody wanted to go home or go to bed. The Inspector left first, when his car came for him.

' Good-night,' he said, ' and many, many thanks for solving this mystery. I hope there will be many more for you to solve. I shall always appreciate your help, if I may say so ! '

' Good-bye ! ' said the Find-Outers, and waved to their big friend. It had been lovely to see him again.

' I bet old Clear-Orf is feeling sick,' said Fatty, getting on his coat to go home with Buster and his parents.

' I feel a bit sorry for him,' said tender-hearted Bets. ' You know—to feel he's failed again—and has an awful cold too—and got locked in that dirty cellar and lost his helmet.'

' Yes. It was awful for him, I suppose,' said Daisy. ' Well, we can afford to be generous—shall we take him some flowers or something, if he's in bed to-morrow ? I don't like him, and I never shall, but I can't help feeling a bit sorry for him, like Bets.'

' Take old Clear-Orf flowers ! You must be mad ! ' said Fatty scornfully. ' I don't mind going and looking for his helmet for him—or even giving him some soap to clean his uniform—but not *flowers* ! Flowers and Clear-Orf don't go together, somehow.'

'All right—we'll give him some soap, then—and find his helmet,' said Daisy. 'Won't he be surprised ?

'I bet he will ! ' said Fatty. 'All right, Mother, I'm coming. Just give me a minute to say good-bye. Now don't you go finding some wonderful soap like Sweet Violets or Sweet-pea Buds, Daisy. Carbolic for old Clear-Orf, see ? '

The others laughed. Buster barked, and Bets patted him. 'Good-bye, Buster. See you to-morrow.'

'Good-bye,' said Fatty. 'And I say—let's . . . All right, Mother, just coming ! Half a minute ! '

'Let's what ? ' asked the other Find-Outers.

'Let's solve another mystery as soon as ever we can ! ' said Fatty, going down the steps. 'And a thumping big one too. See ? '

'Oh *yes* ! ' shouted the Find-Outers in joy. 'We will, Fatty, we will ! '

Enid Blyton

Malory Towers

containing

First Term at Malory Towers

Second Form at Malory Towers

Third Year at Malory Towers

When Darrell Rivers first arrives at Malory Towers, she has lots of exciting adventures in store! She makes many new friends, there are practical jokes and plenty of fun, but some problems too for Darrell in controlling her dreadful temper. We meet Mam'zelle, a great favourite with the girls, trying to be strict but not succeeding, as well as lots of new girls who all have something special to add to life at Malory Towers.

This immensely readable book takes us through the ups and downs of the first three forms at a girls' boarding school.

Enid Blyton

Back To Malory Towers

containing

Upper Fourth at Malory Towers
In the Fifth at Malory Towers
Last Term at Malory Towers

Darrell Rivers and her friends Sally, Alicia
and all the others are back at Malory Towers,
this time as senior girls taking their exams, but
also having lots of fun organising the school
pantomime, playing tennis and lacrosse,
having midnight feasts and trying more tricks
on Mam'zelle. Darrell's sister Felicity arrives
with other new girls who bring their share of
problems, but it helps to make the final three
years more exciting than ever, before the girls
finally have to say goodbye to Malory Towers.

Enid Blyton

The Twins at St Clare's

containing

The Twins at St Clare's

The O'Sullivan Twins

Summer Term at St Clare's

Twins Pat and Isobel O'Sullivan are dreading going to St Clare's. Life is not nearly so easy as at their old school and the 'stuck-up twins' have several unpleasant shocks and arguments before they realise their difficulties are of their own making. Problems resolved, the girls soon find friends and settle down. Each term brings more fun and games, as well as plenty of new girls and lots of surprises. Pat and Isobel don't regret for a moment having gone to school at St Clare's!

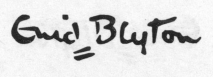

A Collection

containing

The Naughtiest Girl in the School

The Naughtiest Girl Again

The Naughtiest Girl is a Monitor

When Elizabeth is told that she is pretty and rich, but that she has been spoilt, she is astonished. When she is told that she is to go to school at Whyteleafe, she rebels. Elizabeth is determined to behave so badly at school that she will be sent home. During her first term Elizabeth puts her plan into action, but how much we enjoy reading about it! Then we see what happens next...

Enid Blyton

A Collection

containing

Adventures of the Wishing Chair

The Wishing Chair Again

Stories for Bedtime

The adventure really begins for Peter and Mollie when they are looking for a birthday present! They find the present – but tucked away in the strange little shop there are lots of other things and, most exciting of all – the Wishing Chair. They meet giants and pixies, witches and wizards, and share many wonderful journeys together.

Stories for Bedtime is a delightful collection, where we meet Mr Twiddle and Amelia Jane as well as Captain Puss, Hop Around, Mr Tiptap and lots of other good – and naughty characters!

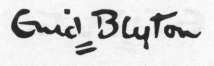

A Collection

containing

The Adventurous Four

The Adventurous Four Again

The Children of Willow Farm

The Adventurous Four have lively holiday adventures when they are staying in a fishing village on the north-east coast of Scotland. Often there is danger all around them – and not only from storms at sea!

The Children of Willow Farm is quite different, but equally exciting. These children move with their parents to a farm, and we follow them through the first year with all its problems and joys too.

Enid Blyton

A Collection

containing

The Enchanted Wood

The Magic Faraway Tree

The Folk of the Faraway Tree

When Jo, Bessie and Fanny move with their
parents to live in the country, they expect all
sorts of adventures and they find them! The
wood looks quite ordinary, except perhaps that
the trees are a darker green than usual – but
they soon realise that it is a magic wood, and
there are dozens of people and animals living
there who become their friends, and with
whom they visit the exciting lands at the top
of the mysterious Faraway Tree.